Web of Deceit

Book One: Agents Under Fire Series

by

Susan Sleeman

Bell Bridge Books

This is a work of fiction. Names, characters, places and incidents are either the products of the author's imagination or are used fictitiously. Any resemblance to actual persons (living or dead), events or locations is entirely coincidental.

Bell Bridge Books
PO BOX 300921
Memphis, TN 38130
Print ISBN: 978-1-61194-468-6

Bell Bridge Books is an Imprint of BelleBooks, Inc.

The author is represented by MacGregor Literary Inc. of Manzanita, Oregon.

Published in the United States of America.

We at BelleBooks enjoy hearing from readers.
Visit our websites
BelleBooks.com
BellBridgeBooks.com
ImaJinnBooks.com

10 9 8 7 6 5 4 3 2 1

Cover design: Debra Dixon
Interior design: Hank Smith
Photo/Art credits:
Interior scene (manipulated) © Citalliance | Dreamstime.com
Exterior scene (manipulated) © Konstantin Sutyagin | Dreamstime.com

:Ldwe:01:

Dedication

For my ever-patient and understanding husband Mark, who always believes in me and is by my side through good times and bad. I couldn't do any of this without you.

Chapter One

Portland, Oregon

KAIT KNIGHT MET her brother-in-law's piercing black eyes. The façade he'd lived for the last two years peeled away, revealing the cold, harsh eyes of a murderer.

"Why are you doing this, Fenton?" She tried to take a deep breath in a room that felt as if it was closing in on her.

"Why are you doing this, Fenton?" he mimicked, his voice going high and shrill as he pointed his 9mm Sig in her direction.

"No, seriously." She eased closer, one inch at a time, her hands raised so he could see her every move. The last thing she needed was for him to panic and pull the trigger. "What are you hoping to accomplish here?"

"You know exactly why I'm doing this. I'm not letting you or anyone else at your prized FBI office arrest me." He came around the desk, his hand trembling as a nervous finger flicked off the gun's safety. "Now go over there and lock the door before your family hears us and someone comes running."

Kait thought to ignore him, but she heard her twin sister Abby and their parents in the other room cooing over Abby and Fenton's infant daughter. Kait could still smell Lily's sweet, powdery scent clinging to her shirt from their cuddle, and she'd do anything to protect this precious child from her deviant father. She had to follow his directions.

For now.

She twisted the deadbolt, setting the tumblers in place with a firm click before turning to face the traitor. He was sweating now, soaking his tailored shirt though her father's study hovered at a cool seventy degrees. He couldn't seem to focus on one thing, his gaze darting around like a pinball.

"Now get over here," he insisted. "Slowly. No false moves. You got that?"

She started across the room, her footfalls soft on the thick carpet. She'd spent countless hours playing at her father's feet, and Lily deserved the chance to play here, too. To know the joy of family. The love of her grandfather. And Kait deserved the chance to watch her. That meant smiling, pretending, promising. Working the process until she negotiated Fenton off the mental ledge of insanity he teetered on.

Easy now. She made sure her voice was gentle and reassuring as she approached. "Think about Abby. How would she feel if she saw this?"

"Don't try to pin this on me. This's all your fault for taking your partner's call when you should be enjoying your niece. Always working. Living for that stupid job." He pressed his gun against her forehead and leaned closer, his minty breath fanning over her face as his lips parted in a hideous smile.

"And now you'll pay for it." He jerked her gun from her holster and dropped it on the desk behind him. The solid thunk of the Glock 17 reverberated through the space as he ground the barrel of his weapon into her forehead.

Dread coiled in her stomach, churning her lunch, and burning up her throat. In her four years as an FBI agent, she'd never been this close to death. She swallowed hard.

Don't panic. Keep working the plan. One step at a time. Work the plan.

She fixed her gaze on him, willing him to listen. "Don't make Abby and Lily go through this." Uncertainty flickered in his dark eyes. *Good.* She was finally on the right track. "Abby loves you, Fenton. This will destroy her."

"I don't want to hurt her." He raised his eyes for a fraction of a second, not long enough for Kait to disarm him.

"I know you don't. You love her. And Lily, too. So give me the gun, and we'll forget this ever happened."

His hand relaxed a bit, a whisper of air sliding between the barrel and her skin. "But not the rest, right? You'll still turn me in."

"I don't want to," she lied as the bitterness over what he was doing to her family expanded in her chest, making it hard to breathe. "Put the gun down, and I won't tell anyone you drew on me. That way it won't be added to your charges."

"Hah! The minute I give this up—" He pressed the cool steel deeper into her flesh. "—is the minute I run out of negotiating power."

"There's really no one to negotiate with. Just me having a conversation with you. So let's sit down and work through this. I'm sure we can reach a compromise."

He watched her, indecision playing on the sharp features of his face as he stroked a thin white scar on his chin.

Good. She had a chance here. Just a few more minutes of talking softly and reminding him of the people he loved, and she'd get him to surrender.

The doorknob rattled.

"Fenton," Abby called from the hallway. "Fenton, is everything okay?"

His gaze shot to the door, then back to Kait. Panic wedged in his eyes, and they darted about before settling on her again. Now, mean and ugly, they darkened, and a slow, sick smile spread across his lips.

Oh, no.

He'd given in. Let evil prevail, taking him to the same deranged place he'd inhabited when he'd murdered his partner.

Kait had lost.

A terrorizing coldness iced her heart. "Tell Abby to go away, Fenton. That you have work to do. I won't move, and we'll keep this just between us."

"Fenton?" Abby knocked this time, her fists rattling the door. "Fenton, why is the door locked?"

"Sorry, honey," he yelled back, the smile spreading wider. "I'm coming to open it."

"Please, Fenton, don't involve Abby in this," Kait said, losing her professional tone and imploring him with every bit of love she felt for her twin. "She doesn't need to be a part of this."

Kait watched, waited for him to react. He backed away from her, his steps sure and strong as if on a mission. She wanted to jump him and take her chances, but if they scuffled and he killed her, there'd be no one left to protect her family.

"Don't move, or I'll kill Abby." Gun barrel still pointed in Kait's direction, he pulled the door open and stepped aside.

Abby entered the room, large brown eyes just like Kait's landing on Fenton, on his weapon, then going wide before settling on Kait. "Kait, what are . . ." She cut her eyes back to Fenton. "What's going on here?"

Fenton jerked the gun. "Get over there, Abby. By your sister."

"Fenton?"

"Do as I say." He gave her a little shove, and she stumbled.

Kait took a few steps toward her twin who now looked lost and pale with shock.

"Come any closer, Kait, and I'll kill her." Fenton's glassy eyes locked on Kait, and she knew with certainty this man—this monster masquerading as her brother-in-law—wouldn't hesitate to fire.

"C'mon, Abby." Kait held out her hand. "Over here."

Abby crossed the room in a daze, stepping cautiously as if she couldn't decide who to trust. "What's going on, Kait?"

Kait wrapped her arm around Abby's shoulders and pulled her into the protective circle that felt like a lie. A big, bold lie. She couldn't control Fenton or protect Abby. He was holding on by the barest of threads and could snap at any moment.

"Kait?" Abby asked again.

"Fenton isn't who he claimed," Kait replied. "He's involved in a huge

Internet scam. Nina just called to tell me about it, and he overheard the call." Kait decided to withhold the part about him being a murderer . . . for now, anyway.

"Tell her it's not true, Fenton." Abby's eyes pleaded with her husband. "Tell her."

He didn't move. Not a flinch. Not a twitch, but a hint of sadness deepened eyes that only moments ago had flirted with madness. Maybe he really did care about Abby.

Too bad.

When he'd bilked thousands of people out of their money and killed a fellow hacker, he'd lost the right to care about her sister. As much as Abby loved her husband, she needed to know the truth.

"It's true, Abby, and he's decided to make a run for it." Kait peered at Fenton, hoping he would find her suggestion of running more palatable than opening fire. "You *are* planning on running, Fenton, aren't you?"

"You'll just come after me."

"I'll stay here with Abby."

A guttural laugh rumbled from his chest, his true colors revealed in a single burst. "I know you. Remember, Kait. You like nothing more than the chase, and when it ends, you get sullen. So, no . . . you won't stay put." He raised the gun and sighted it on Kait. "You may let me get out of the room, but then you'll hunt me down." His finger slowly squeezed.

"No, Fenton, don't!" Abby pushed in front of Kait, knocking her to the floor.

The gun exploded, a deafening sound ripping through her parents' quiet suburban home. Abby jerked back as her chest flooded with crimson, the circle growing and saturating her white blouse.

"No!" Kait screamed.

Surprise etched Fenton's face. He stared for a moment before turning away. Kait pushed to her knees and lunged for the desk. She grabbed her weapon and fired. Two kill shots, aiming for center mass, then holding her fire in the event her parents or Abby came running.

Had she hit him? She could only hope, but her awkward position meant the odds weren't in her favor. She holstered her weapon and scrambled to Abby who lay on her back. There was blood. So much blood. Covering her chest and staining the thick wool carpet. Kait ripped off her blazer and pressed it against the wound. Sticky, warm, it oozed through her fingers.

Bile crawled up the back of her throat. She looked away to stave it off and dialed 911, the operator promising a swift EMT response.

Kait dropped her phone and turned to Abby, whose face was ashen and drawn. Her mouth opened and closed as if she needed to speak. Terror for Abby threatened to take Kait down.

Hold on. Stay in control. She needs you.

Abby moaned, the sound cutting to Kait's core.

"Hang in there, Abs." Kait bent low to look into her twin's eyes. "I love you. Don't leave me."

"I . . . Lily. Take care of her. Promise me."

"You'll be fine."

"No, promise me, Kaitie. Promise," Abby said then her eyes lost their luster.

"No." Kait pressed harder on the jacket, her sister's lifeblood slipping through her fingers. "Hang in there. Please, Abby, hang on. For me. For you. For Lily. She's just a baby, Abs. She needs you."

Abby's throat gurgled, and she shuddered. Kait was losing her sister. Her best friend. Her life.

"No," Kait cried to the empty room, forgetting all of her FBI training and searching for her next step. How could she help her sister? Her family. Her niece. Lily. *Oh, God, Lily!*

"Mom! Dad!" Kait screamed. "Help!"

She listened. Heard only her heart pounding. Abby's labored gasps for air.

They had to have heard the gunshots, so where were they? Had Fenton taken one of them hostage?

"Don't let him take them. Please, no. Please." The whispered plea joined Abby's last breath.

Kait sagged to the floor.

"I'll get Fenton, Abby. Don't worry. I'll get him," she whispered as Abby's eyes glazed over and fixed in a lifeless stare. "No matter how long or what it takes, I'll get him, and he will pay."

Chapter Two

Beaverton, Oregon, Three Years Later
Monday, August 10, 1:00 a.m.

THE FRANTIC SCREAM startled Kait from her sleep. She shot up and swung her legs toward the floor.

"Nantie Kait." Lily's terrified cry came from her bedroom on the other side of the house.

Kait clawed at tangled sheets entwining her legs. "Calm down," she told herself. "She's fine. It's just another bad dream."

So what? Her sweet little niece really believed the man came into her room. She was afraid and needed Kait. She finally ripped free of the fabric and ran through the family room, flipping on the light as she went. The hazy beam drifted through the open doorway and settled over Lily's soft blond curls. Huddled in her bed, her little bottom pointed in the air, she cried softly, her tiny body shuddering under the Dora quilt. Mr. Bear was snuggled tightly under her trembling chin, her eyes scrunched closed.

"I'm here, pumpkin." Kait quickly swept the room, looking for the man she knew Lily would say had lurked in the doorway. Empty as suspected. She scooped her three-year-old niece into her arms.

"I saw him." Lily's voice shook.

Kait pressed the terrified child's head against her chest and stroked her baby-fine hair. The sweet fragrance of her strawberry shampoo enveloped Kait, reminding her of her niece's bath time giggles just a few hours ago. What a difference a few hours could make.

Kait dragged in a deep breath to still her racing heart. "Remember, pumpkin. There's no man. It's just a bad dream."

"Nuh-uh. He was here. I saw him."

"Shh. No one else is here, pumpkin. Just you and me." Kait's gaze drifted around the room the two of them had such fun decorating together. Dora, Swiper, and Boots smiled from walls painted in bright primary colors. Now the space held terror for Lily, and Kait didn't know what to do about these recent bad dreams.

She believed the nightmares were related to an incident at Lily's preschool when a non-custodial father tried to abduct his daughter a month ago. At least, that was the only incident in Lily's protected life that could have incited such dreams.

At first, Kait had retrieved her weapon from her gun safe and checked the house. She found the security system set and no sign of forced entry. Still, to be safe, each time she'd changed her security code.

Better safe than sorry, right?

Now, beyond the initial panic and terror, Kait accepted the incidents as a normal part of parenting she hadn't been prepared to handle.

Parenting. Right.

How could Abby have named Kait as her daughter's guardian? True, Kait was thirty when Abby had died and Kait should have been ready for motherhood, but she didn't have a motherly bone in her body. Put a gun in her hands and give her a lowlife breaking the law. That she could handle. That she did well. This mommy stuff . . .

Lily's sobbing stilled, and her little body shuddered a final time. She drew away, plopped her thumb into her mouth, and fixed sleepy eyes on Kait.

"All better?" Kait asked as her heart melted into a river of love.

Lily nodded.

"Okay, then let's get some sleep."

"Stay here."

"Of course I'll stay, pumpkin." Kait settled her niece under the covers and slid down next to her.

"Love you, Nantie Kait."

The sweetness of Lily's voice split Kait's heart. "I love you too, pumpkin."

Her poor, poor baby girl. This couldn't continue. It was time to find a way to end these nightmares. Kait needed to talk to an expert. Tomorrow she'd make a few phone calls.

She yawned and moved into a more comfortable position, why, she didn't know. After the terror of waking up to her little sweetheart screaming, it'd be a few nights before Kait would sleep soundly again.

WITH LILY'S SCREAM still echoing in his head, Fenton Rhodes crouched in the underbrush outside. He watched the windows. Kait's bedroom. Lily's room. The family room. Waiting for the lights to go out. Then he could hightail it out of there without being seen. Out of the nasty, damp fog—the swirling vapor blanketing the area and inflaming every nerve ending in his leg. The one Kait had destroyed in her lame attempt to stop him with a bullet three years ago. Three long years while he got his financial house in order freeing him to seek revenge.

He rubbed the damaged muscles, the pain firing his anger. He fisted his hand and slammed it into moist ground. Pain, pain, and more pain. He shouldn't have to live with it. *And* he shouldn't have to sneak around just to make sure his baby girl was okay.

It was all Kait's fault. Stupid, stupid, Kait. She would pay.

Starting tomorrow.

Oh, yeah. Tomorrow. She'd be surprised. He'd planned it to perfection. Now all she had to do was play her predictable role. And she would, of that he was certain. She never veered from her schedule. Even after the sleepless night she'd have tonight, courtesy of his clumsy attempt at stealing a quick kiss from his child, Kait would be up at sunup, sitting on her deck with a cup of coffee and the newspaper before taking his darling girl to daycare.

Daycare, hah!

His daughter didn't deserve to spend her days in the care of strangers. She deserved a mother who coddled and cherished her all day long. Abby would have done that. She wouldn't have been like *his* mother, bailing on her son when a man came along who promised a lifestyle dear old dad could never provide. Money. A decent home, not a rat-infested one. Freedom from the man who belittled everyone and inflicted physical pain when they'd failed to meet his standards. Or like Kait. A workaholic. No, Abby wouldn't have been like them. She'd have been the perfect mother, but Kait had ruined it all by meddling in his business.

The last light snapped off.

Good. One step closer to the moment he'd rescue Lily from her surrogate mother, who didn't have time for his precious baby. But first, Kait deserved to know his pain.

He struggled to his feet, stretching his leg and easing out the stiffness. He started to leave, then turned back to the window and saluted.

Game on, Kait. Tomorrow you will pay, and soon, very soon, my sweet little Lily will know life as she was meant to experience it.

With her father.

KAIT'S LACK OF sleep last night had taken a toll. She yawned and rolled her stiff, cramping neck. Her fault, of course. She should have been sitting at her cubicle working on her latest case. Not standing behind an FBI analyst, staring down at a computer monitor and hoping to get a lead on her AWOL brother-in-law.

She watched the code scroll across the screen like a slot machine in Vegas. Rows and rows of gibberish, rolling up and disappearing like Fenton. Was his trademark code in there somewhere, or was this another false lead like so many since he'd disappeared down her parents' hallway?

Time to find out.

She approached the analyst sitting with her legs wrapped around a backless chair, her body hunched over the keyboard, fingers flying. "Any luck, Jae?"

"Minute," she mumbled and held up a finger tipped in green nail polish.

Trying to be patient and not push an already overworked analyst, Kait practiced a deep breathing technique she'd seen on a TV morning show. She didn't know how much longer she could keep this up without losing it. Keep up the pretense of being okay while her co-workers gave her pitiful looks. If they looked her in the eye at all.

But what choice did she have?

She could still feel the stickiness of Abby's blood on her hands. Hear her sister's last gasp and their parents' wailing cries when they'd come into the room. She had to keep looking for Fenton. Make sure he paid. He'd gone so far underground that they'd never had a hint of his existence, but she'd continue to check in with analysts at all hours of the day and urge them to keep working the case. To work harder. Dig deeper.

Jae suddenly sat back and stretched out legs encased in skinny jeans. "Man, I thought I had something."

"So this is another dead end, then." Kait tried not to sound disappointed.

Jae's eyes, lined in thick kohl, remained fixed on Kait. "We want to catch him, too, you know."

"I know you do." Kait blew out a sigh. "Not that it's an excuse for pushing you so hard, but I didn't get much sleep last night." Kait squeezed Jae's shoulder, but the analyst's attention had already returned to the screen.

She started pounding the keyboard again. "For everyone's sake, go do something, Kait. You know we hate backseat drivers."

Jae was right. Staying would only distract them.

Kait left the steady hum of computers for an eerily quiet hallway. Usually, the bullpen buzzed with activity. Sure, it neared four o'clock, but agents never went home this early in the day.

Something was up.

As she passed the conference room fondly dubbed the war room, the scent of scorched coffee drifted under the door and tainted the air with its acrid smell. She spotted Rolland Sulyard, the Assistant Special Agent in Charge of the Portland office and her immediate supervisor, standing at the head of the long table. Figured. He was famous for leaving the last dregs of coffee in the pot to burn while he held his staff captive in endless meetings.

Fellow agents and Cyber Crime Action Team members Becca Lange and Nina Brandt sat with three other agents in the dimly lit space, and Kait stopped to assess the situation. A flat screen mounted on the wall flashed through slides, the light reflecting off Sulyard's shaved head, shadowing his face. The slides held tactical details for a raid. Not a case she recognized, but it was obvious they were getting ready to arrest someone without her. Purposefully without her? No page. No call or text summoning her to the room. Even good friends Nina and Becca had left her out.

She'd never been excluded before, so why was it happening now?

Sulyard clicked off the screen, and the occupants turned toward the window. Most of her co-workers wore sheepish expressions as if she'd caught them with their hands in the cookie jar.

Great. Everyone knew the reason for the shutout except her.

Becca started to rise, but Nina placed a hand on Becca's shoulder, stilling her, and headed for the door. Not surprising. Becca would march out here and blurt out the problem in her straightforward, often brash way. Not Nina. She was the essence of discretion in public.

Which meant they thought Kait needed handling and this situation required kid gloves.

Nina stepped into the hallway, quietly closing the door behind her and staring at a folder she'd grabbed on the way out.

"Nina?" Kait asked, but her friend didn't respond, keeping her gaze trained on the folder.

Not good. Nina's grandmother had raised her in the true southern tradition and taught her to make eye contact. To smile at all times. Even if Nina was as angry as a mad wasp, she didn't show it in public. Becca and Kait were the only ones in this office who'd ever seen Nina reveal a temper to match her fiery red hair.

"What gives, Nina?" Kait asked. "Why wasn't I included in the meeting?"

Nina looked up. Blue eyes usually vibrant and clear were dark with guilt. "I'm sorry. I asked to have you join us, but Sulyard forbid it."

Kait's unease moved toward full-blown worry. "Why? What's happening?"

"A small ISP was tracking communications traffic when they noticed a huge surge in traffic." Nina drew a report from the folder and handed it to Kait.

Kait studied the printout from ValCom, a local Internet service provider, showing that an unusually large number of computers had accessed ValCom's network at the exact same time.

"A botnet," Kait said, referring to a network of computers controlled by an unscrupulous individual.

Nina nodded. "The good news is we've tracked it through a myriad of servers to the source where the attack originated. We're about to make an arrest."

"And the bad news?"

"The code contains Rhodes's signature," Nina said, using Fenton's last name as all agents in the office did.

"Fenton? He's finally surfaced." Kait's stomach fluttered with excitement. *Finally!* "Wait? How is this bad news?"

"Sulyard is making you sit this one out."

"You're kidding, right?"

Nina shook her head, a wayward curl springing into action. She gently tucked it behind her ear when Kait would have slapped it out of the way. "I'm sorry, Kait, but he says you're too personally involved and might do something to jeopardize the prosecution."

"He's not going to keep me here!" Kait tried to push past Nina to the door.

Nina clamped her hand on Kait's arm; her long nails polished an outrageous orange, looking out of place against Kait's simple gray suit.

"Let me go, Nina," Kait warned.

"If you go in there upset, you'll regret it."

"I'll regret not being there to arrest Fenton even more."

"You could lose your job." Nina's eyes flashed with determination.

"Then I'll lose my job." Kait glared back and shook off Nina's hand.

"Look, honey." Nina took a breath and came back with a softer tone. "The odds of this being Rhodes are slim to none. He knows we're on to his trademark code so it's doubtful he'd use it again. This is most likely someone impersonating him."

Not Fenton? No. Kait refused to believe that. "If it's a copycat, Sulyard wouldn't be so adamant about me staying here."

"He has to cover himself just in case it *is* Rhodes." Nina paused, and seemed to consider her next words carefully. "You know we all want to see him pay, don't you?"

"Yes."

"Then trust us to handle this."

Oh, how Kait wanted to put this heavy burden in someone else's hands, but it was her battle to wage. Her revenge to exact. Her mission. Her reason for getting up each morning and moving on after Abby's death. If Kait let anyone else do it for her, she'd never forgive herself. "I can't, Nina. I just can't."

"Fine. Then let me talk to Sulyard. Maybe I can convince him to let you ride along if you promise to stay in the car."

"I can't promise that."

"You know Sulyard." Nina stepped closer and lowered her voice. "No matter what you say to him, he won't reverse his decision and let you in on the arrest. It's either stay in the car or miss out altogether."

Kait studied her friend, looking for any hint of dishonesty. "Was this his plan all along? To let me think I can't go so I'll be happy to ride along?"

"You know me better than that." A heavy sigh slipped from Nina's mouth, and it cut Kait to the core that she was lashing out at one of her best friends. "You've become so suspicious since Abby died."

Kait winced at Nina's comment, but she was right. Kait hardly trusted anyone. Not since Fenton had taught her the toughest lesson of her life. She could never fully know another person. They could hide secrets and turn on her in a flash. But Nina? Not Nina. She wasn't harboring anything. She was Kait's friend. And if she said Kait wasn't being played, then she wasn't being played.

"I'm sorry." Kait made sure her expression carried her remorse for doubting Nina's intentions.

"No biggie." Nina smiled, wrinkling her nose covered with freckles that had multiplied in the summer sun. "I can handle your suspicions without melting. So you want me to talk to him?"

Kait didn't want to sit in the car. Worse, she didn't want to be left behind and miss seeing Fenton dragged out of the house in handcuffs. This option was better than nothing. "Fine. Ask him."

"Then give us some space to work this out. Head over to your cubicle and I'll come find you after Sulyard makes a decision." Nina didn't wait for Kait's agreement but went into the room.

Kait should do as Nina suggested. Walk away. Let them hash it out. But she couldn't leave without seeing Sulyard's initial reaction to the request.

Kait turned to the window. The overhead lights burned brightly now, displaying the pitying looks of her co-workers. Not from Becca, though. She offered a tremulous smile. Kait tried to return it but failed. Instead, she watched Nina march up to the boss. Her gestures were big and animated as she made Kait's case for her, forcing Sulyard to take a step back in defense of his personal space. He shifted his focus to Kait, his eyes burning with intensity. Assessing. Weighing. Processing. She resisted squirming and stood firm. If she let him see any hint that she wasn't clearheaded and strong, or that she would fall apart in the field, he'd deny Nina's request. Deny the one thing Kait desperately wanted, and after three long years of waiting for this day to come, she wouldn't be present to witness Fenton's takedown.

Chapter Three

KAIT WAITED IN her cubicle, pacing back and forth, her palms coated in perspiration. She felt like a little kid sent to her room while her parents discussed her fate. Ten minutes had passed. Going on eleven now. Then twelve. Ticking by as slow as an eternity.

Finally, she heard the meeting break up and she hung at the edge of her cubicle, waiting to see who Sulyard had dispatched to share the news. If Nina rounded the corner, Kait was out. Anyone else except Sulyard meant she was in.

She held her breath. Stared. Waiting.

Becca charged around the corner in her usual head down, get to the problem and solve it mode. Kait resisted shooting her hand up in victory until Becca delivered the official verdict. A runner and all-around athlete, she was solid muscle, her legs powering her down the hallway in rapid strides. With blond hair pulled into a ponytail, she looked every bit an agent. Tough and in charge.

"You're in," she said without fanfare. "So start getting your things together. The team departs in fifteen minutes." She held out her fist for a bump.

Kait pounded it and exhaled emotions that threatened to bring tears.

Becca appraised her. "I'm sorry about meeting without you. Sulyard personally escorted us to the room so we couldn't tell you."

"I understand," Kait said as she worked to control the tears.

"You're not mad?" Becca asked. "Honestly, I mean."

Kait shook her head, her mind already going to the items she would need to bring along on the raid.

Becca glanced at her chunky sports watch and frowned. "You know there's nothing I'd like more than to go on the raid with you, right? I'd be all over it if I didn't have the CASA conference in Eugene. Maybe I should get someone else to do the keynote speech."

Kait shook her head. No way would she be the cause of Becca missing her speaking engagement. A former foster child, Becca volunteered as a Court Appointed Special Advocate for foster children. She was a tireless defender of abused or neglected children and was a sought-after speaker for the volunteer organization.

Kait appreciated her friend's concern, but if Becca chose to cancel, she'd regret it for days. "Go as planned," Kait said firmly. "I won't have you miss something that's so important to you."

Skepticism lingering on her face, Becca continued to watch Kait. "Is there anything I can do to help before I go?"

"For starters, you can stop looking at me that way." Kait crossed her arms. She hated when anyone thought her as weak and helpless as Fenton made her feel. "I'm fine."

"No, you're not. I can see it in your eyes. I'll try to reschedule."

"Absolutely not. You go to Eugene and wow them. Nina will take good care of me in your absence."

"That's what I'm worried about." Becca wrinkled her nose, her mouth lifting in a smile. "She needs looking after as much as you do."

Kait forced a smile at her friend's attempt to lighten the mood, but nothing short of arresting Fenton would make Kait smile with abandon right now. "Get out of here before you're late."

"Call me if you need me." After one last look, Becca hurried down the hallway, her ponytail swinging in cadence with her steps.

Thankful to have friends who watched her back, Kait gathered her things. As she prepared, anticipation over finally capturing Fenton started in the pit of her stomach. By the time Nina came to tell her they were ready to depart, Kait felt drunk with excitement.

"Don't get your hopes up," Nina whispered as they walked out the door with the other agents. "Remember what I said. Rhodes wouldn't use his code again. This is most likely someone impersonating him. You know how the hacking community idolized him. Everyone wanted to be the infamous Vyper." She nearly spit out Fenton's screen name, her distaste for him obvious.

"I don't know, Nina. It makes sense that he'd surface on the anniversary of Abby's death."

"If that's the case, then why wait until the third year? Why not do something on year one and year two?"

Kait slipped her hand into her pocket and fingered the letter "A" cast in pure silver that she'd taken from Abby's keychain. Kait carried it every day, the sleek metal a reminder of her failure to protect Abby and of letting Fenton escape. She gripped it hard, letting the cool edges bite into her palm. She wouldn't fail again. If there was any chance of capturing him, she was all in. "My gut says it's Fenton. So go with me on this one, okay?"

Nina eyed her. "I just don't want you to be disappointed again if it's someone else."

"I know." Kait tried to smile at her friend, but her lips trembled, so she clamped them together before Sulyard saw her questionable hold on her emotions and left her behind.

She trailed the team into the parking garage. Simmering heat radiated off the concrete, hitting Kait square in the face. The last thing any of them wanted to do in this heat was to strap on a Kevlar vest over suit jackets. They would, though. Safety always trumped comfort. Knowing she'd see no action, she felt foolish retrieving her vest from the trunk, but protocol dictated she wear it, so she chose her newest one and slipped it on.

Sulyard tossed his keys to her. "You're driving."

Interesting. She climbed behind the wheel of his SUV, and he took shotgun. His commanding presence made the vehicle feel smaller than usual. Silence filled the car, and she was conscious of the fine line she was walking with him right now and didn't speak. Once on the highway, he handed a file to Nina in the backseat, and they discussed operation logistics.

Of course. That's why he'd assigned driving to Kait. It didn't matter if she knew the plan. She was sitting on the bench for this one. A bystander while the action went down. She hadn't planned it this way, but so what? Fenton was going down today. That's all that mattered.

On the thirty-minute drive, she listened to them review the operation. Arrive. Disperse over the property they'd carefully mapped out. Surround the house. Breach the home if necessary and take him down. Thorough as usual. This was personal for them, too. They were her family. She might be more zealous about hunting down Fenton, but the entire team really did want to see him brought to justice.

"What's our ETA, Knight?" Sulyard asked, using Kait's last name as he did with all his subordinates.

"We're five minutes out."

He dug out his phone. "Time to give the locals a heads up."

Kait nodded her understanding of the standard protocol, but Sulyard was already asking to speak to the watch commander. They wouldn't include locals on the arrest today, but neighbors often flooded 911 with calls when agents rushed out of cars wielding weapons. It was only prudent to keep the police in the loop.

"It's not a good day to be yanking my chain, Vance." Sulyard's voice rose, and Kait glanced at him. "Yes, that's our address." As he listened, he worked the muscles in his jaw hard. "Fine, we'll check in with the detective." He hung up and slammed a fist into the dashboard.

"Everything okay, sir?" she asked, a hard knot of dread filling her throat.

"Do I look like it's okay?" He faced the side window.

She opened her mouth to delve deeper, but he'd clamped his jaw tight. No point in irritating him even more. If he wanted to tell them what was going on, he would. Nothing she could say would draw it out of him until he was ready to share.

She focused on her driving, making the last few turns until she reached their target's street in an older residential area of Portland's east side. Sulyard swiveled in his seat. She felt his eyes on her and wanted to look at him, but there was something going on up ahead, keeping her attention on the road.

"If Rhodes is indeed our suspect, we won't be arresting him today," Sulyard finally said, his tone surprisingly gentle.

Kait's heart dropped, and she bit her tongue before blurting out something she'd regret.

"I'm sorry, Knight," he continued. "But PPB dispatched a homicide detective to our address not more than fifteen minutes ago."

Homicide? The blood drained from Kait's head, and the car seemed to close in on her. She lowered the window and drew hot steamy air into her lungs. "Fenton's dead?" she asked when she could speak again.

"Looks like it." Sulyard pointed in the distance at two police cars with light bars flashing.

Sucking in more air, she took a long look at the pair of uniformed officers standing duty inside fluttering yellow tape and acting as sentries to the modest home. FED was on scene already, snapping overall photos of the exterior. The Forensic Evidence Division's custom van and surrounding chaos had drawn a crowd of neighbors.

She slowed the car to a crawl, and then pulled up behind the other Bureau cars. "He can't be dead." Kait's words whispered out.

Sulyard eyed her. "You make it sound like a bad thing."

"Death is too easy for him. He needs to spend the rest of his life in jail and suffer for the pain he's caused my family."

Nina leaned between the bucket seats and squeezed Kait's shoulder. "At least he finally paid for it. It's better than running free."

Hah! Nina couldn't possibly understand Kait's disappointment. No one could. Arriving to find Fenton dead was not how she thought this would go down. He'd eluded their top-notch team for three years. So how could he be careless enough to let someone kill him today? The Fenton she knew was too smart for that. Too crafty and devious.

"Wait," Kait blurted out. "Maybe Fenton isn't the victim. It might be someone else. Nina, you said yourself that Fenton wouldn't use his code."

"She could be right, sir," Nina said, catching Kait's enthusiasm. "We knew finding Rhodes here was a long shot."

"It's possible," Sulyard answered. "Hopefully, Detective Murdock has ID'd the vic by now."

Did he mean *the* Sam Murdock? The cop who'd comforted her the night of Abby's murder?

Kait searched the scene. There, on the porch. She recognized the transplanted Texan's dark jeans, distressed cowboy boots, and thick belt buckle. Perfect. He was Kait's key to getting in on the action. All she needed was Sulyard's approval.

She schooled her voice to remove any remaining tension. "I get that you don't want me involved in this, sir, but I know Murdock. He'll balk at someone in your position asking for information. If I talk to him, I could get more out of him." At least she hoped he'd be amenable to talking with her. Though locals and feds got along much better than TV and the media often portrayed, they didn't always mix well, and she couldn't be certain Sam would be open-minded.

Sulyard looked at her, weighing his decision before lifting his shoulder. "Why not? This case is going nowhere with our suspect possibly headed to the morgue." He pointed ahead. "I'll update the other team members while you question Murdock."

Kait reached for the door handle, her palms moist and her hands unsteady. She was looking forward to seeing Sam Murdock again, but seeing Fenton Rhodes . . .

Three years of imagining his arrest and she still wasn't prepared for the sick feeling rising up in her stomach. Even if he was dead, getting out of this car and walking across the street to identify him would be one of the hardest things she'd ever done.

DETECTIVE SAM Murdock took a quick break on the victim's front porch as he waited for the medical examiner to arrive. He rolled to the balls of his feet, stretching as far as the stiff leather of his boots allowed. It was hotter than blue blazes inside the house and felt less brutal out here, but the stench of death still clung to his pores and nose as it permeated the sticky air.

He turned away from the house in an effort to block out the image of the man handcuffed to sturdy bolts drilled into the floor. Not that it helped. The sight of the victim chained and left to rot for days remained burned into Sam's brain. He took a deep breath, the horrible smell making him wish he hadn't. Bad enough to catch a case this gory, but on the hottest day of the year?

He heard a ruckus at the street. Hoping it was the medical examiner, he turned to find a news crew scrambling through the growing crowd hugging the crime scene tape. Across the road, he spotted four SUVs lining up at the curb like a mini army. The front door of the lead vehicle opened and a woman stepped out wearing a Kevlar vest. Not local law enforcement. She had the look of a fed.

DEA? FBI?

Playing nice with the feds was the last thing Sam needed today. Better to head her off at the pass and send her packing.

He jogged down the steps as she marched down the street. *Great.* She moved like an officer bent on taking charge. That was so not happening on his watch. He stopped and planted his feet, staking claim to his territory and forcing her to come to him.

Tall, maybe five ten or eleven, she wore a white blouse and gray jacket under the vest. Matching gray slacks emphasized legs that seemed to go on forever. Something about her posture was familiar, but from this distance, he couldn't place her.

Holding a hand over her eyes, she finally looked at him.

What was *she* doing here?

She wasn't just a fed, she was Agent Kaitlyn Knight. The woman with haunted eyes that had once connected with his, telling him they shared pain only a terrible loss could bring. The same kind of agony and despair he'd seen in the eyes of family members on his death notification calls.

He forgot about the noisy crowd and the stench of death and took a long hard look at her. She slowed, her shoulders thrown back and chin raised in a dancer's carriage. He'd never seen her slouch. Even when her sister had been murdered—a horrific day that would take most people down—she'd stood tall, and he'd instantly recognized the depth of her strength.

Strong and stunning. The kind of woman who caught men's attention. Her regal posture made her seem unapproachable and yet, if other men were like Sam, they couldn't help wanting to try.

So what? None of that mattered here. Not at his crime scene.

"Ms. Knight," he said, trying to sound detached when she glided to a stop.

She quirked a brow and studied him for long moments as if she were questioning how he knew her name. Not surprising. They'd never been officially introduced.

He held out his hand. "Sam Murdock. Homicide."

"I remember you, Detective." She slipped slender fingers into his and shook.

Despite the heat, they were like ice. Same as the night of her sister's death when he'd taken her hand to express his condolences.

He released her hand. "What brings you here, Ms. Knight?"

"Kait, please." Her tone was clipped and all business as she side-stepped his question.

He tipped his head at her cohorts. "I take it y'all have a professional interest in this location, *Kait*." He drew out her name, letting his Texas accent make it seem like her answer held little importance for him.

She raised a brow again. She had to know he was purposefully keeping the focus on her reason for being here to avoid sharing information about his crime scene. Problem was, she simply stared at him as if looking for a way to get him to open up. Too bad. He wouldn't be the first to cave. He returned her stare and waited.

"We have an arrest warrant for the code name of Vyper," she finally said, sounding a bit peeved at him. "We believe Vyper is occupying this house."

"Elliot Congdon?" he asked, though at this point in the investigation they hadn't confirmed that the deceased was the man listed on the property deed.

"We're aware that he's the owner of the home, but we have reason to believe he has a guest who possesses a specific computer background."

Interesting. Maybe Congdon wasn't the deceased after all. Many detectives would have searched the body for a wallet by now, but that was sloppy. Could disturb and destroy forensic evidence. The victim was going nowhere. Sam could afford to wait for the medical examiner who was pulling up to the curb right now.

He nodded at the van. "Now that the ME's here, we'll search the body for ID. No sense in all y'all waiting around. Give me your card. I'll call you when I know something."

"Nice try, Detective, but I'm not going anywhere."

Spunky. "Sam. Call me Sam."

"Sam, then. I'll be patient and wait with my co-workers until you get that ID before I insist on seeing the crime scene." She rested a hand on her weapon, and he couldn't help but notice she didn't wear a wedding ring.

Still single. A single mother, if her niece remained in her custody, as he'd once heard on the grapevine. Not that he was interested. Of course not. Just an observation made by a police detective. As was noting the spark in her eyes and the flash of independence and strength that managed to jumpstart his heart after years in mothballs. "I'll let you know what we find."

She took a few steps, then turned back. "Don't take too long, Sam." Her good-humored tone held a hint of warning. "I've been known to bite when I'm kept waiting." Her gaze lingered on his for a long moment until she suddenly broke contact and walked away.

Very spunky and an interesting addition to his case.

Making sure no one saw him smile, he watched her return to her posse, hoping with each step that she'd turn and look at him one more time. She didn't, but kept going, a definite sway in her hips raising his interest. Maybe it wouldn't be such a bad thing to cooperate with the feds for once. Not a bad thing at all.

WHAT WAS SHE DOING?

Fenton gaped at Kait's back. This wasn't right. She shouldn't have walked away from the detective. She should be stepping inside the house, not heading back to the other FBI goons.

Who did she think she was? Ruining this. He'd set up everything perfectly. Sending the code. Giving the ISP enough time to contact her office. Making the anonymous call about Congdon. All at the right time.

So why didn't she care enough to dive in and investigate?

Because she didn't care about Abby's death, that's why. No surprise there. Kait had let her sister die in her place. Then she took his baby girl, leaving him alone.

He should set her straight. Right here. Right now. He took a step in her direction.

No. That's what she's hoping for. You're smarter. More patient.

Lily would be his soon enough. He had a plan. Even if Kait didn't play her part, he'd improvise and she'd pay.

She'd pay all right.

He lowered the binoculars and climbed into Brian's van. If you could even call it a van. The hunk of junk was held together by rust. He cranked the engine, white smoke billowing out the tailpipe and contaminating the air. He chuckled. He was just like the smoke. Soon, he'd contaminate every aspect of Kait's life, then disappear in a wisp of air. All starting with the second surprise tomorrow morning. Too bad he couldn't be a fly on the wall in her office when all hell broke loose.

Chapter Four

"THOUGHT YOU were off for the afternoon." Deputy medical examiner Marcie Jensen paused on the porch and looked up at Sam.

"I was." He smiled at the petite, fifty-year-old woman wearing white coveralls. She was not only the Lead Deputy Medical Examiner for Multnomah County, but she was the best forensic pathologist on staff and a good friend. He was lucky she caught the case with him.

She frowned at him as she snapped on her gloves. "You get to the cemetery before coming in?"

He shook his head and entered the stifling house. He had no intention of discussing the fourth anniversary of his wife's death or his interrupted trip to visit Hannah's grave. Though they'd spent their married life in Austin, she'd been raised in Portland. He'd brought her home to be buried near her family and decided to stick around.

"Maybe you'll have time to go after we finish up." Marcie stepped into the back bedroom that the victim had used as an office. After setting her field kit on the floor, she squatted near the body. "Where's Connor?"

"Out of town. His grandmother died this morning."

"He's had a tough time lately."

"Yeah." Sam pushed the questions about his missing partner from his mind to concentrate on the crime scene.

One wall of the ten by ten room was lined with computer equipment and other gizmos he couldn't identify. He'd have to request a computer tech from the Regional Computer Forensics Laboratory to dismantle and process it all. That was, if Kait didn't try to wrestle this case out from under him, which was entirely possible. At least she was likely to try. The thought of going toe-to-toe with her on this made him smile again.

"What're you grinning about?" Marcie asked.

"Nothing," he said and focused on the victim.

Heavy blackout drapes covered the only window in the space, letting in a sliver of sunlight near the hem and highlighting the victim. He was propped against a wall, his wrists handcuffed to thick bolts protruding from the wooden floor. He wore baggy jeans and a dingy T-shirt boasting the slogan, "Insufficient Memory". No doubt a salute to his profession, if the many computers in the room could be trusted to tell his story. The left side of his chest and the floor below were saturated with dried blood.

As Marcie studied the body, Sam wandered the room. This was the oddest scene he'd ever worked. The oddity wasn't in what was in the room, but what was missing. Plenty of people went overboard with computer equipment these days. Very few people had nothing else in their office space. No papers, files, supplies, file cabinets, no printer. Not even a pen.

So what had this guy been up to?

"Clean," Sam whispered. "Too clean." Not clean as in an obsessive person, but a professional killer who knew to remove all evidence and anything that would give Sam's team a place to start their investigation.

"Hmm." Marcie sat back and stretched out the vic's shirt. "No damage to the fabric. With all this blood, that's odd."

"You're telling me. I wanted to look under the shirt, but I waited for you."

"Good boy," she said, and he almost expected her to turn and pat him on the head like an obedient dog. She leaned over the body again. "You really need to move on, Sam. Hannah would want you to be happy again."

Marcie often flitted from topic to topic, and now she'd returned to his aborted trip to the cemetery. "Not having this conversation, Marcie."

"What in the world?" Her hand rested on the victim's chest, a frown marring her usual cheerful mood. "This isn't good. Not good at all."

"What?" Sam moved closer.

She pressed on the chest. "There's a huge hole where his heart should be."

"The killer removed the heart?"

"Looks like it." She lifted the shirt and examined the body. "It's missing all right. Looks like the killer used a saw of some sort to remove it." She leaned back on her heels and looked up. "This is just sick. I see murder vics all the time, but nothing like this. Shackled to the floor. The heart missing."

"Definitely out of the ordinary." Sam swallowed hard as he pondered the discovery. He was like Marcie—used to seeing murder victims, but cutting out a heart? They were dealing with a depraved individual here. And it was Sam's job to catch him.

"Who would do such a thing?" Marcie continued to peer at Sam as if he had all the answers.

"Maybe our killer's a trophy taker. Or it's meant as a message."

"Message, like what? You broke my heart, so I'm taking yours?"

"Could be."

"Which could also mean our killer might be a woman jilted by this guy."

"So you're thinking she lures him back here for a little fun and games, then kills him?"

"Maybe. Though, he surely had to wonder why she shackled him to the floor in the office instead of a bed."

"Or it's some creepy serial killer," Sam said, hoping he was wrong. "But if that was the case, we probably would have heard about another murder like this. Still, I'll run it through ViCAP."

After seven years as a homicide detective, Sam was all too familiar with the FBI's ViCAP database designed to track and correlate information on violent crime, especially murder. Current cases could be matched to others to see if their killer had struck before.

He opened his mouth to speculate further, when a deadbolt on the door caught his interest. Odd. Who puts a deadbolt on a bedroom? He'd been too wrapped up in looking at the body to see it before, so he went to investigate.

In the hallway, he found a hook near the top of the doorframe with a key dangling from it. He checked the lock again. It carried the shine of a newer lockset. He'd like to make sure the key fit the lock, but he didn't want to risk smudging any fingerprints.

He pulled out his notepad and jotted down the brand of the lock, then snapped a picture with his cell phone. "Did you see this deadbolt? Key's hanging in the hallway. Either the vic routinely secured his equipment, or our killer locked up the vic."

"Curiousier and curiousier," Marcie mumbled, her gaze never leaving the body.

Curious and disturbing. The kind of thing that, combined with the missing heart, took this case from a routine homicide and pushed it to top priority status. One he needed to alert his commanding officer to before the press got wind of it. But the first thing his lieutenant would for ask was the vic's identity.

Sam rejoined Marcie. "Mind looking for an ID so I can get to work on finding the sicko who did this?"

"My pleasure." She withdrew a wallet from the vic's back pocket and handed it to him.

He flipped through the cheap nylon billfold. "No driver's license. Not surprising. Didn't find a car in the garage either. Now if I was investigating this case in Texas, that in itself would be a red flag. Since everything's so spread out there, you need a car, but—"

"With Portland's solid public transit system, plenty of people don't own cars here," Marcie finished for him.

He pulled out a warehouse club card. "ID's for Elliot Congdon. House is registered to him, too." He held the photo out for Marcie.

She looked at it, then at the body. "That picture is so small and grainy, I wouldn't bet my job on this being Congdon."

Sam slipped the card back in the wallet and bagged it. He didn't mind giving his lieutenant an unverified ID, but going to the next of kin without being positive was something he worked hard to avoid. And he sure as shootin' didn't like to bring people to the morgue for an ID when the body was in such a decomposed state.

In hopes of finding a better picture, Sam would search DMV records just in case the vic had a license but didn't carry it. They'd also fingerprint the body and search databases. If their vic had been arrested, had completed a background check, or was in the military, his prints would be readily searchable. Though from his rumpled clothing, Sam doubted the deceased had served in the military.

The process would take time, but it was time well spent. He'd rather do a bit more legwork instead of mistakenly telling the wrong person their loved one had been brutally murdered.

SULYARD HAD LOST all patience with Kait, but she wasn't giving up. Not when a chance existed—albeit a miniscule one—that Fenton had been murdered in the house across the street.

"May I remind you, sir," she said keeping her tone free of emotion, "that with our suspect headed to the morgue, you said I couldn't do any damage to the case. And I know you *never* go back on your word." She held her breath and waited for him to knock her down a peg. He simply let his icy look do the work for him. She'd pushed him too far, and she was certain she'd blown it.

"She's right, sir. You did say that when we arrived," Nina said, surprising Kait. Nina often soothed ruffled feathers in the office, her kindness legendary to all who worked with her, and she rarely rocked the boat. Now here she was standing up for Kait.

Kait waited for Sulyard to freeze Nina with the same stare. If he was a kinder, gentler supervisor, like many others Kait had worked with at the FBI, he'd take this in stride. But he was old school. Rigid. Unyielding and always in control.

He focused on Kait. "You can stay until the vic is ID'd. But report in the minute that happens. You got that?"

"Yes, sir," she said, and immediately clamped her mouth closed on a victory smile begging for release.

"And Brandt." He swung his gaze to Nina. "No more double teaming me if you know what's good for you." He clapped his hands, the sound reverberating through the neighborhood and sending birds flying. "Let's go, people." He pivoted and climbed into his vehicle.

Nina hung back.

"Thanks for that," Kait said. "But you should go, before he gets angrier. I can handle myself, and I don't want you to get in trouble for me."

Ignoring Kait, Nina turned to face the crime scene. "So, Sam Murdock, huh? He's the cop who was so kind to you the night Abby died, right?"

Wondering where Nina was going with this, Kait nodded.

"Then your job here won't be too difficult." Nina gestured across the street where Sam had stepped around the forensics van. "That guy's not hard on the eyes. Not hard on them at all."

"You want me to introduce you?" Kait asked in jest. Nina's recent difficult breakup with Navy SEAL Quinn Stone had left her wary of all relationships.

"Oh, no, honey. With the way he's looking at you, I'd say he's all yours." Laughing, she dropped her car keys into Kait's hand and walked away, but honestly, with Sam's gaze locked on Kait, she hardly noticed her friend leaving.

She'd like to say she was so focused on the case, that when they'd talked earlier, his barely veiled interest hadn't piqued her curiosity, but the connection she'd felt continued to simmer under the surface. Not that she'd do a thing about it. She only had eyes for the victim today.

Pocketing the keys, she worked her way through the crowd to talk to Sam. By the time she reached him, he'd casually leaned his shoulder against the van. His ankles were crossed, his gaze still intently watching. She was sure he'd meant his relaxed posture to catch her off guard, but his laser-sharp focus gave away his intensity.

"Kait." Her name oozed out like warm honey.

"Do you have an ID for the deceased?" she asked, ignoring his attempt to charm her.

He cast an equally languid look across the road. "Where's the rest of your team going?"

So that's the way they were going to play it. She'd thought they were over the local versus fed dance. Obviously not. Too bad. She wasn't all that good at dancing. She had the long lean body of a dancer, but she was much better at stepping on toes.

"You first," she said. "Is the deceased Congdon?"

"We're still not positive." He watched her for a moment. "Seems like a good time for you to tell me what's going on here."

They could ride this seesaw of redirection forever if she allowed it, but she needed to know if Fenton had died, so she'd get this conversation started. "We tracked a bot herder named Fenton Rhodes to this location.

The code was indicative of something he would write. He's the creep who killed my sister. He's evaded us for three years. Not even a hint of his activity until today."

"I remember Rhodes, but I won't pretend to know what a bot herder is."

"It's—"

Sam held up his hands, horror, or maybe disgust, on his face. "If it turns out I need to know about this bot herder thingy for the case, then you can explain. But please, spare me the details until then."

"Not into technology, huh?"

He patted the smartphone case on his belt. "I still haven't totally figured this thing out, much less understand all that computer jargon."

Despite her desire not to succumb to the charms of this dashing Texan, she couldn't help smiling at his technophobia. It was oddly intriguing, and under normal circumstances, she'd consider exploring it, but her life had been far from normal the last three years. "So is it possible that Fenton Rhodes is the victim? He's six feet. One hundred eighty pounds. Jet black hair. Prominent nose. Blue eyes."

"He fits the description of our vic, but we have tentatively ID'd him as the homeowner, Elliot Congdon."

"But you're not positive on the ID."

"Not one hundred percent, no."

"Since there's a chance it could be Fenton, I'd like to do a physical confirmation."

"Shoot, Kait." He pushed off the van and planted his boots wide apart, making him seem bigger and more imposing. Likely his intent. "You don't want to go in there. Not unless you have to. This one is grimmer than most. It's not a pretty sight. And with the heat . . ."

Kait's irritation flared over his assumption that she was fragile. "I can handle it, *detective*."

"I know you can, but why would you want to when there's no need? I'll update you on what we find."

"I need to see him." She met Sam's gaze and saw him warring with indecision. "Please," she added, wishing she could draw out the word for emphasis the way he did.

He gave a sad shake of his head. "If you insist, but don't say I didn't warn you."

"I wouldn't dream of it."

"Right." He rolled his eyes and held up the yellow tape, allowing her to duck under.

She followed him to the officer of record stationed at the end of the walkway and registered her information in the official logbook.

"That's the ME on the porch." Sam gestured at the redhead Kait had seen him talking with earlier. She wore white coveralls and squatted to dig something out of a tote bag. "We'll talk to her first to see if she's discovered anything helpful."

He handed Kait a pair of latex gloves, then took off. His long legs cut across the grass, but she matched him stride for stride. At the house, she followed him up the stairs. The awful decaying smell of death greeted her at the top, sending her lurching back. If Sam saw her squeamishness, he didn't comment, and for that, she was grateful.

"Marcie," he said, his voice carrying a note of fondness for the woman. "This is Kaitlyn Knight. FBI. She might know our vic." Sam shared Kait and Abby's story.

"I'm so sorry for your loss." Marcie snapped off a glove and thrust out her hand to Kait. "Marcie Jensen. Deputy Medical Examiner."

"Any luck in narrowing down the time of death?" Sam asked while Kait shook hands with Marcie.

Marcie frowned. "Won't know until I get him back to the morgue, and I'm not sure I'll be able to give you an accurate time even then."

"A guess, then?"

Marcie sighed.

"I know, I know," Sam said as if he read her mind. "You don't like to guess, but it could help us solve this case faster and give Kait the closure she needs."

Marcie eyed him for a long time. With the way he patiently stood under her study, Kait suspected these two were friends outside of work.

"Fine," she finally said. "If I *have* to guess, the best I can do is two or three days. The large blisters on the skin and the abdominal bloating would normally tell me he's been dead three or four days. But this heat wave speeds up decomp, so I doubt it's been that long."

The smell, combined with Marcie's graphic description, made Kait's stomach churn. "Do you have a cause of death?"

"We don't need to—"

"No clue at this point," Marcie interrupted. "I'd like to say it's not a gunshot or stabbing. Especially since the deceased's shirt wasn't damaged, but with the removal of his heart, I can't be sure of that."

"Someone cut out his heart?" Kait's voice raised two octaves, catching the attention of a forensic photographer standing near the corner of the house. The threatening nausea intensified, and her stomach roiled with unease. She'd been so cocky, saying she could handle seeing the body, but could she? Could she really?

"You didn't tell her?" Marcie flashed Sam an irritated look. "Guess I need to stop telling people you're one of the good guys."

"I didn't tell her because I hoped she'd make a quick ID and leave before she had to hear about that."

"Hello, I'm right here." Kait tried to sound frustrated instead of nauseated.

"Sorry, sweetie." Marcie patted Kait's arm. "With the heat wave, we're all a little bit on edge here. Sounds like Sam's just looking out for your best interests. Which is a good thing, I suppose. This isn't going to be an easy case. Everything I've seen so far points to a professional, or at least a very experienced killer."

Rivulets of perspiration rolled down Kait's back, and she wasn't sure if it was from the heat or because this case was starting to make her skin crawl. "Are you suggesting a serial killer?"

"No, not serial." Marcie pushed a stray curl from her sweaty forehead. "I'm just saying, though I think the heart was taken postmortem, the killer shackled our vic to the floor, which suggests premeditation. Plus, he has to be a real sicko to mutilate the body, and then abscond with the heart."

"He not only cut it out, but it's missing, too?" Kait turned to Sam for an answer. "And the poor guy was restrained?"

Sam nodded, his expression grimmer. "Still sound like Rhodes? Or someone he might be involved with?"

She had no idea how to answer his question. Before Abby's death, Kait would have said absolutely not, but now she knew the real Fenton. The one who would do anything to keep his status as the supreme hacker—and that could make him a target of others who wanted to dethrone him.

But a murder as brutal as this one . . .

She peered at Sam. "Fenton shot another hacker point-blank in the back of the skull. That's why our team tried to arrest him three years ago. So what Marcie describes isn't out of the question, I suppose."

"There's only one way to find out." Sam donned a pair of disposable booties and entered the house.

Swallowing hard, Kait grabbed a pair, too, her pulse hammering in her neck. She was finally going to see if Fenton was shackled to the floor, his heart removed by some ruthless killer. Fitting, she supposed, since Fenton was as heartless as they came. Very fitting indeed.

Chapter Five

KAIT WOULDN'T have a chance to inspect the crime scene again, so she took a quick look at the flaking paint clinging to the front door which held a tarnished brass mail slot. She examined the lock and found no sign of forced entry, but the deadbolt had seen better days. That, coupled with the worn boards on the porch and weather-beaten siding, said Congdon didn't maintain his property in this neighborhood of pricey homes. Must have made the neighbors angry. Angry enough to kill him and cut out his heart? Not likely.

From the small entryway, she saw Sam waiting for her in the living room. He watched her, but it felt more like one professional law enforcement officer evaluating another. Nothing personal. Nothing like the moments between them outside, so she took her time.

She noted the absence of mail on the garish sixties ceramic tile. If the victim had died a few days ago, there should be envelopes and brochures strewn across the floor. Either the mail was moved, or none had been delivered for days. With the abundance of junk mail these days, that would be unlikely.

She looked at Sam. "No mail, or has it been bagged already?"

"There wasn't any. The post office must have stopped delivering for some reason, or the trusty postal worker would have smelled the body sooner and reported it."

She jotted a note on her pad and took the single step up to the living room. A sixty-inch flat screen mounted above the fireplace was the first thing that caught her attention. Next, she noted a gaming console and two controllers on the floor beside a denim beanbag chair. The rest of the room was empty. No pictures on the wall, no knickknacks on the fireplace mantel. No clue about who Elliot Congdon was other than a single guy who liked gaming. Nothing unusual, she supposed.

She took a closer look at the walls, finding holes where pictures had once hung, and her pulse tripped faster.

Sam's focus honed in on her. "You want to tell me what put that look on your face?"

He'd think she was crazy, but she had to be forthright if she wanted him to share his findings with her. "Fenton was a neat freak. Pictures collected dust, so he wouldn't let Abby hang any."

"And you think because there's nothing on the walls that he's our vic?"

She did, but she had nothing to base it on other than a hunch, so she shrugged and moved on. "You never mentioned how the murder was reported."

"I didn't, did I?" he said, once again back to the avoidance dance.

"C'mon, detective." She planted a hand on her hip. "What's the point in this? I'm not going to steal your investigation out from under you. Even if I wanted to, you have jurisdiction here."

He continued to appraise her, maybe trying to see if she was playing him. "But you thought about it, right?"

She laughed. "Honestly, no. But even if Fenton's not the deceased, the code we intercepted suggests his involvement, and I'll be doing my best to take possession of the computer equipment."

"Expected as much, and I'm okay with that. Once you get proper approval, and, of course, *if* you play nice and share what you find."

"What?" She clutched her chest in feigned offense. "You make it sound like agents don't know how to share."

He tilted his head and stared at her. "So you're saying you'll play nice?"

"I will as long as you'll agree to put up with me on this investigation until the killer is caught. Think you can handle that?"

"I'd be lying if I said it'd be a hardship." A slow dawning smile spread across his lips.

She should turn away—especially with the forensic techs entering the room and dropping off equipment, but she couldn't seem to pull free. Sam must have noticed the others as he abruptly jerked his gaze away and stepped to the other side of the room.

Crazy. She was just plain crazy for reacting to him this way. Here, of all places. Now, of all times. Her mission wasn't over. She still had to see Fenton pay, and even then, she wasn't free. Not until she honestly worked through Abby's loss. Through Fenton's betrayal. Only then could Kait trust a man again. And besides, she was likely the one being played here. He had to know his southern charm and good looks captivated women, and he was more likely trying to divert her attention from his case. Something she wouldn't allow to happen.

She caught up to him. "Nice try at distracting me. Now, how did you say the murder was reported?"

He looked half-impressed and half-irritated that he hadn't successfully avoided her question. "It was an anonymous call from a payphone."

"Strange. That doesn't happen every day."

"No, it doesn't. And it stays between us for now. Okay?"

"Sure." Thinking about all the possibilities of who would make an anonymous call, she followed him around the corner to a hallway.

The putrid smell hit her full on, and her footsteps faltered. She'd never smelled anything this nauseating in her life, and she was sure she was going to hurl right here.

Unfazed, Sam stopped near a gurney standing sentry outside a bedroom door and looked back at her. "Coming, Kait?"

She resisted taking a cleansing breath, which she knew would only worsen her problem, and followed him into a bedroom that had been used as an office. Sam lingered near the door as if waiting to be sure she made it into the room without passing out. Marcie squatted on the far side of the body. A skinny young man with a bad case of acne knelt on the side closest to Kait and blocked her view of the deceased's face.

Marcie looked up then nudged the guy. "Tim. This is Special Agent Kaitlyn Knight with the FBI."

"Yo." Clearly unimpressed that she was an agent, Tim didn't bother to look up.

"She's here to ID the body, and you're in the way."

"Have at it." Tim moved, giving Kait a clear view of the man who was handcuffed to metal bolts in the floor.

Her stomach roiling, she couldn't handle seeing the oozing sores Marcie described, so she avoided his face and started with his clothes. He wore a wrinkled T-shirt and baggy jeans that looked like he'd retrieved them from a heap on the floor. Fenton wouldn't dress this way. Even in death, his clothes would be tailored, pressed, and expensive.

Disappointment or relief—she wasn't sure which—settled in. She hadn't wanted him to be dead, but she also didn't want him to elude capture.

She looked at the head. Her stomach threatened to empty as she took in the black hair, broad face, and dark eyes staring lifelessly up at the ceiling. She could mistake this guy for Fenton at a distance, but even with the darkened color of the skin and accelerated decomp, she knew for sure this wasn't her brother-in-law.

"He has a similar build and facial features to Fenton, but it's not him." Saying it aloud forced the truth to sink in, bringing the pain of losing Abby rushing up, and robbing Kait of the ability to breath. She'd failed. Not only herself, but her sister. Again.

The space started to close in, and all she could hear was the throbbing of her own heart. She was instantly back at her parents' house the day Abby had died. The police watching her when she refused to let go of Abby's body. Her mother dragging Kait away as she nearly suffocated with grief. Like now, the air too thick to breathe. She couldn't lose it in front of the others, but she *was* going to lose it. Of that, she was certain.

With no idea where she'd go, she bolted from the room. There were too many people to see her fall apart out front. She'd find the back door. She charged down the hall, through a spotless kitchen, and down a few steps.

Finally outside, she dropped onto a redwood bench under a tall pine, hung her head between her knees, and gulped air. Her whole body shook, and she could barely think, let alone stand again. She continued to pull in big, chest-heaving gulps of air, and when she could form a cohesive thought, she realized her work here was finished, sending her into another tailspin. She'd bombed. Failed. Was back to square one in the search for her sister's killer.

Or was she?

Just because the man inside wasn't Fenton didn't mean Fenton wasn't involved. He could have killed Congdon and sent the code from this location.

A flicker of hope took purchase in her heart. Fenton could be the killer. He could really and truly be the man who'd left Congdon to rot in the heat.

The thought didn't diminish her hope, but it sickened her beyond belief. She hoped, no, prayed, that if he killed Congdon, she would find him and bring him to justice. Quickly, before he committed such a heinous act again and another person lost their life.

SAM LOOKED AT the ugly popcorn ceiling and fought his desire to follow Kait. That was the last thing she needed right now. Him, too. He was working a crime scene, for crying out loud, and they were both professional law enforcement officers. He'd embarrass her more by making a big deal of her abrupt departure.

"Seriously, that was lame." Tim stood and stretched. "Never thought I'd see a mighty fed run at the sight of a body."

"Give it a rest, Tim." Sam tried to keep his warning casual, but he was ready to deck the guy for his insensitivity.

"I'm just saying, I thought agents were supposed to be the gods of law enforcement." Tim rolled his eyes. "This one seems all too mortal."

Sam spun on him. "I said lay off."

Tim held up his hands. "What's your problem, man? I'm just giving my opinion."

"Well, your opinion is way off the mark." Sam poked Tim in his bony chest. "For your information, Agent Knight's sister was murdered in front of her, and the killer's never been found. She came in here thinking our vic might be that man. Now she knows he's still free. So cut her some slack. You got it?"

"Yeah. Geez." Tim backed away.

"Why don't you get some fresh air, Tim?" Marcie suggested.

With a glare for Sam, Tim stomped out. His sneakers covered in paper booties whispered over the wood floor as he slunk off.

Sam shoved his hands into his pockets and felt Marcie staring up at him.

"What?" he asked defensively.

Her eyes narrowed. "That was a little over the top, don't you think?"

"No," he snapped out, wondering what had gotten into him, losing his professional edge and defending Kait like that. "I don't know . . . maybe."

"Would you like to talk about it?"

"No."

"Why not? I'm a good listener and there's obviously something bothering you or you wouldn't have blown up at Tim."

Sam groaned. "I don't suppose it'd help if I told you to focus on the job."

An impish smile spread across her face. "You know me better than that."

He shook his head in frustration. "I don't know how Paul puts up with you."

"If there's anyone doing any *putting up* with someone in my marriage, it's me." She sounded peeved, but Sam knew it was all talk. Her marriage to his friend and veteran officer Paul Jensen was strong, and an example of a shared life Sam often missed in the late hours of the night. A life he would never know again. A thought that made him sadder today than it had in some time. The last thing he needed when working a homicide. He shoved it into the back of his mind and looked at Marcie.

She lifted the vic's hand. "I need you to unlock the cuffs."

Thankful she'd moved on, Sam dug out his universal handcuff key and bent down, instantly wishing he hadn't caught this case and wasn't squatting next to this poor man whose life had been so ruthlessly extinguished. He clicked the lock open and moved to the other one.

"Odd," Marcie said. "No bruising under the cuffs. He didn't struggle or fight at all."

"He trusted whoever cuffed him." Sam stood up. "Or he was drugged. Can you—"

"Rush the tox screen?" she finished for him, and he nodded. "I should have results for you by morning when I do the cut."

"What time?"

"Eight too early for you?"

Any time was too early to attend an autopsy, but it was part of the job. "I'll be there. Hopefully by then, we'll have more than a club card as ID."

"I'll get the criminalist to photograph the deceased so we can get the body out of here." Marcie got up and snapped off her gloves. "You track down that cute agent and see if she's all right."

He thought to ignore Marcie and stay right here, but as long as Kait was on site, he'd like to get her input on the computers lining the wall. He found her in the kitchen, standing in front of an opened refrigerator and absently staring at the contents.

"What's up?" he asked.

"He was here." Her voice was barely more than a whisper. "Fenton always meticulously organized his refrigerator like this. When Abby moved anything, even a fraction of an inch, he fixed it."

Sam glanced at the refrigerator's neatly aligned contents. "Plenty of people with obsessive disorders live this way."

"I suppose," she said, obviously not convinced. "But don't you think it's odd that this house is so neat, and yet the deceased is dressed like a real slob."

"Yeah, it's odd, but that doesn't mean Rhodes is our killer."

"He murdered another bot herder when he wanted to take over his bots. He could have done the same thing here."

"Seriously, are you speaking English?" he asked to lighten the mood, but her expression remained guarded. "Okay, so I guess it's time for you to tell me about this bot stuff." He mocked a shudder, and she rewarded him with a smile just as he'd hoped, but it was gone in a flash.

She stared over his shoulder. "Cyber criminals use the Internet to gain access to unsuspecting people's computers and take control of them via remote access."

"Unsuspecting people like who?"

"Anyone who uses the Internet. You, your neighbor, a teenager, an office worker. Even your mother or grandmother. If a computer connects to the Internet, it's vulnerable to attack and control. The criminals call the computers they control bots and the criminal is called a bot herder."

"Herder, huh," Sam said, letting the idea roll around in his head. "Like ranchers in Texas with their cattle."

"Exactly. The rancher controls his cattle. The criminal controls his computers." She paused and seemed to think before speaking. "Of course, this is a very simplified version of what happens."

"And we both know I need simple when it comes to this stuff." He eased the refrigerator door closed, giving her time to step back. "I could really use your expertise on the computers. Would you mind?"

She lingered for a few moments longer before striding toward the hallway. He understood her reluctance to let this go. Now that she knew the deceased wasn't Rhodes, she was hoping he was the killer, and they'd catch him. Sam got it more than most people would. If the drunk who'd plowed into and killed his wife and unborn son wasn't serving time, Sam would still be hunting the creep down just like Kait was hunting Rhodes. But that didn't mean she was right about this case.

Back in the office, Sam stood out of the way as Kait hurried past the victim and approached the three computers sitting on the scuffed wood floor.

"So what is all this stuff?" he asked, hoping to get her mind on the equipment.

She pointed at a black device with cables running from it. "This is a modem. It's used to connect this house to the Internet service provider." She gestured at a similar white one. "This is a wireless router, which allows you to access the Internet without plugging in your computer. And this," she gave him a sweet little smile as she moved on, "you might recognize. It's a telephone."

He laughed, glad to see her mood changed. "What would I do without you here?"

His question earned him a raised eyebrow before she squatted next to the equipment. "Generic cases. He built these himself. Only one box running, the others are silent."

Sam took a step closer to see what she was talking about, but he really didn't have a clue what he was looking for.

"Seems odd that he left one powered up," she said without looking up at him. "I'm guessing this computer is the source of our investigation. It's almost as if he was hoping it would lead us here."

"So you think the killer wanted us to find the body?"

She craned her neck to look behind the computer. "I don't know. Maybe there'll be a lead on the hard drives when we look at them."

"Can't you just look at it now?"

She shook her head. "Protocol requires us to create an image of the computer hard drive as we found it, which means waiting for an experienced forensic tech to arrive and take it back to the lab. Plus, if I wake up the machine, I may kick off some malicious code meant to destroy the information on the hard drive."

She angled her body, moving closer without touching the equipment. "Hard drive's been pulled on this one. Wouldn't be surprised if the same thing was true of the other one not running, but I can't get close enough to see." She sat back and stared at the equipment.

"And that would happen why?" he asked.

"As I mentioned, the code we intercepted suggests the victim is a bot herder. If so, these machines were most likely used to mine financial information from unsuspecting people. The killer probably stored the information on these drives and took off with the data."

"When you say data, you mean what exactly?"

"Credit card and banking information. Passwords to online accounts, etc." Her phone rang, and she snapped off her glove to dig it from her jacket pocket. "Great. My supervisor. Once I tell him it isn't Fenton, I'll be off the case." She stood and lifted the phone to her ear. "Knight here."

Sam didn't like hearing their collaboration might end, but maybe it was a good thing. He had a murder to solve and the very lovely Kaitlyn Knight distracted him.

Even now. In the room of death. In the sweltering heat, his mind disgusted by the crime. She distracted him. Something he couldn't afford. Not when he had a heart-stealing monster to hunt down.

Chapter Six

KAIT WANTED TO fling her phone across the room. But why? It wouldn't change Sulyard's decision. He wouldn't allow her to work on this case with Sam. Period. End of discussion. She should just be grateful that Sulyard had at least agreed to take the computers in-house for analysis. Even if he had ordered her to leave the crime scene as soon as the tech arrived and secured the machines. That meant she somehow had to convince Sam to keep her in the loop on his investigation. Which, she knew from their interaction so far, was going to be a challenge.

She turned and found him studying the floor by the victim. She joined him for a closer look, but she still couldn't see anything of interest.

"We're taking the computers into evidence," she said to get his attention. "We'll have a tech here in thirty minutes."

He looked up. "Guess that means your agency has completed the official paperwork."

"Not yet."

"And if I refuse to let you take them without it?"

"Then we'll have a fight on our hands." She smiled at him, making sure it was a megawatt-get-everything-she-wanted smile. "So avoid all the hassles and give in."

"Does anyone ever say no to you and get away with it?" His tone was tinged with amusement.

She tapped a nail against her chin as if she was seriously contemplating his question. "I can't think of anyone in recent months other than my supervisor."

"I hate to break your record, Kait, but you're not walking out of here with the computers unless I receive a directive from my lieutenant." His lips curled up, matching her smile with one of equal voltage.

Her heart took a little tumble, but she ignored it. "Already taken care of. They should be speaking right about now."

A loud thump sounded from the hallway, pulling his focus from her.

"Ouch," Tim whined from the other side of the wall. "You smashed my fingers."

"Be a man for once, Tim, and suck it up," Marcie said backing into the room while pulling a gurney.

"I love working with her." Sam grinned and stood. "But we don't want to be in here when they move the body."

"Yeah," the pipsqueak said from the doorway, a sneer forming on his long face. "If you couldn't handle the scene before, the stench we release when we move the dude will send you running for sure."

Why was there always one guy at a crime scene who insisted she prove herself? As if staying put, while an even more horrific smell filled the room, proved anything other than she was dumb enough to stay within range while they did it.

She met the pipsqueak's gaze, ordering him to get out of her way with a look she often used on noncompliant suspects. He held up his hands and backed off. She heard Sam chuckle as he followed her out of the room. Many guys in law enforcement were intimidated by strong women, but after his comment about Marcie and his laugh just now, she guessed he wasn't one of them.

On the porch, a thin young man with a buzzed haircut hurried up to Sam. He wore a knit shirt with the PPB logo on his chest. He'd covered his pants with a pair of white coveralls, but left the suit's upper portion hanging around his waist. The coveralls suggested he was part of the forensics team, but he wore a sidearm, so she couldn't be positive of his job.

"Marcie's ready for me to photograph the body." He shrugged his shoulders into the coverall sleeves then hung a camera around his neck and stared pointedly at Kait.

"Oh, sorry," Sam said. "Criminalist Dane Harwell, meet Agent Kaitlyn Knight with the FBI."

Dane whistled. "Must be some case if the feds are involved."

"They're not involved," Sam said. "This is just a courtesy visit."

Sam looked at Kait as if he wanted her to confirm her unofficial capacity, but she kept her mouth shut. If Dane thought she was officially involved, then if she wanted information from him, he was more likely to cooperate.

Sam didn't look pleased with her, but turned his focus back to Dane. "Be sure to print the key hanging outside the bedroom door. Then check to see if it fits the deadbolt."

"Okay. Any other special instructions?"

"Just give it your best. This place is clean. Freaky clean. It'll take your best effort to find any evidence, much less anything of value."

"Gotta love a challenge." Dane saluted and gave Kait a quick once-over before disappearing inside.

"I'm assuming, since he's carrying, that his job is a sworn position at PPB," Kait said, knowing they had both sworn employees who had taken an oath to carry out law enforcement duties with full arrest powers, and non-sworn staff.

Sam nodded. "The department requires criminalists to serve on patrol for five years before they're eligible for the job. Dane put in seven, and he had a stellar rep as a cop."

"He must keep detectives on their toes."

"He does, but I appreciate it. I've worked with non-sworn staff in Texas, and I'll take the experience a sworn tech brings to the table every time."

"You think it's that important?"

"One of the toughest things to learn as a tech is to stop thinking like the average Joe and start thinking like a criminal. No better way to learn how criminals think than working a patrol job."

"Then I look forward to talking with Dane about his findings," she said, ignoring Sulyard's command to return to the office when it popped into her mind.

Sam lifted his boot to the porch railing and brushed something off his pant leg. "Your supervisor clear your involvement in the investigation with my lieutenant, too?"

Kait forced herself to meet Sam's eyes. "Something like that."

"Something like that, or exactly like that?"

She didn't know what to say so she said nothing and let him form his own conclusion.

"So," he said moving on. "What you're not saying is your supervisor approved taking the computers, but doesn't want you to have anything to do with the murder investigation."

Touché. Sam was a far better opponent than she'd given him credit for, but she wouldn't back down. "I'm not leaving."

His boot fell to the floor with a thud, and he came to his full height. "You're not staying. Not without approval."

She took a step closer to him and cast him a pleading look. "I can't leave, Sam. Fenton killed my sister, and if he has anything to do with this case, I have to be involved."

He didn't immediately agree, but his eyes narrowed as if considering it. "If we discover a connection to Rhodes, I'll be happy to keep you updated." He kept watching her, his eyes burrowing deep.

She met his watchful stare with a defiant look. "If your sister was murdered, would you accept a kindly pat on the head by a detective in charge, or would you fight to stay?"

"Kindly pat?" He grinned at her. "Pretty sure if I tried to pat you on the head, you'd have me on the ground with my arm behind my back in seconds."

She returned his smile. "So I'm staying then."

He appraised her for a long, silent moment, then nodded. "Fine, Kaitlyn Knight who no one says no to. Today only. You observe. Do as I ask. Keep to the letter of the law and buy me a cup of coffee in the wee hours of the night when I'll be wishing I was anywhere but here."

"Deal," she said and relaxed for the first time since Nina told her about Fenton. "So, have you canvassed the neighborhood?"

His eyebrow shot up. "We may not be the FBI, *Agent* Knight, but we know how to run a murder investigation."

"I wasn't questioning your ability, *Detective*." She caught a faint glimmer of humor in his eyes. He obviously loved to spar as much as she did, and she felt a rush of excitement over spending the afternoon with him. "I just wondered if we still needed to question neighbors."

He gestured at the small bungalow on the other side of Congdon's crumbling concrete drive. "Our initial canvass is complete, except for Yolanda Pierce who lives next door. She's not home."

"And did the other neighbors share anything of interest?"

"Not really. Just background info." He settled on the porch railing. "Congdon's lived here all his life. His mother moved to an assisted living apartment in Tualatin a year or so ago and gave him the house. He's single, works in computers, as I'm sure you already figured out, and never leaves home. He even has his groceries delivered."

"Doesn't he visit his mother?"

"The uniforms said no."

"What kind of person doesn't visit their mom?" she asked but needn't have. If it weren't for Lily, Kait wouldn't visit her mother very often, but that was a story for another day, if then.

"So basically, we have a computer geek," she said. "A real loner who no one has missed for days. Sounds like he's the perfect victim."

"And since he never goes out, it's likely he didn't meet his killer in person, but online." Sam looked out over the street, his focus zeroing in on something or someone.

"A perfect place to run into Fenton." Kait followed Sam's gaze, but once again, she couldn't figure out what he was looking at.

"Or someone else." Sam swung his focus back to her. "If our vic meets and chats with his friends online, it will be more difficult to find his killer's identity."

Didn't take a rocket scientist to see the opening Sam left to point out her skills. "With your phobia of anything tech related, you'll need a guide to show you around the Internet." She felt the thrill of the hunt beginning to build. "I'm just the person to help. But I warn you, it won't take long before you'll wonder how you can possibly solve this murder without me."

AT THE END OF the day, Sam stood by Congdon's front door, letting the cooler air wash over him and clear his brain. A heavy downpour served as the grand finale to their weeklong scorching temperatures, and Portland had once again returned to the usual moderate summer weather. Sam felt like he could breathe again. Maybe like he had a chance at solving this bizarre homicide.

Carrying a forensic case that looked like an oversized tackle box, Dane stepped through the door. He swiped the back of his hand across his forehead. "Wish we could've gotten some of this cooler air inside."

"Sorry, man. I know this one is brutal."

"At least we're done and we're out of here."

"Did you find anything viable?"

"A few hairs we'll run for DNA, but don't hold out hope. Looks like they could belong to the vic."

"What about the key? Find a print on it?"

"None. And no prints at all. Not even latents." Dane shook his head. "You were right about this place. Spotless. As if the killer vacuumed and scrubbed the place from top to bottom on his way out the door."

Kait's comments about Rhodes's cleanliness fetish came to mind, but Sam thought it more likely their killer was just good at cleaning up a crime scene.

Dane shifted his case. "I'll be glad to come back out if you think of anything else you want processed. Just let me know."

"Thanks, man."

As Dane departed, Sam clamped a hand on his neck and kneaded muscles stiff as iron. He was physically and emotionally spent. Seeing the essence of a man's life boiled down to forensics and facts always took a toll on him. Today was no different. And he still had to confirm Congdon's ID and then notify his mother that she'd lost her only son.

Sam heard Kait's footsteps heading toward him, and he wished she could accompany him to Mrs. Congdon's apartment. But that wasn't possible. Kait had arranged for her mother to pick up her niece from daycare, but now Kait needed to take the girl home and put her to bed. Plus, Kait seemed equally spent. Not that she voluntarily let him see it. Throughout the afternoon, every time he caught her looking whipped, she forced out a half smile and went back to work.

In all honesty, he didn't regret letting her spend the day with him. He should have sent her packing, but her smile had caught him off guard, and he'd caved. She got to him in a way no one had in years. One innocent—maybe flirtatious—smile, and he was like a junkie jonesing for the next fix, wanting to see her smile again. His lieutenant was going to pitch a royal fit as soon as he found out about her, but Sam figured it was worth it.

Kait joined him, a wave of freshly applied perfume momentarily clouding the other smells. "Thanks for letting me stay."

He nodded. "This is it, though. If you want in on the case after today, you'll need to get your supervisor's buy-in."

"Then you don't want me to try to trace Congdon's online movements for you?'

"If you still want to do that, even knowing you can't be a part of the investigation, I'd be glad for the help." He paused and looked into her eyes. "But unless my LT gives me the approval to discuss the case with you, I won't be able to share anything else."

She averted her gaze.

"You can look away, Kait, but that's not going to make the rules disappear."

She whipped her head around. "Don't you ever get tired of rules and procedures and just want to do the right thing for an investigation?"

"Sure, all the time. But procedures are there for a reason. It keeps us safe. Keeps us from making mistakes, and ensures that the bad guys go away for a long time."

She looked at him, her face shadowed with regret.

"You know I'm right."

"I know," she said, but the sadness in her voice made Sam wish he could ignore the rulebook and give this woman, who'd been through so much, exactly what she wanted.

Chapter Seven

SAM PARKED IN front of Kait's warmly lit home, catching the time on the clock as he turned off the engine. Nine p.m. He shouldn't be here, and not just because of the time. Stopping at her house was a bad idea on so many levels he couldn't begin to name them all.

"Then get of here before you do something stupid." He reached for the key in the ignition. A vision of Mrs. Congdon's grief flashed before his eyes, and his hand fell away. He'd broken the news as gently as he could to the elderly woman, but no matter how skilled he'd become at death notifications, her only son had been brutally murdered, and nothing prepared a parent for that.

He oughta know. He'd lived it.

Sure, his son had still been in the womb when he died, but the visceral pain was the same.

His hand went to the chain around his neck holding a dog tag. He ran his fingers over the metal tag, feeling the letters of Danny's name. His son.

Sam ached with the loss. Danny and Hannah had both died the same day. His fault. All his fault. A stupid argument had forced Hannah into the car and onto a street with the crazed drunk driver. Couple that with losing his partner Stacie, and he'd experienced the trifecta of life events no one wanted to experience.

If he went home right now, he'd wander around the house—their house—and think about the night he'd lost them. He sure didn't want to sit in a lonely bar, and his partner was out of town. What did that leave?

Talking to someone who understood the pain of loss. Talking to Kait.

He jerked out his keys and jogged to her front door before he changed his mind again. He punched the doorbell and waited, his foot tapping nervously. Footsteps sounded from inside, and he still didn't have a clue what he was going to say. *Dumb.* He was charged on a daily basis with finding killers. Why hadn't he been smart enough to come up with a cover story?

He saw the space under the door darken and guessed she was standing on the other side watching him through the peephole. Maybe deciding if she should let him in. Regardless, it was too late to leave.

She opened the door and leaned against the rich cherry wood. She'd changed into stretchy black pants and a baby blue tank top like the kind he'd seen women wear to yoga class. All those curves he'd wondered about under the suit jacket she'd worn even in the sweltering heat today were present and accounted for. Her hair was no longer constrained in a clip, but hung in loose curls around her shoulders, and the overhead light lent a reddish glint to the dark auburn. Altogether, she made a drop-dead gorgeous picture. Too gorgeous for his own good.

"What are you doing here?" Her voice was deep and husky as if he'd woken her.

Not knowing what to say, he didn't wait for an invitation but stepped into the soaring two-story family room with a wall of windows. "Nice house."

"Thanks," she answered, clearly baffled by his presence.

He shoved his hands into the pockets of fresh jeans he'd put on after he'd showered away the crime scene and looked around the room in hopes of finding something to say. His gaze landed on the far wall holding three large paint swatches in various shades of gray.

"I see you're painting." *Duh! State the obvious. Good opener.*

"And, as you can see, I had a hard time deciding on the color."

He looked around the room holding modern leather furniture with colorful pillows that went perfectly with the current mushroom color. "What's wrong with the color on the walls now?"

"Painting and remodeling is my way of getting rid of stress."

"With your job you must be painting all the time, then," he joked.

She didn't smile, but held onto the door as if she might ask him to leave.

"Can we talk for a few minutes?" he asked.

She eyed him for a long moment. He was a first-class idiot for coming here. He was about to blurt out some lame comment and bolt, but her pensive expression vanished. "I was just going to take a break and have a glass of wine on the deck. You want one?"

Wine with a captivating woman, or an empty house filled with unrelenting memories? The decision was easy. "Wine sounds good."

She closed the door, and he followed her down a hall to a state-of-the-art kitchen overlooking a family room strewn with toys.

"Excuse the mess. I was just too beat to enforce picking toys up tonight."

"No problem." He knew she had custody of her niece, but after spending the day with her, he couldn't really picture her as anything but a tough agent haunted by her sister's death. Correction. He could easily picture her in his arms, but he was refusing to do that again.

He turned his attention to the kitchen. It smelled like warm cinnamon, and her décor made the place feel welcoming. Homey and inviting, like his house had once felt. Black granite counters and cool stainless appliances were warmed with dark brown cabinets and a muted green paint color. Classy. Just like her.

"Nice kitchen," he said.

"Thanks. I just finished remodeling it a few months ago." She retrieved a bottle of red wine from a small wine cooler. "Merlot okay?"

He nodded and watched her graceful movements as she reached for a glass from the top shelf, stretching out a muscular body. Muscular and curvy all at the same time.

Knock it off, Murdock. You can't go there. Won't go there. This's a professional arrangement, for crying out loud. Keep your libido in check.

He forced his focus to the intricate tile backsplash. "Did you do the remodeling or hire someone?"

"Except for installing the countertop, I did it all with the help of a few friends." She poured the rich, red wine into a large glass and handed it to him.

"Thanks," he said and hoped by the time that they got out to the deck, he'd figure out what in the world he was going to say and quit sounding like a complete idiot.

"BIG MISTAKE, KAIT," Fenton said as left his perch behind Kait's house and headed for Brian's van. He climbed into the dark interior and fired up the rumbling engine.

"Big mistake," he repeated as he took one last look at her house in the rearview mirror and floored the gas. The balding tires spun on wet pavement until they gripped and propelled him forward, laying down a screech that reverberated through her sedate neighborhood.

Kait couldn't be trusted to do anything right. She had no business letting a man into her home, much less a cop. Or smiling up at him on the deck with the same sultry smile Abby had reserved for him. It felt like eternities since her warmth had chased away the darkness. But he could still see her, feel her. Almost reach out and touch her.

Except when Kait was around.

Stupid Kait, always ruining everything. Her abrasive personality always taking over and erasing the memories of Abby—everything they'd shared vanished, and all he had left was darkness.

Kait had to know that same darkness. First as he toyed with her, then in death.

Yes. Darkness in death. Permanent.

He patted the cooler on the passenger seat and felt his mood lift. He'd wanted to leave his little surprise tonight, but tomorrow would do as well.

There was always tomorrow. Except for Kait. Her tomorrows would be limited to just a few.

KAIT SETTLED ON a chaise lounge with a plump cushion and tucked her feet up under her body. Sam took in the small backyard, secluded even in the middle of the city with tall trees and bamboo ringing the property. A small play structure took up the middle, and every variety of flowering plant crowded the remaining space, all of it dramatically lit with landscape lighting. His unease about being here disappeared.

"Wow," he said, leaning against the deck rail and inhaling the scent of sweet jasmine that reminded him of her perfume. "I didn't take you for someone who remodeled homes, or gardened, for that matter."

She leaned back, looking relaxed in her space. "I find them both relaxing and therapeutic."

"Hah," he said. "I've seen some reality home renovations shows. Those people were far from serene."

"That's because they didn't take the time to learn about the project they were working on." Warming to the topic, she sat forward. "Gardening and renovating are basic. Use the right tools and materials, follow the steps, don't get lazy and skip any, and you'll get good results."

"Still." He shook his head. "There are so many things that can go wrong in both areas that I figured someone with an analytical brain wouldn't embrace them."

"It's a lot like building a computer or writing code. Sure, I can't control the weather, bugs, or diseases, but I can learn how to deal with them and adjust accordingly." Her lips curved in a playful smirk. "It surprises me that you didn't see that. I thought as a detective, you might be a better judge of people."

He took a sip of his wine, then set the glass on the table. "I'm good at my job. You're just hard to peg."

"How so?" She sounded as if she were enjoying this conversation.

He sat on the end of her lounger and took her free hand in his. The ice-cold fingers surprised him for a moment, but he turned her hand and studied it. "Nails not chipped. Clean. No stains or discolorations at all. Smooth skin. Soft. Not at all what I'd expect from someone who digs in the dirt and lays tile."

"Have you ever heard of gloves?" she asked, sounding slightly breathless.

She met his gaze full on, and a buzz of awareness flared between them. The same buzz that had flickered all day when they'd gotten close. What would it be like to date her? To kiss those lips that were pouting ever so slightly right now. To feel her fingers, soft and warm on his face.

Not something he had a right to think about.

He all but dropped her hand and grabbed his glass, taking a long drink before getting up to rest on the railing. The fresh breeze rustled through the greenery. It should cool him off, clear his head, but it only made him notice the distance between them even more. He wanted to go back. To take her hand and ask her out for dinner or to a movie. But he wouldn't. His gut said she was complicated, deep, and worth knowing. She was the kind of woman you couldn't help fall for. Fall hard. And off limits for him.

He focused on plants swaying in the wind—the landscape lights casting weird shadows through their leaves—and felt her watching him. He didn't have to look at her to know what she was thinking. He was thinking the same thing. They had that instant chemistry. He'd had it with Hannah, too. But look at the way that relationship had ended.

He looked down, caught sight of his empty ring finger.

Face it, Murdock. You fail at important relationships.

Even if Hannah and their son had lived, they would have split up. The job had come between them, like it often did for cops. When he'd lost his partner, he'd let it eat at him until he'd thought about little else. Hannah claimed he'd shut down and was incapable of feeling. She was wrong. Way wrong. He felt plenty. Just none of it positive.

Until he'd learned about her pregnancy. Then he'd started fighting his way back to the living. But it was too late. She didn't trust him to be the father Danny would have needed, and she was going to leave him.

He pressed his fingers on his chest, feeling for Danny's dog tag. Hannah had been right. He wasn't whole back then. Wasn't sure he was whole now.

So this—this thing he felt for Kait—had to stop, and he needed to get out of here before he forgot all about why he'd be leading her on and acted impulsively. He turned back to tell her he was leaving.

"If you're here to find out what I discovered about Congdon on the Internet," she said before he could utter a word. "I can save you the trouble of asking. I didn't get to it."

"I didn't—"

"Lily's having issues adjusting," she rushed ahead. "I was supposed to look for a counselor for her today, but when the whole Fenton thing came up, I forgot about it. So I've been searching the web since I put her to bed."

"Um, actually," he said, wondering why she felt a need to explain. "I wasn't expecting you to do anything tonight."

"Really?" She arched a brow. "You came across as pretty intense at the crime scene. I didn't expect you to be so laid back about this."

He thought to walk away now while he could, but talking about work was safe, and he felt like she needed an explanation. "I'm in this job for the long haul. If I spend every waking hour on a case, I'd burn out. That wouldn't do anyone any good." *Good advice. Even if I don't have much of a life other than the job,* he thought, but kept it to himself.

She nodded as if his comment fit the sage advice category. "Wish I could be like that. I figure the faster I solve a case, the fewer people are victimized, so I have to fight the urge to work all the time. But then there's Lily. She's so amazing." A warm smile lit her face. "My mom's always telling me I neglect her in favor of my job. That I'm not a good mother." She closed her eyes for a moment. "Mom would be all over me if she found out Lily was having issues and I chose a murder scene over finding her help."

"I doubt you're a bad mother, Kait. Just a working one."

She shrugged. "Maybe. I don't know."

"Did your mother work when you were growing up?"

"Nah, she was the quintessential PTA card-carrying, cookie-baking, devote yourself to raising your kid kinda mom." She sighed. "Sorry. That came out all wrong. I totally respect women who make that choice. Abby did, and she was so happy. Shoot, maybe I'd even consider it if I wasn't the only breadwinner in the family."

"You don't seem like the stay-at-home type to me." He smiled. "But then, after seeing your home remodel and this garden, maybe I've read you all wrong."

Their gaze connected again. Things heated up. She bit her lip and tipped her head while studying him. He had to stop this. Stop making her think he was coming on to her when he didn't intend to go anywhere with it.

He took another long drink of wine and set down the glass to leave.

"I'll get to the Internet search first thing in the morning," she said, and he was thankful for the change in topic.

"Don't rush on my account. I have Congdon's autopsy at eight and won't be able to talk to you about it until after that."

"So you've positively ID'd the deceased?"

"Yep, it's Elliot Congdon," he said. "We ended up having to locate his dentist and get him out of bed."

"Don't tell me you drove all the way over here just to tell me you'd officially identified him."

"Turns out I only live a few miles away," he sidestepped. "We're practically neighbors." He watched her, wondering how she'd feel about having him nearby.

Her blank expression didn't even hint at a response. "I was hoping you found something to link Congdon to Fenton."

Ah, yes, Rhodes. Everything is about Rhodes with her.

Sam needn't have worried about hurting her. She wasn't thinking about him in the same vein as he was—just as someone who could help catch her brother-in-law. "At this point, we don't have anything to link Congdon to anyone, much less Rhodes."

"Our team may be on to something," she said, not at all fazed by his statement. "I just got off the phone with one of our analysts. The hard drives were removed from two of the computers like I suspected, but they did find Congdon's screen name on the operational one. It's RebelNinja. That should turn up some leads."

"How's that going to help?"

"Computer geeks bond with others who speak their language. Congdon most likely had an online family of sorts, and if he did, we should be able to track his screen name, and that will lead us to the family." She didn't add, lead them to Rhodes, but Sam knew that was what she was thinking.

Made him angry that she only focused on Rhodes when he couldn't seem to quit thinking about how she looked in the moonlight. "Is that what you do, make friends online?"

"What?" She laughed good-naturedly. "Are you calling me a geek?"

"I guess I am. Although, I'd have to say you have a lot more personality than many techies I've run into over the years."

"I don't live for computers like a lot of my associates do."

"What *do* you live for, Kaitlyn Knight?" he asked, and when her smile fell and she shivered, he wished he hadn't.

Rubbing her arms, she got up and strolled to the railing on the far end of the deck.

He'd said the wrong thing. Gone where she didn't want to go. Somewhere, he kept telling himself, he didn't want to go either. He should mind his own business. Leave it alone. Leave her alone. But he couldn't.

He took off his jacket, went to her, and settled it over her shoulders. "What's bothering you, Kait?"

"It's nothing, really." She looked at him as she tugged the lapels closer, her eyes shimmering with the tears he'd expected to see all afternoon. "You simply reminded me of my priorities. I live to fulfill my promises to Abby. To raise her daughter, find Fenton, and make him pay. Until that happens, nothing else matters. Nothing."

"Is that enough for you?" He hoped she might say no, but he knew she wouldn't.

"It doesn't really matter does it?" Sheer determination washed away the tears and consumed her expression. "I promised Abby I'd find Fenton and make him pay. I never break my promises. Never. No matter the cost."

Chapter Eight

COLD AND CLINICAL, the morgue gave Sam the creeps. Always had. He'd hated it from his first autopsy seven years ago. He'd heaved into a garbage can and seriously thought about going back to patrol. Didn't happen, though. Not once he realized he was skilled at helping people at a horrific time when few others could.

Marcie handled her job the same way. Helping families find closure gave her life meaning. Still, it took a special person to deal with death on a daily basis. At least, without growing sour and jaded. Marcie was neither, and he was thankful each time she caught a case with him. Even if she did nag him about moving on from Hannah.

Dressed in protective clothing, she approached the metal table holding Congdon's lifeless body. She adjusted a lapel microphone used to record her findings, slipped on a plastic face shield, then pulled the instrument tray into place.

"Let's get started." She lifted the sheet, and Sam cringed at the putrid smell filling his nostrils and at the gaping hole in Congdon's chest. Even if done postmortem, this kind of mutilation was brutal and cruel. Kait needed to find closure in her life, but she'd be far better off if this murder had nothing to do with Fenton Rhodes.

"By the way," Marcie said. "I took nail scrapings when we got him back here yesterday. No blood or skin cells."

"He definitely didn't fight, then. If he wasn't drugged, then he knew and trusted the killer."

"But obviously, he shouldn't have." Marcie's lips curled up in disgust, then she started describing the victim into her mic, her tone clinical and robotic.

Sam stood watching as she started her external exam, focusing for a long time on the gaping hole in Congdon's chest. The wall phone rang, the sound echoing through the sterile environment, ending her dictation.

"Get that, will you, Sam?" she asked without looking up.

Sam crossed the room and lifted the receiver, instantly stilling the ringing. "Hello."

"Agent Kaitlyn Knight is here claiming she's supposed to attend the autopsy." The female receptionist who was usually quite pleasant sounded ticked off at having to call them.

Kait? Why was she here? He'd told her about Congdon's positive ID last night, so she couldn't possibly think this was Rhodes lying on the table.

"Who is it?" Marcie asked.

"Agent Knight is here. She wants to view the autopsy."

Marcie looked up. A slow smile spread across her face. "Well, what are you waiting for? Tell them to escort her back."

"I'm not so sure that's a good idea."

"The woman is looking for something, and if she thinks this is what she needs, I'll give it to her."

Sam knew better than to argue with Marcie in her domain. "Bring her back," he said before hanging up.

"This is perfect." Marcie gave him a quick smile and bent over the victim. "Now you can ask her to go out with you."

Sam groaned. "Promise me you won't say anything to her about it."

"I won't." She finished the Y incision on the chest.

"No," Sam said firmly. "Look me in the eye and promise."

She looked up, her eyes as innocent as a child's. He still didn't believe her. He wanted a verbal promise, but before he got it, he caught sight of Kait peering through the viewing window. Her eyes met his for an unguarded moment before going to Congdon. They held the usual sadness and pain he'd come to associate with her.

"She's tougher than she looks," Marcie said. "You have to let her work this out, or she'll end up living in the past like you do."

He wasn't living in the past. He just wasn't moving forward. It was his choice. And he didn't think Kait was living in the past either. She was stuck in limbo, and viewing this autopsy would do nothing to propel her out of it. Maybe he could convince her not to stay.

He went to meet her. A shy smile spread across the gorgeous face that had kept him from sleeping well last night. Regardless of the circumstances, regardless of his loss of sleep, he was happy to see her, and he returned her smile as he took her in from head to toe. She was wearing another of those infernal business suits, black today with a gray blouse that hid all of her curves, but he remembered them from last night. Remembered how she looked with her hair down. Soft and very touchable.

Enough. You're supposed to be telling her to take a hike, not inviting her to spend time with you.

"You shouldn't be here, Kait," he said more gruffly than he intended.

She took a step back, her smile falling. "I guess I should have called first to ask your permission, but since my supervisor still isn't sanctioning my involvement, I figured you wouldn't invite me in."

Sam didn't need a roadmap to understand what she hoped to accomplish, and it frustrated him even more. "So instead, you thought you'd come down here and convince me to let you stay, like you did yesterday?"

She mocked an innocent expression. "Is that what I'm doing?"

Irritation boiled up inside, catching him off guard. Not irritation over her trying to horn in on his case, but annoyance over her using their obvious connection for gain. More annoyance than he wanted to admit. "You don't need my permission to be here. This is Marcie's domain, and she's already agreed to let you in."

"You're mad."

He shrugged.

"I'm sorry, Sam." She lifted a hand then let it fall to her side. "My gut still says Fenton's involved in this case, and the autopsy might give us a clue as to how."

He opened his mouth to argue, but she rushed ahead, "I know Fenton. His habits. His flaws. Everything about him. Better than anyone else. I might see something important here that you'll write off as insignificant."

She had a point. Rhodes being involved was a long shot, but one Sam couldn't dismiss completely without cause. He peered at her, weighing and measuring her ability to handle this. She seemed stronger than yesterday. More resolved. Maybe Marcie was right. Maybe Kait did have the internal strength to observe an autopsy when she was so emotionally involved in the outcome. If she wanted in on it, who was he to stop her?

He opened the door and stood back. "After you."

"Thank you." Her steps purposeful and determined, she headed straight for the table, her shoulders raised in the usual hard line. Though Sam hated to see her exposed to a needless autopsy, he respected her unwavering determination.

"Hello, Kait." Marcie looked up and smiled sincerely. "I can call you Kait, can't I?"

"Please."

Sam opened his mouth, prepared to shut Marcie down if she broached a personal topic.

"And I'm Marcie." She gestured at the body on the table. "You haven't missed much. We've barely started."

Waving a report, Tim poked his head in the door. "Your lab results."

"Perfect timing," Marcie said.

Tim crossed the room, his dirty sneakers slapping on the antiseptic floor, his eyes flashing first to Kait then to Sam before the sneer he seemed to wear frequently found its place on his face. Marcie didn't seem to notice, or maybe she didn't care. Tim was an able assistant, and finding experienced workers in this field was tough. She took the report and was instantly wrapped up in it. She thumbed through pages while Tim sauntered out the door.

"Interesting. Very interesting." Marcie looked up. "Congdon had Rophenol in his system."

"Roofies? One of the date rape drugs," Sam clarified in case, as a cyber expert, Kait wasn't up to speed on current street drugs.

Marcie nodded. "And not something you find in a male victim very often. The tests don't indicate levels high enough to have recently incapacitated him. Either the person administering the dose didn't know what they were doing, or it's been some time since he ingested it. If it's the latter, it's certainly not our cause of death."

"So you still don't think the heart played a part in his death?" Kait asked.

"No. I've confirmed that bit of nastiness was done postmortem." Marcie's attention returned to the body. She grabbed a magnifying glass and adjusted the light then bent closer to Congdon's arm, and her face suddenly lit with excitement.

Sam knew that look. She'd discovered something of interest, and he might just have his first real lead in this case. He stepped closer as she pressed on the inside of Congdon's elbow. She bent even closer.

"Hmm," she said. "A puncture over his vein." She ran her finger up Congdon's arm. "And inflammation running up the vein."

"Which means what, exactly?" Sam asked.

She looked up and twisted the light to shine on the far wall instead of her eyes. "It's called phlebitis." She pointed at a spot where the elbow bent, but Sam couldn't see anything except discolored skin and blisters. "There's tape residue here. Could mean a needle was secured to the skin."

"Secured, as in an IV?" Sam asked.

"Likely." Marcie pressed the skin again. "The redness could indicate chemical phlebitis. It happens sometimes when the vein is irritated by a chemical." She looked up again. "Did he have a recent hospital stay?"

Kait's phone chimed, but she kept her rapt gaze on Marcie and ignored the call. "None of the neighbors mentioned a hospital stay."

"His mother didn't say anything about it either," Sam added. "But then, I didn't know to ask about it, so I'll follow up with her today."

Marcie stared at Congdon while tapping her finger on the edge of the table, a sure sign that she was working through an idea. Unlike many of the other pathologists on staff, she went that extra step to combine details from the case with the forensics she discovered. She'd offered theories over the years that had led to arrests on many of Sam's cases.

Her head suddenly popped up, her eyes gleaming. "You know how the room where we found Congdon had that deadbolt and key?"

Sam nodded.

"What if the killer roofied Congdon so he was compliant enough to get him into the cuffs, then kept him sedated with IV drugs?"

"So you're not saying the roofies were given in the IV, right? You're talking about something else that kept him sedated."

"Right," Marcie said. "There are plenty of intravenous drugs that could keep him sedated for any length of time."

"That would explain why he didn't struggle against the cuffs." Excitement from a potential lead built in Sam's gut. "Not just anyone can put in an IV, right? Which means the killer had to have medical training."

"Yes," Marcie said. "We'd be looking at a doctor, nurse, or even a paramedic."

The color drained from Kait's face. "These IV drugs you mentioned. Can you test for them?"

"Maybe." Marcie looked at the body again. "Normally I'd say I could use tissue to locate any drugs he had onboard, but with the extensive decay, it could go either way. We might find something. We might not."

"But you'll test for it, right?" Sam asked.

"Of course."

Sam realized Kait had dropped out of the conversation. He shifted his focus to her and found her deep in thought. "What're you thinking, Kait?"

"You keep saying everything I mention related to Fenton is a coincidence. Not this, Sam. Not this." She started trembling while running her hands up and down her arms.

His instinct to protect her from any additional pain made him take a step closer. "What is it?"

"Don't you see?" She shivered and grabbed onto the edge of the table. "This is it. Like I told you. The piece of the puzzle that only I would know. Fenton was a medic in the Navy."

THE ROOM SPUN around Kait. She might have had a strong hunch that Fenton had killed Congdon, but now she was positive he was their killer. But man. Knowing—really knowing—that the guy who'd married Abby and fathered Lily was the monster who'd carved out Condon's heart, made Kait's head swim.

"You're awfully pale, Kait," Sam said from across the table. "Why don't you sit down for a minute?"

She never let anyone see her weakness. Her mother drilled that into her. But she didn't care if Sam or Marcie thought her weak, today. The shock was just too much to handle. She crossed the room and dropped onto a metal folding chair. The cold seeped through her slacks, but she barely noticed it. Not when the chill from seeing how Fenton had butchered Congdon had already frozen her solid.

A worried expression on his face, Sam joined her. "Are you all right?"

"Fine." She tried to fill her tone with conviction, but she failed. Failed miserably.

He stepped closer and raised a hand as if planning to rest it on her shoulder, but then let it fall to his side. "You don't have to stay, you know?"

"I know," she said, trying to gain control of her emotions before Marcie or Sam insisted she leave. "I need to stay now more than ever."

He squatted in front of her, reaching for her hands. She let him engulf her hands with his. Strong and warm, his touch started thawing the aching cold. She believed his touch meant he understood her, and he would take her claim seriously. Fenton was their killer. Sam would value her knowledge of Fenton and let her work the case with him to bring Fenton to justice. She waited for him to confirm it.

"Don't jump to conclusions here, Kait." He looked her in the eye. "If Marcie's right about the IV sedation, it significantly narrows our search for the killer, but that still gives us thousands of suspects, and it still doesn't mean Rhodes is our man."

Shocked at his stance, she pulled her hands away and crossed her arms.

"I'm sorry, Kait," he said. "But I have to look at the facts, and they don't yet point to anyone specific. What we have at this point is circumstantial at best."

Her phone rang again for the fourth time in fifteen minutes. Despite her desire to tune out the world and focus on Fenton, she couldn't ignore the incessant ring any longer. She dug out her cell. The screen displayed Nina's icon. The three missed calls were from her, too.

"I really have to take this." Kait accepted the call before Nina hung up again.

Sam stood.

"Kait," Nina said, but Kait kept her focus on Sam until he turned away.

Watching him walk across the room, she felt all alone. His compassion and understanding, and the clear interest he'd shown in her last night, fooled her into thinking maybe she wasn't alone in this. To think he'd help prove Fenton's involvement in the murder. But his reluctance to support her now cleared that up fast.

"Are you there, Kait?" Nina's voice came over the phone.

"Yes."

"You best get in here if you want to keep your job." Nina's forceful whisper grabbed Kait's full attention.

As Kait opened her mouth to get clarification, the sound of raised voices in the background and the thump of a slamming door filtered through the phone. Odd. Sulyard kept the office humming along at an even keel at all times. Chaos meant something big was going down.

Kait glanced at her watch. Shoot. She was two hours late. Fortunately, the office was a straight shot up the freeway, and she didn't have to fight city traffic. "I can be there in twenty minutes."

"Make it faster," Nina snapped. "All hell's breaking loose here, and Sulyard's on a rampage hunting you down."

If Kait wasn't so upset about Fenton, this kind of news might worry her, but she just didn't have room in her brain for work issues right now. "Sounds ominous."

"It is. So get over here, already." Nina exhaled loudly, a sure sign she was flustered. "And bring your detective with you."

"My what?" Kait asked as she stood.

Nina snorted. "Come on, Kait. Didn't you think I could decipher your cryptic comments this morning and figure out you'd be at the morgue?"

Kait shouldn't be surprised that Nina knew her location. Not when they could predict each other's moves with precision. Kait promised to jump in the car right away and said goodbye before joining Sam at the table. "Our presence is requested at my office."

He looked up in surprise. "Our? As in you *and* me?"

"That's what Nina said."

"What for?"

She shrugged and dug out her car keys. "It has to be big if it has Nina flustered. Nothing at work ever flusters her. Nothing."

Chapter Nine

WHO SHOULD DIE NEXT?

Fenton dropped onto Brian's pricey desk chair that resembled an alien with outstretched arms. "Whaddaya think, Brian? Who do you want to join you?"

He slid his chair closer to the shackles holding Brian to the floor in his office. Avoiding his splayed legs, Fenton peered into Brian's eyes. "Messy business, this drug, eh? How does it feel to be paralyzed? Not good, I suppose. It was the only choice since I wanted you restrained but conscious. I guess it's not fair to you, but then, think of it as your contribution to my cause. You want to contribute don't you?"

Fenton took hold of Brian's chin with gloved hands and shook his limp head up and down.

"I knew you'd agree. Now." Fenton clapped his gloved hands together. "I have to decide on your replacement."

Pushing back, he lifted his knees and sent his chair turning. Just like his childhood when his father's cruelty had crowded out all thoughts, and Fenton had needed to find peace. He closed his eyes and kicked up his speed. Faster. Faster, he moved, the chair's frame groaning from exertion.

Screaming with a frenzy, ideas dented his skull, trying to escape. He gave in to the fury. Let his head drop back to concentrate on his thoughts. The even *thump, thump, thump* of Brian's portable ventilator soothed his nerves, and peace cleared his mind. He enjoyed the interlude until gravity pulled his eyes open, and he caught sight of Brian again.

Right, Brian. He couldn't forget Brian. Maybe he could help decide. A few more turns.

Three. Two. One.

He stabbed a toe into the matted carpet and ground to a halt.

"Don't worry. I didn't forget you." Fenton adjusted the strap holding Brian's endotracheal tube and patted his glossy black hair. A lock slid across his high forehead and lay as lifeless as Brian would be in the very near future.

"Back to business." Fenton propelled the chair forward, ramming the desk and jerking to a stop. He ran his index finger down the short list lying next to three hard drives he would exchange after silencing Brian for good.

Andy Baker
Jason Mason
Scott Kepple

He lingered over Jason Mason. "What kind of parent saddles their child with a rhyming name? For the name alone, he deserves to die."

Was that reason enough to choose him? Or was it too arbitrary when deciding to end a life? Fenton's finger hovered. *Choices, choices, choices.*

He ran down each man's background. They were all the same. Computer experts, loners, no family to speak of and, of great importance, they resembled Fenton, so nosy neighbors wouldn't question his coming and going.

Depending on the progress of his plan, they could all die. Soon. So why struggle to decide who went first?

He closed his eyes and swirled his finger in the air. "Eenie meenie minie moe, pick a name, I gotta go." Excitement quickening his breath, he stabbed his finger onto the desk and peeked through slit eyelids. He ground his finger into the name.

Jason Mason. Jason Mason. Jason Mason. Buh bye.

No more Jason Mason—well, nearly. Fenton would assume Jason's name for as long as it served his purpose. Then it would be gone for eternity.

He opened a worn photo album and flipped to page one. He pressed out a crease in the clinging film and swiveled to display the picture for Brian. "This is Abby. Oh, I loved her, Brian. How I loved her. Until her sister killed her. Now it's time for payback. You're a big part of that, Brian. A big part." He quickly flipped past a few pages filled with his failures to Elliot Congdon's photo. "And this is Elliot. My first bit of enticement for Kaitlyn Knight. I wish you could have known him. Not a bit of trouble. And special. I had to experiment a few times, but I perfected the drug dosage and vent settings on Elliot." Fenton flipped another page. "And here. See how handsome you looked in the sunlight?"

He spun back to the desk, turning the page on the way. In a small manila envelope, he shuffled grainy pictures from the Internet then withdrew a mug shot of Jason, or J.J. as he liked to be called in chat rooms.

"There." Fenton inserted J.J. into the album. "Doesn't it feel so much better having made a decision?"

Energized, he jumped to his feet.

Yes, the decision was made.

He could relax and enjoy the day. A day that promised to be very rewarding. After he laid his next trap, Brian Youngblood would retire, too. And Kait's nightmare?

That was just beginning.

AS PROMISED, KAIT waited for Sam in the security office at the FBI building. He crossed the visitors' parking area, his stride reminding her of her ex. It'd been a long time since she'd thought about Owen, but the way Sam moved with the ease and confidence of a man who was secure in himself was reminiscent of Owen. The difference—big difference—was that Owen was superficial. All swagger and brawn. But Sam had been kind and compassionate every time they'd met. That's what really made her heart take a dip around him, as it did now. Even if he didn't embrace her theory.

He hung the visitor pass issued at the security desk around his neck, and a slow-dawning, lopsided grin spread across his face. "Like what you see?"

She felt a blush creep up her neck. She didn't have the time or inclination to get into it with him, so she ignored his question and headed across the courtyard to the main building.

Inside the small lobby, he let out a low whistle. "I haven't been to your new offices before. Impressive."

She agreed. They'd moved into the new building a little over two years ago, and every time she arrived on campus, she appreciated the added security. She slid her keycard over the reader, then pressed her code into the number keypad.

He turned in a circle. "So this is what sixty million bucks buys nowadays."

She heard a hint of outrage in his tone. "Blame terrorists. Our old office wasn't secure enough to withstand an attack, and state-of-the-art security is costly." She led him down the hallway to the elevator.

"Hey," he said on the ride up to her floor. "I'm not saying y'all didn't need a safer environment, I'm just saying it took a hefty chunk of change to provide it."

Feeling defensive about what many people saw as an extravagance, she opted not to comment, and they rode the rest of the way in silence. As she headed for her workstation, a wave of apprehension washed over her. The usual calm atmosphere was charged with uneasy, frantic movements. Phones rang nonstop, but the agents she passed were already engaged in conversation, leaving the shrill ring of incoming calls pealing through the open space.

"Your office always this busy?" Sam asked from behind, making Kait jump.

"No. Let's find Nina and see what's going on." She led Sam though the cubicles. Her fellow agents stared as she passed. Not a questioning stare like "where were you," but irritated, frustrated glares.

Sam whistled again. "Awful early in the morning to have peeved off so many people, isn't it, Knight?"

"That's the thing," she said, rounding the corner to Nina's cubicle. "I didn't even stop in this morning, so I couldn't have done anything to them."

Nina sat in her chair. The white blouse she'd paired with navy slacks had come loose, and she'd discarded her jacket on the back of the chair. A sure sign of trouble. If Nina's grandmother was here to see Nina's disheveled appearance, she'd take her by the arm, march her to the bathroom, and wait until she'd tidied herself up.

She looked up. "Good. You're here. They're waiting for us in the war room. Let's walk and talk." Nina came to her feet and absently tucked the blouse into her waistband, her gaze roaming over the bullpen.

"They?" Kait asked.

Nina ignored Kait's question, grabbed her jacket, and gave Sam a quick once-over, ending with a smile. "Nina Brandt," she said pointedly. Her usual warmth and gentility missing, she stuck out her hand. "And you're the detective Kait has told me so much about."

At Sam's baffled look, Kait said, "Nina likes to invent stories."

He met Kait's gaze with a flirtatious smile. "So you didn't talk about me, then?"

Nina's phone rang, saving Kait from responding.

"As you can hear," Nina said, ignoring the phone and starting down the aisle. "Our phones have been ringing nonstop all morning. People are calling to complain about their computers."

"I don't understand." Kait caught up to Nina. "Why would they call here?"

"The computers were taken down by a virus that left a message on the screen telling the owners to call our office."

"What?" Kait shot Nina a surprised look. "You're joking, right?"

"Wish I was." Kait felt the tension rolling off Nina. "The machines shut down precisely at eight a.m. and rebooted to display a blue screen of death. Only it's not your typical blue screen."

"Blue screen of death," Sam said, dryly. "Don't tell me. It goes with that bot term you tossed out yesterday."

"Ah, no, but it is computer related." Nina wrinkled her forehead as she met Sam's gaze. "When a Windows operating system crashes, a blue screen displays an error message warning the user it might need to be fixed."

"Not that I don't find all these computer things fascinating . . ." Sarcasm dripped from his words. "But why call me in?"

"It's your vic from the homicide," Nina said, her face devoid of expression. "We think the virus was generated by the code we intercepted from his home yesterday."

"How could that happen?" Sam asked, and Kait saw his boredom with the subject completely disappear.

"The code was sent by Congdon, or his killer, from Congdon's residence to a number of computers around town," Nina explained. "It contained a virus scheduled to kick off this morning."

"Couldn't have been Congdon then." Sam looked Nina directly in the eye. "He was most certainly dead yesterday."

"That's not necessarily true," Kait said as they rounded the corner to the war room. "Before Congdon was murdered, he could have scheduled the code to activate."

"Or . . ." Nina turned and backed down the hallway, ". . . the killer could have planted the virus, hoping it would lead us to Congdon's body."

"Then why call 911 to report the murder?" Sam asked.

Nina shrugged. "Maybe someone else discovered the body and called it in."

"Maybe." Kait pondered the situation. Hackers had egos a mile wide and were often driven to brag about their skills and claim the hacks. "Or maybe the killer called 911 to report the murder, and this virus is his way of saying screw you, you'll never catch me.'"

"Actually, none of that's important right now." Nina stopped outside the war room and met Kait's gaze head-on. Her worried expression tightened the knot in Kait's stomach. "It's the actual message that's got everyone around here worked up."

"Then why not just start with that?" Sam asked, clearly as irritated as Kait was with the way Nina was drawing this out.

"I wanted you to see the message for yourself." Nina tipped her head at the war room's open door where Sulyard and the cyber team members sat around the table.

Kait peered past them to the large flat screen mounted on the far wall. Kait quickly noted the bright blue background, but it was the scrolling white letters that made her draw in a breath.

Kaitlyn Knight killed her sister and Elliot Congdon.

Now she killed your computer.

Call the Portland FBI office to stop her from killing again.

A sudden chill iced over Kait's body, and she couldn't move. The letters kept scrolling. One by one on the screen, the message sinking in. She vaguely heard Sam suck in a breath behind her. Her sentiments exactly. Fenton was accusing her of murder. He couldn't possibly set her up to take the fall for killing Congdon as his opening line seemed to indicate, but this little stunt could bring the media into the fray, casting unfounded suspicion her way. Something she didn't need to deal with right now, and something that Sulyard could embrace as a reason to keep her away from this investigation.

"I reckon you're right, Kait," Sam said, his relaxed drawl not a comfort for once. "Rhodes might be involved in Congdon's murder."

"Might be?" Kait spun on him. "He *is* involved. The proof is staring you in the face."

His eyes creased in concern. "I wish I could be as sure as you are, but all this proves is that someone has it out for you, and that person most likely killed Congdon."

"What?" She blinked hard as she tried to comprehend his stance.

"I—" He started to say, but swung his gaze down the hall.

Dressed in his usual dark suit, white shirt, and polished shoes, Sulyard had stepped into the hallway and was watching her carefully. "He's right, Knight. You have arrested any number of people over the years who would want to get back at you."

"But, sir," she replied as she scrambled to figure out how to convince Sulyard and Sam of Fenton's involvement. "The message mentions Abby. It has to be Fenton."

Their unchanging expressions said her impassioned plea fell on deaf ears. She was alone here. Alone in this crusade, and her chest ached from the burden.

"This is exactly why I didn't want you on the case," Sulyard went on. "Stop thinking with your heart and use your head. Evidence is needed here. Something concrete to tie Rhodes to Congdon's murder, not just a computer threat that could have come from anyone."

"No disrespect," Kait said, flinging out a last hope, "but who other than Fenton would know about my sister and have the skills to unleash a virus like this?"

Sulyard lifted his index finger. "First, your sister's murder received extensive press coverage, and it's public knowledge." Up went another finger. "Second, you deal with cyber criminals with exceptional programming skills on a daily basis. So our suspect could be any number of hackers from prior cases who have done their research before seeking revenge."

His points were valid. Too valid.

But she couldn't give up. Not now. Not until Fenton was behind bars. "I doubt many of them have medical training."

Sulyard tilted his head to the side. "What does medical training have to do with it?"

Kait opened her mouth to fire back the answer, but she hadn't been authorized to attend the autopsy, so she hesitated.

"It's looking like the killer used IV drugs to murder Congdon," Sam jumped in, saving her from a reprimand. When he finished explaining the autopsy results, Kait sent him a thankful smile.

Sulyard, however, wasn't smiling. "Granted, adding the medical training to the equation further limits the pool of possible candidates, but odds are someone on your list of prior arrests has a medical background."

Just the opening Kait needed to keep the hope of Fenton's involvement alive. "So, if I review all of my former cases and don't find anyone with medical training, can we put Fenton at the top of our suspect list?"

Sulyard crossed his arms. "Let me be clear, here, Knight. We, and especially you, aren't working the murder investigation. That's PPB's job."

Kait took a step closer to him. "Even after this, you're not going to stake a claim to the murder investigation? You're just going to let the locals keep it?"

He gestured at the team waiting in the war room. "We've already taken charge of the computer investigation, and I've spoken to Lieutenant Vance. We agreed that Detective Murdock would sit in on our meeting today, and he'll continue investigating the murder." Sulyard paused and made strong eye contact, his solid stance a challenge, a warning to back down. "Alone."

Kait knew she was treading on thin ground here, but she'd never give up on actions she thought would help her find Fenton. "But, sir—"

Sulyard held up a hand. "Enough, Knight. I've given you too much leeway on this already. Now let's forget about Rhodes for a minute and logically work our investigation to see if we can figure out who's behind the computer threats." He spun and headed into the conference room.

No matter Sulyard's direction, she'd never forget about Fenton. When the meeting broke up, she'd pore through her past cases to make certain no one else possessed the necessary medical experience to pull off this event. Then Sulyard would be forced to consider Fenton their top suspect.

Chapter Ten

READY TO TACKLE another stack of files, Kait left the break room with a bottle of water. A few hours remained in her workday to go through her remaining records and prove Sulyard was wrong. If she didn't finish before it was time to pick up Lily, Kait would take the files home and work on them after putting Lily to bed.

She turned the corner and spotted Nina seated in her cubicle, staring at her monitor as if mesmerized. *Odd.* She'd gone to the post office to see if she could find out why mail hadn't been delivered to Congdon's address. She'd promised to check in the minute she returned, but here she sat. It could only mean one thing.

A problem.

"You memorizing that screen?" Kait asked jokingly to keep her unease at bay.

Nina looked up, but the vacant, distracted expression remained.

"Uh-oh." Expecting a long discussion, Kait put the icy water bottle down. "What's wrong? Is it Fenton? Something to do with the mail?"

"No." Nina grabbed a sheet of paper from under the many files and reports scattered across her desk and handed it to Kait. "There was an order to hold the mail at Congdon's address. As you can see, it was created online."

Kait reviewed the form but didn't see anything odd. More importantly, she didn't see anything that tied the hold order to Fenton or provided the necessary information to track down the request.

"I realize that report's about as helpful as a pocket on the back of your shirt." Nina shifted in her chair. "I asked for the IP address where the request originated from, but the supervisor clammed up. If you find probable cause to request additional information, we could ask Sulyard to approve a warrant request."

Kait frowned. "No way he'll go for it, since it's not related to our investigation of the computers."

"Sam's bound to request it."

"After Sulyard's warning earlier, it's not likely Sam will share the information either." Kait dropped into the desk chair. "Not that it will do much good even if he did. If Fenton requested the hold, he likely routed it though so many servers it'll take forever to hunt down the address. *If* we can even find it."

Nina picked up a pen and tapped it against the desktop, her face raised in thought. "Let's assume for a minute that Rhodes is behind this. He's not the perfect criminal. No such thing exists. He had to have slipped up somewhere." Her pen stilled midair. "This could be the one little detail that will lead us to him."

"I wish." Kait studied the hold order, hoping to find something had miraculously appeared on the form to lead her to Fenton. Of course, nothing appeared.

Maybe she was wrong. Maybe she should listen to everyone else. Not stop looking for Fenton's role in this investigation, but stop getting her hopes up over every little thing. Fenton wouldn't be careless. It wasn't in his nature.

She dropped the paper on the desk and sighed. "I doubt he erred on anything that would leave an electronic footprint."

"Hey." Nina leaned forward and peered at Kait. "You're not giving up, are you?"

"What? No. Of course not. It's just all these setbacks . . . wishing others could see what I see." A shudder ran through Kait. "I feel so alone."

Nina's fingers brushed against Kait's hand like a butterfly, lighting, then disappearing in a flash. Her touch was meant to comfort, while keeping anyone else from seeing it and reinforcing their belief that Nina was a real softie—something Nina fought all the time in the office. Not a good reputation to have for a tough agent.

"I'm sorry I can't be as certain as you are about Fenton, but you're not alone." Her warm tone helped to soothe Kait's frustration. "I'm with you all the way, and I'll do anything I can to help." Her eyes clouded over. She sat back, circling her arms around her waist and staring at her desk.

Kait followed Nina's line of sight and believed she was looking at the multi-picture photo frame on her desk. One slot held her parents in a severe unsmiling pose. Another, her aged Grandmother Hale, gray hair with a tinge of red and a wide smile much like Nina's. And the last, a blank spot that had once held a casual shot of her former boyfriend Quinn. She'd removed his picture a year ago when they'd split up, and she'd left it blank to remind herself that relationships were more trouble than they were worth.

Could she be focusing on the pictures because something bad had happened with one of her family members? She paid for her Grandmother Hale to live in a lovely assisted living facility in Portland. Maybe she'd gotten a call.

Kait wouldn't be much of a friend if she didn't try to find out so she could help. "The mail hold is nothing to get upset over, Nina. So, what's wrong?"

She didn't speak or make eye contact, and that raised Kait's concern.

"Nina." Kait got in her friend's line of sight. "What happened?"

Her chin trembled, and she blinked hard as if trying to hold back tears. "I ran into Quinn."

"You what?" Kait's voice traveled through the space, drawing attention from their co-workers. She scooted closer and dropped her voice. "Where? When?"

"At the post office. He was there with his brother Tyler." A war of emotions battled in Nina's eyes, and Kait wasn't certain which one would win the skirmish.

Kait didn't care what others thought. She took Nina's hand. "Oh, sweetie, why did you let me babble on and on about Fenton when you were so upset?"

"I'm still processing, you know." Her voice cracked, and she paused to gather her thoughts. "I don't know how I feel about seeing him, and I knew you'd insist on talking about it."

"Of course I want to talk about it. The guy shattered your world. Did you speak to him?"

"Said hi, but that's all." She shook her head in slow, sorrowful arcs. "I thought I was over him, but seeing him again was like a sucker punch. And seeing Ty. I didn't realize how much I missed him, and I . . ." Her voice trailed off.

Kait's heart constricted at her friend's sadness. Nina's brother had drowned when she was young, and she'd embraced Ty as the sibling she'd never had, making the breakup with Quinn doubly painful.

"I'm so sorry, sweetie," Kait said.

Nina pulled her hand free. "It's not something I'm going to dwell on."

"Looked to me like that's exactly what you were doing."

"Not on purpose, I assure you." She pressed her lips together and stared past Kait's shoulder. She seemed to be looking for the resolve to move beyond this. Kait wished she could supply it, but Nina would have to find the strength on her own.

"Do you mind if we table this for now?" Nina asked.

"Of course not." Kait smiled "Let's get together tonight to talk. Okay?"

Nina sighed and nodded. "I'll bring the wine."

Kait's phone rang, but she wouldn't answer until she was sure Nina was doing well enough for Kait to move on.

Nina waved a hand. "Go ahead and get it. I'm okay, I promise." A look of resolve erased her uncertainty, a sure sign she'd be okay. For now, at least.

Kait checked Caller ID. Sam's icon popped up, and she felt a strange little catch in her chest. "It's Sam."

"Figured as much when I saw your face light up." Nina winked.

"My face didn't light up," Kait denied, though she suspected it had. "I'm sure he's calling about the case."

"Right." Nina grinned. "So what are you waiting for? Answer it."

Kait pressed Talk. "Sam. I'm surprised to hear from you."

"I'm surprised to be calling." He didn't sound happy about it.

"Uh oh, that doesn't sound good."

"No . . . no . . . nothing bad has happened in the investigation. I just . . . I shouldn't be calling you about anything related to it." Dead silence filled the phone, but Kait resisted speaking and waited him out. "It's just . . . I have a lead, and you were so down when your supervisor . . . well . . . you know. When he shut you down. I thought . . ."

"Why, Sam Murdock, are you trying to be nice?" She used a joking tone, but she was touched by the fact that he'd gone against protocol to include her.

He quickly snorted. "Don't go all mushy on me, or I'll hang up."

She genuinely laughed, surprised that for the first time today, she could forget about her problems. A warm feeling settled in her heart, all because of Sam Murdock. A feeling too close to Nina's pronouncement a moment ago, and one Kait intended to avoid analyzing.

"So, the lead?" she asked, returning them to the case.

"There's a video of the person, a man, who made the anonymous 911 call. Our tech picked it up from the convenience store, and it's ready for viewing. Thought since I don't have a photo of Rhodes, you might take a look at it. You know, just in case . . ."

"Just in case Fenton made the call?"

"Yeah, that."

"Are you kidding, I'm all over this," she said quickly before he changed his mind about including her. He could have simply requested a photo of Fenton to compare to the video. The fact that he'd asked her to accompany him was a bonus she wouldn't question.

"Great." She heard genuine joy in his voice, widening her smile. "I'm a few miles from your office. I'll pick you up."

"I'll be waiting out front." She stowed her phone and clamped down on her silly ear-to-ear grin. "I'm meeting Sam to look at surveillance video from the 911 call."

Nina arched a brow. "Sounds like you're not the only one smitten."

"Please. He's simply being courteous."

"Uh-huh," Nina said, a knowing grin sliding across her face.

Kait resisted rolling her eyes. "I'll let you know what I find out."

"You do that, honey." Nina smiled earnestly. "And know that I plan to grill you about all the other details over that wine tonight."

UNDER DARK, ominous skies, Sam did a U-turn, pointing his car toward the morgue. Shortly after picking up Kait, Marcie had called and asked to see him ASAP—for a reason she said was best discussed in person. Other than an autopsy, she rarely asked for his presence at the morgue.

The fact that she had not only asked, but requested they drop everything and get down there, put him on edge. Kait, too. He'd let go of the pleasure he'd found in seeing her again—the little hum in his veins that told him he was alive—and they'd made the trip in silence to arrive without even a hint of speculation over the call's implications.

Inside the building, they signed in with the receptionist, then headed straight for Marcie's office where she sat behind her desk. Usually organized, the top was littered with papers and open books.

At their approach, she looked up and offered a tight smile. "Good. You both came. I'm sorry to drag you down here, but I thought you might have questions that would require explanations difficult to cover on the phone." She gestured at the metal chair sitting next to the desk. "Sorry. I only have one chair."

Sam held out his hand. "Go ahead, Kait."

"I'll stand."

"Actually." Marcie's eyes narrowed. "You may want to take a seat."

"Gruesome pictures?" Sam asked.

"No . . . no . . . nothing like that. It's the second tox screen."

Sam pulled out his notepad and perched on the edge of her desk. "You have the results already? Even with a rush order, that's unbelievably fast."

Marcie grinned. "I personally went down to the lab to wait, and they knew better than to mess with me."

Sam chuckled. "As do we all."

"So what did you find?" Kait asked, not joining in their humor. She remained standing, her feet firmly planted and her back rigid.

Marcie slid forward. "My suspicion that Congdon had another drug onboard was confirmed. At least partially." She picked up a report lying in front of her and came around the desk. "The drug we found is called rocuronium, often shortened to roc."

Sam glanced at Kait, and she shrugged.

"I didn't expect either of you would recognize it." Marcie held out the report to Sam, and he jotted the name of the drug on his notepad. "It's not a street or recreational drug, but a strong muscle relaxant usually administered before surgery, or when a patient needs to be intubated quickly. It relaxes the patient and keeps them from fighting the endotracheal tube."

Kait stepped closer, her face rapt with interest. "So this roc relaxed Congdon, and he didn't fight his restraints."

"Exactly," Marcie said. "But this is where it gets odd for me. I have to think that our killer handcuffed Congdon because he wanted him to remain alive for a least some period of time, yet not let him escape. If not, he could have roofied Congdon, then killed him without a need for restraints or a lock on the door."

"Sounds logical," Sam said.

Kait nodded her agreement. "Seems like you don't think this drug fits that scenario, though."

"I don't. Roc is a potentially deadly drug, plus many people are allergic to it. So administering it can be tricky."

"A poor choice if our killer wanted to keep Congdon alive, then." Sam's mind raced with the implication of this news. "What exactly does roc do to the body?"

"Technically, it relaxes all skeletal muscles, but for our discussion, it means Congdon would have been paralyzed."

"Completely unable to move?" Kait asked, then swallowed hard.

Marcie nodded. "Plus, with roc onboard, he wouldn't have been able to breathe without mechanical help. There are plenty of other less risky drugs that would have kept Congdon from fighting his restraints and not stop his breathing."

Completely baffled at the killer's drug choice, Sam met Marcie's gaze. "Knowing you, you have a theory of why the killer chose roc."

"I do, and that's what has me so disturbed." Marcie frowned. "The only reason I can imagine for using this particular drug is because it completely immobilizes a person yet leaves them fully awake and alert."

Sam sat up, a sick feeling cramping his gut. "You're saying the killer wanted Congdon to know what was happening to him the whole time?"

Marcie gave a grim nod.

Kait's eyes widened with horrified understanding. "That's just sick." She grabbed the back of the chair, and Sam figured she was imagining Rhodes, a man who'd once been part of their family, doing something so heinous.

Marcie patted Kait's hand. "I agree, sweetie. I totally agree."

Sam searched for any anomaly that would disprove Marcie's hypothesis, but came up with only one. "Your theory doesn't explain the handcuffs. With Congdon immobilized, why would he need handcuffs?"

Marcie looked at Sam, her expression grim. "I think it was a failsafe.

Roc wears off in about fifty minutes. The discovery of the IV site makes me suspect that the killer used an infusion pump to regularly dose Congdon. But like any mechanical device, a pump can fail. If it did, Congdon would regain use of his muscles and escape. Hence the cuffs. "

"Makes sense," Sam said, not liking the added sick dimension to this case.

"The good news is—"

"Thank goodness, there's good news," Kait interrupted.

"Yes." Marcie sighed. "Thank goodness."

"And that news is?" Sam pressed on.

"This should narrow down the killer's profile. Using roc and a vent to keep Congdon alive without blowing out his lung or causing heart failure would require a doctor or a very skilled medic or nurse. Plus, as I said, roc isn't a street drug, so access to it would be limited as well. We're definitely looking at someone in the medical community."

Kait gripped the chair harder, her fingers going white. "I mentioned yesterday that Fenton was a medic in the Navy."

"Did he see any combat duty?" Marcie asked, her eyes going to the chair as if she still thought Kait should sit.

Kait nodded. "In Iraq."

"Then if he served at a combat hospital, he would have intubated patients and handled portable vents."

"Vents?" Sam asked. "You've mentioned that twice now."

Marcie wrinkled her nose and returned to her chair. "Sorry. Ventilator. It's the machine that the breathing tube is connected to and mechanically breathes for the patient."

"Can you tell if Congdon has been on a vent?" Kait asked.

Marcie opened a folder and pulled out a photo of some internal body part, but Sam hadn't a clue which one. She tapped her finger in a reddened section. "As you can see, his trachea was abraded and irritated. A sure sign of an endotracheal tube."

Kait released the chair and ran her hand over her face. "Okay, say you're right, Marcie. If Congdon was alive and awake with a machine breathing for him, then how did he die?"

"I've classified the cause of death as asphyxia secondary to drug-induced respiratory depression."

"Which means what in our language?" Sam asked.

Marcie dropped the photo and carefully folded her hands on the desk as if buying time. "The killer removed the tube while Congdon had roc onboard. While still fully conscious and alert, Congdon would be able to see and hear everything as he struggled for two or three minutes to breathe before his blood became oxygen-depleted. It'd take another few minutes before he'd lose consciousness, eventually become brain dead, and slip away."

Kait shuddered. "That sounds like a horrible way to die."

Sam met her horrified gaze. "Does this still sound like Rhodes to you?"

"He liked to be in control, and this would be the ultimate way to control someone else, wouldn't it?" Kait opened her mouth as if she wanted to add something, then closed her mouth without speaking and looked down.

Sam figured she was thinking about the mental instability that would be needed to kill someone in this heinous way. Rhodes had once been an integral part of her family. If he actually was their killer, she had to be struggling with that realization.

"One other thing," Marcie said, a hint of caution in her tone. "Because there are no real physical signs on the body from this type of death, it's possible I'm wrong about the cause of death. Though I've found nothing else that could explain his demise, it is possible that I've missed something. And the tube and roc could be from a recent hospital procedure that has nothing to do with his murder."

For everyone's sake in this investigation, Sam hoped that was true. "Then it's even more important that I get back with Congdon's mother."

"The procedure would have occurred a day or less before he died, or his system would be clear of the roc or the levels too low to cause his death. This wouldn't be a simple in and out procedure or something done at a dentist's office."

Sam nodded his understanding. "If the mother doesn't know anything about a surgery, I'll also check with the hospitals and surgery centers."

"Let's say you were right the first time, Marcie." Kait's eyebrows gathered in a frown. "That Congdon didn't have surgery, and he was kept on this vent by the killer. Where would the killer get that kind of equipment and the drug?"

"Good question." Marcie leaned back and looked up at the ceiling. "Anyone with the right credentials could likely buy the vent online from a medical equipment dealer or eBay."

"eBay?" Kait asked.

"Yeah, believe it or not, you can buy all types of medical equipment there. Of course, you can't vouch for the working condition of said equipment, and the sale is regulated, so not just anyone can bid on it."

"Could he have stolen the vent?" Sam asked.

"Hmm, maybe. But it'd be difficult."

"If he did steal one"—Kait lifted her chin, a likely attempt to look confident, but Sam saw the concern lingering in her eyes—"where are the most logical places to find one?"

"Hospitals, of course, or an ambulance." Marcie kept the pen going as she thought. "Maybe an air ambulance, helicopter . . . or even a medical transport plane. Plus, some ERs store backup equipment for their helicopter and might keep one in a locked storeroom. Vents are pricey, so if it was taken from a hospital or EMS company, they surely would have reported it."

"If we're talking Rhodes here, he could have used his military connections to get one," Sam added as he jotted down her other suggestions.

Marcie nodded. "That's an excellent possibility as well."

Sam closed his notepad. "First, we'll rule out Congdon's hospitalization before checking for stolen equipment."

"Let me know if you want me to put feelers out to the local medical community in case anyone's heard of a vent or any roc that's gone missing." Marcie stood. "Sorry to be the bearer of such unfortunate news, but I thought it important you hear about it right away." She met Sam's gaze, and he saw the toll this case was taking on her. "I could use some fresh air, so I'll walk you out."

In the hallway, Kait tipped her head in the opposite direction from the exit. "I need to make a quick trip to the restroom before we go. I'll meet you out front." She spun and all but ran down the hallway.

Her posture was sure and true as usual, but he'd seen the look of despair on her face before she fled. He didn't want to examine too closely how her dejection made him feel, but he did know he wanted to go after her and offer comfort. But he also didn't want to give Marcie additional ammunition to use in her matchmaking attempts, so he started for the lobby.

Marcie caught up to him. "You ask the fine agent out yet?"

"Marcie," Sam warned as frustration coiled tightly in his chest. "After what you just told us, I'm in no mood for this."

"I'm just trying to help."

He struggled to keep his annoyance in check. "I have no interest in a relationship, and I don't need your help."

Instead of backing off as he'd intended, she grabbed his arm and jerked him to a stop. "That's what has me worried, Sam. You don't do anything but work. What kind of life is that? Dealing with sickos like this all the time and nothing else to balance it out. Except for your empathy for victims and their families, you've shut down. I honestly wonder if you're even capable of feeling anything but pain anymore."

Her words, so similar to Hannah's the night she died, made him pull away and head for the exit alone. A lump formed in his throat, and he had a hard time swallowing it down. He was the person Hannah had accused him of being and more, and as much as he wanted to change and let go of the pain to see where these feelings for Kait might lead, God help him, he didn't know if he could.

Chapter Eleven

TURNING HIS vehicle into a downtown parking garage, Sam listened to Kait's phone conversation. Not that he made it a habit to eavesdrop, but he wanted to stop Marcie's comment from replaying in his brain. And apparently, Kait's mother was the perfect person to distract him as her shrill voice cut through the phone, and he could hear her every word. Kait had asked her to pick up Lily from daycare again today, but her mother refused. She claimed she wouldn't enable Kait's workaholic tendency any longer.

"Mom. Mom." Kait looked at her phone. "No signal."

"Sorry." Sam pulled into a parking space. "I should have warned you that the signal in the garage is iffy."

"No biggie. It's not like I haven't heard that same argument a hundred times before." Kait shoved her phone into her pocket. "I was hoping she'd give me a bit more time this afternoon, but I can only take a quick look at that video, and then I need to pick up Lily."

Sam climbed out of his car, and Kait followed him onto the busy Portland street. He led the way down a few blocks to the Central Precinct. Normally, he enjoyed this short walk from the private police department parking to the office, but he was cranky, and it irritated him to have to jostle through people to get there.

Inside, he went straight to the elevator, and they rode to the ninth floor housing the Forensic Science Division's media room.

Technician Wally Edwards sat behind his computer. His messy dark hair, sticking out at odd angles, was visible above the monitor. He looked up and frowned. "Figures you'd show up before I had a chance to preview the video for you."

"No worries," Sam replied. "I didn't expect you'd have time to look at it. I'm just thankful you were able to retrieve it."

"Figured I should go out and get it myself before the store owner or a detective botched the job," he grumbled.

Many detectives would take offense at Wally's comment, but Sam knew he spoke the truth. Very few owners and equally few detectives—Sam being one of them—possessed skills to locate and correctly transfer video files, not only for viewing but also for potential use in court.

"I'll cue it up for you and . . ." Wally's voice trailed off, and he looked pointedly at Kait.

She stepped forward and stuck out her hand. "Special Agent Kaitlyn Knight. FBI."

"Wally Edwards." He shook, then started to pull his hand away, but Kait held on and looked directly in his eyes.

"I can see you're extremely busy, Wally," she said warmly. "Thank you for taking the time to retrieve the video." She released his hand.

He turned away, but not before Sam caught a smile and blush creeping over the techie's face. Kait's genuine warmth had easily subdued the old curmudgeon. Just the way she often caught Sam unaware. He'd tell Wally not to be embarrassed at letting her disarm him, but that would only cause Wally to blush more.

He settled behind another computer at the end of the worktable and soon had the video file open. He paused the program and pushed to his feet, keeping his focus on Sam. "Let me know if you want a copy." He retreated to his own computer.

Kait slipped onto the stool Wally had vacated and started the video playing. The camera angle faced the street, providing a clear view of the payphone mounted to a gas station on the opposite corner. A man climbed from a tan Chrysler Imperial that Sam guessed to be from the early nineties and stepped toward the building. The camera was too far away to identify any facial features, but gave them a clear view of an olive-green pea coat slung over one of the guy's shoulders and a brown leather bag hanging from the other.

Sam pointed at the jacket. "What's with the pea coat, do you think? It's been in the nineties all week, so he didn't need it."

"Does seem odd," Kait responded, but her focus didn't leave the monitor.

The caller's back was to the camera, and Sam noted the guy was dark haired, over six feet tall, had a muscular build, and dressed impeccably—if you didn't count the ratty coat. Sam kept his eyes on the man as he dialed and then engaged in an animated conversation.

Kait shifted on the stool. "It's like he knows the camera's there and is purposely avoiding showing his face."

After hanging up, he rifled through his bag and removed something. He peered at it for a moment then flipped it around.

Sam squinted. "Is that cardboard?"

Kait shrugged.

Holding the item over his face, the guy spun. Sam quickly figured out it was a sign, but he couldn't read it. "Can you get us a closer look?"

Kait clicked a few keys, and the video zoomed in to reveal the message.

Hope you enjoyed meeting Elliot, Kait.

Come and get me, if you can, before I strike again.

Before I pay you back. Before you get what you deserve.

Kait gasped, but didn't look away. Sam kept his eyes glued to the screen, too, looking for anything to give them a lead on this man's identity, but he seemed too shrewd to reveal his face.

He suddenly jerked the sign down, proving Sam wrong. He looked directly into the camera.

Kait lurched back, her hand flying to her mouth.

"Rhodes, I take it," Sam said, not liking the feeling of dread building in his gut.

She nodded woodenly.

Sam studied Rhodes's face. His eyes were wild and unfocused, his smile more of a smirk, his expression taunting. He suddenly saluted the camera. A lingering smile followed before he strutted off, his lips puckered in a whistle.

A whistle. The creep was whistling.

It took a cool and calculating person to leave that kind of message and walk calmly away. Of course, it took a sociopath to let a man die the way Marcie theorized Congdon had died. And now, they could assume the sociopath was none other than Fenton Rhodes. Just like Kait had been trying to tell all of them.

"I need to get going." Kait pushed off the chair and handed Wally a business card. "Can you e-mail a copy of the video to me?"

Wally looked at Sam for approval.

Sam nodded. "E-mail one to me as well."

"I'll need a ride back to my car," Kait said evenly, and headed out the door.

Baffled, Sam followed. If he'd just gotten confirmation that a relative had likely committed a heinous crime like this, and then threatened him or someone close to him, he'd be railing or slamming things. Not taking a stoical walk to the elevator.

Sam joined her. "Why don't I take you to pick Lily up and drive you both home?"

"I'm fine on my own, Sam." She calmly pressed the button.

"Still, I'd like to be sure Rhodes isn't waiting there for you."

"We've seen no signs that he wants to physically harm me." Her voice was strong and assured, but her expression didn't carry the same message.

"His eyes in the video were glassy. He's unbalanced. Plus, he clearly threatened you, and there's no telling what he might do."

She took a deep breath and stabbed the button a few more times. "If I'm vigilant, I'll be fine."

"Then think about Lily."

She whipped her head around to look at him, her expression a mix of surprise and hurt, but Sam wouldn't be deterred.

"You don't want to risk exposing her to Rhodes, do you?" he continued.

Her shoulders sagged. Gone was the perfect posture. Gone was the self-assurance. Sam had won. She would let him escort her home. But at what cost?

KAIT CLOSED LILY'S bedroom door and stopped into her own room to retrieve her gun from the bedside safe. She wouldn't carry while Lily was awake, but even if Sam hadn't followed them home and waited while she confirmed her home was secure, the feral look in Fenton's eyes would urge her to take extra precautions now.

In the kitchen, she checked the patio lock one more time. Twisting. Tugging. Looking out into the darkness of night. Wondering if he was watching.

"Get a grip," she warned herself, and checked the deadbolt in the family room—just to be sure—then started picking up toys. She tossed them into the basket, the crack of blocks hitting each other reminding her of Lily. Of positive thoughts. Her mind drifted back to Sam's protective behavior. She was a tough agent and didn't appreciate the way he'd treated her like a victim needing to be watched. But the woman in her? She appreciated his concern. And it was the woman who seemed to be winning where Sam Murdock was concerned.

The woman had almost invited him in for dinner. The agent fought it and sent him on his way. Like it had done much good. He'd been on her mind since then, and nothing, not even Fenton's threats, had managed to displace Sam for long. What was it about him that captivated her so? He was attractive, sure. But she'd run into her share of good-looking men the last few years. Not a one had stuck with her. She'd forgotten about them as fast as she'd met them. So why Sam?

Her phone rang, and, thankful for the interruption in her thoughts, she looked at the screen. Becca's icon popped up, and Kait eagerly grabbed the phone. "Bex. How'd your speech go?"

"Perfect, if I do say so myself." Becca laughed, but it rang false.

She was trying to downplay her contribution to CASA to keep people from commending her tireless work on behalf of children. She rarely relaxed, never let her guard down, and always had a cause to champion. A child to defend. She was trying to make up for her foster sister's disappearance. Molly had never been found, and Becca took the blame. She'd introduced her to the chat room where she'd met the lowlife who was suspected of abducting her. Becca couldn't help Molly, so Becca worked tirelessly on behalf of other children to atone for it. No matter Nina and Kait's attempt to help Becca let go of the guilt, she clung to it.

Like you're clinging to blame for Abby?

"So what's happening with the investigation?" Becca asked.

Kait continued to pick up toys as she relayed Marcie's discovery and described the video of Fenton. "Of course, with this concrete proof of Fenton's involvement, I called Sulyard the minute I got home."

"And let me guess," Becca's voice was loaded with skepticism. "He didn't believe you until he actually saw the video?"

"Exactly." Kait grabbed the last few Duplos and threw them into the bucket a little harder than necessary to relieve her frustration with Sulyard. "But after watching it, he agreed Fenton's our guy and phoned Sam's lieutenant. They convened a task force to work the murder. We meet first thing in the morning."

"We? Really? You mean Sulyard's actually letting you work the case? With your personal connection, I thought he'd keep you benched."

"He says my insight into Fenton is invaluable to the team, so I can consult." Kait rolled her eyes though no one was there to see it. "Whatever that means. Nina will take lead."

"Well, that's good news," Becca said, trying to put the best spin on things as usual. "She has your back. Can't say that about everyone else in the office. Plus, even if you can't play an active role, you'll be kept in the loop on the investigation."

"Agreed." Kait stowed the bucket on a small cubby shelf and dropped onto the sofa.

"But?"

"But what?"

"I hear a but in your voice."

"But,"—Kait tried to settle into the sofa, shifting and pushing against the plush pillows to get comfortable—"I want first hand access to all the files, which you know only supervisors on the team will have."

Becca snorted. "A supervisor? You're hoping Sulyard will make you a supervisor?"

"He could."

"Hah! If you think you can convince him of that, you've gone off the deep end, my friend."

Becca's logic was right on track, but Kait had to try. For Abby. "I'll do my best to convince him."

"It'll take a miracle."

"I have plenty of time to come up with a solid argument before the meeting tomorrow." Too antsy to sit, Kait got up and stared at her wall of paint samples. "Plus I have lots of mindless painting to do, where you know I do my best work."

"Well good luck with coming up with something." Becca's tone said Kait had a snowball's chance in hell of getting Sulyard to agree. "Just be careful you don't tick him off, or he won't let you participate at all."

A sliver of apprehension wormed its way to the surface, but Kait tamped it down. "I get that it's a risk to talk to him. If this wasn't about Abby, I might not, but you know I'll do everything humanly possible to fulfill my promise."

"That's what has me worried, Kait," Becca said sadly. "You've got to think things through instead of letting your feelings control you."

"I wish I could be more like you and plan things out, but that won't work with Fenton. I'm going to have to take risks to bring him in."

"I get that you think my ways are rigid, but they work." Becca paused, silence filling the phone. "Take a minute to step back from this and analyze your steps. You'll see the risk in talking to Sulyard is greater than the possible reward."

Becca often offered solid advice, and Kait appreciated it. She just couldn't think logically about Fenton. Not after he'd killed her sister. Her steps were driven purely by need. Deep, unsettling need. Becca understood these driving emotions when it came to her causes, but often couldn't comprehend the same need in others.

Time to move on, before they argued. "So tell me more about the conference."

A long sigh filtered through the phone, but Kait waited it out. Becca began describing her day, but soon had to go. "Please reconsider your talk with Sulyard, okay?"

"I will," Kait promised before saying goodbye.

She shoved her phone into her pocket and headed down the hallway to get started on her painting. At least she didn't have to spend the night reviewing files to find a suspect with a medical background. Fenton took care of her need to do that, just like he'd taken care of stealing her peace. So painting would fill her time and help her regain some semblance of calm. At least, she hoped it would.

She stepped into the garage to gather her paint supplies, the crisp evening air invigorating her. She stirred the paint delivered by a local hardware store and cleared her mind of everything but the thoughts of a fresh start in her family room. The subtle gray of Empire Porcelain, which she'd chosen over Matrix and Twilight, swirled together. She stood back and looked at it.

Light. Maybe too light. Lighter than she usually chose, and Twilight would have reflected her tastes better.

Maybe it was a sign that she wanted to lighten up her life.

Hah! Now she'd taken her painting to extremes, assigning importance to the color that it clearly didn't have. She gathered her well-used brushes plus drop cloth and roller, putting everything into a tote so she could carry it and the paint in one trip. As she took the stairs to the house, headlights swung into her driveway and shimmered under her garage door.

Fenton?

A frisson of fear shot through her.

No. He wouldn't pull into her driveway, headlights blazing. Still, she was Lily's protector and wouldn't take any chances. She rushed inside and peeked out the peephole. Nina climbed from her Mazda, the hood of a blue slicker covering her hair as she hurried through the rain to the passenger door.

Kait exhaled the fear tightening her chest. She settled her supplies on the canvas drop cloth covered in bright splotches of pink and orange from painting Lily's room, before opening the door.

Nina turned, holding out a box. "I could use your help."

Kait slipped into her Birkenstock clogs and jogged to the car, rain instantly dampening her T-shirt and chilling her skin. She grabbed the box, and the warm scent of Nina's famous peach cobbler rose up to meet her. She ran back inside and heard Nina's ever-present heels clipping along behind.

In the kitchen, Kait opened the box and found the perfectly browned cobbler with tips of luscious peaches breaking through. Next to it sat one of Kait's favorite southern treats—a bowl of saltine crackers soaked overnight in oil with ranch dressing and spices.

"Firecrackers." Kait popped one in her mouth and moaned over the crispy, salty flavor.

Nina set the wine on the table and *tsk*ed. "You're painting. Not a good sign."

"How'd you know?"

"Your hands." She pointed at gray blobs already tipping several of Kait's fingers. "I never understood how such a fastidious person could be such a messy painter."

Kait turned to the sink to wash her hands. "And I never understood how a woman who looks so put together could be so disorganized."

"Honey, my Grandmother Hale and mama may have drilled into me never to go out in public without my best face on," Nina paused to push off her hood and run a hand over her hair, smoothing the soft curls, "but they were fine with my messes as long as I kept them behind closed doors.

Which I do. Most of the time, anyway."

Kait grabbed another cracker that she lovingly called crack, as she suspected they were as addictive as the drug. "I'm just thankful you haven't taken it as far as putting on lipstick before making an arrest."

"At least not that you know of." Nina winked and picked up the corkscrew.

Kait lifted the still-warm cobbler from the box and grabbed plates while Nina uncorked a bottle of Shiraz Cabernet. She kicked off her heels and climbed onto a barstool, swirling her glass and staring into it.

"You doing okay?" Kait asked.

Nina shrugged.

Kait sat next to her. "Talk to me. It'll help."

"I'm not sure that's true." She took a long sip of her wine. "Nothing's changed. Quinn's still charging off to God knows where, doing God knows what. And I can't handle not knowing where he is and if he's all right."

"And you don't think he has any intention of settling into a more stable job?"

"We haven't talked about it since our last big fight, but he's still a SEAL, so what do you think?" Tears glistened in her eyes, and she shook her head. "Still hurts that he chose the team over me."

Kait hated to upset her friend more, but she couldn't let her put this spin on the breakup. "You know it's not that cut and dried, sweetie. He really didn't choose the team."

"Right," she said. "He just chose to do nothing, so I had to act."

"Maybe it would be better to remember that if you hadn't walked away, he'd still be with you."

"How will that help?" she snapped. "It's not like I can change how I feel. Mama made sure of that after Daddy took us rafting, and Garrett died."

Nina sipped her wine and stared off into the distance. Kait knew Nina was reliving growing up with a mother who let her fear of losing another child control their lives. She'd monitored Nina's every move, keeping her home and warning her to be careful every time she went out, making her afraid to do anything. She'd finally revolted and went away to college and, even then, she'd had to struggle to separate herself from her mother's fears. Nina was better now, as long as she could stay in control, but running into Quinn today brought back all the issues.

All this pain was because of Fenton. He was hurting people Kait cared about, and his threats were escalating.

Take a minute to step back from this and analyze your steps. You'll see the risks with talking to Sulyard are greater than the possible reward. Becca's words came back to Kait. Becca was right. She couldn't let her emotions get in the way and cloud her judgment. She'd accept Sulyard's decision and not risk her place on the team. They needed her. Without her intimate knowledge of Fenton, he would get the best of them and go free. Something Kait could never let happen.

Chapter Twelve

A LOUSY TASK FORCE.

Sam didn't want to work his case with a big team. It meant endless reports and meetings instead of nose to the grindstone investigating, but he couldn't turn down the FBI's vast resources. That, and the fact his lieutenant gave him no choice, put him in the FBI conference room for the eight a.m. briefing, one of the many status meetings that would occur daily until Rhodes was caught.

Waiting for the rest of his team to arrive, Sam took a good look at the closest of three whiteboards. Someone had jotted Elliot Congdon's name across the top, then sketched a schematic of the murder scene and other neighborhood homes, leaving space for notes from the police canvass of the area. They'd also left metallic clips for crime scene photos and designated a spot to list suspects.

There would be no reason to create a murder board unless they were planning to get involved in the murder investigation. Could mean their promise of a cooperative intra-agency team was all talk. Not unexpected. Working with feds was unpredictable. Just like cops, some wanted to work together, others could get pushy and territorial. Sam could deal with either one, but this case was centered on electronic technology, already putting Sam's team at a disadvantage. Then there was the FBI's past knowledge of Rhodes's criminal activities that Sam hadn't been privy to.

He crossed to another whiteboard holding the name Vadik Kozlov, the hacker Rhodes had killed three years ago. Sam flipped through crime scene photos. He cringed at the gruesome scene. As Kait had mentioned, Kozlov had been shot execution style in the back of the head, his brains splattered around the room filled with computer equipment. Nothing like Congdon's murder, save the computer equipment.

A list of Rhodes's known associates and their online nicknames had been jotted below. An empty column remained to note people linked to Congdon as the investigation progressed. Sam didn't have a clue how to navigate the cyber world to look into these associations. That would be Nina and Kait's job. He suspected they'd work with the group of excited geeks sitting at the table and speaking in a language only someone with a computer degree could understand, while he'd be boots on the ground tracking down local leads.

Sulyard suddenly ended his conversation with Kait and Nina and clapped his hands. He made eye contact with Sam. "Briefing starts in five. If your people are here, great. If not, we'll start without them."

Sam lifted his shoulders in a whatever-you-say shrug, but the man's dictatorial behavior put Sam on edge. The guy looked as haughty as he sounded. He wore a crisp white shirt, power tie, and a Brooks Brothers suit that would cost at least a week's salary for Sam. Sulyard's black wingtips were polished to a sheen, his head shaved, his blue eyes icy, and his expression self-important.

He pivoted toward the door where Sam's co-workers made a noisy entrance. Lieutenant Vance, along with long-term detectives Frank Yates, George Adams, and Olivia Lee, plus criminalist Dane, stepped into the room and headed straight for Sam, completely ignoring Sulyard. He didn't seem too happy about the snub, but he'd have to deal. Vance was a force to be reckoned with, too.

Vance perused the whiteboard then tipped his head at it. "They fill you in on any details yet?"

"Just that Kozlov was a hacker who Rhodes killed to take over his business."

Yates hitched his pants up on his beer belly and looked around the room. "I don't like this."

Vance's high forehead furrowed, accentuating lines and creases earned on the job. "Meaning what, exactly?"

"Meaning all this hacking business." Yates mocked a shudder. "Give me a real case where I can see the evidence and talk to real people. Not this shadowy online stuff without a face."

Vance looked at the board again and stroked his perfectly trimmed mustache. "Granted, we're behind the eight ball here, but let's gather as much information as possible this morning, and take it back to our tech department. I have them on standby for the assist." Vance plastered a fake smile on his face. "I'll say hello to Sulyard, and then we'll get started."

Sam knew that would take a few minutes, so he made himself comfortable in a thickly padded chair, and the rest of his team joined him.

Adams, looking uneasy and out of place, planted his elbows on the table. "Never worked a serial case before."

"This isn't your typical serial case," Sam said.

"Right, this guy's got some nerve," Yates jumped in. "Never heard of a serial killer out and out giving his identity away."

Lee batted away a stray strand of hair that had escaped a clip. "Or it's not him."

Sam shook his head. "It's him."

"Maybe Rhodes is begging to get caught," Dane suggested.

"That's a misconception many people have about serials," Sam said. "It's not like they want to get caught. They just figure that, after they get away with a few killings, they *can't* be caught. That's what causes them to get sloppy."

"Good." Yates pounded a thick fist on the table. "That means Rhodes might have already gotten sloppy."

Dane pointed at the video screen still blue with Congdon's message. "That from the virus he set off?"

Sam nodded and ran down the timeline of events leading up to the blue screen for the others. "Anyone need further clarification before we begin?"

"We're good," Adams said while Yates ground his teeth.

A normal reaction for any murder investigation, but even more deserved when the killer committed some depraved act like cutting out a heart, and then threatened to commit another one. At least, a normal reaction for the homicide team.

Not so normal for the geeks sitting across the table. The geek speak flying between them made Sam's head feel like it might explode.

"It's showtime." Yates leaned back in his chair and jabbed a thumb at their lieutenant.

Vance, along with Kait, Nina, and Sulyard, crossed the room. Nina and Kait sat near the geek trio, and Vance took a seat next to Sam.

Sulyard stood at the head of the table. "For those who don't know, I'm Rolland Sulyard, one of the Assistant Special Agents in Charge of this office. Before I get to the other team introductions, I'd like to say a word." He stood taller. "Law enforcement attracts individuals with strong personalities."

"Yeah, man," Yates said plugging his nose. "Some stronger than others."

Sulyard frowned at Yates who clamped his mouth shut. "A strong personality is great for our line of work, but on a joint task force, it's best if we all check our egos at the door. The only person who'll be served by battles of will is Fenton Rhodes, and none of us want him to win."

Sulyard nodded at Vance who introduced their team. Sulyard followed suit, then spun and tapped a marker on Congdon's whiteboard. "Vance will head up the local team, while I'll take charge for the Bureau."

"Meaning what, exactly?" Yates asked skeptically.

Sam wondered the same thing as it was odd for an ASAC or a lieutenant to take lead on an investigation when they had so many supervisory duties.

"Meaning this case is top priority for both agencies, and Vance and I will lead the charge. That includes talking to the media. We can hope news of Rhodes's trophy-taking doesn't get out, but if it does, the media will beat down our door. All communications go through Vance or me. Is that clear?"

The group nodded.

"All data will be compiled in this office," Sulyard went on. "Our analysts will review and collate the incoming information on a timely basis, then provide regular reports allowing us to assign leads. Which means, a daily report by all involved and any strong leads reported immediately."

Vance eyed Yates. "That includes you, Yates."

He grumbled his acknowledgement.

"Additionally," Sulyard said, "Murdock will serve as lead investigator on the murder, focusing on Rhodes with assistance provided by us when he requests it. Detective Lee will run a parallel murder investigation looking for any other possible suspects."

"Other suspects." Kait's eyes widened. "Fenton all but admitted he killed Congdon."

"Without a confession or hard evidence proving Rhodes's guilt, we'd be negligent if we didn't pursue all possibilities," Vance said.

"Please." Kait fired a terse look at Vance. "I know how to run an investigation. I just hate to see any resources diverted to what is likely a dead end."

"Be that as it may, we will proceed as planned." Sulyard eyed Kait, and Sam knew that, with her emotional attachment to Rhodes, she was treading on thin ice with her supervisor. "Moving on. The computers will remain our property and," he nodded at Nina, "Agent Brandt will serve as the official case agent. She will coordinate our effort to track Rhodes's online movements as well as find any connection between Congdon and Kozlov."

Sam saw Kait's jaw clench. She obviously wasn't pleased Sulyard had made Nina lead on this case, but Kait was too close to the situation to be in charge, and Sam agreed with Sulyard's decision. He didn't agree with the last statement though.

"Excuse me," he said. "But it seems to me, Congdon's murder is all about revenging his wife's death. His transmission made sure Kait would show up on scene, and the message on the blue screen of death proves he wants her to pay. And the MO for Congdon's death has no correlation to Kozlov. Of course, I don't pretend to understand Rhodes's motives for killing Kozlov, so maybe you know something we don't, and it's not a waste of time and resources trying to connect Congdon to Kozlov."

"As I said earlier,"—Sulyard narrowed his eyes—"we need to explore every avenue."

"Plus, you have these computer nerds sitting around twiddling their thumbs anyway." Yates's tone was filled with sarcasm as he eyed the geeks. "Might as well give 'em something to do."

"I'm sure by the time this case wraps up, you'll be most happy we've included our very qualified analysts in the investigation." A hint of Nina's warm accent hid her displeasure with Yates, but Sam saw it in her eyes.

Sam didn't like Yates's behavior either. For the most part, there was great cooperation between PPB and the local FBI office, but Yates was what they called an OG. Old guys often operate as they had in the past, carrying an antagonistic attitude toward the Bureau. Sam knew Vance had counseled Yates about it, and yet, he couldn't leave the past in the past. If he didn't have such a high closure rate on his homicide cases, Sam suspected Vance would let Yates go.

Sulyard tapped a stack of folders. "Rhodes's profile from our earlier case. Take one when you leave, but for now, Knight will provide a brief intro to Rhodes's personality."

Kait sat up higher and seemed to organize her thoughts before starting. "Fenton's meticulously clean. Cleans to clear his head. He claimed this tendency came from his time in the Navy, but I suspect it came from his childhood. His mother ran off when he was a preschooler, and his father was a taskmaster. He grew up in a working-class neighborhood. When I visited his father three years ago, I found their house rundown but spotless. Fenton joined the military right out of high school to get out from under his father's control, and when I spoke to his father, he said he hadn't heard from Fenton since he took off—and he wasn't broken up about it."

"So he probably has daddy issues," Yates mumbled, as if he were processing this bit of news.

"Yes, but it doesn't seem to control him. At least, not that he let on. Of course, he could have hidden it like everything else he kept from our family. He's cunning and manipulative. *That* he hides very well. You know there's something off about him, but you can't put your finger on it. I chalked it up to just being odd."

Yates snorted. "Whatdcha expect? He's a geek, after all."

The geek trio glared at Yates, but Kait continued. "He's not odd in the way you seem to think of all of us." She smiled at her fellow geeks. "In hindsight, I can see he was always acting, hiding his methodical and calculating personality under a charming, charismatic veneer and we couldn't help but like him."

"So what motivates him?" Sam asked.

"He likes to be in control and be the best at what he does. Has to win at everything. He also likes to live the good life. Designer clothes. Expensive restaurants and wines. That kind of thing. Like, if he owns the best, that means he *is* the best." Kait paused and let her gaze move around the group.

"In my opinion, there's only one thing that keeps him going on a daily basis. Money, and he'll never have enough. So I believe tracking his bot business is as viable a way to hunt him down as is pursuing the revenge aspect."

"See, that's where you lost me," Sam admitted. "The whole bot thingy. Street crimes I understand. Agent Knight explained bots to me, but I still don't see how that translates into income."

Sulyard cast an appraising look at Sam and seemed to appreciate his honesty. His lieutenant, not so much. He just looked upset about being in fed territory where one of his men admitted ignorance on any subject.

"It's all a matter of numbers." Sulyard planted his palms on the table, but kept his shoulders pinned back in way only a former military man would do. "Three years ago when we were set to arrest Rhodes, he controlled around a million computers and installed nearly thirty different malicious programs on them. The largest bot network by far. He used the bots in a variety of moneymaking schemes that included stealing accounts and passwords, and renting out the bots to other hackers to use in conducting spam and phishing campaigns."

Sam groaned. "If it's not too much to ask, can you translate that into English, please? I mean, how's it even possible to remotely control other people's computers without their permission?"

Nina opened her mouth to answer, but Sulyard nodded at Kait. "Knight, you're the best one to communicate this in lay terms."

"Glad to." Kait got up and took the marker from Sulyard as he sat. All eyes were on her, yet she seemed comfortable and relaxed as if she did this all the time. "With all the security breaches in retail stores and banks of late, you've all heard about hackers and know they illegally break into computer networks, right?"

A murmur of agreement traveled around the table.

"In the past, hackers set out to cause computers to crash. This was more of a malicious attack that caused companies and individuals money to rectify the problem, but that's changed. Now, in addition to hacking these big companies, they also install software on the average Internet user's computer without the owner's knowledge, then they use the software to earn money."

"As Murdock asked, how is that even possible?" Yates sounded bored as he leaned back in his chair and clasped his hands behind his head.

At the whiteboard, Kait drew a rudimentary sketch of a house with a front door standing open. "I'd like you to think of the Internet as a house. Houses contain valuables and people needing to be protected. Your computer's the same. Passwords for financial accounts such as banks, credit cards, etcetera, are stored on your computer's hard drive and need to be protected. So you have to lock down a computer just like you'd lock your house to keep others from breaking in and stealing the actual credit cards.

As police officers, you'd never leave your door wide open, right?"

She got a few half-hearted nods from Sam's co-workers.

"And if someone came to your door, you'd look out the peephole before you opened it."

Yates dropped his arms and started at Kait. "What's that got to do with those bot things?"

"If you'll be patient, Detective, I'm getting to that." Her soft tone mellowed Yates's antagonistic look. "So there's a stranger at your door. Before opening it, you'd ask a few questions to be sure it's safe."

"Or I'd open it and be sure the dude sees my gun." Yates elbowed his partner in the ribs, and Sam couldn't help but feel sorry for Kait. Yates didn't think highly of women in law enforcement, but Kait didn't seem to notice. Or maybe she was used to this kind of heckling.

She just smiled and waited until she had their attention again. "Okay, so maybe you wouldn't check first, but say you have a teenaged daughter. Would you want her to open the door for anyone without asking a question?"

Yates sobered. "Nah. Not with all the lowlifes out there."

"Exactly. The same thing is true of the Internet. There are a lot of lowlifes there, too, but they're even more of a threat because you can't see them. Every time you connect to the Internet, it's like opening the door to allow all of them to access your computer." She tapped her marker on the whiteboard. "In this example, we asked the person physically standing outside our house a question before opening the door. He wasn't automatically allowed in. The door served as a wall between us, and, based on his answer, we decided if we wanted to open it. But the minute you connect to the Internet, a door to your computer flies open and, unless you put the right safety measures—firewalls, antivirus programs and the like—in place, others can access your computer. Just like an unprotected house is tempting to a thief, an unprotected computer is tempting to a hacker."

She paused and made eye contact with each of the PPB team members, ending with Sam. She lingered a fraction longer, and he caught the enthusiasm for her subject. She obviously loved her work. And she was good at it. Making something complicated easy to understand.

"And from there, they can control it?" Sam asked.

She nodded. "Gaining access to your computer allows them to download a program that works in the background, running undetected, but performs basic instructions that allow the hacker to earn money. There are many more ways for them to make money with your computer beyond what ASAC Sulyard said, but it's not relevant at the moment so I won't list them."

"So how do you stop them?" Lee asked.

"If you have a firewall installed, it will block some of the hackers, but they know how to get around firewalls quite easily. You—"

Yates snorted loudly. "I don't buy it. My kids and I have been on the web for years, and nothing bad has happened to us."

Kait raised her eyebrow and settled a hand on her hip. "Are you sure?"

"Of course, I'm sure. Our computers run just fine."

"But is the computer really fine, or have your kids allowed someone like Fenton Rhodes to take control of their machine?"

Yates snapped his chair forward. "Hey, I'm not a complete computer novice like Sam here. I might be an OG, but I do all the things I'm supposed to do. I have one of those firewalls you mentioned and an antivirus program that I update regularly. And I do those dumb Windows updates, too. So I'm protected."

"Good." Kait smiled. "That's a great start. But what about thinking before clicking on a link on the Internet that downloads something to your machine? Or opening an attachment or link in an e-mail from someone you don't know? Or, if you have a laptop, tablet, or smartphone, logging onto an unsecured network in a coffee shop? How about downloading pirated music or books? Have you or your kids done that?"

He shrugged. "Maybe. I guess."

"And what about ensuring that your browser—Internet Explorer, Firefox, Safari, Chrome, etc.—is the current version? Do you update them regularly?"

He scoffed. "Are you kidding me? I just get one set up the way I like it, and then they change it."

Mumbled agreement came from the PPB staff, bringing scathing stares from the geeks.

"If you want your computer to be vulnerable to attack, keep using that old browser," Kait went on despite the charged atmosphere in the room. "They have known security vulnerabilities that hackers love to exploit."

"That's freakin' impossible." Yates's voice erupted from his mouth. "I'd know if that was happening on my computer."

"Are you sure?"

"Well, yeah . . . I mean, yeah, I'm pretty sure." His gaze locked on Kait's face. "You're just trying to intimidate us with all this computer stuff to get the upper hand on this case."

Kait shook her head. "No we're not, Detective. We're just trying to help you understand that the problem is pervasive and why men like Fenton Rhodes are willing to kill to keep their networks intact." She wrote eight to ten billion on the white board. "This is the estimated number of devices connected to the Internet last year. A recent study says that nearly thirty percent of them are infected with malware. Imagine three billion computers under the control of criminals."

Yates's jaw dropped open.

"So tell me, Detective Yates," Kait said, then paused dramatically. "Do you think it's likely that three billion people know their machines are infected, and they're willingly turning a blind eye to criminals who use their computers to commit crimes?"

Yates crossed his arms. "Of course not."

"So you'll concede the fact that your computer might be infected and you don't know it?"

Sam would have gloated here, but Kait didn't show any sign of winning.

"I guess it's possible," Yates admitted.

"And this is how Rhodes got the virus with the message on so many computers," Sam clarified.

"Yes. Men like Fenton have built up a network of computers just waiting to do their bidding." She looked at Sam's team members. "We call them bots, and men like him, bot herders. In this case, he sacrificed the machines that crashed. He can no longer use them."

"So he did all of this to send the message?" Sam peered at her, hoping to see what she was feeling, but he got a blank look. "A message that says to me he has a grudge against you, and he wants you to know it. Maybe wants to do more than tell you about it, too."

"I'm the least of our worries, Detective." She met his gaze directly, not showing an ounce of fear. "Fenton is obsessive about not letting anyone best him. If he blames me for having to go into hiding when Abby died and leave his life behind, then he not only wants to make me pay, but assert his superiority as well. Which to me says, he'll follow through on his threat and kill again, if we don't locate him before he succeeds."

Chapter Thirteen

A DARK CLOUD settled over the room, and Kait hated that her statement about Fenton had been the cause of it.

"As Agent Knight said, time is of the essence." Vance stood, his strong presence seeming to defuse the tension. "I'd like Detective Murdock to provide an update on the murder investigation."

Kait appreciated Vance's adept redirection of the group as she returned to her seat next to Jae, whose leg was bobbing a hundred miles an hour, upping Kait's unease. She'd been hanging on by sheer will since she'd seen the video yesterday, and she couldn't predict if or when she'd let go.

Sam jumped into describing the crime scene, and Kait watched him with unabashed interest. He wore a green checked shirt, his usual jeans, and boots. His hair was messed up as if he'd recently run his fingers through it in frustration. His tone was professional, and his respect for the victim shone through.

"Of course, you all know that Rhodes made the anonymous call to 911," he said, winding down his story. "Clearly, he wanted us to know that he's the mastermind behind the murder. Not clear is why he was carrying a green pea coat in the heat of summer."

"Knowing Fenton, he was trying to tell us something," Kait said.

"Could it have something to do with his Navy background?" Lee asked.

Nina shrugged. "Because his military service wasn't related to Abby's murder investigation, we didn't dig into it."

"Perhaps now's the time to do so," Vance suggested. "Especially if the ME's suspicions about the drug and ventilator turn out to be true. Rhodes could have used his military connection to obtain both of them."

"I agree that investigating Rhodes's military career is a priority," Sam said. "But he's going to kill again soon, and the Navy's red tape will tie up any request. We need info now."

"Where was he last stationed?" Sulyard asked.

"San Diego area," Kait replied.

Sulyard scanned the group. "Anyone have a contact at the Navy who could deliver the background information on Rhodes without making us jump through hoops? Preferably someone stationed in San Diego."

Kait immediately thought of Quinn Stone. She looked at Nina to see if she was thinking about her former boyfriend. Her pinched mouth and scrunched forehead said her thoughts mirrored Kait's.

"Brandt. Knight." Sulyard stared at them. "Something you'd like to share?"

Kait fired an apologetic look at her friend for causing Sulyard to notice them.

Nina lifted her shoulder in a shrug and said, "I know a SEAL. He wouldn't have direct access to the information we're seeking, but he might be able to call in favors from soldiers on his base to get us what we need."

"No," Kait said forcefully. "We should find another way."

Sulyard eyed her. "Care to elaborate on your reasoning?"

Kait shook her head.

Nina sat forward, her fingers going to her necklace. "It's not something relevant to our discussion, but I do want you to know that my friend won't likely go through official channels for this intel. He's a SEAL after all, and he'll use whatever methods he deems necessary to get the information, short of committing a crime."

"Didn't hear a word you said, Brandt," Sulyard replied, condoning this unorthodox approach by disavowing any knowledge of it.

"Okay, then I'll contact him as soon as we break." Nina rubbed the turquoise and stared across the room.

Nice one, Kait. She'd put Nina in an awkward position, where she wouldn't say no to involving Quinn because she was a team player and would take one for the team. And it was all Kait's fault.

"Even if this SEAL is helping out." Vance peered at his team. "We should try to track the drug and ventilator locally."

"I'm all over that," Yates volunteered. "I'll request Congdon's home phone records, too, and let you know if they produce anything concrete."

"Fine." Vance grabbed the marker and eyed Sulyard. "Since you went to all the trouble of creating a murder board for us, we'll go ahead and get some assignments jotted down." He continued to peer at Sulyard, likely waiting for him to react to his jab about the FBI team overstepping the line that had just been established.

Kait didn't know if Sulyard meant to push the boundaries by creating the board or if he was just being thorough as usual. In either case, he didn't react.

Vance frowned, then noted Yates's assignment and turned back to Sam. "Get over to the mother's apartment right after we break up and find out if Congdon was hospitalized. Even if she claims her son hasn't had a hospital stay, Yates, I want you go ahead and check hospitals and surgery centers. We can't be too thorough on this lead." Yates nodded, and Vance noted the assignment on the board. "If we learn Congdon didn't have a procedure, we'll pursue locating a local source for the roc and vent."

Jae shook her head, her eyes narrowed. "Here's the thing I don't get. Why did Rhodes wait a few days after he killed Congdon to kick off the virus and call 911? I mean, what's the point of waiting?"

Sam shrugged. "Maybe he thought a decomposed body would better make his point."

Adams scratched what little hair remained on his head. "Speaking of gruesome, any leads on the missing heart?"

"None," Sam said.

"I've worked a few serials," Sulyard jumped in. "And trust me, there's a purpose for it, and his reasons will most definitely surface when Rhodes is ready for us to discover them."

The tone in the room darkened again. Silence, heavy and thick, settled over the table.

"Has anyone searched ViCAP for similar cases?" Sulyard asked, moving them on.

Sam nodded. "For both the heart and the handcuffs. No hearts. Quite a few with cuffs, but they all involved beds and sexual activity. Not Rhodes's MO at all."

"What about the neighborhood canvass?" Sulyard asked. "Any leads there?"

Sam shook his head. "Nothing of interest, other than Congdon was a loner who worked from home and rarely went out. Yates and Adams will broaden the canvass out a block and profile the residents this afternoon. I'll also interview the next-door neighbor who wasn't available yesterday, but since Congdon rarely left the house, my gut says his killer is an online connection."

"I already have Jae tracking that," Kait added, earning both her and Jae a frown from Sulyard.

Jae fired a feisty look back at Sulyard, as if daring him to call her on working for Kait behind his back.

"What have you located, Jae?" His tone was more civil than Kait would have expected.

"I don't have anything but Congdon's screen name so far. RebelNinja. Can you believe it?" She shook her head. "So not appropriate for what you all are saying about this dude, but whatever. I'm following his tracks, and I'm also working on enhancing the video from the payphone to see if we can focus the plate number for the car Rhodes was driving."

"If you can make them out, have someone call me immediately, and I'll issue an alert for the vehicle." Vance jotted the assignments on the board.

"Any chance Rhodes could be driving Congdon's car?" Yates asked.

"Not likely," Sam said. "Congdon didn't have a driver's license, nor is there a car registered to him, so we have no reason to believe it's Congdon's car."

"Moving on to Rhodes." Vance looked at Sulyard. "I think your team would be best equipped to look into any possible addresses and gather financial information for him."

"We've already exhausted that avenue," Sulyard said. "We've kept after him all these years. There hasn't been a hint of any financial transactions tied to his social security number. Nor did we find any addresses associated with him."

Jae's eyes brightened. "We have alerts set everywhere. If anything pop up on the dude, we'll be all over it. But the guy has rad hacking skills, so he's probably stolen an identity to live under."

Vance frowned as he surveyed the group. "So, is that it, people?"

"I've been working on the lack of mail at Congdon's house," Nina volunteered, drawing a questioning look from Sam and Sulyard. "The post office confirmed Congdon's mail was held. The request was completed online. Now that we're officially onboard with the case, I'll prepare the warrant paperwork so we can see where the request originated."

Sulyard gave her a we'll-talk-about-this-later-look then swung his gaze to Sam. "What about employer and co-workers? Anyone talk with them?"

Sam shook his head. "With no personal records at the house, we haven't located his employer."

"Ah, Detective," one of the analysts named Pete said. "He worked as tech support for MedSoft. It's a small local company that designs medical equipment for hospitals. We got the name from his computer before it crashed yesterday."

Vance glared at Pete. "And you didn't feel a need to share this with us?"

Pete looked to Sulyard. "We were just following orders."

Vance whipped his head around to stare at Sulyard. "Not my idea of teamwork."

"Each of us has our priorities. Yesterday, mine was a computer attack launched from Congdon's address. I'm pretty sure you didn't give my priority a second thought yesterday either." Vance opened his mouth, but Sulyard held up a hand. "Today is different. My priorities have changed."

"Adams, you get to MedSoft," Vance said, not taking his eyes off Sulyard. "Talk to his supervisor and associates. This could be where Rhodes got the portable vent. Be sure to ask about it."

Adams nodded vigorously, sending his double chin wobbling. "Would totally bite if it turns out Congdon procured the vent that was used on him."

"No reason to speculate about that at this point in the investigation," Nina said, glossing over the negativity Adams left behind. "Where do you stand on trace evidence?"

"At the moment, we don't have much," Dane admitted reluctantly. "The scene was squeaky clean. Only recovered two hair strands that I've sent in for DNA processing. To be completely transparent, though, Congdon and Rhodes have similar hair coloring, so this might not lead anywhere."

Sulyard cleared his throat, drawing everyone's attention. "I find it hard to believe this is the only evidence recovered. Perhaps a fresh look at the scene by our Evidence Recovery Team is in order."

Dane crossed his arms, and Kait watched Vance war with letting ERT onto what was still a crime scene under his jurisdiction. She knew he was struggling with defending his territory and letting the Bureau's team on the scene. If ERT showed up and found evidence Dane had missed, it could make Dane look bad and hurt team morale. But it could also lead to bringing Fenton to justice.

"We could send FED back out there to do a joint visit with ERT," Sam suggested, and both supervisors shot him a look. "I'm just saying, the feds have all the cool toys, and working together on this might yield better results."

Kait's admiration for Sam skyrocketed. His willingness to forge a strong working relationship, despite Sulyard's attitude, displayed his cooperative and honorable traits. He really was one of the good guys, and she would support his effort.

"He has a point," she said, looking directly at Sulyard. "Fenton doesn't make idle threats. He's a killer, plain and simple. If we're going to stop him, we need to set aside our egos and do everything we can to find him." She paused and looked around the group. "I hope all of you will do the same thing."

"SCORE." FENTON pumped his latex gloved hand in the air. "I knew J.J. would meet me for a drink tonight, didn't you, Brian?"

Fenton scanned the screen again and reread the e-mail from Jason Mason. "Listen to what he says. 'Dude, you know I'll meet the legendary Vyper. Anytime. Anywhere.'" Fenton peered at Brian. "I promised him the same peek at my bot program that I made to you. He can't resist."

Fenton slid his chair closer to Brian, the wheels rumbling on the wood floor. He leaned down. "Now, now. I can see you're jealous. Don't be. Your contribution to the mission will always be special to me. Remember, I put you in the scrapbook. But I have to move on before that hideous detective takes up with Kait and decides he must guard her night and day. If I can't get to her, how am I going to let her feel the same things you're feeling?"

Fenton pushed away and held his feet in the air as the chair zoomed across the floor to the bookshelf. He needed to shower before his meeting, but first, he'd prepare his package for Kait so when he had J.J. securely trussed up, Fenton could swing by her house to deliver her next surprise.

Since she'd foiled his first delivery attempt, he'd had time to improve his presentation. First the tissue paper. He riffled through the supplies he'd purchased yesterday.

"I think white would be good, don't you, Brian?" He glanced at his companion of the last few days. "White will emphasize my gift." He gently folded the paper and laid it in the bottom of the box.

He scooted back to the cooler sitting on the floor by Brian and lifted out the zipper bag with Elliot's heart. He checked to be sure plenty of ice remained to keep it cold until he was ready to deliver his gift.

Satisfied, he looked deep into Brian's eyes and smiled. "Now don't be jealous, Brian. Kait will receive Elliot's souvenir first, but I promise you have nothing to worry about. Yours will be the very next one she gets."

KAIT STOPPED at Nina's cubicle. Sam had asked Kait to accompany him when he went to question Mrs. Congdon. Kait wouldn't turn down the opportunity, but first she wanted to make sure Nina was okay with bringing Quinn in on the investigation. Nina was on the phone, so Kait dropped into the chair by the cluttered desk to wait. Nina was smooth-talking the judge's clerk, trying to convince him to fast-track the warrant for the post office.

Kait made herself comfortable and plucked out the latest edition of *Garden & Gun* magazine that was peeking out of Nina's Vera Bradley tote bag. The magazine title fit Nina to a T. As much as she loved living in Portland, she missed home, and embraced her heritage in her off hours. The three of them had often talked about taking a trip to Nina's hometown of Mobile, but hadn't done so. Maybe after Fenton was firmly locked behind bars, Kait would suggest it again. After all, she'd have plenty of free time that she'd been devoting to finding Fenton the last few years. She flipped through the magazine, enjoying yet another insight into her friend's unique tastes until she ended the call.

"I'm sorry about the Quinn thing," Kait said quickly, to preempt any objection Nina might want to raise. "If I hadn't given you that look in the meeting, his name never would have been mentioned. I hope you're not mad."

Nina swiveled her chair and crossed her leg, letting a pricey red pump dangle from her foot. "Mad about what? It's not like you volunteered me to talk to Quinn."

"Still, I can't help but think you're doing this because of me."

"Don't take this the wrong way, honey." Nina gave Kait a sugary smile, her way of making bad news palatable. "But this has nothing to do with you. Sure, I want Rhodes caught so you can put this behind you, but I volunteered because he's going to kill again if we don't stop him. I couldn't live with myself if he succeeded when I could have done something to stop it and let a silly little spat stop me."

"This thing with Quinn is a lot bigger than a silly spat." Kait eyed her friend, digging beyond the front she was putting on. "At least, that's how you acted yesterday."

She waved a hand. "Yesterday, I was just fit to be tied, but I've had a night to work through it and have things in perspective today."

"You're sure?"

"Positive. You don't get anywhere pretending the world is something it isn't." She pulled back her shoulders, and Kait was reminded of Nina's strong-willed grandmother. "I may not accept things I can't change all the time, but this situation calls for acceptance. Quinn wants to be a SEAL more than he wants to be with me, so why focus on that? Better to set my sights on the things I can control. Asking him to help falls in that category."

Kait appraised Nina. "Since when did you become such a grown-up?"

Nina smirked. "I didn't, but it sounds good, doesn't it? And hopefully, it'll help me get through seeing Quinn again."

"Do you really think he can get the info we need on Fenton?"

"He was never very open about his life as a SEAL, but one thing I am certain about. They command an amazing amount of respect. Even officers give them a wide berth. So, asking a clerk for a little information should be no problem."

"Then the real problem is you having to face him again." Kait looked for any hint of unease in Nina's expression. "I could go with you when you talk to him, if that would help."

Nina gave a firm shake of her head. "I can handle this alone."

"Are you sure?" Kait asked. "I mean, after the post office and all."

"That was different. I wasn't expecting to see him there. I'm more prepared for our meeting this afternoon."

"You've already arranged to talk to him?"

"Figured I'd just keep stewing about it until I did. We're meeting at TeaTime this afternoon." Nina mocked an innocent look that failed completely.

"Nina, no." Kait sat forward. "You're not really making him meet you there, are you? Talk about a bull in a china shop. He hates that place."

Nina wrinkled her nose. "I know."

Kait swatted a hand at her friend. "You're so bad."

"Hey. He broke up with me, so he should be the uncomfortable one."

"Ah, sweetie," Kait said. "You need to quit saying he broke up with you."

"Close enough."

Kait didn't think it was close at all, but she was looking at it from an outside perspective, not from the heart as Nina was doing.

She heard the soft thump of footsteps approaching and swiveled in time to catch Sam stepping up to the cubicle, his gaze shooting between them. "Am I interrupting something?"

"We're done," Nina said pointedly.

Sam focused on Kait. "Sulyard's already arranged for ERT to meet Dane at Congdon's house to process it. I plan to meet them there, but we should still have enough time to question Mrs. Congdon first."

Kait smiled up at him, eliciting a similar grin. After Sulyard had forbidden her from investigating on her own, she was thankful that Sam had asked her to accompany him. And maybe, just maybe, she was excited to be spending more time with him.

She stood, turned her attention to Nina, and felt guilty about the flutter in her stomach Sam caused when Nina was still suffering over Quinn. "Call me after you talk to Quinn, okay?"

"I'm thinking this will require another girl's night. You game?"

Kait nodded enthusiastically. "I'll have Lily, so you'll have to come to my house."

"Don't we always," Nina said. "I'll bring the bottle and a little something to snack on."

A little something to snack on—in Nina's world—took hours to prepare at home and was loaded with calories just like the treats last night. Kait would need extra time on the treadmill for sure. "If you need me before then, just call or text."

Nina's smile waned. Maybe she wasn't as okay with talking to Quinn as she'd claimed. She was very good at putting on a front when something was troubling her. Especially here at the office.

Perhaps Kait should insist on accompanying Nina to the meeting. After all, Nina had been there for Kait every moment after Abby died. Since Nina had lost her brother in a white-water rafting accident, she understood the aching loss of a sibling. So she'd supported Kait year after year, helping chase down false leads on Fenton and keeping Kait sane when they didn't pan out.

"We've gotta go, Kait," Sam said.

"Go on." Nina waved at her, her salmon-colored nails catching the overhead light. "I'll be fine, and you have a killer to catch."

Kait squeezed Nina's hand. Kait hoped she wasn't letting down her best friend, and Nina really would come through a visit with her ex in one piece.

Chapter Fourteen

ON THE DRIVE TO Mrs. Congdon's home, Sam glanced at Kait from behind the wheel. She was deep in thought, and her clenched jaw said it wasn't a pleasant daydream. She had to be thinking about the case. Maybe wondering how she could be more involved in it, but Sulyard made it clear he wouldn't let her do more unless he or Nina requested help.

Sam nearly snorted. She would no more stand back and let him lead this case than he'd stand back in her position. And he preferred it that way. He liked her spunk and determination. He just didn't like seeing the lingering look of despair on her face, and wanted to do something about it.

"You did a good job back there," he said, hoping to engage her in conversation and take her mind off her thoughts. "I finally understand something about computers and get how Rhodes makes his money."

She looked at him warily. "I'm not sure Detective Yates will agree with you."

"He's a jerk."

"I hadn't noticed." She gave him a wry smile.

"I'm being serious, Kait. You have a knack for explaining hard to understand concepts."

"I get a lot of practice. I volunteer with a team of computer professionals to teach people how to protect themselves on the Internet."

He had no idea how she found time in her busy schedule to volunteer. "How did you get involved with computers, anyway?"

"You make it sound like that's a bad thing."

"No, not bad. Just . . . well . . . you know. You aren't the typical geek."

She crossed her arms. "I'm assuming that was meant as a compliment."

"I'm really putting my foot in it, aren't I?"

"Don't worry. I won't hold it against you." She looked out her window. "You can't see this today, but I have always been shy. Painfully shy, and much more of an introverted geek than I seem now."

"Really?"

She nodded. "Abby was the opposite. She was outgoing, and others flocked to her. When we were little, she made sure I was included in things, but when we got older, her friends didn't want me hanging around as much.

So I retreated. My cousin was a lot like me. He bought one of the first Apple computers. I got hooked, so it was natural for me to get a computer science degree."

Surprised, he glanced at her. "So how did a shy girl with a computer degree become an FBI agent?"

She sighed. "That's a long story."

"And you don't want to talk about that."

"Very perceptive, Detective." She smiled. "What about you? How'd you decide to become a police officer?"

"Smooth move, turning the tables on me."

"I'm an agent, remember? We're good at getting information out of people." She chuckled, giving him a glimpse of her playful side. "Seriously, why a cop?"

He frowned, knowing she'd be like a pit bull until he gave it up. The last person he wanted to talk, or even think about when a crazy murderer was running free, was his dad. The man who'd gladly defend Rhodes and put him back on the street to kill again. "It's a long story."

She gestured at cars clogging the highway ahead. "We have nothing but time."

"Good," he said, smirking. "So you can tell me why you chose the FBI, then."

He hoped she'd continue to play along, but instead of a smart retort, he received a pained look, and she reached for her soda to take a long pull on the straw.

The last thing he wanted to do was hurt her more. He took a breath and launched into his story. "My dad was a buttoned-down suit like Sulyard. Arrogant. Always right. Demanding. Except, he was a defense attorney, getting every slime ball off for their crimes, and he kept pressuring me to follow in his footsteps."

"Seriously?" She squeezed his arm, her fingers cold from her drink, before she self-consciously dropped it to her lap. "You becoming a cop had to be one of the worst things you could to him, then."

"Precisely." Sam would never forget the day he told his father, and Sam had all but been disowned. "I was young and hot-headed when it came to Dad. So I figured he'd go ballistic if I become a cop."

She shifted, facing him, her face rapt with interest. "And did he?"

"Oh, yeah," Sam answered. "I hit the mark."

She studied him intently for a moment. "Even if you took the job to make your dad mad, it seems like you really like it."

"Most days I do," he said, not willing to go any further. He used to enjoy the detective work all the time. Even days where they found a fellow human being brutally murdered. He felt useful. Needed. By the victim who couldn't speak, and by their families who could. And that had been enough for him for a long time.

Until Stacie and Hannah's deaths rocked everything he believed in. Now he just felt empty. On the job and at home. Marcie's comment at the morgue came to mind, but he shoved it away and focused on the road.

"Did I say something wrong?" Kait asked, clearly confused at his change in attitude.

"No, we're good," he said, then clamped his mouth shut for the remainder of the drive. He'd already said too much. She didn't need to hear about his baggage. And he didn't need to see her pity him when it was becoming clearer by the minute that he wanted something else from her.

At the assisted living building, Kait got out of the car the minute Sam parked.

"What's the rush?" he asked when he joined her on the sidewalk.

She simply shrugged, straightened her jacket, and ran a hand over her hair. Not that either was necessary. Nothing was out of place. A stressful two-hour meeting and he was rumpled, but she looked as fresh as the moment he'd first laid eyes on her that morning.

She headed up the walk of the new and very pricey assisted living building. He hung back, noticing how her pants fit her generous curves like a glove. He didn't feel guilty keeping his eyes on her all the way to the apartment. Watching her was strictly business, and he needed to make sure she stayed safe from Rhodes.

Right.

Nearing the front door, she looked over her shoulder. "Stop looking at me like that, Detective. I've shot men for doing far less." She fired off a wicked grin.

"I don't know." He grinned back. "I'm pretty sure it's worth taking a bullet for." He wasn't sure how he expected her to respond to his open flirting, but a blush creeping up her neck wasn't it.

Interesting.

They signed in at the front desk, and the receptionist buzzed them through. Kait avoided eye contact for the elevator ride to the fifteenth floor. He had to smile at the insecurity he hadn't seen in her until now. After her reaction to his flirting, he could actually believe her story about growing up shy. He should do something crazy like kiss her, just to see how she reacted. But they were on the job, and he'd honor that.

The elevator dinged. She stepped into the hallway but lingered by the door and chewed on her lip. "You're taking point on this, right?"

He hoped his flirting wasn't to blame for the disappearance of her usual confidence. "I can if you want me to."

"It's just . . ." Her voice fell off, and she shrugged. "In cyber crimes, I don't often deal with talking to people about murdered family members."

"Don't worry, I got it." He squeezed her arm.

She smiled. Softly. Sweetly, like he was the only person in her world. Before he could react, she started down the hallway. She seemed oblivious to the effect such a smile could have on a guy, but he wasn't. His pulse kicked up, and he had to force himself to focus on their mission as he knocked on Mrs. Congdon's door. It wasn't long before the drone of her mobility cart whirred toward them, and the deadbolt clicked open.

"I didn't expect to see you again, Detective." Mrs. Congdon peered up at Sam through thick glasses that made her eyes look unusually large. She wore a flowery housecoat similar to the one she'd worn at the death notification call, and her eyes were puffy and red from crying.

"I'm sorry to bother you, ma'am," Sam said. "But I have a few more questions for you."

"Of course." She changed her focus to Kait. "And you are?"

"Sorry, Mrs. Congdon," Sam stepped in. "I should have introduced the two of you. This is Agent Knight with the FBI. She's working the case with me."

"I'm so sorry for your loss, Mrs. Congdon." Kait offered a tight smile.

"Thank you." She lifted a gnarled hand to the control knobs on her cart. "Please come in."

She reversed direction and pointed her cart toward the miniscule living room. She gestured at the same loveseat covered in a worn flowery fabric where Sam had sat two nights ago.

"Can I get you anything?" she asked.

"Thank you for asking, but no." Kait perched on the edge of the loveseat.

Sam shook his head and settled next to Kait.

Mrs. Congdon shifted on her cart. She weighed all of ninety pounds, and that was being generous. "You said you have additional questions."

"I do," Sam said. "When I spoke to you the other night, you were having a hard time remembering when you last talked to Elliot. Has that become clearer for you?"

"A little. Nothing much goes on around here, so I sometimes lose track of days." Tears glistened in her eyes. "I think it was a few weeks. He called to tell me he'd made a new friend who would be coming to stay with him for a few days."

"Did he mention the friend's name or where he lived?" Kait asked, her voice soft and compassionate, though Sam knew she had to be eager to learn more about this friend.

"No. Is that important?" She looked from Kait to Sam. "Did this friend have something to do with his death?"

"We're not sure yet," Sam answered.

Her hand flew to her chest, and she grabbed onto a gold locket dangling from a thick chain. "I knew it. Just knew it. Elliot didn't make friends. I warned him that this man might take advantage of him, but he didn't listen. My poor, poor Elliot."

Kait took Mrs. Congdon's hand and held it until the older woman calmed down.

"What about Elliot's health?" Sam asked. "Did he have any recent medical procedures that might have included an IV? Maybe in the last week or so?"

"Medical procedures?" Her eyes widened behind the thick lenses, and her hand dropped to her knees. "No. Why do you ask?"

"No procedures involving a hospital stay?" Sam quickly followed up.

"No. Nothing." Her gaze darted between Sam and Kait, searching for explanations.

Sam smiled at Mrs. Congdon to ease her concern. "I had a minor procedure once and didn't tell my parents because I didn't want them to worry. Could Elliot have done the same thing, do you think?"

She shook her head almost violently. "Not my Elliot. He was so squeamish about needles. Passed out at the sight of them. Even as a boy. If he was going to have anything done that involved a needle, I'd have been there by his side." She smiled as if a fond memory had come to mind. "Besides, he never got his driver's license, and he was afraid to leave the neighborhood on the bus. He would have needed someone to transport him. Wait, do you think this mysterious friend took him?"

"He could have taken a cab," Sam suggested.

She frowned. "Since I no longer drive, we often took a cab. But again, even with this new friend, I'm sure he'd want me there with him, holding his hand."

Poor Elliot Congdon. So afraid of life that he hid in his home. A virtual recluse, yet Rhodes had found him and killed him anyway.

Mrs. Congdon sat up straighter. "Now suppose you tell me what this is all about, Detective."

"The medical examiner believes Elliot recently had an IV," Sam answered.

She shook her head hard. "That's not possible. Not for my Elliot. At least, not without me there."

"Still," Kait said. "We'd like to follow up with his doctor. Do you have his contact information?"

"I'll get it." She pressed forward on the cart's controls, wheeling out of the room.

"I'd bet that friend was Fenton," Kait whispered as she leaned close to Sam.

"Unless Congdon wasn't as much of a hermit as his mother thinks."

"We need to interview the neighbor who wasn't available before. She might be able to give us a description of this friend. Plus, if Congdon did leave home, she'd have been the most likely person to see him." Kait glanced at her watch. "Hopefully, we have enough time to talk to her before meeting ERT."

Sam nodded. "I'll text my LT when we get out of here, so he can assign someone to question Congdon's doctor while we talk to the neighbor."

Mrs. Congdon came back into the room, a worn address book resting on her lap. She flipped it open to the doctor's information, and Sam jotted it down.

She ran her fingers across the page, tears pooling in her eyes. "I can't believe I'll never take my boy to see this fine doctor again. Never do anything with Elliot again."

Her grief pulled Sam toward that dark time in his life when it had swamped him. He couldn't leave without trying to help her. He dug out a card for a grief support group and squatted next to her. He would have given it to her the other night, but she was too shocked to process his offer.

"I know the pain you're feeling, Mrs. Congdon." He pressed the card into her hand. "I not only suddenly lost a former partner, but my wife, too. And I want you to know there are others who can help you get through it. I sponsor a grief support group. We meet every Monday night. When you're ready, I hope you'll join us."

She dropped the card on her lap and squeezed Sam's hand. "That's so kind of you, Detective."

Sam wished he could do more for her, but he was already stepping outside of department guidelines. "If you want to attend a meeting and have any issues getting there, call me at the number on the back of the card. I'll find transportation for you." He stood, and she smiled up at him.

"God bless you, Detective. You're a good man."

Kait rose, and Mrs. Congdon looked up at her. "God bless you, too, Agent Knight."

Sam saw Kait's eyes shining with unshed tears. If he could sweep her into his arms and kiss them away, he would, but he couldn't ignore Marcie's comment the other day. She was right on target when she said he was no longer able to feel anything but pain. Sure, he had flashes of warmth and happiness with Kait, but he couldn't sustain that long-term. His past could still bring him down, and he didn't think he possessed what was needed to make a committed relationship work. Until he did, he had no business even thinking about Kait in that way, and that made him sadder than he'd been in a long time.

Chapter Fifteen

KAIT SAT ACROSS the table from Sam at a small café near Congdon's house. ERT had been delayed at another scene, giving her and Sam the luxury of having lunch before visiting Congdon's neighbor. They'd already placed their orders, and Sam was checking his e-mail. Kait had nothing to do but think about his bombshell of losing a partner and his wife. Not that he'd even said a word about them. He could have explained about them on the ride over, but he'd left her to imagine the worst. She got that he didn't want to discuss lost loved ones. It was easier to focus on her losses. But it would also have been natural for him to talk about it, and it stung that he hadn't confided anything. Not even a hint.

She sipped her iced tea, trying to put aside her feelings. But like it or not, his unwillingness to share bothered her. More that she'd admit to anyone but herself.

Then there was the support group. Never would she see him as the type to attend a support group, let alone host one. Obviously, something he hadn't been involved with until after Abby died, or Kait suspected he would have suggested the group to her, too.

He looked up and caught her staring at him. "So tell me the story of how you hooked up with the FBI."

Great. Another foray into her personal life while ignoring everything he'd revealed at Mrs. Congdon's place. Maybe he'd let it go if she made light of it. "You're so predictable. After I changed the subject in the car, I knew you'd pounce as soon as possible."

"Pounce?" He gave her a devilish grin that, heaven help her, sent her pulse skittering higher. "That's a little strong, isn't it?"

"Maybe, but you've let very little time pass since first asking about it."

"You're avoiding it again, aren't you?"

"Me, avoiding?" She gave him a pointed look.

He didn't catch her inference. "Yeah, you."

She sighed. "You're not going to let this go until I tell you."

"Nope. The more you avoid the question, the more I'll press." That grin came back while he leaned closer. "I have to know what's so bad that you feel a need to hide it."

"I'm not hiding it." *Not like you.*

"Me thinks thou dost protest too much."

"Fine," she gave in. "I'll give you the CliffNotes version, but I assure you, you'll be disappointed in the story. It's nothing very exciting."

He sat back with a satisfied smile. "Go on. I can do boring."

"Okay, but don't say I didn't warn you." She took a long drink of her tea then started. "After getting my master's in information technology, I spent five years working for a major IT company as a software engineer. And speaking of unexciting, it got boring real quick. I'd get up each morning, go to work, sit behind a computer screen for ten to twelve hours and come home. Do the same thing every day. On the weekend, I'd have dinner with my parents, Abby, and my boyfriend, if I happened to be dating at the time."

The thought of happier times with Abby brought a smile. "Abby was working as a rare art buyer. She had such exciting stories to tell about her travels and purchases. I sat back and listened. Watched, seeing how my dad's eyes lit up when listening to her. One day, I asked him about it. Not in a mean way, like why don't you get excited over my life, but why was he so thrilled with hers."

"And what did he say?" Sam grabbed his tea glass and added two packets of sugar.

"He said he had to live through her. He's an accountant, and he'd always wished he could have done something more thrilling." She paused and had to force herself to go on. "And then he said something that changed my life."

"What?" Sam sipped the tea and grimaced at the taste.

"He said that he and I were exactly alike. Not cut out for the exciting things of the world. We were made to be slow steady workhorses who kept people like Abby grounded." Her voice trembled, giving away her inner turmoil when she'd hoped to hide it.

Sam poured another packet of sugar in the glass. "And that bothered you."

Since she'd already given more than the CliffNotes version, part of her wanted to stop talking, but it truly felt good to let it out. "So much I could hardly breathe. I love my dad, but I'd always said I wouldn't be like him. Wouldn't settle for average. Wouldn't hide away in my office and only come out when forced. And there I was. His spitting image."

"So you had to change." He took another long drink and grabbed the sugar again.

She nodded. "I searched the Internet for an IT career with some excitement. Saw the FBI was looking for people with IT expertise, and I thought nothing could be more adventurous than that."

"You sound disappointed."

"No, not at all. I love my job. But honestly, agents don't live the kinds of lives you see on TV. Especially ones who work in cyber crimes. Our hunt is done behind the scenes most of the time, not in the field."

He tried his tea again and added more sugar.

"Seriously, are you going to put that whole container of sugar in your glass?" she asked.

"We like our tea sweet in the south." He smiled. "Guess if we drink enough of it, we figure we'll be sweet as pie."

"Then you best ask our waitress for more, 'cause I'm sure there's not enough in there to sweeten you up." She grinned at him.

He rolled his eyes. "So if you're a desk jockey most of the time, then this field work is new for you."

"For the most part, yeah. I mean, I've interviewed plenty of people in the field and participated in my share of raids, but honestly." She paused and looked him in the eye. "I'm kind of worried that maybe I don't have the skills to keep Fenton from getting to me or Lily. You know . . . that I won't be able to protect her when she needs me the most."

"I won't let anything happen to either of you." His voice went low and husky, his eyes dark, and he engulfed her hand in his. "No one's getting hurt again on my watch."

She felt safe, and loved the warmth of his callused hands, to feel that connection between them even stronger. She watched him for a moment. Waiting. Hoping he'd expound on his last statement, but he stared over her shoulder, silent, a brooding expression drawing down his mouth. He'd expected her to open up all the time, and yet, he had no intention of reciprocating.

She pulled her hand free and sat back.

He glanced at her. "What's wrong?"

"You want me to spill my guts, but whenever we venture close to your personal life, you just offer cryptic comments and then clam up."

"What, you mean the 'on my watch' thing?" he honestly sounded surprised.

"Yes, that's exactly what I mean. You told Mrs. Congdon about your partner and wife and didn't bother to share it with me." Hurt lingered in her tone, but she didn't care. She was getting mad.

Didn't seem to matter to him as his expression said he was warring with what to tell her.

Fine. So he didn't want to open up. At least she now knew this was a one-way street, and she could stop letting her emotions run wild and think he might be someone she'd want to get to know.

"Forget it." She looked away, staring at a small child across the restaurant.

"My partner, Stacie," he said so quietly Kait almost missed it, "was gunned down on my watch."

She snapped her head to look at him, his pain visible in his eyes. "I'm sorry, Sam. You want to tell me about it?" She thought about taking his hand, but he pulled it away and shoved his fingers into his hair.

"Not much to tell. We were patrol cops. She was a rookie." His hand drifted down the back of his neck. "We'd only been together for a few days when we responded to an alarm at a warehouse. It was late. Around midnight. Dark and deserted. We saw a flashlight in a window. We waited for backup and when they arrived, we went in. The suspect ran. I went after him, but twisted my ankle."

He stopped speaking and looked down. "Stacie took up the pursuit. She forgot all about being cautious and barreled around a corner, right into a bullet. One of the other officers plugged the shooter. Now he's six feet under, as is Stacie. All for a load of copper." He cupped his fingers around his glass, turning it round and round, his head remaining down and watching it. "I replay it over and over. Thinking there's something I could have done differently, you know?"

"You're not to blame, Sam." She threw commonsense to the wind and laid her hand over his.

He looked up. "I know it's not my fault. At least, I keep telling myself that, but I was the senior officer. She was my responsibility."

"And so you take it personally."

"Yeah," he said, threading his fingers in hers. "Just like you and your sister. The loss is personal."

"And your wife?" she asked.

He shrugged, that shutter coming down over his eyes again. Kait wanted to pry, to push him, but he'd shared something today. That was enough. For now, anyway.

"MRS. PIERCE." ON the neatly kept porch of Congdon's neighbor, Kait held her ID near the peephole. "I'm Special Agent Kaitlyn Knight with the FBI, and this is Detective Sam Murdock. Could we speak to you for a moment?"

A deadbolt clicked, and the door whipped open, revealing a rotund woman Kait guessed to be in her seventies. She raised painted-on eyebrows above watery eyes. "You're here about Elliot, aren't you?"

"We are. Do you have time for a few questions, Mrs. Pierce?" Kait offered her a sympathetic smile.

"Please call me Yolanda. And if you don't mind, I'd like to sit down." Cane in hand, she waddled onto the porch and sat on a metal chair. It groaned under her weight, tipping dangerously to the side, but she balanced with one elbow on the handle of her cane.

"Such a tragedy." She pulled out a lacy handkerchief from her apron pocket. "Dear, sweet Elliot never hurt a flea. He didn't deserve this."

To soften her approach, Kait knelt on one knee in front of Yolanda. "When was the last time you saw Elliot?"

"It's been awhile." Her voice broke, and she held the hankie to her mouth. "My sister Ida has been staying with me for the last month, so I didn't pay much attention to Elliot during that time. Sure, I saw him coming and going, but I didn't check up on him."

"And that was unusual for you?" Sam took a few steps closer, and Kait recognized it as his way of inserting himself into the conversation in a nonthreatening way.

Yolanda nodded and looked up at him. "After his mother moved, I tried to stop in at least once a week to see how he was getting on."

"You mentioned not checking up on him for a month or so," Sam said. "But did you talk to him at all since then?"

Yolanda shifted on the chair. "I've been thinking about that very thing. The last time we had one of our up close and personal chats was on his birthday, July first. I had him over for dinner. His favorite—roast beef, mashed potatoes, and gravy. He ate supper and a piece of my famous chocolate buttermilk cake, then took the rest home." She shook her head.

"Let me get this straight," Kait clarified as Yolanda sounded like she might have spoken to Elliot, just not up close and personal as she called it. "You didn't talk to Elliot after his birthday on July first?"

Yolanda peered down at Kait, her expression thoughtful. "Yes. That's right. That was the last time I *really* talked to him. I saw him come home after that, but we only yelled across the yard. You know, the 'how are you' kind of stuff."

"And do you recall the last time that occurred?" Kait asked, trying to keep Yolanda moving forward.

She tipped her head in thought. "I suppose it was when I was out walking Fluffy one night. I'd been gone all day, and Fluffy was hyper. I spotted Elliot climbing into his car. I yelled to him, but—"

"His car?" Kait interrupted. "There wasn't one in the garage, and we couldn't find one registered to him. We also know he didn't have a driver's license."

"I don't know about the license, but when his mother moved, she left her old Chrysler Imperial behind."

"Chrysler Imperial?" Sam's voice purred over the words, drawing out Imperial. He could have reacted to the importance of the car, but he remained cool and didn't alert Yolanda.

A smile claimed her lips for a moment as she raised her eyes in thought. "It was a big old tan car they bought in '91. I know the year because my Earl and her Lester went out and bought one together. Same color and all. I had it until he passed, but then I didn't need such a monster for little ole me, and I traded it in for a hybrid."

"But you're sure it was Elliot?" Kait asked.

"Yes, I'm sure." Yolanda thumped her cane as if she couldn't believe they were doubting her. "Who else would it be?"

Sam bent closer. "Do you remember what night that was?"

"Of course I do. It was the day of the annual church bazaar. We can usually count on clear skies by the fourth, so we always hold it the first Saturday following the fourth." She tapped her chin. "I believe that was the twelfth this year."

Kait shifted to her other knee, impatience with Yolanda building. "Have you seen Elliot drive off in the car at other times?"

"Now that you mention it, I did. He'd recently started going out. A lot. All times of the day. I was hoping he'd met a woman. Though I don't know where that could have happened. Maybe in one of those newfangled online talk places."

"Do you know if Elliot was planning a trip out of town this month?" Sam asked.

"Elliot?" Yolanda's eyes widened. "No. As far as I know, he's never even spent the night away from home." She suddenly sat up and slapped her hand against her forehead. "Oh, my stars, how did I forget this? I picked up Ida at the airport. I'd just loaded her five bags . . . five . . . can you believe it, five?" She *tsk*ed. "The woman might be skinny as a rail, but she brings enough luggage for an army. Anyway, I was loading the bags into my car when I saw Elliot pass by the doors inside baggage claim. He shook hands with another fellow."

"You're sure it was Elliot?" Sam asked

"Positive," she replied. "He was wearing that ratty old green pea coat of his. In July, mind you. He hid behind that coat. I tried to get him to toss that thing out a hundred times, but it was like his security blanket, and he never stepped outside without it on. I guess seeing him at the airport means he could have been heading out of town, right?"

Kait felt her adrenaline kick in, but kept it from her voice. "If he was at baggage claim, he was more likely picking up the man you saw him with."

"We'll need details of your sister's arrival," Sam added. "Day, time, airline."

"Let me run in and get my calendar." She didn't wait for agreement, but bolted faster than Kait could imagine she could move, her cane thumping inside then fading away.

Kait came to her feet. For a time, she stood next to Sam, the sun high in the sky, spilling warm rays over the railing and casting shadows at their feet. A soft breeze played over her skin.

Sam settled on the porch rail, one boot dangling, the other firmly planted on the weathered boards. "It's looking like this guy Congdon picked up was the friend his mother mentioned."

Kait nodded her agreement. "Once Yolanda provides flight details, I'll report it to Sulyard. He'll assign someone to follow up on the flight manifests and get the video footage for the baggage claim area."

Sam leaned forward, planting a hand on his knee as he looked at her. "And you caught the pea coat comment, right?"

She nodded, but couldn't embrace his excitement. "It's helpful to know Congdon owned a pea coat, but it doesn't explain why Fenton had it at the phone booth."

"Maybe he didn't think we'd believe he'd killed Congdon and the coat would tie him to the case."

"Maybe," Kait said, her mind wandering back through the conversation with Yolanda. "I think we're better off getting the tags for the Imperial and issuing an alert than trying to figure out the importance of the coat."

Sam nodded. "I'll look up the registration information, and get a BOLO out on the car."

Kait nodded. Being able to issue a "Be On the Look Out" alert quickly to every PPB officer in town was one of the advantages to working on a joint taskforce. Each organization had their specialty, and bringing them together made things work so much more efficiently.

Her specialty was retrieving and analyzing data. "I'll have our analysts pull footage from street cams in the general vicinity. Maybe we'll catch the car on one of these mysterious trips Yolanda mentioned, and that will give us another lead."

The screen door burst open and slammed against the wall. Yolanda rushed outside, an Anne Geddes calendar tucked under her arm. After sitting, she pressed it open on her lap and stabbed a chubby finger on Wednesday, July 3rd. "Here it is. Alaska Air from Medford. See the flight number?"

Kait grabbed her phone and typed the details into a note. "Do you remember what carousel the bags came in on?"

"No. I met Ida at the curb. She might know."

"About this man Elliot met," Kait said. "Can you describe him?'

Yolanda closed the calendar, her eyes creased in thought. "He was about the same size as Elliot. Dark hair, too. He was dressed nice. A suit, I think. He had one of those computer bags hanging over his shoulder."

Kait thumbed through her phone and showed Yolanda a photo of

Fenton. "Is this the man you saw?"

She studied the picture. "Could be, but I'm not sure. I just wasn't close enough. But Ida mentioned seeing Elliot, so maybe she saw the other guy, too."

"We'll want to talk to her." Sam pulled out his notepad. "I'll need her last name and phone number."

"Ida Nance. She never married, poor thing." Yolanda *tsk*ed, then rattled off Ida's phone number. "Don't be surprised if she gives you a hard time. She's suspicious by nature, so she'll want proof of who you are before she'll say a thing. I'll phone her to tell her to expect your call."

"I'd appreciate it if you didn't call her," Kait said. "If the two of you talk about that day, she might get confused about the details and inadvertently repeat your account of the events instead."

"Oh, heavens, it's like you know her. She would do just that. I'm the older one, and she's always tried to be just like me." Yolanda frowned. "But honestly, if I don't call her first, she's not going to answer your questions. Unless of course you plan to hike to Medford to show her your badges."

"How about I call her right now?" Sam offered. "You can get on the phone and tell her you saw our ID." Sam snapped his from a belt clip. "We can use mine." He dialed Ida's number and handed the phone to Yolanda.

She held it away from her body as if it might bite. "Do I just talk into it, or do I have to push a button?"

"Just talk after Ida answers."

"Oh my stars, Ida, you'll never guess what I'm talking on?" Yolanda's eyes twinkled. "A cell phone. Can you believe it? It's not mine. Belongs to a Detective Sam Murdock with the Portland police. He's here on my porch with Special Agent Kaitlyn Knight with the FBI." She took a breath and listened for a moment. "No. I'm fine. It's Elliot. You know my next-door neighbor. He was murdered."

Sam heard Ida's cry of surprise.

"They want to talk to you, too. In case you saw anything while you were visiting. You're so careful; I knew you wouldn't talk to them without seeing their badges, so I wanted to make sure you knew they were okay." Yolanda listened again. "I suppose that's okay. Let me ask." She looked at Sam. "Ida's got the girls over for bridge, and she wondered if you could call her back in fifteen minutes or so."

"That's fine," Sam said, and Yolanda relayed the message as her gaze drifted off down the street.

Kait followed her line of vision. A white truck with the FBI logo and Evidence Response Team in bold blue letters on the side pulled down the street and stopped in front of Congdon's house. Soon, neighbors would pour out of their homes to gawk as they had the day Congdon's body was discovered.

When Yolanda returned the phone to Sam, Kait handed her a business card. "Thank you for the help, Yolanda. Call me if you think of anything else. Anything at all."

Yolanda's head bobbed. "You can be sure I will."

Before Yolanda started asking questions about the ERT truck, Kait jogged down the stairs, the heavy thud of Sam's boots following behind.

He caught up to her. "She was something else, wasn't she?"

"Memorable, that's for sure. She's shed a whole new light on Congdon."

"Sounds like you think everything she told us is significant."

"Don't you?"

He shrugged.

"Think about it, Sam." She turned to him, stopping to gain his attention. "Yolanda tells us that Congdon suddenly changes his routine. Starts going out more frequently. What if the reason Fenton chained up Congdon was to take over his life? You know, impersonate Congdon so he could move about freely without worrying about getting caught?"

"That would take identity theft to a whole new level, and I'm not sure I buy it."

"But it *is* possible. Congdon's a loner. No friends, no family to check on him, works at home, rarely goes out. The only person who kept in regular touch with him was Yolanda, and even she'd left him alone lately."

"Your theory is solid, but I just don't see what Rhodes had to gain from impersonating Congdon. And if it was working so well for Rhodes, why did he up and kill Congdon? Why not keep going?"

She resisted the urge to grab his arm to make him see her point. "Because it was time to unleash this crazy plan."

"I suppose you could be right." He glanced at his watch and pressed a few buttons. "I've set a reminder to call Ida. If she can identify Rhodes, then I'll give your theory more consideration."

"Even if she can't, we might get lucky and catch him on security footage at the baggage carousel."

"Let's hope at least one thing from this conversation pans out."

"It will," Kait said with a certainty she didn't quite feel. "It's about time we catch a break on this case."

Chapter Sixteen

AT TEATIME, NINA passed the closely grouped tables for two and chose a booth in the back for privacy. Her hands shook as she slid onto the bench facing the door. She wanted to see Quinn the minute he entered. She'd acted confident when talking to Kait, but Nina dreaded seeing him as much as she dreaded trying to get a brush through her tight curls. An impossible task and a painful one at that.

The bells above the door tinkled. Nina could sense Quinn's presence filling the space before she saw him enter and stop by the door, his feet planted wide as he perused the room. His eyes looking. Seeking. Searching for any danger and assessing his escape routes. The same survey most law enforcement officers completed when entering a public space. Even Nina. But Nina had been too nervous when she'd come in to do so. Not that TeaTime harbored any real danger. Except maybe now, in the form of Quinn Stone.

An anemic-looking waitress named Betty stepped to the table, blocking Nina's view of Quinn. "What can I get you?"

A frequent customer, Nina didn't need to look at a menu. "I'll have a one-person pot of Darjeeling and a plate of mini-pastries. My associate," she tipped her head at Quinn, "will have the organic French press coffee."

"Not a tea drinker, huh?" Betty glanced at Quinn then did a double take before departing.

Nina didn't blame the woman. Even though he'd stomped all over her emotions, she stared at his wide shoulders, trim waist, and a face made for commercials—a package that sent her senses reeling.

Business, Nina. You're here on business.

She focused on the table, straightening items that didn't need adjusting, and waiting for him to cross the room. She conjured up the smile she'd practiced in front of the mirror hundreds of times to ensure proper manners while Grandmother Hale looked on. Southern stereotypes of women might be disappearing, but many Alabama mamas and grandmothers still raised their daughters with the same code they were raised by. And at the moment, all the sweet-talking and smiling to say nothing's wrong when the world was falling apart was going to come in handy.

Nina heard Quinn's boots clomp closer on the worn wooden floor. He wanted her to hear him coming. If he didn't, he'd use the stalking training he'd completed in sniper school, allowing him to cross the room without a sound.

"Scoot over," he said, as he stopped at the end of the booth.

She shifted her gaze to the edge of the table. His hiking boots came into focus, and she let her eyes travel up his body. She noted the oddity of his long-sleeved shirt on a summer day and his hands shoved in his pockets, but it was the familiar face that she'd once been sure she'd see for the rest of her life, that left her tongue-tied.

She tried to come up with a good reason for him to sit on the other side of the table, but nothing came to mind except how great he looked. "I'm good."

"Well I'm not. Not with my back to the door."

"Who's going to jump you in a teashop, for goodness sake?"

He stared down on her. "Guess you're the only one who might want to plunge a Ka-Bar in my back in a place like this."

In the time she'd spent with him, she'd learned that he used Ka-Bar as a generic term for a knife, but that was about all she'd gleaned from the tight-lipped SEAL about his Navy way of life.

"I don't want to kill you, Quinn," she said, infusing her words with as much grace as she could muster. "But I wouldn't mind seeing you suffer for a while."

She watched and waited for his reaction, expecting him to get mad, but he threw back his head and laughed, bringing a smile out of her when that was the last thing she wanted to do around him. Or maybe sitting thigh to thigh with him was the last thing.

She slid out of the booth and quickly took the other side. "It's all yours."

He took the spot she'd just vacated. "It's not like you to give in so easily."

"There's no point in arguing. I'd like to get down to business and get out of here."

He pressed his shoulders back against the worn leather and settled his hands in his lap. "Must be some business if you didn't want to talk about it on the phone."

She brought him up to speed on Rhodes and their need for information. "Anything you could do would be helpful."

He opened his mouth to reply, but Betty arrived with their food. She quickly set the tea and pastries in front of Nina but took her time placing the coffee in front of Quinn. "Anything else I can get you?" she asked, purring like a well-loved cat.

Quinn shook his head, but didn't look at her. Nina had seen waitresses fawn over him many times. Experience told him if he didn't make eye contact, they went away faster.

Betty slid the bill under his cup, and Nina noted she'd added her phone number.

Nina grabbed the bill. "Thanks, but we don't need anything else." Nina waited for Betty to depart and pushed the plate of pastries over to Quinn. "I see you're still a chick magnet."

He chose an éclair dripping with chocolate. "Is that your way of asking if I'm dating? 'Cause if it is, I'm not . . . I haven't."

A thrill shot through her at his news, and he watched her, maybe waiting for her to update him on her relationship status, but she wouldn't give him the satisfaction. She took a long sip of tea, letting the soothing liquid calm her jitters. "Do you think you can help us with Rhodes?"

"I'll need his particulars. Like his social, date of birth, etc." He shifted in his seat, clearly uncomfortable. Maybe with Nina's choice of meeting places, or her, or both.

She picked up a file from the seat and slid it across the table. "It's all in here."

"If you brought that along, you must have felt confident I'd help." He chomped down on the éclair, leaving a spot of chocolate on his upper lip.

She wanted to wipe it away and that made her mad. "I don't pretend to know what you'll do," she snapped. "But I did hope you'd want to help us take a killer off the street before he kills again."

"Geez, Nina. Lighten up, already. When did you get all serious on me?"

When you broke my heart. "This is business, Quinn. Will you do this or not?"

He set down the éclair, his fingers tipped in chocolate. "Of course I will."

"Soon, or are you and your precious team off on a mission?" She hadn't wanted to sound bitter, but there it was in her words.

He didn't reply but picked up his cup with the chocolate-free hand, and Nina couldn't miss seeing the angry, raw flesh from burns on his hand.

"Oh my gosh, it was *you.*" The tea swam in her stomach as she met his gaze, her frustration with him forgotten. "You were you the SEAL who was hurt in that hostage rescue."

"It was nothing. I'm fine." He pulled his hand back as if intending to hide it, but she took it in hers and looked at the tender, pink scars. He had such amazing hands. Long fingers. Gentle fingers for such a big guy. Now they were scarred for life. The very thing she feared for him.

No, that wasn't true. She feared his death. She gently set his hand on the table and vowed again to get over this man before her fears became a reality.

"How soon do you think you'll be able to get on this?" she asked, noting how breathless she sounded.

He picked up on it and tilted his head to watch her. "I'll need to go back to base, so as soon as I can schedule a flight."

"We'll compensate you for the flight."

"No need. My time here was about up, and I'd be going back anyway."

"Back to active duty."

"Yes."

Her gut tightened. "At least the injury allowed you to spend time with your family."

He snorted. "Like that was a good thing. Ty's entered a junior in high school rebellion phase. Skipping classes. Pulling pranks. Mom asked me to come knock some sense into him. Didn't work. He thinks he knows everything."

A techie at heart, Ty didn't want to be like his brother, but he'd once idolized Quinn. "So a typical teen, then."

"Exactly, and I'm ready to get away from it for a while." The big strong SEAL who faced knife-and gun-wielding terrorists shuddered over a teenager, making Nina smile.

"Sounds like this will work out for both of us then." She pulled out a few bills, tossed them on the table, and stood. "So you'll call me the minute you know anything?"

"I could come back." His voice was filled with hope. "Tell you in person."

"That's not a good idea, Quinn." She took a step.

He circled her wrist with his hand, stopping her. He rubbed his thumb over her pulse, which had burst into overdrive at his touch. He looked up at her, his eyes awash with the same longing she was fighting.

"We were good together, sweetheart," he whispered. "So good."

"Were is the operative word, Quinn," she said, and freed her arm before she did something she'd regret. "Remember it."

As she exited the building, she could feel his eyes on her, but she kept going. She was running from him. She was also running from herself when there wasn't any place to escape. That meant reliving the last six months and trying to put him behind her again. This time she'd try harder. This time she'd succeed.

BY THE TIME Sam and Kait reached Congdon's house, the FBI tech had opened the back door of his truck and had climbed in. Sam stopped near the rear of the truck, surprised to find Dane inside, staring at the other guy like he was Dane's favorite celebrity.

"Dane," Sam called. "Have you gone plumb crazy and joined up with the other side?"

"Are you kidding? Look at the place." He gestured at the walls filled with equipment then looked at Kait. "Tell your boss thanks for letting me work with Henry." He nodded at a male tech holding a tripod with a boxy piece of equipment mounted on the end. It looked a lot like an old boom box with the middle indented.

Kait rolled her eyes. "Men and their toys."

"Oh yeah." Dane grinned and jumped down. "And this one's the top of my list."

"If you say so," Kait said, not seeming to have any interest in this kind of technology. "What is it?"

"It's a Leica—"

"ScanStation C10," Henry butted in as he grabbed a laptop case from the back of the truck before smiling at Kait.

She acknowledged him with a nod then turned to Sam. "This is Henry Greco. He's one of our finest evidence recovery techs."

"The guy with all the cool toys," Sam said sarcastically. "So it's a Leica something or other, but what does it do that's so cool?"

Henry climbed down and affectionately patted the piece of equipment. "This baby puts out a pulse of eye-safe laser light fifty thousand times per second as it scans the crime scene and creates a 3-D rendering. When the scan is completed, we upload the file to a computer, and you can look at the scene over and over again."

Sam wasn't impressed. "And this is somehow better than the copious photos we take at crime scenes?"

Henry gave Sam a well-duh look. "3-D captures measurements along with the pics, so the model is scaled. It's a great way for a DA to show the crime scene to a jury, or for you to refresh your memory as time passes."

"But how does it help us solve the case?" Sam hated that he was sounding defensive, but he didn't have access to such equipment, and Henry was intimating that Sam wouldn't do a good job without it.

"Why don't I give you a demonstration?"

Sam didn't have time to waste, but he did like to keep up on the latest forensic technology, even if his department didn't have the budget to purchase expensive new equipment. "Lead the way."

"Can I carry it?" Dane asked like a rock star groupie.

"Um . . ." Henry glanced at Kait who didn't respond. "Um . . . well . . . no . . . I mean it's so expensive and all, and our insurance doesn't cover you."

"Rats."

"I'll let you start the scan running though."

"You're on," Dane said enthusiastically and followed Henry up the walkway.

"After you." Sam held out his hand for Kait. "Nice that they're both so into their jobs."

"Hey." She grinned at him. "I'd act the same way as Dane if someone drove up with a truck loaded with the latest weapons."

"I'm assuming you're not meaning a black market dealer and his weapons."

That earned him an eye roll and a shake of her head, and he couldn't help but laugh.

In the house, Henry set up the camera in the bedroom where they'd found Congdon's body. "Once Dane starts this up, it'll take a few minutes. Then I'll need to upload it to my laptop."

Sam's alarm for the call to Ida chirped. "Perfect timing. I have a call to make while you get this set up."

Kait held up a finger. "One quick question, first. Isn't it a little late for a scan with the body gone?"

Henry shrugged. "It is unusual. In fact, I've never done one at this point in the investigation, but we were told to use everything we have, so we'll scan the rooms to cover all bases."

"Let's hope it's not a waste of time then." Sam took one more look at the camera as it started to rotate and gestured for Kait to join him.

On the patio with the sun beating down on them, she dug out her phone. "I'll follow up on Nina's visit to the SEAL while you call Ida."

Sam nodded and dialed Ida. "This is Detective Sam Murdock with the Portland Police Bureau. Yolanda told you I'd call. Do you have time for my questions now?"

"The girls just left. So fire away."

Sam wedged his phone between his neck and ear and dug out his notepad. "Yolanda told us on July third you were on flight number 2415 from Medford to Portland."

"I was, but what does this have to do with Elliot?" The skepticism Yolanda warned them about came through loud and clear.

"Did you see him at the baggage carousel that day?"

"Yes, I remember seeing him. He was talking to another guy."

"Can you describe the other man?"

"Sure," she said as if he'd offended her by asking. "He was tall. Black hair. He had a scar on his chin. Left side as you looked at him. Yolanda had baked her famous banana bread, and I couldn't wait to get to her car and have a slice. So I kept thinking the scar looked like a banana." She laughed.

"Maybe more of a crescent, but you get the idea."

Sam's adrenaline kicked in. Sounded like a match for Rhodes's scar. "I have a photo I'd like you to look at. If I e-mail it or text it to you, could you tell me if it's the man you saw?"

"I don't text, but I'm not in the dark ages like Yolanda. I at least have a cell phone, and I have e-mail." She spelled out her e-mail address.

Sam jotted it on his notepad. "I'll send the picture as soon as we hang up. Do you recall which baggage claim area your luggage was delivered to?"

Ida rattled off the location.

Sam made another note. "Lastly, did you talk to or see Elliot while staying at Yolanda's house?"

"No, but that was par for the course. He rarely came outside. I *did* notice that he stayed up late at night, which was unusual for him, as he had to work early every morning. You should check with Yolanda about this, though. Nothing, and I mean nothing, escapes her attention in that neighborhood."

Apparently, a murder escaped her attention, Sam thought, but kept it to himself. "I'll e-mail the picture to you along with my phone number. If you recognize him, please call me back as soon as possible."

"You can be sure I will."

Sam hung up and thumbed to his e-mail, the one advanced skill he'd learned on his phone. Still, it took him a few tries to get Rhodes's picture attached to the message. When he looked up, he found Kait's eyes crinkled in humor.

"E-mailing Rhodes's pic to Ida," he said.

She grinned at him. "I could tell what you were doing was far more complicated than a phone call."

"Hey." He smiled back at her good-natured teasing. "I told you I wasn't very good with this thing." He shoved his phone into his pocket. "Did you connect with Nina?"

Kait frowned. "Her appointment must have run long. I left a message."

Henry poked his head out the door. "Got the 3-D rendering ready for viewing in the kitchen."

As they strolled inside, Sam considered telling Kait about Ida's mention of the scar, but chose to wait for a positive ID from Ida first. In the kitchen, Dane stood at the counter, his finger on a laptop track pad, his eyes glued to the screen until Sam approached.

"Check this out, Sam." Dane's enthusiasm had increased, which Sam hadn't thought possible. "I just have to move the cursor, and we have a perfect 3-D picture of the room. We can extract any measurement that's of interest and view this at any time. What a great way to see the scene from a witness's viewpoint."

Sam watched the screen scroll past, and he had to admit the tool would be valuable in weeding out witnesses with sketchy stories.

"And, though it's not important in this case," Henry added, "you could use it for shooting reconstructions."

Thinking about the practical applications, Sam kept his eyes on the monitor. A small fleck of blue in the corner of the room caught his attention. He stabbed his finger at the screen. "What's that?"

"I'll zoom in." Henry clicked the mouse, enlarging the shadowed corner of the bedroom.

"There's definitely something there." Sam squinted, trying to identify the object peeking from behind the leg of the desk. "Can't make out what it is, though."

"No problem. We'll just go look," Dane offered.

They all tromped to the bedroom. Dane snapped on gloves before crawling under the desk. He came out holding a round iron-on patch in blue with an embroidered gold crest.

Kait grabbed a glove from her pocket and took the patch. She turned it over. "World of Warcraft."

Sam had no idea what she was talking about. "What's that?"

She looked up. "It's an MMORPG."

"Thanks." Sam resisted rolling his eyes at her. "That helped clear up my confusion."

"It stands for massively multiplayer online role-playing game," Kait said. "Which means it's an online video game where groups of people play at the same time. Gamers call it WoW, pronounced like the word wow but written with capital W's and a lower case o. It's one of the originals and still has the largest number of paid subscribers."

Now they were getting somewhere. "Could the patch belong to Rhodes?"

She shrugged. "He didn't play. At least, not that I know of. Plus, this patch is for the Alliance guild, and I can't see him being part of that group. I'd place him in the Hoard. So this more likely belongs to Congdon."

"We could use the M-Vac to extract DNA from the patch," Henry offered. "If we find only one person's DNA, it could tell us who it belonged to."

"Oh, yeah." Dane grinned. "Bring it on."

Sam looked at Dane. "I take it this is another toy we don't have."

"I've only seen it online."

"Then it's time you see one in action." Henry clamped his hand on Dane's shoulder. "Let's retrieve it, and I can show you how it gets into nooks and crannies and releases stubborn cells in places where swabs don't work as well."

The duo departed, and Sam turned to Kait. "Is this lead worth following up on beyond the DNA?"

"It's possible Fenton and Congdon met on WoW. They might even have been in the same guild."

"You keep mentioning guild and Alliance and Horde. Is this something I need to know about?"

"Guilds are groups of players," Kait explained. "Alliance and Horde, two factions of races. Alliance is the goody-two-shoes side, and the Horde is a darker, more twisted version. That's why I think Fenton wouldn't be in the Alliance. This is very simplified explanation, but WoW is so complicated that I won't bore you with more details unless we find it's relevant to the case." She dug out her phone. "I'll call Sulyard and get the team started on looking for a WoW connection."

"Thanks for sparing me," he said sincerely.

She eyed him. "If you want to keep up with investigations, one of these days you'll need to join the rest of the technologically savvy world."

"Are you offering to help?"

"Sure. After we have Fenton behind bars."

Right. It was always about Fenton Rhodes. Get the man at all costs.

As Kait talked with Sulyard, Sam's phone rang, and he was soon speaking with Ida about the photo.

"That's the guy," she blurted out. "The one with Elliot that day."

"You're sure?"

"Positive. The scar is unmistakably the same as the one on the guy I saw."

"Thanks, Ida. I appreciate your help." Sam hung up and looked at the bolts still protruding from the floor. He couldn't help but wonder if Rhodes had taken Congdon captive as soon as he flew into town. If he had, Congdon could have been held prisoner in this room far longer than they'd first thought.

Sam didn't have a hard time visualizing Congdon in chains. Paralyzed for two full weeks. Terrified. Day after day, wondering when he was going to die. Or worse, maybe wondering how long he was going to live like that. Seeing, feeling, but not being able to move.

Sam's gut churned as he watched Kait talk with Dane. Strong, beautiful Kait. The woman who'd found her way through his resolve to avoid relationships. How on earth was he going to tell her that, if he was right about this theory, Rhodes could be even more of a monster than she or any of them had first thought?

Chapter Seventeen

THE SUN NOW low on the horizon, the vivid reds and oranges warned of coming nightfall. Sam scoured Kait's property for anything out of the ordinary. Landscape lighting hadn't kicked in yet, leaving shadows clinging to the shrubs and plants in her backyard. Moving large plants aside, he searched behind them. When he was certain no hidden danger existed, he followed the stone path along the side of the house, stepped through a solid gate, and joined her in the driveway.

She opened her car door, looking him square in the eye. If she feared Rhodes coming after her, she wasn't showing it. "We good?"

"We're clear," he replied.

She exhaled a breath, the first hint that she might be concerned, as she grabbed her purse and briefcase. He opened the back door and stood blocking any attack from the road.

"I want out," Lily complained from the backseat.

Sam kept his focus ahead and moved back so Kait could exit the vehicle and access Lily. Should Rhodes be foolish enough to try something, Sam remained in his human shield mode. Kait shouldered her case and leaned inside the car.

"My friend Sam is going to come inside for little while tonight," she said to Lily, sounding like this was a happy event.

"To play?" Lily looked up, anticipation widening her eyes.

Her hopeful attitude was just what Sam needed after the last few days. This was what it would have been like coming home to Danny. A son to brighten a dismal day. Sam was smart enough to know being a parent wasn't all rainbows and sunshine. There would have been the usual stresses of parenting, but to have had the chance . . .

Kait backed out of the car holding Lily's hand, and he stepped back, allowing them to exit. He waited until the car door slammed then said, "Straight inside, Kait."

"He's grumpy," Lily said seriously. "Don't like grumpy."

"He's just in a hurry to get inside." Kait headed up the walkway.

"Can we play?" Lily asked.

"We'll see."

Sam followed them up the walk lined in tall purple flowers, the sweet scent filling the air. Lily chatted nonstop about her day and waved an art project at Sam. He couldn't identify the green blob glued to a large sheet, but she claimed it was a turtle from the book *La Tortuga.*

"It's nice," he said.

"Kait said it was bootiful."

"That it is." He wanted to stand here, smiling at her pudgy little face, maybe tug on her curly pigtails, but he'd already lost too many people in his life. He wouldn't take his focus off his job and risk their lives.

The minute Kait had the door open, he shooed Lily inside and locked the door while Kait disarmed her security system.

Lily took a step, but Kait clutched her hand. "Sam wants to look at our house, but he wants to do it alone."

He made a quick, but thorough tour around Kait's home—checking closets and under beds, and confirming windows were locked before returning to the entryway. "We're clear."

Kait sighed, and let go of Lily's hand. Lily immediately slipped it into his and looked up at him again. "Are your grumps gone?"

"Yes." He gave in to her sweet smile and grinned at her.

"Want to play?"

As an only child, Sam didn't have nieces or nephews, so he had little experience with children and didn't know how to answer. But it was hard to say no to eyes that looked just like Kait's, and even harder to say no when, after wavering for a few moments, Lily's lower lip popped out and trembled.

"Maybe another day, Lily," Kait suggested. "Sam and I have some work to do."

"Please." She looked at him; brown eyes the size of saucers pleading.

Crack, went Sam's heart as he let the innocence he hadn't experienced in his life for so many years settle around him. "Maybe we can play for just a minute."

"Yay!" She jumped up and down, jerking his hand.

"Thank you," Kait mouthed and then flashed a warm smile.

Memories of her gazing up at him on the deck the other night assaulted him, and his pulse leapfrogged. He was drawn to her in a way he couldn't put words to, and she got to him. Big time, burrowing under his common sense and making him want things he couldn't have.

"C'mon." Lily tugged on his hand, bringing him back. "Play in my room."

Kait's eyes crinkled in apology. "I'll get dinner going. We can work on the case after we eat."

Dinner, huh? He hadn't expected a dinner invite. It *would* give him a chance to be sure Kait and Lily were safe. And . . . a home-cooked meal, which he hadn't had for a long time? Bonus.

He let Lily drag him down the hallway and into a room painted a cheery yellow. The walls held characters he guessed were from a TV show or book, their clothes painted in bright orange, purple, and green. Lily dropped his hand and went to a low shelf filled with toys. She pulled out the board game Candyland and plopped down on the floor.

Sam knelt on a plush area rug and helped her set up the board. "I'm not sure I remember how to play this game."

"I'll show you." She pulled her legs in and scooted closer to the board. "Me first." She took a white card from the pile and turned it over, revealing two red squares. She picked up her plastic man and hovered the piece over the second red square without settling it in place. Her face scrunched up, and she looked like she might cry.

Afraid he'd done something to cause this reaction, Sam asked, "What's wrong?"

"Lord Licorice and the bats." Her lip trembled.

Sam looked at the man dressed in black, located next to the red square. "It's okay, sweetheart. It's just a picture."

"He's real," she whispered. "I saw him in my room."

"In your room?" Sam asked so forcefully Lily jerked back. "In your room?" he repeated softly.

"Nantie Kait says he's pretend. I know he's real. I saw him in my room at night." Her tiny voice filled with resolve, and Sam believed her. At least, he believed she thought she was seeing a man.

"Want you to stay tonight," she said. "To keep him away."

Sam's chest constricted from the fear in her voice "I'll talk to Kait about it."

"She'll say no." That adorable lip popped out again.

"We'll see." He got up and ruffled her hair, then went in search of Kait. He found her in the kitchen chopping large ripe tomatoes.

"That was quick." She turned. "Don't expect a lot for dinner, we're just having . . . what's wrong?"

"Why didn't you tell me Lily thinks a man comes here at night?" he demanded.

Kait's shoulders rose into that hard line he'd seen every time she felt threatened. "I'm not sure why you think I'd tell you about our private lives."

"What if it's Rhodes?"

"First of all," she set down the spoon and crossed her arms, "this started long before we heard a peep from Fenton. Right after an incident at Lily's preschool when a non-custodial father tried to abduct his daughter. That's what I think is fueling these dreams. Second, there's no proof anyone has been in the house. When I check, the security system is always on. The doors are locked, and I've changed the password multiple times. Besides, if Fenton snuck in here, I'm sure he would do something other than look at Lily and sneak back out."

"I suppose you're right," Sam admitted, although it was reluctantly. "Just promise me you'll set your alarm and double-check the doors when you go to bed tonight."

She saluted and the doorbell rang. Sam's hand shot to his gun.

"Relax," she said. "It's just Nina."

"You stay here. I'll make sure."

Kait turned back to the stove, but he caught the roll of her eyes before she did. She thought he was overreacting. Maybe she was right. Maybe he was, but after losing Stacie and his family, he wouldn't take any chances.

ANOTHER CONQUEST. Another step closer. The warmth spread through Fenton's body, and he felt flushed all over. Across the booth sat J.J., the fool slurring his words as the roofie oozed its way through his blood stream.

Fenton tossed a few bills onto the table and used a napkin to wipe fingerprints from his and J.J.'s glasses. Not that anyone would come here to check on J.J., but Fenton always believed it was better to be safe than sorry.

And now, it was time to take J.J. home.

Their waitress knew J.J. had only consumed one beer, casting suspicion on his altered state, so Fenton waited for her to schlep into the kitchen before helping J.J. to his feet. He staggered. Fenton slipped an arm under J.J.'s and walked calmly to the door.

"Is he okay?" asked the hostess with hair as high as Mount Hood.

Fenton rolled his eyes. "My brother just can't hold his liquor."

They shared a knowing look, and she pushed open the door. He hurried J.J. through the cool of the night and found his sleek red Dodge Challenger. Within minutes, Fenton had J.J. shoved in the passenger seat and roared onto the road.

"You played your part perfectly, J.J.," Fenton said, noting the quick acceleration of J.J.'s car. "Much easier than Brian. He looks to be our size, but he's deceptively heavy."

Fenton hummed for the remainder of the drive, enjoying the feel of the powerful engine under his hands and running through his night one more time to be sure he hadn't screwed up anywhere. He'd arrived at the restaurant fifteen minutes early, stashing Brian's van down the street where it would take weeks for the police to locate it. Then he'd hoofed it to the dive he couldn't believe dared to call themselves a restaurant. He'd chosen the dumpy little place due to their lack of security cameras. He'd ordered drinks, laced J.J.'s with Rophenol, and made sure he drank it down by toasting to his computer skills until the last drop had been consumed.

All that was left to do was settle J.J. in the cuffs, hook up his IV and vent, then Fenton could bring Kait her little gift. Maybe he'd show it to J.J. first. He might not fully understand, what with his drugged state and all, but it was only fair for J.J. to see the important role he would play in this long-overdue revenge.

KAIT HEARD SAM talking with Nina as they headed for the kitchen. Nina's voice was tight, her expression dour.

Kait started to pull down wine glasses, but stopped when she saw Nina carried the fixings for a Hamilton Cobbler, her new favorite cocktail. "I take it things didn't go so well."

"On the contrary. As I was telling Sam, Quinn will head back to California today to see what he can find out about Rhodes." Nina might claim her meeting went well, but the cocktail mix told a different story.

Kait turned to Sam. "Dinner's not for another thirty minutes. Would you mind if Nina and I talked alone? You could wait out on the deck."

"Or I could go back and play with Lily."

"Don't think you have to."

"Are you kidding? And miss seeing her smile when she gets out of the swamp? No way." He grinned and departed.

"Oh, girl," Nina said watching Sam leave. "A man who looks like that *and* volunteers to play with Lily? You cannot let this one get away."

Kait was thinking the same thing, but she wouldn't speak it aloud, or maybe she'd start to believe she could actually have a normal life at some point in the future. She grabbed three mint julep glasses, a gift from Nina, and set them on the counter. "How did it really go with Quinn?"

"Nice change of subject." Nina started mixing the drinks.

"And nice try at avoiding it."

Nina opened the bottle of sherry, her eyes fixed on the cap. "Remember that hostage rescue six months ago? The one where a SEAL was injured in an explosion? It was Quinn."

"Oh, no." Kait came around the island to sit with Nina. "Is he okay?"

"He says he is. His hand was pretty badly burned. The scars. Bless his heart, they looked so painful." Nina's eyes filled with tears. "He was wearing a long-sleeved shirt, so I don't know how high the scars go."

Kait took the sherry from Nina, set it on the counter, and held Nina's hands. "I'm so sorry, sweetie."

"Look at me crying." Nina sniffed. "I have no reason to be this upset. It's not like we're together or anything."

Kait hadn't had a man in her life for years. She couldn't really imagine the pain Nina experienced wanting Quinn in her life, but fearing his loss so badly that she couldn't be with him.

Sam and Lily's laughter rang down the hallway, drawing Kait's attention. She put aside Sam's role as a law enforcement officer and thought of the man she was getting to know and respect.

What if he was injured in their hunt for Fenton?

The sweet, gentle, caring man who was strong when needed, and yet, seemed to know when to back off. To give her the space she required.

It wasn't difficult to imagine coming home to him and Lily. A life filled with laughter and fun, contentment that was missing from her life.

But him getting hurt? Taking a bullet like Abby? Lying there, struggling for life then dying. That was a kick in the gut.

So, great. She'd started to care for him. Not just a little bit like she'd thought, but more than she wanted. More than was good for her.

Watch your step, girl, she warned herself. If she didn't, she'd find herself in Nina's shoes. In love with a guy when there was no hope of a future together.

Chapter Eighteen

KAIT RETURNED TO the family room after showing Nina to the door. She sat next to Sam on the sofa, being sure to leave a goodly amount of space between them. She'd put Lily to bed hours ago, and they'd spent the time since then discussing the case. Nina mentioned her team had worked all day tracking Congdon's online movements, but hadn't connected him to Kozlov or Fenton. A bust, but they'd also had a victory. They'd reviewed security tapes and confirmed Congdon had picked Fenton up at the airport. Since then, Kait's mind was consumed with questions of what Fenton had been doing since he'd arrived in town.

Sam's phone chimed, and he jerked it from his belt. "It's a text from Yates. Congdon's doctor and dentist confirmed he didn't have any procedures involving an IV."

"So Marcie's theory about the roc is holding weight," Kait said, her thoughts going back to Fenton's time with Congdon.

Sam shifted to face her. "You look deep in thought."

"I've been thinking about those two weeks after Fenton arrived, and hoping he didn't keep Congdon shackled all that time." She shook her head. "I mean, how did this all go down? Did he arrive at Congdon's house under the guise of friendship, they settle down to share a drink, only Fenton has put a little surprise in Congdon's glass?"

"The Rophenol."

"Right, the roofie. When Congdon is out of it, Fenton installs the floor bolts then shackles Congdon with handcuffs. Before he wakes up, Fenton inserts the IV, gives him the roc, and puts in the breathing tube. Then leaves him like that for weeks?"

"We shouldn't get ahead of ourselves. It may not even be physically possible to keep someone paralyzed for so long."

"You could call Marcie."

"I don't want to bother her at home. I'll call her tomorrow." Sam propped his ankle on his knee and leaned back. "What I still don't get is what Rhodes hopes to gain from all of this."

"Other than making me feel helpless as I try to catch him before he kills again." She sighed.

"Yeah."

"I've been thinking about that, too. If Congdon was also a bot herder, then it could be about taking over his business while challenging me to catch him. At the same time, letting me know he thinks I can't succeed."

"We don't have anything that suggests Congdon was in the same business."

She grinned at him. "You're such a technophobe you can't even say the word bot, can you?"

"Never." He gave an exaggerated shudder.

She mocked twisting the ends of a long mustache. "Spend enough time with me, and I'll change that."

She expected him to laugh. Instead, he frowned. "I think it's time you consider the fact that Congdon was just a tool in Rhodes's plan to taunt you. That his ultimate goal is to pay you back." He slid closer, quickly filling that space she'd purposefully left open and took her hand. "I won't let him anywhere near you, you know."

"I know." She tried to make it sound as if she believed it. But even with Sam holding her hand, after the way Fenton had planned this case to perfection, she didn't know if anyone could stop him.

"I should never have told you about Stacie. Now you don't trust me to protect you." He started to pull away.

"What? No." She reversed their hands and gave his a quick squeeze. "This has nothing to do with Stacie. I trust in your protection. It's Fenton I don't trust."

"And well you shouldn't. Especially when we don't know what his endgame is."

"But it sounds like you really think it's to kill me."

"He wouldn't need such an elaborate scheme if his goal was simply to kill you, but I do think he'll try."

"It's seeming more and more like he wants to watch me suffer first."

Sam pulled his hand free to rub his forehead. "Okay, so say that's true and he does want to see you suffer. Then he has to be watching you to see the effect he's having on you."

"Maybe he was at the crime scene."

"That would be risky."

"For a sane person, but not for someone like Fenton. The video at the phone booth says he's unhinged. We need to look at the crowd photos." Kait had reviewed the pics Dane had taken of the crowd—as was always done at crime scenes. Killers often returned to see the damage they inflicted, but she hadn't been looking for Fenton, and it was worth another look.

"If he really is watching, then the real shock and awe came at your office when you learned about the virus, and he wasn't there to see your reaction."

"Or was he?" She shot to her feet. "The computer. The one we took in. He could have rigged up a camera or a recorder in the case, hoping to see or hear our reactions when the phones started ringing." Wishing she could go check the machine right now, she started pacing.

Sam got up and stepped in her path, forcing her to stop. "Get that gleam out of your eye, Kait. It's almost midnight, and I don't babysit, so the only place you're going is to walk me to the door."

Surprised he could read her mind, her mouth dropped open. He laughed, deep and joyous, so different from the serious guy she'd seen so far. As she went to the front door, she found herself wishing she could see this side of him more often.

She stepped outside and stared at the star-filled sky, letting the cool breeze wash over her face. "I love summer and how clear the skies are."

Sam snorted. "Tell me about it. I moved here in December. Talk about rain. I didn't think I'd ever see stars again. I still miss sitting under the Texas sky."

The longing in his tone drew her eyes toward him. "What part of Texas are you from?"

"Born and raised in Brenham. Went to college in Austin."

"You're a long way from home. I thought Texans never left the state."

That shutter, the one that said whatever he was thinking was off limits, dropped over his eyes, the good mood instantly gone. But she wouldn't let it go. "Why did you move here, Sam?"

He pondered her question for a moment. "I needed a change. I saw the Keep Portland Weird website, and Austin has a similar slogan, so I thought it would be a good fit."

"Are we weird enough for you?" she asked, though she really wanted to ask if he came here to get away from the memories of losing Stacie and his wife.

"I wasn't sure. Until I met you." He cocked an eyebrow and tugged on her ponytail. "But you are the epitome of weird. So, yeah. Portland fits all my needs."

She playfully socked his shoulder. He grabbed her wrist, pulling her against him. She rested her hands on his chest, the feel of him solid under her fingers. His gaze met hers and held. Pulling. Seeking. Heating up. His eyes darkened, and he lowered his head. Inch by inch. Closer. Hardly able to think, she waited for him to kiss her. She wanted him to. How she wanted him to.

"Sleep tight, Kait," he whispered, his breath soft against her neck. After running his hands down her arms and looking into her eyes for a long, heat-charged moment, he jogged to his car.

She leaned against the doorjamb and watched him back onto the street. She swallowed hard, her body still tingling from his touch. Fenton wasn't the only one tormenting her tonight. Sam Murdock knew how to drive a woman crazy, too. After the way he'd messed with her emotions, she'd be tossing and turning all night, wondering how it would feel to let go of her past. To forget her promise to Abby. To kiss him. To really kiss him.

WHAT WAS THAT detective doing here again? Touching Abby that way?

Fisting his hand, Fenton took a step closer to the house, but the loser detective backed his car onto the road, so Fenton planted his feet on the dewy grass to wait. The detective stopped and rolled down his window.

"Go inside, Kait and lock the door," he called over the idling engine sending a mist of exhaust into the foggy night.

Kait? Fenton rubbed his eyes and looked again.

Of course, it was Kait standing there. Not Abby.

He shook his head hard to clear out the cobwebs.

Foolish mistake. Unbelievable mistake. How could he make such a blunder?

Kait and Abby were nothing alike. Kait was evil. Harsh. A career woman. Abby softness and light. Perfect. Dead.

He melded back into the shadows and watched Kait wave at the man, then close the door with a simpering little smile on her face. A lovesick face. Sickly sweet.

So Kait liked the detective.

Not fair. Totally not fair with Fenton's heart still a blistering mass of loss.

He wanted to march up to her and end things now. Here. This moment. Seek his release. He looked down. Saw the cooler.

No. Stick with the plan. So much more painful for Kait if he toyed with her first.

Instead of getting angry, he smiled. A woman in love was more vulnerable. Absentminded. Fenton could use that to his advantage, and he could also do away with Mr. Cop first, letting Kait experience the ultimate in pain and heartache.

The lights went out in her house, and Fenton settled in for the tortuous wait for her to fall asleep. Time passed. The temp fell—chilly at first, then downright cold. The pain in his leg grew. Unbearable. He could take it no more.

He woke up his phone and remotely silenced Kait's alarm system by logging onto her security company's server. She thought the little box on the wall was keeping her safe. But why? She should realize nothing could stop him. He was the supreme hacker. And nothing, especially not an alarm provided by a security company he could hack in his sleep, would keep him from his daughter and making Kait pay.

He grabbed the cooler and moved his present to the tissue resting in the box he'd wrapped in Dora paper. With the package under his arm, he hobbled through the damp, chilly air to the front door, easing, stretching his leg with each step. He inserted his key into the lock and entered.

He pressed the door closed, silently, and paused to enjoy the feel of invading Kait's sanctuary. This would be the last time he'd enter her house. After tonight, she'd realize that Lily hadn't dreamt his visits. Kait would try so hard to learn where he got a key. She'd wouldn't figure it out. He'd been careful at the park as his mother-in-law played with Lily. So careful. Made an impression of Rosalind's key when she'd left her purse in the car to play with Lily.

He tiptoed to Kait's room and watched her back lift and fall in the even breaths of sleep. His fingers itched to circle her neck. To put an end to this, but he retreated. Always retreated. Seeing her lying there, vulnerable, and then walking away was nearly the hardest part of these visits. Leaving Lily trumped it.

He crept into Lily's room and set the package on her nightstand, then took a small wireless camera from his pocket. He inserted the camera into the blinds. Using his phone to view the feed, he aimed the lens at the door. Perfect. Kait would discover the box in the morning. He'd capture Kait's reaction. Savor every moment as if it were a meal in the finest of restaurants.

Just like he intended to do tonight before he departed. He went to the kitchen, selected the most expensive wine and grabbed a glass. He took them, along with the Waterford crystal bowl Kait had inherited from her grandmother, and returned to Lily's room. He pulled a plump chair up to the bedside and lit a cigarette.

He shouldn't smoke around Lily, but a few cigarettes while he enjoyed his wine wouldn't harm her. Not like the second-hand smoke he'd been exposed to from birth until he signed on for an adventure in the Navy.

But his greatest adventure was yet to come.

Being a father.

Not like *his* father. Anything but. His child would never know fists raised in anger. The life he created, the baby girl softly breathing and snuggling Mr. Bear not more than three feet from him, would be cherished. Loved.

And most of all, *his,* once again.

Chapter Nineteen

KAIT LOVED THE early morning hour before Lily got up and life became hectic—birds chirping outside her bedroom window, sun drifting through the cracks of her blinds as it ascended in the sky. A few final minutes of peace before her day as a single mother commenced.

A hint of fresh coffee she'd set to brew via a timer last night snaked under her door. Perfect. She'd grab a cup of coffee and start her day on the deck as usual. She followed the tantalizing aroma down the hallway. A quick stop at the security panel to disarm it, then she padded over the wooden floor she'd patiently restored to her kitchen. As her favorite Columbian blend ground fresh every night splashed into her cup, she inhaled the nutty scent. A quick sip drew a groan of pleasure from her throat.

She put the mug and her phone on a tray with a power bar and headed outside. The air was crisp and fresh, and it smelled like new beginnings. Like hope. She settled in her favorite chair, the sun rising into the sky, the rays warming her body. Ahh, golden rays beating down. The scent of jasmine rising up. The hum of honeybees. She stretched her arms high and took in the blooming perennials, delicate Japanese maples, and vegetables ripe for picking. All she saw was the work that needed doing. She was behind in deadheading flowers and thinning overgrown drifts of perennials. Hours of work she'd lovingly tend to, but not today. Not until Fenton was behind bars.

"Get over it," she whispered to herself and sipped her coffee. No price was too high to pay to find him.

She ate the power bar, then grabbed her phone and fired off an e-mail to Sulyard, requesting the analysts review crime scene photos in search of Fenton in the crowd. She didn't bother asking them to look at Congdon's computer for a camera, because now that she'd had time to think about it, she knew they would have already located it and reported the discovery. Thankfully, she hadn't asked last night. Sulyard would've rolled his eyes at that request. Today, she'd keep her emotions in check. She'd stop jumping at any little hint of a lead and work the investigation dispassionately. Just the way she'd been taught. The way Becca would handle it. Kait couldn't risk being yanked off the case.

Her phone vibrated in her hand. Caller ID displayed an unlisted number. Too early in the morning for a telemarketer, but it could be about the case. About Fenton.

"Kaitlyn Knight," she answered.

"Hello, Kait. Enjoying your coffee on the deck?" The familiar voice slid through the phone like a viper slithering up to its prey.

Kait jumped to her feet, her free hand going for her gun. "What do you want, Fenton?" she asked nearly choking on his name.

He chuckled, that same sick, maniacal sound lingering in her mind from the day he'd murdered Abby. "Not going to ask me how I know what you're doing?"

She desperately wanted to know, but she wouldn't give him the satisfaction of asking. Besides, there were only two options. Either he was watching her, or he'd bugged her house. She was pretty sure he hadn't planted a bug, so that meant he had to be watching.

A wave of revulsion swept over her body. Coffee churned in her stomach. She jerked out her gun, eased off the deck, and crept into her garden. She quickly searched the space then made her way along the side of the house.

"Aren't you going to ask me?" he went on, sounding mad at her failure to play his game.

"No." She slid along the building, her jacket catching on the rough Hardiplank siding. She watched for any movement. Any sign of life. At the gate, she peeked through the wooden slats and scanned the road.

He laughed again. "That's the Kait I remember. Stubborn to a fault."

His familiar tone sent a torrent of revulsion firing through her body. She wanted to throw something or burst through the gate and fire round after round at anything that moved. But she had to keep her cool.

Clenching her teeth, she slowly opened the gate and let her eyes track up and down the street. No one. Not even a neighbor walking a dog.

"Okay, then. I guess I better come right out and tell you why I phoned." He sounded mad. *Good. Let him suffer for once.* "I wanted to ask if you found my package yet."

"Your package," she replied, keeping the surprise from her voice as she retraced her route to the deck.

"I guess that means no." Anger now clearly bit into his words. "That's okay. It's safe. I left it in Lily's room, and I'm sure *no one* could get past your security and break into her room."

"You're lying," she said, letting all of her disgust for him darken her tone.

"Am I?" he taunted. "The box is right next to the Dora lamp you leave on for my precious baby every night."

How could he know about the lamp? Was he in Lily's room?

Heart hammering, Kait charged back into the house, dodging her dining table and running through the kitchen into the hallway.

"I hear you breathing, Kait. You must almost be to her room now." His chuckle was low and oddly excited.

Fear barreled through her, threatening to take over. *No. Lily needs you to stay calm.*

She wedged the phone in the crook of her neck. Started down the hallway to Lily's room. Inch by inch. Step by step. Cautious. Gun outstretched. She reached the open doorway. Glanced into the room. Lily lay in her bed, hands under her tummy, her knees up, sound asleep. Alone.

Relief swept through Kait, but disappeared in a flash.

He could be hiding.

She stepped into the room. Whipped open the closet door. Flipped up the pink dust ruffle and glanced under the bed.

Empty. He wasn't here.

Her breath whooshed out as she looked around the space. The chair had been moved from the corner next to Lily's nightstand. A small box wrapped in bright red Dora paper sat next to an empty wine glass, and Kait's precious bowl from her grandmother held several cigarette butts.

He'd been here. In the night. Not just a quick in and out to drop off a package. No, that would have been bad enough, but he'd sat here in the rocker. Drinking. Smoking. Watching Lily sleep. Violating their privacy.

"Do you see it yet?" he asked, his voice alive with excitement.

Did she see it? her mind screamed. Of course, she saw the box. It sent her heart thumping against her chest. But what did it hold?

Alarm snaked up and over her back, but she wouldn't speak and let him hear the terror in her voice.

"Fine. Don't say anything." He laughed, but it held no mirth. "Enjoy the package. Until we meet again."

The line went dead. Just as well. She had to figure out what to do. She stowed her phone in her pocket. Her hand trembled like a frightened child. But she couldn't act like a child when one depended on her to keep her safe.

"You're an agent," she said as she sought answers. "Think like one."

She went on autopilot, remembering her law enforcement training.

Step one, protect life at all costs. That meant thinking of worst-case scenarios. The unknown box could be a bomb.

Fenton would never kill Lily, would he? Maybe. He sounded mentally unstable on the phone. There was no telling what he might do. That meant they had to evacuate. Now.

She scooped Lily into her arms, making sure to grab Mr. Bear and Blankie before bolting down the hallway.

"Nantie Kait." Lily woke and rubbed her eyes.

"In a minute, pumpkin." Kait flung open the front door and quickly scanned the area. This could be a trap designed to force them out of the house. Should she go?

Prioritize, Kait.

The threat from a bomb outweighed a bullet. She charged down the steps. Faster. Faster. *Hurry.* She ran across the road, hunching her shoulders to cover Lily's precious little body. A large utility box sat at the curb, a green space behind it. She took cover behind the drab green box, sinking to the ground wet with morning dew.

"I need you to pretend we're playing hide and seek," she said to Lily, settling her next to the box. "Dora is coming to look for you and Mr. Bear. She doesn't know you're hiding here, okay?"

Lily looked up, her face a mass of confusion, but she nodded.

Kait pointed at a tall tree. "See that tree? I'm going over there to make a phone call. You stay here."

"'K," Lily said, but plopped her thumb in her mouth as she always did when uneasy.

Kait hated leaving her niece in distress, but letting Lily hear her report a suspicious package and possible bomb would scare her far worse. Ducking behind the tree, Kait glanced at her watch. 7:00. Too early to call the office. Sam? Maybe, but he'd just call dispatch. 911 was her best bet.

She punched the numbers and said, "This is Special Agent Kaitlyn Knight with the FBI. A suspicious package was left in my home sometime during the night. I need MEDU to check it out." She hoped that a specific request for the Metro Explosives Disposal Unit would bring them out faster and this could all be over sooner.

"Can you tell me more about this suspicious package?" the operator asked.

"I'm in the middle of a murder investigation where I've been targeted by the killer. He called me to tell me about a package he'd left in my niece's room. I don't know if it's a bomb, but I've evacuated the house, and I'm waiting across the street." She rattled off her address and waited for the operator to repeat it. "That's all I'm at liberty to share. I need to tend to my niece, so I won't be holding while you make the arrangements."

Kait disconnected and looked over her familiar neighborhood with the eyes of a professional law enforcement officer. On one side of her home, the Roseburgs' boxy car sat in their driveway. On the other side, Sandra and Mel's minivan was parked on the street as usual so their teenage sons could play basketball in the drive.

When the bomb unit arrived, they'd at a minimum evacuate anyone within one hundred feet of her home. Should Kait go tell them to evacuate now?

She couldn't talk to them without moving Lily from the protected spot, which could put her in jeopardy. Besides, Kait couldn't be certain the box contained a bomb. She'd wait for the impartial opinion of a patrol officer who was bound to respond in a few minutes. She went to sit with Lily, easing down beside her and smiling.

"Did Dora find you?" she asked, forcing false cheer into her voice.

Lily pulled out her thumb with a sucking noise. "Nuh-uh."

"Well, I did." Kait scooped Lily into her arms and hugged her close. "I'm sorry to wake you up this way, pumpkin."

Lily leaned back and looked up, the three-year-old's eyes picking up on more than she needed to see at her young age. Kait pulled her close again. She inhaled the calming scent of her strawberry shampoo and felt like weeping for everything this child had been through. Kait couldn't let her be traumatized even more. She surely shouldn't see the bomb squad's voluminous green suits and heavy helmets approaching her place of sanctuary, or hear their raised voices as they barked warnings to the neighbors to move back.

She pulled away from Lily. "Would you like to go to Nana's house instead of daycare today?"

Her eyes lit up. "Really? Can I?"

"Let's call her and see." Preparing for a lecture, Kait retrieved her phone and dialed her mother.

"I need a favor, Mom," Kait said hoping her mother was in an agreeable mood for once.

"What's wrong, Kaitlyn?" The worry that lived in her voice since Abby died was thick in her tone.

"I just wanted to see if Lily could spend the day at your house."

Silence, solid and heavy, filled the phone.

"Before you lecture me, Mom, I'm not calling because I can't get a babysitter or because the day care is closed."

"But this *is* about your job, isn't it?"

Kait sighed at her mother's suspicions that were right on target as usual. "I can't get into this right now. I need you to come get Lily right away. Can you do that?" The panic and alarm that had threatened to take over her voice since Fenton's call laced through it now.

"You're scaring me, Kaitlyn."

"Everything will be okay," Kait soothed. "Just come. Now. As quickly as you can." Kait hated that her voice rose in desperation, but she couldn't explain the situation in front of Lily.

"I'm on my way." Her mother didn't say she was disappointed in Kait, but it came through loud and clear. Her ongoing judgment wasn't fair. Kait had to work to support Lily. And sometimes that meant working odd hours. She wouldn't apologize for that.

She tucked her phone into her pocket and smiled at Lily. "Nana is on her way. What do you think you'll do all day?"

"Make cookies. We always make cookies. And pick flowers." She giggled as if the thought brought pure joy. "Swing with Papa, too." She shoved her thumb back into her mouth, her tiny fingers skimming the silky edge of her blanket as she laid her head on Kait's shoulder.

They sat together, the calm before the storm, until the first siren swirled through the neighborhood, bringing Lily's head up. Kait stroked her hair and urged her head back down to still the questions Kait knew her curious niece would ask. When the siren grew loud enough for the patrol car to have reached their street, she smiled at Lily again. "That's one of my friends from work. I asked them to come help me. Can you stay here for a few minutes like a big girl?"

Lily loved being called a big girl, and she nodded enthusiastically. Kait settled her on the grass again and went to meet the officer. An unmarked car flew down the street and, before Kait could recover from the surprise of a detective arriving sooner than a patrol car, Sam was climbing out of the car and jogging toward her.

"What's going on?" His eyes searched the area with practiced ease.

"I didn't expect you."

"Heard it on my radio on the way in." His gaze landed on her, his eyes razor-sharp. "What's going on?"

"Fenton was in my house last night."

"What?" He choked the word out as if he'd tried to strangle it on the way up.

"He called this morning and told me to go to Lily's room. I found a package on the nightstand along with a wine glass and a bowl filled with cigarette butts." Her voice trembled, and she vowed to take better control of it by the time the other officers arrived.

"And you think it's a bomb?"

She shrugged. "Better to be safe, right?"

"Definitely. What about Lily? Is she at daycare already?"

"My mother's on her way to pick her up, but for now, she's waiting behind the box." Kait pointed at the utility box. "I don't want her to see the patrol cars or the bomb squad."

"Good plan."

At least Kait had done one thing right. "Somehow, Fenton knew I was on my deck drinking coffee. I searched the outside for him or for a camera, but spotted nothing."

"Do you follow the same routine every morning?"

"Yes."

"If he's been watching you, then he'd know exactly where you'd be at this time of day."

Of course. Why hadn't she thought of that?

Sam's gaze lingered on her, and he touched her arm. "Will you be okay alone if I go meet the bomb squad?"

Okay? After this? Not likely, but she responded with a clipped nod, so he would leave her alone before she lost all composure and started bawling like a baby.

Chapter Twenty

FENTON HELD his breath while Kait lifted Lily into her arms and crossed over to Rosalind, or as he liked to call her, the wicked witch. He should've planned to pay her back for her interference in his short marriage, too. Why hadn't he? Or would taking Lily be payback enough? She adored his daughter. He'd watched them at the park—had seen her love for Lily. Rosalind might be a difficult woman to most, but to his daughter, she was a doting grandmother.

He shifted to get more comfortable. His leg throbbed. A groan of agony slipped out as he peered through the waist-high grass in the green space. When Kait had gone inside, he'd left his perch overlooking her backyard to sit in this cramped little spot in the woods near a utility box to watch the police arrive. A box that he could almost reach out and touch.

If he'd known she would run like a bat out of hell over here, he'd have chosen a more secure hiding spot. But maybe the universe had a bigger plan in bringing her close enough for him to smell her perfume.

This was good. So good. How could he not be drooling like a baby?

Despite her bravado with the detective, terror held firm in her eyes, and the rush left Fenton lightheaded. But he wanted to get closer. To smell her fear. To taste it. To relish all the pain he'd inflicted.

Patience. You will.

Soon. Just a little longer. A few more kills. Then she'd be his. He'd take his time. Relish that, too.

He dug out his phone and played the video feed from Lily's bedroom. Just the few seconds when Kait had discovered the box. Lurching back. Fear thick on her face. *Delightful.* He rewound and played it again. And again. It'd been so hard not to say anything about her reaction on his call, but she would have stifled her emotions if she'd known he was watching.

Ooh, this is nice. So nice. The terror. Her trembling hands. Her frantic rush to scoop up Lily.

He'd accomplished his purpose. She now knew beyond a shadow of a doubt that he was not only involved, but planning to include her in his revenge. And after his next move, she'd be certain he was coming for her, and no one could protect her.

KAIT WAS A STRONG, vibrant woman, but right now, she'd strayed as far from herself as Sam thought possible. Hands planted on her hips, she argued with her mother. Loud, boisterous, the way Sam knew she'd argue. Even as thoughts of going toe to toe with her sometime in the future brought a smile to his mouth, it disappeared when he caught sight of Lily sitting at the curb, her head hanging as she worried her fingers over her silky blanket.

The urge to intervene for Lily's sake tugged at Sam. But he couldn't get involved. No. Correction. He *could,* but he wouldn't.

"She should never have left her to you," Kait's mother shouted.

Lily's head popped up, and her lower lip slipped out and quivered much like it had with Lord Licorice.

Thump went Sam's heart.

No, dang it. He didn't want this. Didn't want to feel anything.

"So what? You do," he mumbled as he reluctantly pushed off the tree and headed up the hill.

Coming up on Kait, he cleared his throat loud enough to break through the argument. She didn't acknowledge him, but kept her focus on her mother now spewing even harsher comments about Kait's lack of parenting skills.

Taken aback at the vehemence in her mother's tone, Sam decided not to come between them, but to rescue Lily on his own. He stepped to her and squatted down. Forlorn eyes locked on his, and his heart split wider.

"Are you hungry?" he asked, figuring food was a safe topic for a person of any age.

She nodded weakly.

"I have a chocolate chip muffin and orange juice in my car. Should we share it?"

Her eyes brightened a bit, and her head bobbed faster.

He stood and held out his hand. She laid soft little fingers against his palm, sending his heart thumping harder, and the truth to his brain.

He *did* want this. All of this. A wife. Kids. He wanted them badly.

So at least be honest with yourself. But never, ever forget you're not father material.

He headed toward his car, now farther up the hill and out of the blast radius. The squad determined the safe zone based on the size of the box inside, and the uniforms had set another perimeter beyond that. He crested the hill and spotted a news van arriving on scene.

Great. That's all Kait needed to deal with today.

He opened the passenger door of his sedan. Lily scrambled in as if eager to get away from the argument that had escalated to a new level. He ran around the front, trying to get Kait's attention so when she came to her senses and realized she was holding WWIII within hearing distance of Lily, she'd know where to find her.

Despite waving at her, she didn't acknowledge him. He climbed behind the wheel and snatched up the paper bag on the console. He split the muffin in half and gave a piece to Lily. Her miniature hand couldn't hold all of it, so he halved it again.

"I'll set the rest on the napkin for when you're ready," he said when she looked disappointed.

She chomped down on the muffin, and he opened the orange juice, then set it in the holder by her leg.

"Good?" he asked.

She offered a tentative smile, and he relaxed a bit. He could do this. At least until Kait's mom was done belittling her.

He watched them, so alike in appearance. Kait would likely age as gracefully as her mother. Her posture was still perfect, her figure trim, and if she smiled, he'd bet she was pretty. She stepped back, and the anger suddenly disappeared, her eyes holding the same pain and regret that Kait carried. The same regret he lived with.

Kait turned and met his eyes through the windshield. Her anguish put a physical ache in his gut. He pointed at the spot where Lily had sat, and then at his passenger seat hoping she understood Lily was safe.

She glanced at the curb. Her eyes going wide, panic taking over.

Sam popped out of the car. "She's with me."

"Oh, my gosh," Kait called out. "I didn't . . . I forgot . . . oh, my gosh." She clamped a hand on the back of her neck and turned in circles before pulling her shoulders back and coming over to the car. She knelt at the open door, and Sam joined them.

"I'm sorry, sweetie," she said to Lily. "Nana and I shouldn't have been arguing."

"You were mad," Lily said around a mouth filled with muffin.

"I was. But I'm not anymore." She scooped Lily into her arms and held her close, stroking her hair and cooing assurances. "I'll bring you to Nana, and she can take you home."

She looked up at Sam. "Sam take me."

"Me?" Sam asked.

"Uh-huh." A wide smile lifted her crestfallen face. "I like you." She reached her arms for him.

Kait arched a brow and studied him, but didn't comment.

"What can I say? I'm irresistible to the ladies." He grinned.

"Puh-lease," Kait said jokingly, but distress remained lodged in her eyes.

"I'm a girl. Not a lady." Lily threw her arms around his neck.

"I know, Squirt." He ruffled her soft hair and followed Kait over to her mother.

"Mom, this is Detective Sam Murdock."

"Nice to meet you, Mrs. Knight." Sam offered his hand.

She grasped it firmly. "Mrs. Knight is my mother-in-law. Please call me Rosalind."

"Rosalind it is, then," Sam said, though he doubted he'd ever see her again. At least with the way she'd treated Kait, he doubted he'd ever want to see her again.

"Thank you for taking care of Lily while we were occupied." She cast a quick disapproving look at Kait.

"Saying we were occupied doesn't make our actions any less wrong." Kait stepped closer to her mother and glanced at Lily who was distracted by the crowd building behind the barriers. "Neither one of us considered Lily at all today, and we've put her through enough already. I'm done battling with you. I'll relinquish custody."

"You what?" Rosalind asked, clearly dumbfounded

"Take Lily to your house, and I'll come by tonight to discuss the details."

Sam's mouth fell open. How could she agree to give up Lily? Just like that. Permanently.

He thought to protest, but this wasn't a discussion to have in front of Lily. Once she was gone, that was another story all together. He'd be glad to give Kait his opinion.

Rosalind snatched the muffin from Lily's hand. "We don't eat chocolate chips for breakfast."

"Sam does," Lily said.

"Mr. Murdock to you," Rosalind chided.

"It's okay, honey," he said before thinking. "I asked you to call me Sam, and that's what I want you to do."

Rosalind scowled at him, and he thought he saw a hint of a smile flash on Kait's face as she leaned close to give Lily a kiss on the cheek. "See you later, pumpkin. Listen to Nana, okay?"

"'K." Lily gave him a big hug before he transferred her into her grandmother's arms, her scowl still firmly in place.

"Please call before you come over, Kait," she tossed over her shoulder as she departed.

When she was out of earshot, Sam faced Kait. "You're a wonderful mother. Don't let her tell you otherwise."

"You've only spent a few minutes with us. Mom has spent years."

"Do you really think you're a bad parent?"

"Bad, no. Lacking, yes. My job often has to come before Lily. I live a life that can put her in danger. This morning adequately proved that."

"So you're saying law enforcement professionals shouldn't have children."

"No, of course not."

"Don't do this, Kait." He moved closer, but resisted taking her hand like he wanted to do. "Don't make less of yourself than you are. You're an amazing, strong woman who can have a child and a career, too. As long as you don't have knock-down drag-outs like this in front of the kid, she'll be fine."

She glanced around, a mortified expression taking over. "I couldn't have been any less professional."

"Relax. Everyone else is too busy checking out the bomb to notice."

"Everyone but you."

He started to say he noticed everything about her, but that would be akin to flinging open Pandora's Box.

She touched his arm as lightly as a butterfly. "We haven't known each other very long, but your support means a lot to me."

"No problem." He could feel his mouth turn up in a dopey grin, and yet, he couldn't stop it.

She smiled. "If we see my mother again while on the case, I promise to remain in control."

"Not that I'm disparaging your mother, but from what I've seen, it would take patience beyond the average person not to get testy around her. You sure you want her to take care of Lily?"

"She's not usually like this when I'm not around."

"You do something to make her mad?"

"Yeah. I lived instead of Abby."

She sounded so sad and lost that Sam had to shove his hands into his pockets to keep from taking her into his arms. "Seems to me she should be happy that you're alive and embrace you instead of alienating and blaming you."

"You'd think, wouldn't you?" A low, long sigh escaped from her mouth as if trying to exhale her pain. "So . . . where do we stand with the bomb?"

He wanted to pursue her comment, but talking about her mother wishing she'd died instead of Abby was a conversation for another time and place. "Why don't we go find out?"

She stepped past him then turned back. "Thank you, Sam. You're an amazing person, too." She smiled, softly, sweetly, her full lips torturing him.

Thud—his heart tripped over. He wanted to throw his arms around her and kiss her right in front of the entire bomb squad. Crazy. Sheer will forced him to offer a simple thanks and move toward two MEDU officers scrambling around their van.

They stepped into ugly green suits with rigid ballistic panels covered in flame-resistant Nomex and body-protecting Kevlar. The team leader, Sergeant Charlie Zamsky, barked orders like a drill sergeant. He often exploded like the bombs they disarmed, but he was a good cop. He'd served on an explosive ordnance disposal team in the military before graduating from the FBI's Hazardous Devices School like all certified bomb techs are required to do.

By the time they joined Zamsky, he'd set a nearly indestructible laptop on the hood of his vehicle. Using a remote control that resembled popular gaming remotes, he maneuvered a large silver robot toward Kait's front door. Two arms protruded out front with long pincers acting as hands ready to seek out the package.

Zamsky would follow protocol by taking an initial x-ray of the suspicious device. If the x-ray proved the item wasn't explosive, he'd give the all clear, and Sam would take over the scene to ensure the recovery of any evidence left behind by Rhodes.

The robot whirred into the house, the camera displaying the interior of Kait's home on the laptop.

"Which direction?" Zamsky asked.

Kait didn't take her attention from the screen to answer. "Left down the hall, then the first room on the right."

The robot entered Lily's room, and Kait stiffened. Sam took a step closer to her, hoping his nearness might help her deal with whatever Zamsky discovered. The robot slowly approached the neatly wrapped package.

"Some nerve using kid's wrapping paper," Zamsky muttered as he clicked the controls to shoot an x-ray. A few seconds later, the image appeared on screen. Zamsky let out a shaky laugh. "Not a bomb."

Sam expected Kait to relax but she continued to stare at the x-ray. "What is it?"

The object was four or five inches long and looked like a large clenched fist.

"I'm not a doctor," Zamsky said, and then looked up at them, his expression making Sam's body tense. "But I hunt enough to be fairly certain it's a heart."

Kait gasped and stepped back.

"Human?" Sam asked.

"Not sure. We'll need the ME to confirm." Zamsky's voice held no emotion as he pointed at the screen. "Looks like a note's enclosed, too."

Kait turned to Sam, sheer pain slicing through her eyes. His gut started hurting even more.

"Congdon's missing heart," she said soberly.

"Likely," Sam said.

This was a warning to Kait. A serious warning. Fenton Rhodes meant business. He was coming for her, and so far, God help him, Sam had done nothing to stand in the monster's way.

Chapter Twenty-One

KAIT FORCED HERSELF to take the walkway to her front door, leaving Sam outside to phone his Lieutenant and report the recent development. Development, hah! How could she call the package something that innocuous? A development in a case was the discovery of trace evidence. Or a murder weapon recovered. It surely wasn't a heart in a box, sitting smack dab in the middle of Lily's room.

She dragged her feet up the steps and wished Sam was with her, holding her hand. How she wished it. But it couldn't be. She was an agent, and needed to portray strength in front of other law enforcement officers watching.

She stopped at the door and spotted Zamsky with one of his men moving the robot down the hallway. They were joking while her heart was breaking. She didn't take offense. Their adrenaline was still flowing, and they relieved the pent-up tension by joking. She'd done it herself at a crime scene.

She stepped into her house, her fight or flight response intensified, and adrenaline coursed through her veins, making her jittery.

Zamsky caught sight of her and sobered. "We opened the box to confirm my initial thoughts."

"A heart?"

"Yep. Size leads me to believe it's human. Your ME will have to confirm." He gestured at the FED van pulling down her driveway. "We'll be turning the scene over to the detectives now, but you better prepare yourself for the criminalists. They're bound to make a real mess."

Kait nodded her understanding, but she didn't care about the techs invading her home. Nothing could be more invasive than Fenton entering Lily's bedroom last night. Except maybe the fact that he'd done it before. Several times. Hacking her alarm as he must have done last night. Standing outside Lily's door while Kait slept down the hall. While Kait discounted Lily's fears.

"Figured FED and Murdock would have my hide if I touched the note," Zamsky went on. "So I left it alone."

Kait nodded. She shouldn't touch the note either, but she didn't have the same self-control. If Fenton left a message for her, nothing would stop her from reading it now. Nothing.

SAM FOUND KAIT in the corner of Lily's room, sitting on the floor, hugging a large stuffed dog. She'd been crying, but her eyes were dry now. He entered the room, and she looked up, despair muffling her very expressive eyes.

He knelt next to her. "We'll catch him, you know."

"I know. But it's not going to take away the feeling of being violated." She pointed at the box. "I realize I shouldn't have, but I read his note."

Sam looked at the nightstand and noted a pair of discarded latex gloves. "At least you wore gloves and didn't contaminate the evidence."

"Even if protocol didn't dictate it, I didn't want to touch anything from him."

"What'd it say?"

"It's best if you read for yourself."

Sam got up and snapped on gloves. He lifted the heavyweight card-stock in a bright pink color.

You shattered my heart, Kait, when you let your sister die in your place.

How many hearts do you think I'll have to take before mine is whole again?

Are you smart enough to catch me before I take another one, Kait? Are you?

"As if this lunatic is even capable of love," Sam mumbled.

"Actually, I think he is. At least in his way, he loved Abby, and he loves Lily."

"It's just that *his way* is sick and disgusting."

"Regardless," Kait said. "He's definitely going to kill again."

"He could just be trying to scare you."

"I'm not scared. Creeped out. Sick to my stomach, but not scared."

You should be, Sam thought but kept it to himself. A killer who was willing to admit to his crimes and taunt the woman he blamed for his wife's death was more than willing to expand his murderous circle to include Kait.

As he watched her, a violent shudder claimed her body. He crossed the room. "Looks like you're more bothered by this than you're willing to admit."

Her eyes flashed with anger. "Of course I'm bothered. He was here. In my house. In Lily's room. I'm not sure I can even live here anymore."

"That feeling will pass in time."

"Will it? Or will I always blame myself for not taking care of Lily the way I promised Abby?"

"Lily is fine."

"No thanks to me." She shook her head. "My mom is right. I'm not fit to care for her."

"That's not true."

"Isn't it?" She wrapped her arms around her stomach. "Lily told you all about his visits. You believed her, until I talked you out of it. What if this is about kidnapping her? Taking her away from me?"

"He obviously doesn't want to do that, or she'd already be gone."

"After the way he talked about her on the phone, I'm not so sure about that. My gut says when the time is right, he plans to take her from me." Kait shivered again, but her shoulders lifted higher. "I won't let that happen. I'll make sure she's taken to a safe house today."

A good plan. "Can I help with that?"

"My team can handle it."

Sam wanted to take both Lily and Kait away from here. Away from Rhodes. At the very least, he wanted to be part of Lily's detail, but he'd settle for having one of his guys on the team. A man he could trust, count on. "I'll sleep better at night if you let me assign one of our men to the house, too."

"Sure, why not? One more person will help keep Fenton from getting his hands on her."

"I'll arrange it then," he said, his earlier comment returning to his mind. "You said when the time was right, he'd take her. What do you think needs to happen before he does that?"

Her eyes flashed up to his. "Good question."

Sam really needn't have asked. His years as a homicide detective told him the answer. He just had to be willing to admit it.

Kait had to suffer. First, Rhodes wanted her to feel guilty for not being able to keep him away from Lily and not stopping him from killing others. Then, he'd take Lily. Step back and watch Kait writhe in anguish over her loss.

And when he was done toying with her? Then . . . then he would revel in ending her life.

THE ACHE IN Fenton's gut propelled him forward, the pain in his leg forgotten. He should be thrilled with watching the chaos he'd created, and salivating over Kait's anguish. But she'd failed him again. Not falling apart at the discovery of his gift. Looking strong and in control as she'd marched into the house. This wasn't how he'd planned it, and her reaction did nothing to stem the pressure threatening to burst his skull.

He pounded his hands on his temples. *Stop. Please. Please, stop.* It had to end. Soon. He thought it would have by now—that each little step would provide the patience to wait for the grand finale. But he needed more.

Now!

Something to take the edge off. Just to tide him over until he had Lily in his care and Kait in shackles. Since Kait refused to show the agony he'd caused her, he'd keep inflicting more until she had to release it.

He looked around the area, searching, seeking anything to dull the throbbing ache. He spotted a reporter frantically looking for a story to build her career. She was mingling in the crowd. Far from the police officers at the barricade. He could smell her desperation twenty feet away. She'd do. Yes, she'd do. For now.

It'd be risky, but he'd take a gamble. Law enforcement hadn't distributed his picture to the media yet, so the reporter wouldn't recognize him. Plus, he'd quit shaving and wore a cap pulled low over his face. He'd be fine.

He slipped through the onlookers milling around the news crew. He set his sights on the Barbie doll reporter, nearly foaming at the mouth for her next story, but he wouldn't make it easy for her. He'd make her work for it, too. Yes! A bonus. Doubling his pleasure.

He just needed a patsy to help him out. He stepped up to a stubby little man. "Wow. Can you believe this happened in our neighborhood? I mean a bomb threat at the same woman's house who's accused of killing that man and cutting out his heart?" he asked, though in fact, he was the only who accused her of killing Congdon in his delicious blue screen of death virus. This guy didn't need to know that. "Too surreal."

"She killed someone and cut out his heart?" The man's voice spiraled above the crowd.

Perfect.

The reporter latched her opportunistic eyes on them and rushed over. "Cut out a heart?"

Fenton flashed an irritated look at her. "I don't believe I was talking to you."

"I'm sorry. With such close quarters, I couldn't help but overhear you." She planted a hand on a curvy hip and jutted it toward him.

Ah, yes. Sex appeal. Her go-to move. But after Abby, he was immune to other women.

She laid blood-red nails on his arm. "I'm Eva Waters. I'd love to get your story for a breaking news feature."

"I don't know," he said, playing his part convincingly enough to garner an Oscar.

"Please," she whined unbecomingly. "Everyone deserves to know if this woman is dangerous."

"Yeah, man," the stubby guy said. "Tell us."

"I suppose you're right." Fenton took a step closer as if reserving his comments just for her. "What do you want to know?"

"Let's start with your name and telling me how you're associated with Ms. Knight," she purred.

Name? Fenton thought for minute. A brilliant plan unfolded. "I'm Brian Youngblood. I was one of the victims of the computer crash yesterday."

"Crash?"

Fenton *tsk*ed. "Just like the feds to keep this quiet." He recounted the situation, embellishing the genius behind his virus. "I can't believe they didn't arrest her. But it *is* the government, after all. Guess they're trying to quash any negative publicity and protect one of their own."

With each word, Eva's eyes grew rounder. "Perfect. I need to check a few facts, and then we'll film the interview."

"Facts? I don't have time for any fact-checking." Fenton glanced at his watch, the diamond-encrusted one Abby had given him on their first wedding anniversary. "I need to get going."

"Won't take me long." She charged over to her cameraman, and the two of them powwowed for a few minutes before she raced back. "I don't want to hold you up, Brian. I'll do the interview now."

"Great," Fenton said. "Where do you want me?"

"Over by the van."

Fenton followed her, the ache still swirling through his head with hurricane force. He fought the urge to clap his hands over his ears and shoved his hands in his pockets.

Don't worry. It'll go away after the interview.

If it didn't, he'd have to consider escalating his plan for the ultimate payback.

SAM ACHED TO help Kait, but she wouldn't let him. He'd had to pry her out of Lily's room so Dane could comb the space, but despite Sam's attempts to get her involved in processing the scene, she sat listless and lost in her thoughts. She'd provided the phone number from Rhodes's phone call, but otherwise, she'd said very little in the last two hours. She'd simply settled at the kitchen island, her hands cupped around an ice-cold mug of coffee, her eyes staring into space as if she were alone.

Sam started to cross the room to her, but Dane came down the hallway, stepping in his path. He shouldered his case. "We're done with the bedroom. We'll take the box and note to the lab to work them for prints. We lifted a few prints throughout the room, but after the way our suspect left Congdon's house so clean, I have to think we'll discover they belong to family and friends."

"I'd have to agree."

"I've also printed all the entrances, and we'll get the heart to Marcie. She'll grab a DNA sample to confirm it belongs to Congdon." Dane rooted around in his case and came up holding a plastic evidence bag with a mini wireless camera in it. "Found this in the blinds in the child's bedroom. I thought maybe it was a nanny cam, but Agent Knight says she didn't put it there."

Sam stifled a curse. "So Rhodes has been watching her."

Dane nodded. "We'll try to track the camera's serial number to see where he purchased it, but these things are dime a dozen and odds aren't good." He stowed the camera in his case. "Anything else you want done before we take off?"

"You get the alarm panel?"

He nodded. "Only found Kait's prints."

"Rhodes knew exactly where Kait would be this morning, so we should check the rest of the house for cameras."

"Already done. Nothing."

"Okay, then," Sam said, searching for anything else that could help them locate Rhodes. "If he only had eyes in Lily's room, he had to have been hanging out somewhere watching Kait. Mind taking a walk with me to see if we can find evidence of his hiding spot?"

"Glad to help," Dane replied.

Sam's phone rang. He jerked it from the holder and spotted the number for his office on Caller ID. "I've got to take this."

"No problem," Dane said. "I'll grab a few markers from the rig while you take the call, and we'll be good to go."

"Murdock," Sam answered, but kept his eyes on Kait. Hearing about the camera in Lily's room must have freaked her out even more, and could serve as her breaking point.

"The phone Rhodes used to call Knight this morning is a burner." Yates's voice was higher than normal. "And before you ask for any other updates, we struck out on finding Rhodes's source of roc. We've checked all the hospitals and surgery centers, and none of them will admit to losing the drug. They could be covering up, or he could have brought drugs with him."

Great. Another dead end. Sam wouldn't let it get to him. "Nina's

SEAL is still following up on the roc. Hopefully, he'll turn up a military connection. What about MedSoft? Get anything from them?"

"Nothing useful beyond the fact that Congdon worked for them. The fibbie analysts also bombed on finding Congdon's vehicle on any of the security footage. Now ask me what I *do* have for you?"

"I'll bite. What do you have?"

"Got an Officer Diaz on the line. He has Congdon's vehicle under surveillance."

Yes, finally! A solid lead. Sam knew Diaz from his patrol days. They couldn't ask for a better cop to find the car. "Can you patch Diaz through to me?"

"Yeah." Yates's enthusiasm died. He couldn't seriously think Sam would let him take this call, could he?

"So put him on." Sam waited for the officer to come on the line. "What's your 10-20, Diaz?"

Diaz announced an address a few miles away. Sam knew Diaz wouldn't do anything stupid, but after seeing the depravity Rhodes was capable of, Sam had to warn Diaz. "Call for backup."

"I plan to when we hang up." Resentment flowed through Diaz's tone.

Diaz miffed or not, Sam wouldn't be responsible for another officer losing his life, so he added, "Maintain your distance. Do not under any circumstances approach the vehicle."

"I haven't, I—" Silence filled the phone.

"Diaz?" Sam asked, his concern ramping up. "Diaz, are you there?"

No answer. Sam looked at his screen to make sure the call hadn't dropped and found a strong signal. "Diaz," Sam said again.

"Hey, you!" Diaz shouted. "Police! Stop!"

"What's going on, Diaz?"

"Suspect in sight," he snapped out. "Gotta go."

Sam wanted Rhodes captured, but Diaz needed to follow protocol. "Call for backup, Diaz, and wait."

A loud clunk sounded through the phone, then silence. Had Diaz dropped his phone? Maybe to draw his weapon and go after Rhodes? A foolish move after Sam's warning—a move that could get the man killed.

Chapter Twenty-Two

KAIT DIDN'T KNOW what was going on with Sam, but he looked agitated as he rushed across the family room toward her. His unsettled expression sent her radar clanging.

What's happened now? Could she possibly handle more bad news?

"I've gotta go," he said as soon as he reached her. "Stay here with the officers. Be back soon." He turned to leave.

She grabbed his arm. "Where? What's wrong?"

He looked mad at having to explain. "An officer spotted Congdon's vehicle a few miles from here. Then a suspect."

"Fenton?" Her stomach clenched. "Fenton left the car near here?"

Sam nodded. "I was on the phone with Officer Diaz, but lost him. He's not responding. I requested backup for him, but if it's Rhodes, I have to go." Sam took off toward the door.

She wasn't letting him go without her. She caught up to him. "I'm going with you."

He shook his head hard. "You're safer here."

"I'm going." She kept up with his pace.

He sighed out a breath of resignation, but didn't slow. "I can't waste time arguing. You can ride along, but you'll wait in the car."

At the front door, he stopped to give Dane instructions on searching the surrounding area.

Kait listened half-heartedly as she caught sight of the crowd eyeing her with unveiled interest. She'd seen her share of crime scene onlookers in her job, but she'd never been the focus of a group that looked like an angry mob. Were they blaming her for disrupting their lives this morning? Likely. Normally, she wouldn't care, but she'd have to push through them to get to Sam's car.

As if reading her mind, he pulled out his shield and stepped in front of her. "I'll create a path. Stay close behind me."

He barked out instructions for the onlookers to step aside, and she trailed him up the hill. A few neighbors she recognized called out, begging for an explanation to the chaos. She opted to keep her head down and plow ahead without any explanation.

In the car, Sam fired up his lights and siren.

"If you give me the address," she said. "I can help you get there faster."

Sam replied with the location of Congdon's car.

"Say that again," Kait whispered as the blood drained from her head.

Sam repeated the address.

No. Oh. No. She grabbed his arm, but words failed her.

He shot her a look. "What? What is it?"

"The address. It's on my parents' street. Fenton's there. At my parents' house." She clutched his arm like a lifeline. "Oh, Sam. No. This is it. What we suspected. He's gone after Lily."

"STUPID, STUPID, STUPID." Cursing his mistake, Fenton dragged the cop toward the patrol car parked across the street from his in-laws' house.

Why had he come here? So what if the interview hadn't given him the relief he sought? He should never have gone off half-cocked, running to the Knights' house like this. But the urge to up the stakes after the reporter failed to provide relief sent him to Rosalind. He had to make this more personal by letting Kait know her precious law enforcement couldn't stop him from getting to her and those she loved.

He'd been in such a hurry to act, he'd forgotten about leaving Elliot's car here last night for them to find, along with his delectable little surprise inside.

Now he was screwed. So screwed. He had to get the cop in his patrol car. Otherwise, the neighbors would spot the guy sprawled on the ground. They'd call it in. Cops would scream to the area. Maybe arrest Fenton. Not happening.

He shoved the body into the car, the thrill of tying up Rosalind gone, and the pain—that grinding, mind-splitting pain—returned, threatening to explode his head. It was getting to be too much. All of it. This waiting. He'd spent too much time on the sidelines and needed to get into the fray.

You're in the fray now. Knocking out a cop guarantees that.

But it was worth it, right? Seeing Rosalind's eyes. The fear. Wondering if he was going to kill her. If he'd take or harm Lily. He wouldn't hurt her, of course, but Rosalind didn't know that.

He stepped away from the car. The memory of her eyes when he'd restrained her while Lily slept in the next room brought a smile as he raced for J.J.'s sports car. Fenton had backhanded her. Hard. Her head had whipped to the side, the loose flesh on her neck shaking like Jell-O. The witch deserved his treatment for sure. Her interfering ways. Always demanding. Never asking. Just like Kait. They were a pair. If Abby had lived, he'd have found a way to take her away from her family. She was the only sweet one in the bunch.

Abby. He pounded a fist on his forehead.

Focus. Must focus.

Abby needed him to take revenge. His mind clearer now, he picked up his pace. He passed the Knight's house and imagined Kait finding her mother. Then visualized Kait seeing the interview and learning another man had died because of her.

Good. This was better. Much better.

He settled behind the wheel, his mojo quickly resurfacing.

Payback sucks, Kait. But it's oh so satisfying.

KAIT COULDN'T breathe. Couldn't think. Lily. Kait's precious, sweet Lily in danger from Fenton. Again. Kait's parents in danger, too. She slid to the edge of her seat and searched the road ahead. Her eyes straining, her heart slamming against the wall of her chest.

Sam careened the car around the last corner.

Kait held fast and spotted a patrol car with lights flashing, the driver's door open. "There." She jabbed a finger at the cars. "Right behind Congdon's beater."

"Diaz is in the car." Sam slowed, crawling to a stop behind the cruiser.

Diaz wasn't moving. Was he dead? Another person who'd lost their life because of her? Nausea turned her stomach. She didn't really want to learn the answer to her question, but she had to know. She drew her weapon and reached for the door handle.

Sam clamped a hand on her forearm. "You're not going anywhere. This could be a trap to lure you here."

"You don't honestly expect me to sit here with an officer down and Fenton in the house with Lily?" She shrugged off his hand and lurched from the car.

Sam met her at the front of the vehicle, his weapon drawn. Together, they approached the patrol car. Diaz was slumped over the wheel, a dried river of blood on his neck.

"Watch my back while I check him out," Sam said, already leaning into the vehicle.

Despite the palpable urge to charge across the street to check on Lily, Kait couldn't leave Sam unprotected, so she stood her ground. She tracked her gaze up and down the street. The street she'd played on as a child. Tag. Soccer. Roller-skating. All enjoyed right here. Where birds chirped and a soft breeze whispered through the trees.

A direct contrast to the adrenaline coursing through her body. Her hand trembled, and she gripped her gun tighter. She concentrated on holding the weapon still, but her hand continued to shake. She steadied it with the other hand and kept vigil.

"Looks like he's been pistol-whipped." Sam backed out of the car. "His pulse is strong, and I see no other injury."

"Good." Kait was relieved, but quickly moved to thoughts of her parents. To Lily, and the safest way to approach the house.

"I'll call for backup and an ambulance." Sam dug out his phone and dialed.

With Sam now able to defend himself, Kait was free to head inside. Sure, she should wait for Sam to back her up, but he needed to stay with Diaz until help arrived, and every second counted right now. She took a step.

Sam grabbed her arm. "Not a good idea, Kait," he said meeting her gaze.

"Maybe not, but Fenton could be in there with Lily. I won't hang out here until the ambulance arrives."

Sam glanced at Diaz then back at her, the struggle of deciding which person to protect readily visible on his face. She felt a tinge of guilt for forcing him to choose, but her duty to Lily was far stronger. "You have to stay with Diaz. But I can't."

She wrenched her arm free and hustled across the street, keeping her head on a swivel on the way. She took the familiar walkway to the front door and found it open. Her mother was so paranoid about everything since Abby had died that she'd added another deadbolt to the doors and would never willingly leave the door ajar.

Keeping her back against the wall, Kait slid into the foyer, then stopped to listen and inspect the open family room. No one. Where were they? Lily wanted to bake cookies, but Kate's mother's flowery perfume was the only scent lingering in the air. Kait's father had likely left for work at his usual time and knew nothing about this situation.

Dreading what she might find, Kait crossed the room and swung into a chef's dream kitchen. A metal mixing bowl filled with dry cookie ingredients sat forgotten on the massive island, a bag of chocolate chips beside it. They'd started baking only to be interrupted.

Interrupted by Fenton?

Kait's desire to race though the house to find Lily warred with her professional training that said to calm down and methodically clear the property. She'd already risked her life by entering the house alone. She couldn't take any more shortcuts. She tried the back door and found it unlocked. Likely the way Fenton entered. And he could still be here, or he could have grabbed Lily and bailed.

The thought stopped Kait's heart. She backtracked through the family room, the urge to call out begging for release, but she held her tongue and kept her movements slow and purposeful as she entered the hallway.

Her father's study door stood open, soft light spilling onto the hallway floor. Fenton? Maybe. Would be fitting for him to do his dirty work in the room where Abby had lost her life.

Keeping her eyes ahead, her ears tuned for any sound, Kait inched closer. She glanced into the room. Caught sight of her mother sitting in her father's leather chair, duct tape wrapped around her body and her mouth. Fear gripped Kait as she retreated to safety.

"Mmm-mmm," her mother mumbled through the gag, but approaching sirens drowned her out.

Was she trying to warn Kait about danger, or begging her to remove the restraints? Had Fenton set this as a trap to lure Kait into the study? One way to find out. He could only hide under the desk or behind the door. She jumped to the other side of the door where she'd have a better view of the room. Her mother jerked against her restraints and mumbled another plea.

Kait held up a finger to still her mother, then pressed the door until it hit the doorstop. *Good.* Fenton wasn't behind the door. She aimed her weapon at the desk and cast a questioning look at her mother.

She shook her head frantically side to side. A warning not to enter? Maybe. Or telling Kait he wasn't here? Either way, she had to check it out. Weapon still raised, she slipped into the room, cautiously approaching the desk. Step by step. One foot after the other, to the back of the desk by her mother. Kait's eyes went to the cubbyhole. Empty.

Kait could breathe again, but now what? Protocol dictated she leave her mother behind and clear the rest of the house, but her mother might provide information that could save Kait's life.

Kait couldn't just rip the tape from her mother's face. That would be too painful. She would free her mother's hands so she could remove the tape herself. Kait started working on the tape at her mother's wrists, but couldn't wait until she was free to ask about Lily. "I need to know about Lily. Nod if she's okay."

Her mother's head bobbed.

A wave of relief washed over Kait, but she wouldn't relax until she saw Lily with her own two eyes and confirmed Fenton didn't pose an immediate danger. She tugged on the tape. Her mother winced.

"I don't want to hurt you so I'm going to cut the tape around your wrists and body. Then you can take it off your mouth." She found scissors in the desk and snipped the tape. Her mother slowly pulled the strip from her mouth.

"Thank God you're here, Kaitlyn. It was Fenton. He was here. Kept babbling about you and making you pay." Her mother choked on a sob, then broke down and started weeping.

Kait knew her mother was in shock and needed to cry it out, but Kait had no time for hysterics right now. "Where's Lily?" she demanded in a tone that she'd never used with her mother.

It worked, sobering her enough to respond. "Sleeping. We started the cookies, but she was so tired from her early morning wakeup, I had to put her down for a nap. Fenton grabbed me when I came out of her room."

"So you haven't seen her since then?" Anxiety carried Kait's voice higher.

"No, but she was sleeping, so I'm sure she's fine."

"You can't know that. Stay here while I check on her." Kait raised her weapon again and returned to the hallway.

The wails of emergency sirens spiraled though the open door as she hurried to Lily's room. Holding her breath in fear, Kait swung into the room. Lily lay curled in the bed, Mr. Bear and Blankie snuggled under her chin as usual.

Kait sagged against the doorframe, but knew she had to hold it together long enough to check the other bedrooms. She scanned the closet first, then moved down the hall, methodically sweeping each of the three remaining bedrooms. As she exited her parents' room, she noted the absence of sirens.

Sam.

Diaz was in good hands now, and Sam would come looking for her. Maybe bring a team of responding officers with him. Kait needed to let him know she was okay. She stopped in the office to tell her mom Lily was still asleep, and then went to the front door where she spotted Sam across the street in a circle of officers.

"Sam," she called out. "We're clear."

He spun, his focus zooming in on her. He said something to the officers before jogging across the road. Relief flooding his eyes, he grabbed her by the arms and pulled her to him for a fierce hug before setting her away as if he hated himself for hugging her. She was right with him. Hugging in front of other law enforcement professionals made her look weak.

"What were you thinking, coming over here alone? You could have gotten yourself in a heap of trouble." His harsh tone was in direct opposition to the hug and the concern lingering in his eyes.

Fearing he planned to hug her again, she took another step back for good measure. "That's a bit hypocritical, don't you think? You'd have done the same thing."

"Maybe, but we're not talking about me." The protective look, the kind where a man was compelled to take care of a woman, flashed on his face. There it was again. Him in charge. Her, the damsel in distress. She warred with how she felt about it.

The agent in her won, taking over her emotions and erasing her remaining fear. "What you're saying is, you can do it because you're a seasoned cop. I can't because I'm a female FBI agent."

"I didn't say that."

"You didn't have to. It's written all over your face."

"I'm sorry if that's what you think, but if any other officer pulled this stunt, I'd let them have it, too." He gestured at the cops across the road. "Even big burly Smith over there."

"Please." She rolled her eyes and noted how the other officers were watching with interest. "I'd like to see that happen."

"Okay, so maybe it would be a bit different, but I'd still give him a dressing-down for failing to follow protocol."

"Look," she said not liking the way all the officers were jabbing each other and gesturing at her. "There's no point in belaboring this. I'm fine. So are my mother and Lily."

Sam watched her with narrowed eyes, his anger clinging to his face and making it seem like he didn't want to move on.

Too bad. She was ready to process this scene and find Fenton. If Sam couldn't make the transition, she'd do it alone. "Let's agree to disagree and get started processing the house." She made sure her tone was professional. "I found my mother bound and gagged in the study. Lily's in her room sleeping."

Sam shoved his hands in his pockets as if he needed to bind them to keep from throttling her. "Rhodes's handiwork?"

"Yes."

"You think he drugged Lily?"

"No," Kait replied. "Mom said she'd put her down to nap before Fenton arrived. I suspect he watched her again like he's been doing at night."

"At least he didn't take her."

"Not yet," Kait said, as thoughts of Fenton holding Lily worried their way into her brain, making her sick to her stomach.

If they didn't up their vigilance and move Lily to a safe house today, it was just a matter of time before Fenton abducted her.

Chapter Twenty-Three

SAM WAS STILL mad. Worried and mad. The combination made him feel out of control. Kait thought she could move on, forget the scare she put him through and talk about processing the scene, but he wasn't finished warning her to take care.

She headed into the house, her footsteps quick and efficient as if she wanted to get this over with and get out of here. Well, too bad. He got that she didn't want to talk about the danger she'd just faced, but she'd have to hear him out. In the hallway, he tried to stow his irritation as he approached her. "Maybe it's time you think about stepping down from this case, Kait."

"What? Why?" She watched him warily.

"You're too vested in catching Rhodes, and you're not thinking clearly."

She took a breath and jerked back from him as if he'd hit her. "Granted, I may not have waited for backup, but I didn't come running in here like a crazed lunatic."

"You wanted to though, didn't you?"

Another breath. Another huff. She was losing patience with him. "I performed a safe and thorough search of the residence just as protocol dictates."

"Fine. Refuse to acknowledge the fact that you're letting your emotions control you and putting yourself in danger." Sam crossed his arms. "But think of Lily. She needs you."

"I won't let anything happen to her. I fully intend to put her in protective custody."

"That's a good idea, but not what I meant, and you know it. She needs you to be her mother. Long-term. Not looking at another gravestone when she gets older and wondering about you."

Kait rolled her eyes. "You're overreacting, and we have things to do. First off, processing this scene, then arranging a safe house for Lily and my parents."

"But not you?"

She fisted her hands. "How many times do I need to say it? I. Don't. Need. Protection."

Sadness over her refusal to be more cautious had him shaking his head.

"Forget about Rhodes. You need protection from yourself before you go off half-cocked again."

She closed her eyes for a moment then met his gaze. "If I admit racing over here wasn't the smartest move, and promise not to do it again, can we move on?"

"You can promise, but I doubt you can predict how you'll act if something like this happens again."

"You'll just have to trust me to know what's best for me and for Lily." Her shoulders shot into that rigid line that said she was done talking.

His anger flared, and everything he'd held back rushed to come out. "You're right. You didn't put me in harm's way, so it's just like your decision to give up custody of Lily. It's none of my business."

Kait sighed. "Maybe once you have kids of your own, you'll understand."

The sharp ache of losing Danny hit him, and he reacted instinctually, pressing his hand against the dog tag and stepping back.

"I'm sorry, Sam." Kait lifted a hand and let it fall. "I wasn't thinking. After losing your wife, talking about potential children must be painful."

"No biggie." He tried to sound convincing to keep from becoming the focus of this discussion. "Just take my words to heart, Kait. Rhodes has proved his willingness to kill and hurt those you love. You need to be careful before he succeeds again."

Kait opened her mouth as if to reply, but her mother stepped into the hallway, and Kait snapped it shut.

"He's right, you know," she said eyeing Kait and crossing her arms. "Working in this Godforsaken career of yours has brought nothing but danger to our family. Starting with Abby."

Kait fisted her hands and pinched her lips together, but didn't say anything in her defense. Sam had expected her to snap at her mother. He would have if he was Kait. He might want her to step down and take cover, but that was because he cared about her. Not so with Rosalind. She just needed a scapegoat to blame for Abby's death.

Sam's anger at Kait melted, but he wouldn't keep quiet and let Kait take on more guilt. "If you need to blame someone for these attacks, Rosalind, blame Rhodes. He's the one who shot Abby, and he's the one terrorizing your family now. Kait is working her tail off to protect all of you and bring Rhodes to justice. You should be thanking her instead of berating her."

Rosalind marched up to Sam and eyed him. "I don't agree, Detective. If Kait hadn't lost her senses and become an agent, Fenton wouldn't have felt threatened that day and shot my precious child."

Sam wanted to stare her down, but the red blotches around her eyes told him this attack had affected her deeply. He would temper his tone, but not his message. "Rhodes killed long before Abby, and he continues to kill. Just being married to him put her in danger, and it was only a matter of time before something bad happened."

Kait stepped between them. "Arguing about this is keeping us from finding Fenton. Let's focus on the case."

She was right. Surprising. Sam had underestimated her ability to keep her head clear under emotional duress.

"Why don't you tell us what happened, Mom?" Kait's tone was soft and encouraging as he suspected it would be with any other victim. "Even the smallest detail might be important."

Rosalind glared at Kait.

How could a woman as caring and feeling as Kait have ever come from such a bitter, domineering woman? Sure, Kait had bullied her way onto this case, but she'd done so for Lily and because of her promise to her sister. Rosalind was just plain angry at the world and was willing to take it out on everyone around her. Sam didn't like how she was treating Kait, but Rosalind was a victim here, too. A woman who Fenton had terrorized, and Sam needed to continue to hold his temper.

"Tell us what happened," he encouraged, trying to be the compassionate detective he usually sought to be instead of the man who wanted to stave off any additional pain for Kait.

Rosalind stared at her hands, her complexion ashen. "While I was putting Lily down for her nap, Fenton entered the house. I must have left the back door open. Or he broke in somehow. Either way, I didn't hear him." Her voice cracked, and she cleared it hard before going on. "He was waiting in the hallway for me. He had a gun and forced me into the study. As he tied me up, he kept chuckling over how he wished he could be here to see Kaitlyn's face when she found me." She sighed heavily and peered at Kait. "He clearly blames you for Abby's death."

As do you, Sam thought.

"What did he do next?" Kait asked.

"He said he was going to peek in on Lily." Rosalind touched the red welts on her wrists, as if still trying to believe this had really happened, and swung her gaze back to Sam. "He left the study, and I heard him go down the hall for a few minutes. On the way out, he saluted me and said to tell Kaitlyn that it's taken her too long, and he was off to claim another heart—whatever that means."

Kait gasped and clamped a hand over her mouth.

"What are you not telling me, Kaitlyn?" Rosalind asked, with a look that even a convict in a maximum-security prison would wilt under.

Kait cringed, her mouth opening then closing.

"She's unable to share any information related to the case," Sam said, jumping in so Kait wasn't forced to sidestep her mother and draw another harsh response.

"He's right." Kait sounded like she was trying to convince herself of that fact.

Rosalind arched an eyebrow. "Are we in danger beyond Fenton?"

"We'll get you settled in a safe house today, and you'll be fine," Sam said, ignoring her question and taking her focus back off Kait.

Rosalind's chin rose, and the same perfect posture he admired in Kait made Rosalind look haughty. "Make sure the place is up to my cleanliness standards."

The last thing Sam wanted to discuss was how clean the house might be when their lives were in danger, so he ignored her comment. "My forensics team will arrive soon to go through your house. I'm afraid you'll have to be patient with them until they've processed the entire house, and then you'll be free to gather your things and pack."

Her shoulder's sagged a bit. "Is that really necessary? After all, we know it was Fenton, and he wore gloves."

"Gloves or not, he could have left evidence behind."

"Like what?" she challenged

"Dirt tracked in on his shoes or carpet fibers. Or any number of things that will lead us to his location."

"Fine." She looked at Kait. "I'll just get my phone to call your dad and arrange for the housekeeper to clean up after the forensics team."

"Actually," Sam said. "I have one more question before I let you go. Did you happen to notice an older model Chrysler parked across the street?"

"Of course. I first saw it when I went for my nightly walk. A rundown car like that certainly doesn't belong in our neighborhood. I'd planned to call the police if it was here this morning. Then I got Kait's call and then . . . well . . . Is it important?"

"We're unsure at the moment." Sam forced a smile. "I appreciate your help, Rosalind. I know it was difficult to talk about this, but I hope if I have any additional questions, you'll be willing to answer them."

Her arrogant expression faded. "Yes. Of course. Anything to find Fenton and make him pay for Abby's death."

Sam handed her a business card just as he'd do with any other victim. "Let me know if you remember anything else you think might be important."

Sam waited for her to move out of hearing distance before turning to Kait. Her look reminded him of Lily when she'd told him about the man in her room. What Kait needed right now was a hug. Badly. Something her mother should have provided.

Something he'd provide, but it wouldn't be well received. "Is it always this difficult between the two of you?"

Kait gave a sad and dejected nod.

"How do you deal with it?"

"She wasn't always this way," Kait said in support of her mother, but her tone lacked enthusiasm. "I try to remember the good times, growing up."

"Good times?" he probed gently.

"Sometimes it's hard to remember them. Especially since Abby died." Kait's eyes glistened with unshed tears. "But our childhood was pretty normal. She was a good mother. There when Abby and I needed her. More for Abby than me, but then, I had more of Dad."

"Guess that means she'll be good to Lily."

"I suppose so." Kait's chin trembled. "Maybe I shouldn't have made a decision about Lily's custody in the heat of the moment."

Sam reached out to touch her, but thought better of it and let his hand fall. "You can always tell your mother you changed your mind."

"I could also hang from the ceiling by my fingernails," Kait said, looking away. "But I don't plan to do either of those things anytime soon."

"WATCH CAREFULLY, J.J.," Fenton said as he queued up the video. "I know you'll like to see Kait reading my special note as much as I want to see it."

Kait appeared on the screen as she stepped into Lily's bedroom. Fenton relished every moment, every step as she approached the box like it really was the bomb she'd reported. She snapped on gloves, her jaw clenched, her eyes filled with dread. She lifted the lid, paused, and her shoulders rose. She pulled out his card, studied it for a moment. He loved seeing her trembling hands and the way she bit her lower lip. She shot a look around the room, then, seeming as if she couldn't take anymore, she collapsed out of view. He heard her sobbing, her broken cries and agony a balm to his pounding head.

He smiled at J.J. "Perfect. She's starting to know my anguish, isn't she?"

The detective appeared on screen next and warned Kait that he thought Fenton would abduct Lily. Kait agreed.

"Hah, abduct!" Fenton shot to his feet and turned it off. "They're the ones doing the abducting. Taking Lily away from me to put her in a safe house like she's some kind of a victim. She doesn't need protection. She needs me."

He'd planned to take Lily from her house tonight, but with a legion of cops and feds protecting her, he'd have to alter his plans. He had no choice but to let them move her to the safe house. As time passed, they'd grow complacent, and he'd take her from under their noses. It might delay his grand finale, but he had contingencies built into his schedule. Now all he had to do was find out the location of the safe house. Might be a problem for a lesser man, but it wasn't the least bit of a concern for him.

"Foolish of them to think I won't find her." He dropped into the chair and typed his computer password. "You'll be impressed with my idea, J.J. I'll spoof the entire task force with an e-mail that looks like it came from their respective departments. One of them is dumb enough to open it and click on the link I'm including. Hopefully, it'll be Murdock."

Fenton logged into one of many e-mail accounts. "When Murdock clicks on the link, one of my lovely malware programs will download, and I'll have full access to his phone. Then, when he contacts the safe house, Lily's location will be revealed." Fenton looked at J. J. "Don't be sad. I know there's nothing more fun than creating an e-mail that looks like it's from one person when it really isn't, but you're in no shape to help me."

He turned back to the computer. "Let's make the e-mail a warning about opening suspicious e-mails. It'll be a hoot for Murdock to open that, don't you think?" He finished the officially worded message and hit send.

He sat back. "There. It will take some time for them to secure a safe house, but when Murdock takes the bait, I'll know exactly where to find my darling Lily."

Chapter Twenty-Four

AS KAIT'S TEARS threatened to fall, she hugged Lily hard while her mother and father waited to accompany Lily to the safe house. Kait bit the inside of her cheek to keep from falling apart. She wouldn't cry. Not in the office. Not in front of task force members. Their faces were already filled with pity. She needed them to think of her as the professional agent she'd worked so hard to become. Not some sobbing woman who couldn't cope.

"Time to go." Nina approached and bent close to Kait. "Lily will be fine."

Would she? Or would Fenton somehow track them to the safe house? Maybe Kait should listen to Sam and accompany Lily.

The sight of Abby's lifeless body invaded Kait's mind as it always did. Day and night, reminding Kait of her duty. Exactly what she needed right now to be able to let Lily go and stay behind to look for Fenton. Two top agents plus a police officer would ensure Lily's safety, but no one else had Kait's unwavering desire to bring Fenton to justice.

She planted a kiss on Lily's button nose. "I'll miss you. Listen to Nana and Papa, okay?"

Lily nodded and looked up her grandma. "Make cookies now?"

Kait's mother smiled at Lily, that warm welcoming smile Kait remembered from her childhood. "Just as soon as we get to the house."

"House with a big yard." Lily's lower lip slipped out. "Nana says we can't go outside."

Nina bent down to Lily. "You know what, sugar? Baking cookies is far better because you don't have to take a bath afterward." She tweaked Lily's nose. "Plus you'll have cookies to eat."

Lily's expression brightened. Nina stood and shot a pointed look at the war room where the team waited for Kait.

Kait got the hint. She turned to her mother who Kait knew would speak for both of her parents. "Keep me updated, but only use the cell phone we provided."

Her mother rubbed her fingertips as if trying to rid herself of having to be fingerprinted to rule out prints found in Lily's room. "I'm quite capable of following directions, Kaitlyn."

Nina winced, and Kait imagined the others following suit. *Great.* Another reason for them to feel sorry for her.

"Don't worry, honey. We'll take good care of Lily." Kait's father squeezed her shoulder, his kindly eyes bringing her tears to the surface again.

"I know you will, Dad," she said, but her voice caught in her throat.

As they departed, Nina stepped closer. "You'll be together again before you know it."

Would they? Or would Kait actually let her mother take over Lily's care? Something she needed to think through very carefully. With everyone waiting for her, now was not the time. She stepped into the conference room where Adams, Yates, and the analysts quickly averted their eyes. But not Sam. He met her gaze and gestured at the chair next to him.

"Lily get off okay?" he asked.

"Fine." Kait took a seat.

"Good."

"Yes," she replied, not at all missing the fact that after their terse discussion at her parent's house, they'd resorted to using single word answers.

"Okay, people." Nina took the head of the table. "Let's get started. You've had time to think about the package and Rhodes's visit to Kait's mother and niece this morning. Yesterday, his threats were directed at non-family members." She grabbed a marker. "Today, he goes directly for the family instead of delivering on his promise of another heart. Feels a little out of control. Rushed. Why not follow through on his original threat? What's changed?"

"Sorry, Nina, but I don't agree," Kait said. "I think he's still in control. He could have killed my mother today, but he didn't. And trust me, it's pretty easy to want to kill my mother and takes a lot of self-control not to do it."

The team erupted in laughter as Kait hoped, sending the elephant in the room parading out the door.

"Still," Sam said, jumping in. "The break-in at your parents' place did feel unplanned and sloppy. Not at all like Congdon's meticulous murder."

"Agreed," Kait admitted.

Yates cleared his throat. "Maybe Rhodes is tired of playing games, and he's simply escalating his timeframe."

"Or not," Sam said. "He could have killed Kait, her mother, or Lily today, but he didn't. His actions say he's still toying with Kait. Maybe escalating the stakes, but toying with her nonetheless."

"So you don't think he's losing control?" Nina asked.

Sam shrugged. "I don't think we know enough to form a concrete opinion."

The door swung open, and Jae poked her head into the room. Kait saw a glint of excitement in Jae's eyes, and she hoped for good news.

"Sorry for the interruption." Jae grabbed a remote from the credenza. "But you'll want to see this."

Nina turned, her usual smile for a co-worker absent. "It better be important, Jae."

"Don't worry, it is." Jae clicked on the television. "Your hunch about monitoring the news coverage from this morning's bomb threat paid off, Nina. Take a look at who I spotted." She pressed Play.

A stunning female reporter recapped the bomb scare at Kait's house as the camera panned away, searching through the crowd then landing on the face of a monster.

Despite a hat and thick scruffy beard, Kait recognized the man smirking at the camera. The wildness in his eyes, the barely veiled hatred—maybe insanity—sent fear racing through her body.

Sam shot a look at her. "That's—"

"Yes," Kait interrupted, her heartbeat thundering in her ears. "Fenton Rhodes in the flesh."

THE VIDEO CONTINUED to play. Rhodes smiled at the camera and gave his name as Brian Youngblood. He claimed his computer had been hacked, and he'd received the blue screen of death. Then, he announced that Kait had killed Congdon and cut out his heart.

The camera panned the crowd. Bystanders stood in shocked silence, mouths hanging open, and Sam saw red. Big, bull-fighting, rage-blinding red. At Rhodes. At himself for missing Rhodes when he'd stood outside Kait's house today. Sam had been too distracted by thoughts of how Kait was handling the situation to look at the crowd, leaving Rhodes to run free—and it was Sam's fault.

"Okay, people." Nina raised her voice over the buzz of conversation that had spread through the group. "Let's get back to it." She turned to Jae who remained at the door. "So Rhodes has taken on Brian Youngblood as his name. I want to know if he made it up or if Youngblood actually exists."

"Already ahead of you, Obi-Wan." Jae puffed up her chest. "I have a search running and should have that information for you soon."

Nina smiled, her fondness for Jae evident. "Excellent."

"Just keep the energy drinks flowing, and your wish is my command." Jae departed, her laughter ringing behind her.

Sam hoped Jae was as capable as she'd made herself sound. Though, honestly, Sam didn't want to learn that Brian Youngblood was real. Could mean that Rhodes had taken another life.

Adams turned to Kait. "You really think Rhodes would be dumb enough to drop a name that has any bearing on the case?"

Kait nodded. "But only if he wanted us to find Youngblood."

Sam doubted that was Rhodes's only purpose in doing the interview. "Rhodes could have called or e-mailed to tell us about Youngblood. If he's willing to risk an interview with all the cops swarming around, then maybe our discussion has been right on target, and he's not thinking clearly."

"But again, why?" Nina asked. "The man we just saw on the video wasn't calculating and methodical. He was an attention seeker, risking it all. So what's causing Rhodes to change his MO and act outside his normal character?"

"I'm not one of your FBI profilers," Yates said with the sarcasm Sam expected from the caustic detective. "But I get a sense that he's feeling like the victim here."

"It's clear Rhodes blames you for Abby's death." Adams looked at Kait. "Maybe seeing you free and not paying for it is messing with his head. And he needs something to make him feel better until his plan unfolds."

"Maybe," Kait said. "Or maybe he really is mentally ill and coming unhinged."

Nina tapped photos of the gift box posted on the whiteboard. "I think we all agree that there has to be some degree of mental instability to commit murder and remove a heart, then gift it to you."

Sam opened his mouth to say this instability meant they should consider assigning a protection detail to Kait, but Jae burst back into the room and drew the attention. "Some dude's on the phone who says he has a lead in Congdon's investigation. He won't talk to anyone except you, Kait, but everyone's too afraid to bust in here and tell you about the call."

Kait grinned at Jae. "So they sent you."

"Nah." Jae smirked. "I volunteered. You know my day's not complete until I mess with you guys." She picked up the phone and held it out. "He's on line three."

Still smiling, Kait crossed the room and took the handset. "This is Special Agent Kaitlyn Knight. To whom am I speaking?" She listened, her smile disappearing. Her mouth went slack, and she clutched the side of the table. "Where?"

Something bad had happened, and Sam didn't care if the entire room thought he had a thing for Kait. She needed someone by her side. He crossed over to her.

She hung up the phone.

"What is it?" he asked, his hand going to her elbow to steady her.

"That was Fenton." She looked past Sam to Nina. "You can cancel the search on Youngblood. He's very real. I can take you to him, but you're not going to like what you find."

KAIT MOVED THROUGH Brian Youngblood's house. It was the same as Congdon's home had been. Empty. Clean. Meticulous. She knew she'd find Youngblood in the bedroom and was prepared to see his body, but when she headed inside, her steps faltered. The overhead light shone on his contorted face, another life cut short. His body was fresher than Congdon's had been, but in every other aspect the same. Same hair color, size, and build. Cuffed to sturdy bolts. No sign of a struggle. Blood saturated his T-shirt over his heart.

This was so surreal. Every bit of it. Fenton was a vicious killer. A serial killer. Part of a rare group of crazies that boggled Kait's mind and terrified her. It was all so unbelievable, but true. If she didn't stop him, he'd keep killing.

Who would be next? Would it be her, as Sam seemed to think?

She heard his heavy footsteps and Marcie's lighter ones coming down the hall. They were discussing the victim as they stepped into the room. One of Marcie's assistants followed. Fortunately, she was a shy, retiring kind of person, and the grim set of her mouth was the only thing she had in common with surly Tim.

"Good to see you again, Kait." Marcie's usual smile was absent, replaced by a dour look. "Just wish we could meet under different circumstances." She rested a hand on Kait's shoulder, the touch making tears prick at Kait's eyes. "You okay?" Marcie watched Kait carefully. "What with Rhodes calling you and all?"

Kait wasn't okay, and Marcie's solicitous attitude made her want to confide her fear, but she wouldn't. Not with Sam watching her every move. It wouldn't take much for him to demand she be put in protective custody, and it was best not to dwell on the panic that kept threatening to take her down.

"I'm fine." She turned away before the tears flowed and they urged her to step away. "We should get to work."

"Then let's get to it so we can catch this creep." Marcie's no-nonsense tone buoyed Kait's attitude.

Marcie snapped on gloves and knelt by the victim's side. Her focus intense, her hands roved over the extremities. "Youngblood hasn't been dead for more than a few hours."

"So we're not far behind Rhodes, this time." Sam's words whispered out as he squatted next to Marcie. "I've been meaning to ask you. If these victims have indeed been kept alive with a vent, how long could they stay that way?"

"Indefinitely. Assuming a trained professional was managing their care."

Sam frowned at Marcie. "So Rhodes could have kept Congdon on a vent for a few weeks?"

Kait thought to walk away. She didn't want to hear Marcie's answer. Didn't want confirmation that Fenton was not only a murderer, but the monster they were coming to believe him to be. But she stayed put and waited.

"Rhodes clearly has the skills it would take to keep someone on a vent for an extended period of time." Marcie sat back on her heels and looked up at Kait. "I'd hate to think he did it, though."

Me, too, Kait thought but averted her gaze and avoided the subject lest they see how truly upset she was.

Marcie turned back to Youngblood and moved his head. "Is it just me, or does Youngblood look like he could pass as Congdon's twin?"

"It's not just you." Sam shifted his focus to Kait. "I'm starting to buy your theory that Rhodes is impersonating his victims before killing them."

Kait should be glad that Sam was agreeing with her, but it simply made the situation more real, and she couldn't control the tremor that ran through her body. Nor could she stop the guilt. She was responsible for Youngblood's death. If she'd done a better job, done more, sooner, he might still be alive.

She couldn't look at him any longer. She stepped to the window and gazed out over the backyard. A tall pine shaded the postage stamp-sized space with a rusty swing set and empty sandbox. Once upon a time, this house had been filled with the laughter of a child, and now the stench of death had erased it all.

Sam's phone rang, splitting the deathly quiet and making Kait jump. She kept looking out the window, but listened to Sam's conversation. It wasn't hard to figure out he was talking to the Oregon State Police tech processing Congdon's car. Sam's voice grew frustrated, and she turned to watch him.

"Sure. Run the DNA." He massaged the back of his neck, a sure sign he was stressed, too. Of course he was. Sam took this murder personally. He had empathy in droves for those who suffered. He was such an amazing man, and she was fortunate to have him working this case by her side.

He shook his head then stowed his phone, mumbling, "Fat lotta good it'll do us."

"Problem?" Kait asked, though she doubted she wanted to hear his answer.

The tightness of his shoulders and firm set of jaw increased her apprehension. "They've finished processing Congdon's car. Nothing of interest yet, but they found the pea coat. They're running it and the car for Rhodes's DNA."

Not bad news. Not good either, which explained Sam's frustration.

"Since we're fairly certain Fenton stole Congdon's car, the DNA won't do much now, but it will help with his prosecution," Kait said, stepping across the room to join Sam. "I'm more interested in why the coat keeps turning up."

Sam shrugged. "Rhodes might simply want us to think it's important and divert our resources."

"You could be right," she said, as she thought about the events that had transpired today and considered what their next move should be. "Since Fenton abandoned Congdon's car last night, he needs new transportation. We should check for Youngblood's vehicle."

"Already done. The garage is empty." Sam pulled out his notepad and flipped a few pages. "Pulled a registration. He drives a classic 1968 Volkswagen van. Blue and white." He looked at Kait. "I've also issued an alert, and your analysts are reviewing street cam footage. Plus, Yates and Adams are canvassing neighbors near your parents' house again to see if anyone saw the van earlier today."

"I wouldn't be surprised to find it in my driveway when I get home," Kait said, but at Sam's frown, she wished she'd kept the thought to herself.

He kept his hawk-like gaze trained on her for a moment, then suddenly turned to Marcie without commenting. "You have a cause of death yet?"

"Nothing obvious. There's a needle stick and IV tape like Congdon. No sign of a struggle." She came to her feet. "If he was drugged, the sooner I get him on the table, the better my odds of identifying the drug."

"Then get him out of here."

She turned to her assistant. "You heard the man, Sandra. Let's bag him."

Kait stepped closer. "Before you do, can you confirm the missing heart?"

Marcie wrinkled her forehead. "The blood on his shirt makes it pretty obvious."

"Still," Kait said warily. "If I'm going to get another unexpected package, I'd like to be sure about it in advance."

Sam winced, but didn't speak.

Marcie returned to the body and slid her fingers over the chest. Her eyes lifted in surprise. "The heart's gone, but there's something in the cavity."

Kait moved closer, as did Sam, while Marcie raised Youngblood's shirt. She pulled out a neon-pink sheet of cardstock—the same type of paper as the note left with Congdon's heart. This one had heart-shaped stickers on one side and had been laminated.

Marcie's mouth flattened in a hard line as she read the message, then she handed it to Sam.

Kait read over his shoulder.

I thought you were smarter than this, Kait.

Tick, tock. Tick, tock.

Another dies in 24 hours unless you stop me.

Dread coiled in Kait's stomach, and she glanced at Sam who was staring into space. She couldn't get a read on his thoughts, but he had to be wondering who would die next. At least, that's what she was thinking.

Marcie snapped off her gloves, the sound reverberating in the nearly empty room. "If the countdown commenced at the time of death—likely the time Rhodes put the note in Youngblood's chest cavity—then I suggest you subtract about two hours from the clock."

"Two hours." Sam peered at his watch. "That gives us until 5:25 tomorrow afternoon."

"To do what?" Kait asked, her tone plagued with the turmoil churning in her stomach. "We don't even have one solid lead to run down."

"Then we better come up with something quick." Sam met her gaze, and she saw a healthy measure of desperation there. "Or we'll be looking at another victim in twenty-two hours."

Chapter Twenty-Five

THE CLOCK LOOMED over Sam's head. *Tick. Tick. Tick.* It weighed on him as he checked his phone while Dane carried in supplies, and Marcie loaded Youngblood onto the gurney. A voicemail from Yates confirmed Rhodes's call to the FBI office had come from a burner phone. Sam wasn't surprised. Rhodes was a technology expert, and, despite Sam's disgust over the guy's killing spree, he had to admit he was proving to be a worthy opponent.

Sam switched to his e-mail. The first message was from Sulyard, updating task force members on Youngblood's murder. He also noted that the request for the post office mail hold came from Congdon's address. Didn't mean Congdon ordered the hold, just that it was sent from his house. Essentially another dead end.

Sam moved on to a department message telling them to be careful with e-mail.

He rolled his eyes. How ironic was that? An e-mail to warn them about e-mail. The message said something about spoofing, whatever that was. He read the message and tapped the link to acknowledge that he'd received it as was required with department memos.

Marcie crossed to Sam. "Okay, we're good to go. I'll start the autopsy and won't head home until I have something to report."

"Thanks." Sam watched Kait as she stared at the body bag then, with a shake of her head, she left the room.

"I'm worried about her." Marcie's eyes narrowed. "She doesn't seem nearly as together as yesterday."

Sam had the same concern, but he didn't want to admit it. "You said it yourself. She's a strong woman."

Marcie's eyes widened. "Why, Sam Murdock. You've fallen for her. I hear it in your voice."

Sam stepped closer to her. "Keep your voice down."

"Oh, my word." Marcie clasped her hand to her chest. "For the first time ever, you didn't tell me to mind my own business or deny any interest in her, proving my point."

He glanced at the others openly watching him and moved even closer to Marcie to keep them from overhearing him. "If I admit that if I *was* going to get involved with someone, it would be Kait, will you lower your voice?"

"I'm so happy for you." She grabbed him in a hug, and he heard Dane chuckle.

Sam eased out of her arms. "Okay, that's enough, Marcie. We're working, and I have a reputation to maintain."

"Reputation, phooey. Everyone knows you're a big softie."

"She's right," Dane called out.

Sam glared at him. "Who asked you?"

Dane held up his hands and backed away.

"So," Marcie said. "When this case is over, Paul and I will be glad to have you and Kait over for dinner."

"For real, Marcie. Not the time or place for this discussion." Shaking his head, Sam headed for the door.

"I'll set it up with Kait," she shouted after him.

He stifled a groan and went in search of Kait to warn her about Marcie's intentions. He found her staring into the refrigerator again as he had at Congdon's house. This time, she wouldn't need to convince him of Rhodes's involvement.

He approached, but her tense stance said it would be prudent to delay a conversation about Marcie. "Something interesting in there?"

She shook her head. "Pretty much like Congdon's fridge."

He noted the meticulously arranged containers. "Maybe the yogurt says Rhodes hasn't lost it after all."

"Not sure I agree." Kait turned back to the refrigerator. "There's what? A half-dozen or so containers of yogurt? Just like at Congdon's house. Fenton ate a container at precisely ten a.m. each morning. He claimed he needed protein to fuel his brain. If he was on his game, he'd have planned his purchase down to the exact number of containers he needed until he killed each of them."

"That's a good thing then. Rhodes isn't thinking straight. He's bound to slip up, and the perfect crime won't be so perfect any longer."

Her head suddenly shot up. "Perfect. That's it. Just like Nina said."

"That's what?"

"What are the odds of pulling off a perfect crime?"

"Slim to none."

"Yet here we are with very few leads."

"And?" Sam tried to keep the skepticism from his tone, but failed.

She flashed a frustrated look at him. "If Congdon was Fenton's first dance, wouldn't he have screwed up somewhere? It's only after you practice that you can dance like a pro, so maybe there's evidence we're missing."

"Between FED and ERT, I'm positive we haven't missed a thing at Congdon's house, and it doesn't look like there'll be much here either."

She stepped forward and clutched his arm, her gaze locked on his. "I'm not talking about these cases. I mean that a crime this perfect may have been rehearsed a time or two."

He caught her train of thought and didn't like it. Not one bit. "You're thinking Rhodes killed before Congdon. And you don't mean the way he executed Kozlov, but killing someone with the same method he used on Congdon. In preparation."

She nodded. "He always had to be the best at everything. Why not be the best at killing?"

"Could be, I suppose," Sam said, but he hated the thought that Rhodes had taken even more lives.

"One way to find out. ViCAP."

Sam shook his head. "I've already searched the database for the heart and handcuffs."

"Maybe he changed his MO a bit, and the heart has been added as a way of proving his point to me. And if he failed on his trial runs, maybe he removed the handcuffs. Or maybe he never got as far as handcuffing the initial victims." She tightened her grip. "Marcie said something about blowing out someone's lung or causing heart failure if this wasn't done right. What if we should be looking for suspicious deaths involving these medical conditions, instead of a cut-out heart or handcuffs?"

"You have a point," he admitted. "But death by heart attack without any other unusual conditions won't even be in the database."

"We'll add the IV with the rocuronium and the abraded trachea as secondary criteria." Her enthusiasm was contagious.

"Could work," he said warming to the idea. "I suppose since you work for ViCAP's mother ship, you're volunteering for the assignment."

"Absolutely. It's part of my plan to make sure you can't live without me." That smile, the one that made him want something he had no business wanting, slid across her face, and he was already beginning to think life without her after they closed this investigation was going to be far more lonely than it was now. Very lonely indeed.

Dane joined them, his gaze bouncing between them, then settling on Kait. "I just got off the phone with the state police. The tech processing Congdon's car found a flash drive sewed into the lining of his pea coat. But she's the only one on duty, and she's not trained in electronic evidence recovery. Normally, she'd pass the drive on to our department, but I thought since the feds are better equipped to deal with this, you'd want to take it."

"Of course we'll take charge of it." Kait dug out her phone. "Let me get the tech on call down there to pick it up."

"You know how to handle this kind of evidence, right?" Sam asked.

"Wouldn't it be faster if we picked it up, so we could look at it right away?"

Kait thumbed through her phone. "I'd still have to take it back to the office first. Flash drives are notorious hack bombs, and it'll have to be opened in a controlled environment. Plus it'll need to be copied and documented first."

Sam nodded. "Then the sooner we get to your office, the sooner we see what's on that drive."

"STUPID CHARTER plane company!" Fenton screamed at J.J. "How dare they put me off like that when I have a plan? An even stricter one since I don't yet know Lily's location. Delaying my flight for twenty-four hours is not okay. The timeline must be met. Mechanical issues or not, they could find me another plane. Is that so hard?"

His anger begging to explode, he raised his phone, preparing to slam it on the desk. No. This was his pricey smartphone, his lifeline to computer files and banking information, not one of his disposables that he could destroy.

But the anger.

He snatched up his drinking glass and flung it at the wall. The rigid plastic shattered, tiny fragments raining down on the floor.

Better. But not enough.

He clamped his hands over his ears. It hurt. Always hurt. Never relenting. Maybe he should jump the gun. End J.J.'s life. That would bring relief. Finally, sweet relief. But at what cost?

"That's what they want, isn't it, J.J.? They want me to make a mistake so they can win. But I'm better than them. Better than Kait. Better than that stupid detective. I can adjust. Go to plan B." Oh, yes, he was smarter. So much smarter.

He grabbed a paper towel from the desk and crossed the room. "This isn't your fault, J.J. You deserve to have the final hours I planned for you. And thanks to the airplane screw-up, you might get a few more."

Fenton squatted by J.J. to clean up the scattered shards. "What's that? You think I should leave the mess to remember how I nearly lost it and almost did something stupid?" Fenton stood. "You're right. My time is better spent calling up Toby Bradley from the backup list and invoking my contingency plan."

"I knew I could count on you for solid advice." Humming now, Fenton patted J.J.'s head before returning to the desk and opening his photo album. He selected Toby's picture from the envelope and settled it in place. "You haven't met Toby, but he's eager to help. Just like you. See, here he is." He displayed Toby's picture for J.J. "Why the sad face, J.J.? Oh, I get it. You don't want to share your role with Toby. That's priceless, but you'll get your chance in the limelight. I promise."

Fenton's phone emitted a special alarm he'd set to notify him if anyone clicked the link in his spoofed e-mail. He spun to look at his phone. "How delicious." He held out the phone to J.J. "See. It's a text from the detective to the officer at Lily's safe house. Murdock says he's afraid Kait will get hurt and he wants her moved to the safe house, too."

Fenton swiveled the chair back to the desk and logged onto the computer. "A simple trace of the officer's phone, and I'll have the GPS coordinates for Lily before you can blink." He looked at J.J. again. "Sorry, J.J. That was insensitive of me, wasn't it? You can't blink now, can you?"

KAIT STARED AT her computer screen. She was vaguely aware of Sam standing behind her, watching the slide show from the flash drive they'd recovered in Congdon's car. Photo after photo of herself and Lily slipped by on the screen. Lily at daycare. Kait heading to work. Lily and her mom at the park. Kait and Lily grocery shopping. On and on.

"You're too quiet, Kait," Sam said.

"What do you want me to say? That I feel violated again. Sick to my stomach. Because I do." She shuddered. "You have no idea."

Sam perched on the corner of her desk. "I hate that you had to see these pictures on top of everything else, but I'm sure that's what Rhodes is counting on. He wants to show you how vulnerable you are in order to distract you from the case."

She got that—clearly—but it still hurt. Like acid poured in an open wound. Even with the evidence staring her in the face, she could hardly believe it. "The first of these pictures are three weeks old. He tailed me for three weeks. Not simply a day. Three whole weeks or even longer, for all I know. What kind of an agent doesn't know they're being tailed by a sociopath?"

"Stop it, Kait." Sam gripped the arm of her chair and spun her toward him. He got in her face until she looked at him. "You had no reason to suspect a tail, and you sure as shootin' can't go through life feeling paranoid."

"But I—"

"Shh." He pressed his fingers to her lips. "I won't hear you take responsibility for this, too. You're not to blame for any of it. Rhodes is behind it all."

"Right," she replied, though she couldn't put any conviction into her voice.

"Let's not focus on how you feel, but look at the details in the pictures.

Maybe you'll see something that will give us a lead. That's the best way to repay Rhodes."

She turned back to the computer, but no matter how hard she tried to concentrate, she kept seeing her life through Fenton's eyes, and Sam's earlier warning finally rang true.

Fenton was eventually coming after her. If she wasn't prepared, she, too, would wind up chained to a floor, unable to move while Fenton rode off into the sunset with Lily.

Chapter Twenty-Six

FEELING USELESS, Sam paced in the walkway behind Kait and Nina's cubicles. The pictures held nothing of value, so they'd moved on to searching ViCAP. Kait hunted for blown lungs while Nina input the other criteria.

The search was going slowly—too slowly—with Rhodes breathing down their necks.

Marcie had called with Youngblood's official time of death, confirming that they now had precisely seventeen hours before Rhodes killed again. Sam tried to shrug off the tension, but Kait's frantic strokes on the keyboard had made him antsy, and he couldn't stand still.

"Got one," she called out.

He rushed back to her cubicle to find her pointing at the picture on the monitor of a thirty-something male. "Died seven months ago in Salt Lake City. About Fenton's height and weight. Looks like him, too."

Sam scanned the case details. "Victim was a computer programmer."

Kait nodded. "And Fenton hails from Salt Lake City."

"You think he might have moved back there to stay with his family?"

"He has no living family members," Kait said, turning to look up at Sam. "His mother took off when he was a kid and died of an overdose a few years later. His father died a year and a half ago. He had no siblings, which would leave him to inherit the family house, but he never showed up to claim it. So, the city foreclosed on the property and put it up for sale. I personally knocked on the door of the people who bought the place to be sure there was no connection to the Rhodes family."

Sam didn't doubt she'd knocked, and he assumed she'd also run a thorough background check on the family. As consumed as she was with finding Rhodes, she'd have delved into even a hint of a lead.

"What about friends?" Sam asked.

"None that I know of. After Abby died, Nina and I spent a lot of time in Salt Lake City. We went all the way back to Fenton's childhood, and he was a loner then, too. The only person who remembered him very well was his high school technology teacher, but she said Fenton didn't talk to anyone. Not even the other techies."

Not surprising. "But you still think he might have gone back to Salt Lake?"

"If he was hiding out to lick his wounds and plan his revenge, it'd be easier to do so in a familiar place."

"It would also be easier to get caught there."

"True." She tapped the screen. "But this guy died seven months ago, and Fenton could have waited to return to Salt Lake until then. The official investigation had ended long before that, and he wouldn't have been worried about us."

"It's worth following up on." Sam snapped his phone from his belt. "Print out the detective's information for me, and I'll give him a call while you keep searching."

Kait started the printer, then turned back to the screen. Sam stepped away to make his call without disturbing Kait's concentration. He got the detective's voicemail and left a message requesting a return call and a faxed or e-mailed copy of the case file. As he hung up he heard Nina shout, "I may have something, too."

By the time Sam got back to them, Kait was leaning over Nina's cubicle. She'd taken the clip out of her hair, letting it softly fall over her shoulders. Her blouse had come loose from her waistband. She looked a bit disheveled, and he liked the less-than-perfect version of her. Made her seem as if she could lose control and act on the feelings the two of them had bottled up.

He stepped up next to her. She tossed her hair back, sending a hint of vanilla into the air. He was even more aware of her and had to put distance between them. He sidestepped her cubicle and moved closer to Nina who was studying him.

"What did you find?" he asked pointedly, to shift her focus.

She crossed her legs and leaned forward. "A sudden heart failure with trachea abrasion of a thirty-four year old man in Denver."

"Let me guess," he said. "Fits Congdon's height and weight and even looks a bit like him?"

"What do you think?" She turned her screen to face him.

Sam let out a low whistle. "I think Rhodes did indeed have a few dress rehearsals."

"The guy worked in tech support like Congdon," Nina went on. "When he didn't report back to work after his vacation, the supervisor went to his house. Found him on the floor in his office. The ME discovered the trachea abrasion, but didn't find any drugs in his system."

"Doesn't rule him out, though." Kait's voice was filled with conviction. "Marcie said finding rocuronium in a body after a few days could go either way."

"No need to convince me." Nina smiled. "Sounds like a viable lead to me."

Sam got the detective's phone number from the screen and entered it into his phone. "I'll talk to the detective. Plus I'll issue a multi-state broadcast in the event we missed any other suspicious deaths fitting our criteria."

Kait shot him a surprised look. "You really think there are more?"

"Rhodes clearly has no qualms about killing, and these victims might just be the tip of the iceberg," Sam replied, though at the raw pain taking over the enthusiasm in Kait's eyes, he wished he'd kept his big mouth shut.

SAM REMOVED THE Texas-style pizza loaded with chicken, jalapeños, and red peppers from Kait's oven. His mouth watered despite the tension in the air. He glanced at Kait who sat at the counter flipping through the police files they'd received via fax.

After they'd located two additional cases that fit their criteria, one in Minneapolis and one in New Mexico, she'd wanted to stay at the office and work through the night, but he wouldn't let her. They both needed a meal and at least a few hours of sleep. He'd been forced to agree to let her bring the files home, but at some point, he fully intended to take them away from her and slip them under the cushions on the sofa. She'd have to roust him to gain access, because he also intended to sleep there tonight and every night until Rhodes was locked behind bars.

Sam rolled the cutter through the thick dough. "Come and get it."

Kait looked up and smiled. "I didn't think I could eat anything, but it smells so incredible. You'll have to fight me off to get any." She closed the files and stacked them neatly on the corner of the island.

Good. He'd thought he'd have to force her to set them aside. "Let's eat on your deck."

Her smile fell.

Idiot. Remind her of Rhodes's phone call, why don't you. "I didn't mean to make you think about this morning."

"It's okay," she said. "Being here doesn't take much to get me thinking about Fenton. The only spot in the house that's free of him is my bedroom."

He gave her a fiendish smile. "If that means you're inviting me into your—"

"Hold up, sport." She flipped up a hand. "Pizza on the deck will be just fine."

He was glad to see her humor had partially returned. After the photos, he'd thought she might never smile again. "Why don't you take our plates out, and I'll bring the drinks?"

"Let me guess. Now you're trying to get me drunk." She winked at him.

The lighthearted grin that followed kicked his pulse into gear. "Trust me," he said, letting his eyes lock on hers. "If I ever try to get you drunk or really try to get into your bedroom, you'll know about it." He expected her to run the other way. Instead, a shy smile flitted across her mouth.

She nibbled on her lower lip as she picked up the plates. He had to turn away before he snaked an arm around her, jerked her close, and soundly kissed her. He planted his hands on the cool granite and waited until he heard her step outside. He took a few deep breaths, something he'd found himself doing way too often around her. He should leave her to eat alone before he acted on his feelings and then regretted it.

"You waiting for that wine to ferment?" she called from the doorway.

"Be right out," he replied, and poured a glass of the hearty Merlot for her.

He took a long drag on his ice-cold beer, then joined her on the deck. A soft breeze brought the sweet fragrance of jasmine onto the deck, but his mind stubbornly clung to the scent of her shampoo.

She'd sunk into a plush dining chair at a small glass table. He set her wine in front of her. She'd placed his pizza at the seat next to her, but he needed space between them. Lots of space. The whole state of Texas space.

He slid his plate across the table, garnering a questioning look from her, but he ignored it and sat. They ate in silence for a while, both avoiding eye contact. It was awkward and tense, and Sam couldn't stand it. Even stilted small talk was better than this.

"Did you get a chance to phone your mom or Lily today?" he asked, grasping at any safe topic.

She nodded as she chewed.

"They get settled all right?"

"Fine." She picked up her wine glass and took a sip. "They made cookies, and Mom said the house was clean enough."

"A win-win then."

She frowned again. "If you can say putting your parents and niece in a safe house is a win at all."

A cell phone chimed from inside, and she looked at him.

He patted his pocket. "I have mine."

She rushed inside to answer, though he couldn't help but wonder if she was more rushing away from the tension charging the air between them. In truth, he was thankful for the call giving him time to clear his head. But it wouldn't clear. Not a bit.

He kept seeing her after the emotional onslaught of the pictures. Then her resolve surfaced, her shoulders straight and rigid again. Her control back in place, as usual. Ready to tackle ViCAP and find anything to bring Rhodes in. She possessed tenacity in boatloads, and he valued her as a partner in this investigation. Unfortunately, he was beginning to value her in too many other ways and having her around was clouding his thoughts

Twining up her hair, she returned to her chair. The breeze caught strands she'd missed, blowing them softly against her slender neck and tempting Sam to action. He slugged down the last of his beer and waited for her to tell him about the call.

"That was Nina." She snapped a clip in her hair and let her hands fall to her lap. "Quinn got a look at Fenton's medical records. X-rays show fractures consistent with childhood abuse."

He watched her for a moment, gauging how the news was affecting her. All he could see was a surprising wave of sadness. "You feeling bad for him?"

"What?" Her eyes flashed wide. "No! Never! I was thinking about Abby, and wondering if he ever hit her. I never saw any signs of abuse, but he's a monster, so it stands to reason he probably hit her, too." She wrapped her arms around her stomach and sat staring into the distance.

Shoot. She didn't need another thing to eat away at her. And he didn't need another reason to want to offer comfort. For that very reason, he would move on.

"Quinn find anything else?" he asked, but Kait was lost in thought. "Kait?"

She looked up, her sadness deeper. "What?"

He fisted his hands. "The SEAL. He learn anything else about Rhodes?"

She nodded. "A portable ventilator went missing from a Navy base a little over a year ago."

He ran through the dates of the victims they'd discovered tonight. "About the time of the New Mexico killing."

She swirled the wine in her glass. "You're thinking Fenton stole the vent and traveled to New Mexico to claim his first victim."

"Then headed to Minneapolis, Denver, and Salt Lake City before coming here."

"If you're right, then he must have thought moving from state to state would make it harder to catch him, and it has."

"So, other than Salt Lake City, any guesses on how he chose the other locations?"

"Maybe by the people he friended online. Something we can try to track." Kait thumbed through her phone. "Jae was still at the office when we left. I'll text her to add the cities to narrow the focus of her research."

Sam chewed on pizza that now tasted like sawdust and watched her. He'd run into motivated family members in his homicide investigations, but never anyone like Kait. If they didn't find Rhodes, or he didn't kill her, she'd go to her grave feeling guilty for losing her sister. Now, she added Congdon and Youngblood to that list. She'd likely assume guilt for every victim they located. Not a good way to live.

When she got off the phone, he set down his pizza and looked her in the eye. "I meant what I said at the office. You're not to blame for any of this, Kait. You need to let it go before it destroys you."

She arched a brow. "You mean the same way you've let go of the guilt over your former partner?"

He felt bad for letting her think Stacie's death continued to haunt him, but he'd never told anyone about his final argument with Hannah, and he didn't know how to start. Besides, what was the point? He couldn't do anything about it.

"C'mon, admit it," she went on. "You're as eaten up with it as I am about Rhodes, and your every decision is motivated by it."

"I wouldn't go that far," he said, still avoiding spilling his guts. "Maybe you're projecting your own guilt onto me."

"Maybe," she said. "But I don't think so. We're a lot alike, Sam. And if the person who killed your partner wasn't dead, you'd be doing the same thing I'm doing right now."

He felt like a heel for not clarifying that his issues were all about his wife and son, but Kait had enough to deal with without feeling sorry for him, too.

At least, that sounded like a good enough reason to keep his mouth shut.

Chapter Twenty-Seven

IF KAIT WAS GOING to be at her best tomorrow, she needed to sleep, but she couldn't manage it. She'd tried everything. Counting sheep, imagining herself in a happy place, even deep breathing. None of them worked.

With a groan, she climbed out of bed and paced, hoping to eliminate the thoughts buzzing in her head like a mosquito looking for blood. Her mind refused to clear. It remained consumed with thoughts of Lily. Not for her safety—she was with top-notch agents and the decorated officer Sam insisted join them. Lily would be fine. But it was Fenton's serial killer status that was keeping Kait awake. What would happen when Lily grew older and became curious about her birth parents?

Kait would make sure she knew all about Abby, but what should she do about Fenton? News was everywhere these days, and lived on the Internet forever. Lily would surely find posts about these murders. Maybe see the video tape from the TV story this morning. And she'd discover that her father was not only a serial killer, but a taker of hearts. A monster.

Then what? What kind of damage would having a psychopathic killer as a father do to her niece?

Thinking about it was almost more than Kait could bear. She had to do something to free her mind. *Painting.* She could get started on the dining area to blow off this nervous energy then get the sleep she needed.

She jumped into a pair of jeans and an old T-shirt, then padded toward the door leading to the garage. Moonlight filtered through the large overhead window, the soft, hazy light landing on Sam. He was stretched out on the sofa, one arm flung over his eyes, his bare feet hanging over the end. She listened for telltale signs that he was sleeping, but the man didn't snore. Didn't even breathe deeply. Another positive in a list far longer than his negatives, making it hard for her not to think about what it would be like to be in a relationship with him.

Something else to work out with a paintbrush.

She tiptoed to the door and input the first number of her alarm code. The resulting beep sounded through the space.

"Don't even think about it," Sam said before she touched the second button.

Startled, she spun. He was sitting at the end of the couch, his weapon drawn.

"It's just me," she said, trying to catch her breath.

"I know who it is."

"Then why the gun?"

"Ever heard of being prepared?" He sounded angry. "Never know what might happen when you open that door without thorough recon first—which you did not do. Not to mention when you hightail it out of here while you think I'm sleeping." He stood and holstered his weapon. "Mind sharing where you're headed at this time of night? *Alone?*"

"Not that it's any of your business, but I couldn't sleep, and I was going to do some painting. I didn't want to wake you."

"I wasn't sleeping." He approached her. He'd removed his dress shirt and wore a white V neck T-shirt. A thick chain trailed down the vee. A lovely, musky, manly scent clung to him. Even in the dim light, his toned muscles were visible. His belt lay on the table, and his jeans rode on his hips.

"Want to talk about what's keeping you awake?" He'd softened his tone.

Something about him being here in the middle of the night, his shirt off, barefoot and beltless, seemed so intimate. Though she'd be happy to ask him if he had any knowledge about how children of serial killers handled the notoriety, the last thing she needed was to be alone with him. "Not really."

"Oh." One word, but it sounded like he was hurt.

After all he'd done for her, she didn't want him to feel bad. If she put a physical obstacle between them, they could have their little talk, and she'd be fine. "Since we're both up, how about I make a pot of coffee?"

"Sounds good."

In the kitchen, she flipped on the lights and started filling the coffee pot with water. *Better. Less intimate.*

"Have a seat." She gestured at the island and moved to the other side of the kitchen. She poured beans into the grinder and pressed the lid, the whirr of the motor and blades slicing into the beans the only sounds. She dumped the grounds into the basket and flipped the switch on the pot.

"Smells good," he said as he straddled a stool.

She watched coffee fill the carafe while she gathered her thoughts before facing him. She leaned against the counter and recounted her concerns about Lily having a serial killer as a father. "Do you have any experience with this kind of thing? Maybe some advice to share?"

He shook his head. "I've never worked a serial case, but I have seen my share of kids with incarcerated parents come through juvie."

"Great. Juvie. Something to look forward to." Figuring he liked his coffee as sweet at his tea, she put sugar, milk, and a teaspoon on the island.

"Lily isn't going to wind up in juvie, Kait," he said. "She has you and your parents as role models."

"True."

The pot signaled its readiness with a set of shrill beeps. She retrieved mugs from the cupboard and filled them, the steam curling up and evaporating.

She slid a mug across the island to him. "Learning about Fenton is still going to throw Lily for a loop."

He added copious amounts of sugar to the coffee, then cupped his hands around the mug and leaned back on the barstool. "You mentioned looking for a counselor before. He could give you direction in this area, too."

"Actually, I haven't followed through on that. I was looking for someone because I thought Lily was imagining a man coming into her room at night. But now . . ."

"Now we know that she didn't imagine it," he finished for her. "You should still seek professional advice soon. Counselors can help in ways lay people can't."

"That's a surprise coming from a cop. I thought all you guys were too macho to admit counseling's a good thing."

He shrugged. "Sometimes seeing a shrink is the best answer."

She sipped her black coffee and watched him for a moment. He hid his thoughts so well. It frustrated her, yet at the same time she saw it as a challenge. One she would keep plugging away at. "You sound like you're speaking from experience."

He looked down at his hands for a few moments, then seemed to make a mental shrug. "I never realized how hard it is to be a parent."

Right. Change the subject like you always do. His continued evasiveness hurt. Deeply.

"With you in her life," he added, "Lily will be fine."

His comment succeeded where she'd been failing. He pulled her thoughts away from him and the challenge of getting to know him, and put them back where they needed to be. On Lily. On Fenton. And most importantly, on the time ticking down to a murder Fenton had promised to commit.

"AT LAST," FENTON said to J.J. "I didn't think Toby would ever log onto the Internet."

Fenton opened a private chat window on his computer, and his fingers flew over the keyboard. *Would you like to meet for a drink tomorrow, Toby?*

You're in Portland? came Toby's reply.

Fenton typed, *On a layover for business. Staying at a hotel near the Hillsboro airport. Is that convenient for you?* He knew exactly where his ace in the hole, Toby Bradley, lived, but Fenton couldn't very well admit that.

Toby responded, *Sure. When?*

Fenton peered at J.J. "Let's see. I've promised my next surprise for Kait at 5:30 tomorrow, so that means I'll what? Need about two hours to implement by plans for Toby? Yes, two hours should do it."

Fenton looked back at the screen and typed, *3:30 work for you?*

"Sure."

Great, Toby, Fenton typed, the thrill of making a conquest flooding his body. *Then we'll finally meet in person. I'm sure it will be memorable for both of us.*

SAM HELD HIS second cup of coffee and waited for Kait to speak. She'd been hugging that counter across the room and looking at him oddly since they'd come in here. If his cop sense was right, she was thinking about what it was like to have him in her home in the middle of the night. At least, that's what he was thinking about, but it wasn't odd to him. It felt right. Comfortable. Until she'd suddenly clammed up.

She looked up and caught him watching her. "I suppose all of this talk of Lily and juvie has put you off wanting to be a parent."

"Nothing could do that," he said, instantly regretting the longing he'd allowed in his tone.

Her interest intensified. "Were you and your wife planning to have children?"

He was tired of not telling her the truth, but he didn't know if he could get through the story, so he sipped his coffee and ignored her question.

"What is it, Sam?" she asked crossing the room to join him. "Why do you keep shutting me out?"

He shrugged.

Her shoulders drooped. He'd found a vulnerable spot, and he'd hurt her.

"Fine," she said. "I get it. Be that way. Expecting me to share, and then shutting down when the conversation turns to you."

He couldn't add to her pain. He could at least tell her part of the story.

"I was a father. Once," he said, his hand automatically going to the dog tag. "Almost, anyway. Hannah was seven months pregnant when she died in a car accident. A son. We were going to call him Daniel after Hannah's father. Danny for short." He held the tag out for Kait to see. "But Hannah was pinned in the car too long, and they couldn't save him."

"Oh, Sam." She laid her hand on his arm, the warmth giving comfort.

"I'm so sorry. I can't imagine the pain of losing a child."

"Worst part is, I'm the one who sent them out that night. We argued. Hannah took off. It was my fault." He dropped the tag and met her eyes, dark with pity just as he'd expected. Raw, empathetic pity. The very opposite of what he wanted from her.

He wanted her. Plain and simple. As a woman. In his life for as long as she'd have him. But with his issues, how long would that be? She might not want to get involved with anyone right now, but after they apprehended Rhodes, she'd heal and be ready to move on. He knew that. Could feel that. And she'd want children of her own. Children he had no right even to begin to think about fathering. Not after Hannah's warning.

"Did I say something wrong?" Kait asked, clearly confused.

"No."

"But you—"

"It's nothing you've done or said. It's all about me." He smiled to ease her concern, but confusion lingered in her eyes, and it hurt to see her this way. Like a boxing glove to the gut.

Without thinking it through, he ran his thumb over her cheek. He'd meant the touch innocently, but it quickly changed, and he cupped the side of her face. Her breathing sped up, and a small "Oh" of surprise slipped from her lips. He slid his fingers into her hair, the silky stands caressing his fingers. His mind consumed with kissing her no matter the consequences, he moved his hand to the back of her neck and drew her closer. Her lips were inches from his. Her sweet fragrance wrapped around him, her lips open and waiting.

His heart beating a wild rhythm, he lowered his head the remaining distance.

She suddenly stiffened and stepped free. Her chest heaved as she drew in air. She obviously wanted the kiss as much as he did, but she was walking away. "We can't do this, Sam."

"Do what?" he asked.

"Pursue this thing between us."

He knew she was right. Now, anyway. After she'd put space between them and commonsense prevailed. He wouldn't follow through on his feelings, but he wanted—no, needed—to know why she didn't want him to. "As far as I know, I'm single and you're single, so why don't you think something between us would work?"

"Because . . ." Her voice trailed off, and she watched him for a long moment, that raw pain back. "When I look in your eyes, I see myself."

"So I'm letting my feminine side out?" he asked, hoping to lighten things up when he knew what was coming next.

"I'm serious, Sam."

"Sorry. Go on."

"I see my pain. The anguish that never leaves. And now that you've told me about your wife and son, I know the reason for yours. You haven't put your loss behind you, just as I haven't."

She *did* see him. Better than he could imagine. Deep inside where the pain lingered. And, despite her plan to push him away, it made him even more attracted to her.

"And that means we need to put these feelings on the shelf." She shrugged. "Who knows, things could change someday. But for now . . . now, we're colleagues only."

She started to walk away.

He slipped his hand around her wrist. Lightly, so she could pull away if she really wanted to. "I'll still be sleeping on your couch tonight. That's not optional."

She looked at him long and hard. "That doesn't mean I'll do anything about the other."

"Got it," he said.

"It's nothing personal, Sam. You're a great guy. We're both just in bad places."

"Don't worry. I'm good." He smiled and dropped her wrist.

Surprisingly, he really *was* good. It had been a long time since a woman had told him she was interested in him. An even longer time since it really mattered. For the first time in eons, he had hope for the future he desperately wanted.

Chapter Twenty-Eight

FENTON LOOKED at the clock. An hour. Toby had an hour to live and the idiot sat there behind his monitor, three sheets to the wind, oblivious to his upcoming fate.

Of course, Toby wasn't all that much different from Fenton's other conquests. They hadn't seen their maker coming either.

Fenton wouldn't use the vent on Toby, though. J.J. was still using it. Plus, Fenton didn't need Toby for anything other than this house. A place to hole up close to the airport until his plane was ready to depart. So, after Toby's starring role in a World of Warcraft game, and a quick shot of roc, he would slip away. Fenton would rush back to J.J.'s house, retrieve his belongings, and set up Toby's basement to receive Lily and Kait.

Ah, yes, Kait. He couldn't forget Kait. She needed one last scare to distract her while Fenton freed his baby from the feds. Then, and only then, would his grand plan unfold so his daughter once again lived with him, and his darling Abby could finally rest in peace.

KAIT CHECKED HER watch. The day had flown by. Of course it had. Fenton's deadline saw to that. Each disappearing second more important than the last. A mere thirty minutes until he killed again, and they were no closer to stopping him. At the morning task force meeting, they'd decided to focus on the World of Warcraft lead, find Youngblood's van, and follow up with detectives in the cities of Fenton's initial killing spree.

Never leaving the war room except for short breaks, Kait and Jae researched WoW while Sam and Nina worked with the detectives. The table, littered with coffee cups, candy wrappers, and takeout containers, spoke to their frustrations.

Sam lifted his focus from dog-eared files spread in front of him to Jae who sat behind her laptop. "Can you turn that blasted thing down?" he snapped.

"Crabby much?" Jae said above the WoW audio. She wadded up a piece of paper and threw it at him. "Everyone's gone to the dark side in here."

"Not everyone," Nina said, her drawl thick. "I'm still my usual charming self."

"Right, keep telling yourself that." Jae suddenly jerked her gaze to the computer screen.

Hope coursed through Kait's body. "You have something?"

"Maybe."

Kait couldn't sit and wait, so she got up.

Jae eyed her. "You know how I feel about backseat drivers. When I'm sure of what I have, I'll show you."

Kait lowered herself back into the chair.

"Don't look so down," Nina said. "I'm following a promising lead on Minneapolis." They'd taken to calling the out-of-state victims by their city to keep them straight. "He was questioned by our Minneapolis office for a hacking case before he died, and I'm just waiting for the case agent to call me back."

Kait looked at her watch. "With the time zone difference, the agent's likely gone for the night."

"Ooh, ooh, ooh," Jae said.

Kait started to rise.

Jae held up a hand. "Not yet."

"She always this aggressive?" Sam asked, scowling at her.

"Hey, what can I say?" Jae grinned. "I'm good, and I know it."

"Which means we give her a lot of leeway," Nina added.

"No freakin' way!" Jae shot to her feet, her eyes glued to her screen. "It's better than I thought."

Kait resisted the urge to stand.

"Well what're you guys waiting for?" Jae's grin widened. "This is it."

Kait hurried around the table, but Sam had beaten her to Jae. He looked at the screen and frowned. "Exactly, what am I looking at?"

"World of Warcraft." Jae's well-duh tone showed her lack of understanding for non-gamers.

"Have at it, Kait." Sam stepped aside. "You can explain it to me."

Kait quickly took in the WoW scene where several characters stood in a grassy spot outside the city of Stormwind. A human character named Abby4Ever and another called AgentOfDoom stood facing each other.

Kait cringed and took a step back.

"What?" Sam asked. "What is it?"

Jae tapped her finger on each woman. "They're identical, and look at their names. Abby4Ever is obviously Abby, and the other, AgentOfDoom, is a play on Kait's status as an agent."

As Kait watched, the characters both walked toward the city. "Fenton can't be playing both characters at the same time."

"No, he can't," Jae said.

"Since I'm sure he'd want to be the Abby character, he's conned someone else into being me."

"Can someone explain this to me?" Sam asked sounding frustrated.

"When you start playing WoW, you choose and customize an avatar—an electronic image of a person or thing." Jae pointed at the Abby4Ever character. "Rhodes created a human avatar that resembles Abby, and it looks like he had someone else create Kait."

"Are you sure this is right?" Sam squinted at the screen. "Wanting to be a woman while playing a game doesn't sound like Rhodes."

"Actually, it's quite common for guys to choose attractive females as their avatars," Nina answered without looking away from the screen. "Gives them something sexy to look at while they play."

"And naming the character Abby4Ever means he was likely paying homage to Abby," Kait said.

"Or fantasizing that she's still alive," Nina added.

Sam eyed Jae. "How did you find this, and how can you be sure Rhodes is behind it?"

"I trailed Congdon all over the web, leading me to his WoW account. That gave me his character name, AgentOfDoom. I figured the agent part meant something, so I checked out the players in his guild and found Abby4Ever. That name couldn't possibly be a coincidence, so I started looking for the names of Rhodes's other victims in his guild, but didn't find any. Then I got to thinking maybe Rhodes played with other guilds, too, so I searched for other Abby4Ever characters."

Kait listened to the discussion, but couldn't take her eyes off her character. Her avatar look-alike was attacked by a character from the other guild, and she suddenly dropped to the ground. Kait gasped and waited for the avatar to get up, but she lay in a heap on the stones. "Do you think—"

"He just killed another one?" Jae asked. "Yeah. I think so."

"For real killed someone?" Sam asked clearly confused.

Kait glanced at the clock. "His twenty-four hour deadline just passed, so it's reasonable to assume he'll soon lead us to the body of the man he conned into playing me in this game."

"I don't get it." Sam stared at the screen. "You said he doesn't control other characters, so he couldn't arrange to have AgentOfDoom be attacked and die like this."

"Actually," Nina corrected. "Abby4Ever's job in the game is to protect Kait, but clearly that didn't happen. Which means, if Rhodes is controlling Abby4Ever like we think he is, he withheld support from Abby4Ever and let Kait's avatar die."

Like in life, Kait thought.

As a heavy cloud settled over the room, Jae dropped into her chair and navigated to a WoW stats page that displayed a list of Abby4Ever and AgentOfDoom characters.

Kait counted down the screen. "Nine. He's killed nine?"

"Not yet," Jae said. "But you're looking at the list of all of his victims. Looks like he role-played Kait's death with each of them in WoW."

"How do you know?" Sam asked sounding skeptical.

"I looked at the individual stats of each AgentOfDoom character. The date each character was last seen in the game is the same day one of Rhodes's victims died." Jae tapped the bottom AgentOfDoom name. "This one corresponds with New Mexico's death." She moved up the screen and tapped the next one. "Minneapolis." She continued to move up the list. "Denver. Salt Lake City, Congdon, Youngblood, and the one we just saw. The last two are still active and might still be alive."

Kait squeezed Jae's shoulder. "Amazing work, Jae. He played in all these guilds, but you found the connection."

Sam frowned. "Give us the address for each guy, and we'll track Rhodes that way."

Jae's hand dropped to her side. "Sorry. I don't have access to private accounts, so I don't have their addresses. I'll need a warrant to obtain that information."

Sam came to his full height, resolve burning in his eyes. "Then get one, and let's find him. And while you're at it, get one for Rhodes's credit card information, too."

"We'll request it," Nina said. "But there's no way Rhodes was sloppy enough to give WoW any legit information."

"What about the IP address or whatever you call that thingy that tells us where he logs onto the Internet?" Sam asked, surprising Kait that he was the one to bring up technology.

Nina shook her head. "By the time we get any actionable information, he'll be long gone."

"But we have to do something, or he's going to kill the others." Sam swung his gaze to Kait.

She focused on her dead avatar look-alike and couldn't dispute Sam's logic. There were two more guys on Fenton's list, and then they had to assume he was coming for her.

THE CONFERENCE room walls closed in on Sam. The nasty, irritating smell of burnt microwave popcorn clung to the air, and the atmosphere in the war room had grown more tense—if that was possible—after seeing Kait's look-alike falling to the ground. He'd expected to see blood oozing from her body, but at least they were spared that sight.

Needing water, Sam started to get up, but paused when a woman he didn't recognize stepped into the room.

"Why the long faces?" she asked.

"Becca!" Kait jumped to her feet and hurried across the room.

Ah, the missing cyber crimes team member.

"The three of them are inseparable," Jae said as she packed up her laptop. "They sometimes let me tag along, but it's hard to get into the inner sanctum. Not that I'm jealous or anything, but if you're thinking what I think you're thinking about Kait, good luck."

Sam ignored her comment, and, as he waited for an introduction, he watched the trio. All three were tall, nearly six feet, but that's where the similarity ended. Nina was all curves. Kait, long and lean, moved with grace, and then there was that very regal posture. Becca was muscular, tomboyish, with no makeup. She wore jogging shorts, a Portland FBI T-shirt, and had blond hair scraped back in a ponytail.

Jae slung her computer case over her shoulder and stopped next to the women. "Let me know when the warrant comes in with the names from WoW, and I'll run their backgrounds."

"Thanks." Kait smiled at Jae. "We couldn't have done this without you."

Sam stepped up to them. "*This* isn't done until we bring Rhodes in, so don't start celebrating yet," he said, hoping Kait hadn't pinned her hopes on this lead. Sure, it was a good one, but his years on the job told him good leads could evaporate quickly.

Becca turned and gave him a quick once-over. "You must be the detective I've heard so much about." She stuck out her hand. "I'm Becca Lange."

Surprised Kait would have mentioned him, he glanced at her as he shook hands with Becca.

Kait's face colored. "We should get back to work."

Sam would have to be blind to miss her obvious avoidance of Becca's comment, but he wouldn't pursue it now.

"What can I do to help?" Becca took a rigid stance and peered at Kait as if she was raring to go even at this late hour.

"I was just about to tell Kait to get out of here," Nina said, and quickly held up her hand. "And before you say no, Kait, even if we get the warrant tonight, it's not likely we'll receive any response from WoW until after their lawyers look at it in the morning."

Kait shook her head. "I'll stay just in case."

Becca planted her hands on Kait's shoulders. "No offense, Kait, but you look worn out. Nina and I will hold down the fort while you take a break. I'll call you the second we get any information."

Kait's shoulders sagged a fraction. "Promise?"

"Promise."

Nina faced Sam. "You are escorting Kait home again, right?"

"Won't let her out of my sight," Sam replied, and though he knew Kait would balk at his need to hover over her, he'd be there by her side. Day and night, keeping her safe from the lowlife who remained out of their reach.

Chapter Twenty-Nine

KAIT STARED AT her plate. She usually loved Kung Pao Chicken, but the Chinese takeout sat untouched. Sam didn't have the same problem. He'd powered through his food, and his plate was almost empty. They'd decided to have a casual meal in front of the TV for distraction, but Kait had paid little attention to the movie.

She set her plate on the coffee table, tucked her feet up under her, and tried to figure out what was happening on the screen.

Sam looked at her. "You've been quiet all through dinner."

"Just thinking," she said.

"Talking about whatever's bothering you might clear your mind." He watched her carefully. Intently. Like he was seeing her from the inside out. And, instead of feeling uncomfortable, she liked knowing he cared enough to want to understand.

"Is it the World of Warcraft thing?" he went on. "I mean, I gotta admit it was kind of creepy seeing you killed, even if it was just an avatar."

She shook her head. "We're finally getting close to locating Fenton, I can feel, it, you know? And that has me thinking about what will happen after we bring him in."

"You mean his trial?"

"No, no. It's . . . I've just . . . the last few years . . . revenge has kept me going. I never thought about what life would be like without that driving me." She planted her hands firmly on her knees and forced herself to continue. "Then tonight, out of the blue, it hit me. I'd have my life back. No more living for someone else. So what might my life look like then?"

"And?"

"Other than Nina and Becca, I realized I've shut everyone else out." *Except you*, she thought but didn't say. "Without them and Lily, my life would be pretty empty."

"So you're rethinking giving up Lily to your mom."

She nodded. "I'd be a fool to let her go. I should never have let Mom get to me. Maybe it was the stress. Or maybe I needed to spend the night away from Lily to see how much I'd miss her. I don't know which, but I know I want to raise her. Not because of some promise made to Abby, but because I love her. Really love her. She brings meaning to my life."

"No offense to your mother, but thinking about breaking this kind of news to her would keep me from eating, too." He grinned.

"There's that," she said and smiled at him for a moment. "But I can handle my mom."

"Okay, so why can't you eat, then?"

She took a moment to take a drink of water and gather her thoughts. "I was so close to losing it when Abby died. Really losing it—like mental hospital losing it. So maybe I've used the hunt for Fenton to keep that from happening—from really grieving for Abby. You know what I mean? And once this is all over, I'll fall apart."

"That's not really something you can predict." He shifted closer and took her hand.

She sat for a moment, feeling the rough calluses on his fingers grazing hers, enjoying his touch, wishing she could let go of everything and move on. "I'm afraid I'll totally collapse. Then what?"

"Then you pick yourself up." He moved closer. "It's all natural. All about a process you have to go through."

"Still, after three years?"

"There's no expiration date for grief. We all have our timelines and ways of getting through it. You'll just have to see what happens." He squeezed her hand. "You're strong, Kait. Exceptionally strong. Nothing in the last few days has bested you, and I know you can deal with anything."

She smiled her thanks at him and was rewarded with a sincere smile that lit up his face and captured her breath for a moment. "I figured if anyone got this, it'd be you. I mean, since you're still not over losing your wife and all."

He twined his fingers with hers. "I'll always miss Hannah, but after a solid year of counseling, I've made peace with the loss."

So he *had* gone to counseling. "Then why the sadness I see in your eyes all the time?"

He let go of her hand and looked away, retreating as he always did.

"Do I have to remind you, confiding is a two way street?" she asked, somewhat irritated.

He looked back at her. "I'm sorry, it's just—" He shrugged. "I've never told anyone about this."

"Trust me, with my issues, I'm in no place to judge." She rested a hand on his knee for reassurance. "As someone said just a few minutes ago, tell me and maybe it'll clear your head."

"You're going to use my own words against me, huh?" A crooked grin washed the pain from his face.

As much as she liked seeing him smile, she wouldn't fall for his diversionary tactics. "Don't try to change the subject."

"Fine. You asked for it." He freed his hand and shoved it into his hair. "After Stacie died, I let all the questions of life and death get to me. You know what I mean? Those questions, like why her, why not me? What's the point of living? Things like that, and I shut down."

"A normal reaction to death. I did the same thing."

"Maybe, but I didn't deal with it. Instead, I let the problem escalate. So much so, that I shut Hannah out, and we had some problems. She couldn't understand why I didn't just snap out of it. I clammed up more." He shook his head. "When she found out she was pregnant, she said I was emotionally bankrupt and in no frame of mind to raise a child."

His pain cut a knife through Kait's heart. "That was kind of harsh."

"But true. I *was* bankrupt. Totally." His face was tight with emotion. "But the thing is, once Hannah told me about Danny, I started to feel something. Like maybe he could give me back what I'd lost, you know? When things got rough, I hung onto that."

"And then she was killed."

"Yeah . . . I mean, not exactly." He got up, went to the window, and stared out, when Kait knew all he could see was the wall of black reflecting from the glass. "I thought I'd made progress in our relationship—been there more for her. But the night she died, she told me I hadn't changed enough. Couldn't change enough. She said I had no business ever being a father, and she wanted a divorce."

Kait joined him, and at the completely exposed pain in his eyes, she realized how much she wanted to help him heal. Maybe heal herself at the same time. "It's not true, you know. I've only spent a few days with you, but I saw you with Lily. I see you with Marcie and your co-workers and how you offered to help Mrs. Congdon. How gentle and patient you've been with me." She pressed a hand over his heart. "You have a kind and generous heart, Sam, and any child would be happy to call you dad."

He locked eyes with her. "You're just telling me what you think I want to hear."

"No, I'm not. I mean it." She took his hand in hers. "All of it. If we were together, I'd be proud to have you as Lily's father and to have your child."

He watched her, his eyes seeming to drink in everything about her.

"You're a good man, Sam Murdock, and it's about time you know that."

He suddenly dropped her hand and slid his arms around her waist to pull her closer. Her heart thumped like a conga drum.

"Kait," he whispered and searched her eyes for a long moment before lowering his mouth toward hers.

She should step away, run away. But suddenly, this thing between them felt right. His lips, warm and urgent settled on hers. Her body exploded with emotions long dormant, and time stood still as his lips caressed hers. He drew her even closer, and she slid her arms around his neck, clinging to him like a life preserver. Maybe he was her lifesaver—put in her life to bring her back from the brink of despair. Maybe she was supposed to bring him back, too.

FENTON PARKED on the street behind Kait's house and grabbed his binoculars from the backseat. Perfect. Everything was going according to plan. If you didn't count the airline. No matter. It had all been rescheduled, and he'd soon be on his way to Mexico with Lily.

But first, another delivery.

He darted into the neighbor's yard behind Kait's house. The all-expense-paid vacation he'd given to the occupants as a bogus contest prize guaranteed they'd been cruising all week, and he had full run of their property. He climbed onto a small bench near the fence that abutted Kait's backyard and pointed his binoculars at her picture window.

"What in the world?" he whispered and blinked hard.

The detective held her in his arms, kissing her as if he never intended to let her go.

No! This was not in Fenton's plan. How dare she enjoy a man's touch when his one true love was buried?

Abby, I miss you so much.

He missed everything, but he especially missed kissing her. Her lips were so soft. Sweet. Like nectar. He wanted her here instead of Kait. Desperately. Not this temptress moving against the detective, making Fenton ache for Abby's body pressed against his.

"Abby," he closed his eyes and whispered. "Are you there, sweetheart?"

"Of course," he heard her say.

"Really there?"

"Yes. You killed Kait, remember? She died on the field outside Stormwind. You vanquished her forever."

"You're right, love." He opened his eyes and looked through the binoculars. He rubbed his eyes and looked again, anger frothing up his throat.

"Get your grubby mitts off my wife," he snarled. "She's mine. All mine."

No man kissed Abby and lived to tell about it. He climbed down and hurried to his vehicle, spotting the patrol car sitting out front of Kait's house.

Hah! The cop could sit there all night, and Fenton would still get to Kait. Didn't they know by now that they couldn't stop him?

Wait. Kait. Kait was kissing the detective, not Abby, right?

Seriously, he needed to get some sleep, but there was no time. He'd have to make do with energy drinks. He swigged the last of an open can then popped the trunk of J.J.'s Challenger and retrieved his rifle. He settled the ammo in the chamber, picturing the detective's face with each slug he inserted.

Better. He was feeling better already—even if this wasn't exactly how he'd planned to leave the package for Kait. Rifle in hand, he grabbed the box, then returned to the neighbor's backyard. He climbed up on the same bench facing Kait's property and focused the binoculars.

It *was* Kait with the detective. At least Fenton thought so.

No matter. Either way, the detective needed to die.

Fenton jumped to the ground and removed fence boards he'd loosened earlier in the week. He slipped through the opening hidden behind tall bamboo stalks on Kait's property and crept toward her deck. The closer he came to her picture window, the clearer he could see them and their sickening infatuation with each other. Fenton itched to pummel the detective, but Fenton wasn't ready for Kait to see him.

Not yet.

He set the box under a bench built into the railing on Kait's deck, then slid it forward for good measure.

"There you go, Brian," he whispered as he retreated. "Your contribution won't be as meaningful as I had hoped—what with killing the detective and all, but it will still prove a point."

Back at the fence, he lifted the weapon and sighted it in. Perfect. He could get off a few good shots, then he'd have to hightail it out of there before the cop sitting sentry out front reacted.

Now Fenton just needed the lovebirds to step apart and . . . *bang.* Life would end for one of them, and Kait's grief would make her wish hers had ended as well.

Chapter Thirty

A GUNSHOT shattered the silence and pulverized the window. Glass peppered Sam's neck as a lancing pain razored through his chest. Kait spun toward the window, a bewildered look on her face.

Pop.

Another bullet grazed his arm. The pain cut him to the quick, but he ground his teeth to fight it off and used his good arm to tackle Kait to the floor. He dragged her from the window and under the table.

Another bullet whizzed overhead. The table exploded. Glass rained down on both of them, shards clinging to Kait's hair and the folds in her clothing. She started to rise.

"Stay down," he commanded, covering her body as completely as possible.

"Is that blood I feel on my back?" She tried to turn over, but he held her fast. "Are you hit?"

"It's just a scratch," he said, though he felt his blood soaking his shirt. At this rate, it wouldn't be long until he lost consciousness.

Before he did, he had to ensure she was protected. He searched the room for his walkie-talkie. Spotted it a few feet away where it had landed after the table came crashing down. He couldn't go for it or he'd leave Kait unprotected—the last thing he'd do.

She raised her back, throwing him off and rolling out from under him. He was too weak to stop her from standing, but thankfully, she remained lying there, staring at him, her lips puckered as she reached out to touch his shirt.

She frowned. "It's more than a scratch. Let me get something to apply pressure."

"No." He clamped a hand on her wrist, but his strength was already receding and would do little to hold her here. "Rhodes wants to kill you, and I won't risk you getting up."

"Murdock, report," Officer Taylor said over the walkie-talkie.

Sam bit down on his lips and crawled a few feet, pain burning through his body with every movement. The room swam before him. He blinked and breathed deep, then grabbed the comm device.

"I should call 911," Kait said, obviously not thinking clearly.

"Your phone's in the other room, and I have Taylor right outside." He tried to lift the walkie-talkie, but it felt like a boulder sat on his arm, and he couldn't manage it.

She moved as if to stand.

Too weak to stop her, Sam said, "Don't get up. I can't lose you, Kait. Not now. Not when I . . ." The strength to talk evaporated.

She slid over to him and took his hand, her gaze hungrily seeking his. "Don't worry, you won't lose me. And before you pass out, get it through your thick head, Sam Murdock, I'm not letting you die either. You got that? You are not going to die today or any day soon."

Darkness circled his vision, and he knew he only had a moment before losing consciousness. He lifted his arm, painfully, slowly, the black cloak taking his vision nearly winning.

"Officer down," he said into his walkie-talkie and focused on Kait as he let the darkness claim him.

WOW, MAN! THAT was something! Fierce. Intense. Fenton wanted to do it again, but he had to get out of there. He floored the gas and peeled out of Kait's neighborhood.

"Awesome ride, J.J.," Fenton said, thankful the guy needed to prove his masculinity with a sports car.

Fenton's heart hammered against his chest, but he felt more alive than he had in years. Sure, taking lives with roc had been sweet, but besting a cop? A homicide detective at that? Well, that just proved who was superior, didn't it?

"I am."

Sirens cut through the quiet as a police car raced toward Kait's house. Fenton slowed his ride. Wouldn't due to draw attention to the flashy car. Another siren joined the fray. Then another. And another.

Of course. He'd shot a cop. One of their own. They'd leave no stone unturned until they found him.

Problem?

Maybe, or maybe it was another chance to prove who was superior. Not that there was any question. He was the best. He'd come out of this just fine.

THE SMELL, THE one of death, clung in the air at the hospital. So like the day they'd rushed Abby to the same ER. The family speeding here. Hope, though it was futile, had lingered in Kait's brain. She'd arrived, held Lily, heard the doctor pronounce Abby dead. Not a surprise, but the finality of the pronouncement had taken Kait down.

Now she hated hospitals, but so what? She might be uncomfortable here, but she wouldn't leave Sam. Even though he'd made it through surgery and the doctor had said he'd recover. She'd stay by his side until all danger had passed.

She went to his bed. Afraid to touch him. Afraid not to. "Sam," she whispered. "I need to hear your voice. Just to be sure you're okay." She took his hand. "Please?"

His eyes fluttered briefly before his lashes settled again. Not letting go of his hand, she took a seat. She could still feel his kiss on her lips. Feel her heart swell with happiness. For the briefest of moments, she'd dared to hope, to believe she could finally move ahead, let someone into her life. And now . . . now this? Him lying in bed, pale and clinging to life.

Was she meant to live life alone? Was that what God wanted for her?

Maybe she should back off now while she could—before she fully vested herself in this man. That was the wise thing to do. The sensible thing. So why didn't she want to heed her own advice?

He stirred and moaned, pulling his hand free. His eyes opened. He blinked hard a few times, then a weak smile played over his mouth.

"Hey there," he said so quietly she could barely hear him. His southern drawl was thick with sleep, bringing up thoughts of what it would feel like to wake up next to him every morning. That sweet smile the first thing she saw, followed by his honey voice warming her to the core. How amazing that would be.

Could she really be happy in life? Let go of the fears and regrets to have it all?

"Guess we both made it out okay," he said.

"Guess so." She grabbed the container holding the slug removed from his chest and stood to show it to him. "And you even have a souvenir to prove it. Of course, Nina's coming by to get it and lock it up in an evidence locker, but once Fenton's behind bars and all the appeals are over, I'm guessing you'll find a way to get hold of it."

"Kait," he said.

"Yes?"

That smile returned again. "Mind giving me a kiss? Just so I know I'm really alive."

A kiss? She couldn't kiss him. That would make him think after she responded so freely to his kiss at her house that she wanted a relationship with him. But she was far from making any commitment to him. At least, not now. There was still so much to do. To process.

He frowned. "Is it too much to get a kiss? Just one."

She couldn't deny him. Not when he was lying there so pale and helpless, all because he'd been drawn into the drama that was her life. She settled her lips on his for a chaste kiss and pulled back.

"You call that a kiss?" His arm came around her back like an iron band. His strength took her by surprise, as did the passionate kiss that followed.

He released her and sighed contentedly. "Oh, yeah, I'm alive, baby. So alive."

She wanted to feel alive, too. Really, she did. To experience everything she'd put on hold for her quest to find Fenton. Question was, did she want it badly enough to do something about it, or had the last three years of soul-crushing loss taken away her ability to embrace and enjoy life?

HUMMING, FENTON parked in J.J.'s driveway. It had felt so satisfying to kill the cop. What was he going to do after Kait was dead? Would he still need that zing, that excitement, or would he finally be at peace? His revenge would be complete, and he'd have Lily. What more did he need?

In the house, the sound of movement coming from the bedroom stopped him cold. He listened.

Scratching, clawing, mixed with jingling.

Was J.J. awake somehow, or was someone else here?

He eased down the hallway and found the door locked just the way he'd left it. J.J. had to be awake. But how?

Fenton opened the padlock and pushed open the door. J.J. looked up, his eyes alert, terror clinging in the depths. He jerked harder at his cuffs.

"How did you wake up?" Fenton asked as he stepped into the room.

J.J.'s eyes cut up to Fenton. He tried to talk, but the tube in his throat left only a gurgling sound

Fenton *tsk*ed. "Don't struggle. It will only make things worse."

He checked the infusion pump and found it malfunctioning. "Here's the problem." He peered at J.J. "Don't worry. This won't change your starring role at all."

As J.J. squirmed and bucked, Fenton retrieved a syringe from his bag, drew in a vial of rocuronium, and inserted it into the IV. He smiled down on J.J. whose facial muscles instantly relaxed. "There, that's better, isn't it? Stress isn't good for you. Not now. Not when it's near the end. In fact, why don't I let the drug work into your system while I locate Kait?"

Fenton sat in the desk chair and checked the GPS for the detective's cell phone. He cross-referenced the data with an Internet map, and confirmed they'd taken Murdock to the hospital. He had to assume Kait accompanied him. If Murdock was still alive, she'd be there. By his side. Fawning like a woman in love.

That had to end. Now.

He got comfortable in front of the computer and worked his way through the hospital's firewalls.

"How disappointing, J.J. Their security's better than many institutions, but even you could hack it." He sighed. "No one ever lives up to the challenge. It's getting boring. I need something bigger. Better. A high-stakes target. Maybe the defense department. Wouldn't that be fun once I'm settled with Lily?"

"Let's see, now." He clicked through the records, soon locating Murdock's file. "So he's alive and the prognosis is a full recovery. That's unfortunate." Fenton made note of the detective's room number, then looked at J.J. "You know, I thought this would make me mad, but I just don't care. I'm so close to my goal. Plus, I have your starring role to look forward to."

He watched J.J., wishing he hadn't drugged him. With J.J. awake and conscious, Fenton could see the man's fear. Taste it. Revel in it. He supposed he could wait for the drug to wear off. But he had a timeline. And with Murdock in the hospital, it meant Kait would be there, too, and it would take more time get to her.

"You know," he said to J.J. "I'd have liked to see the detective die, but maybe his living is an unexpected bonus for both of us. I can give your special contribution to Kait while she's at the hospital. What a rush it'll be to move around unseen while she's surrounded by all the cops who came to see Murdock. And it'll get everyone talking about you. You'll be famous." He looked at J.J. "I know what you're thinking. It's a risk to show up there, but then, the biggest risks have the biggest payoffs. A quick change in my appearance, and I'll blend in perfectly."

Pumped up, Fenton grabbed his reciprocating saw. He checked to be sure the blade was seated correctly, then squeezed the trigger. The powerful motor hummed in his hand as the blade sawed through the air.

"Perfect," he said, releasing the trigger and squatting next to J.J. "This ending will be just right, J.J. Just perfect. It's time to say goodbye, my friend. Kait needs your gift."

SAM WATCHED Kait sleep in the recliner. Her head was tilted at an awkward angle, her breathing even and deep. He'd never seen the strong in-charge woman at rest. This Kait seemed approachable. Reachable.

His for the asking.

He imagined her waking up and stretching. Looking at him as she had before the gunfire, the interest mixed with surprise smoldering in her eyes. Not like the questions lurking there when he'd woken from the surgery. She was rethinking her willingness to open up. To get hurt again.

Not him. Not any longer. His near brush with death took care of that. He didn't even want to close his eyes again. He wanted to live. To simply live life to its fullest. She'd touched a part of him that he didn't know existed anymore. A part that told him he could be the father Kait said he'd be. A part that made him feel. Deeply. Wonderfully. And he had to see where this thing with Kait took them—after they brought Rhodes in. Anything before that would go nowhere. She had to finish her mission first.

Sam closed his eyes and concentrated on sleeping. He needed to gain his strength so tomorrow, he could be by her side again and track down Rhodes with renewed vengeance.

FENTON PARKED in the hospital lot, adjusting the soft white cotton shirt of his EMT uniform, courtesy of a gig with a private ambulance company. After leaving the Navy, he'd given the job a chance for a full month, but really . . . no one could live on those wages. At least, no one who wanted to eat anything but macaroni and cheese and hot dogs. So, he'd quit. Kept the uniform, though, and it had come in handy several times. But tonight would be the crowning jewel.

Expecting to see a parking lot full of cop cars and unmarked vehicles, he climbed out. Surprisingly, he spotted only civilian cars. Perhaps Murdock had only a few friends. Fenton certainly didn't like him, if that was any indication.

Fenton grabbed the box containing J.J.'s contribution and a disposable cell phone, then picked up the present he'd brought to ensure the nurse's cooperation. He strolled across the empty lot. At this time of night, the building was nearly deserted, and he made it to the elevator without notice. Without human notice, but security cameras everywhere recorded his movements. At least he hoped they did, giving Murdock something to stew over when he discovered Lily and Kait were missing.

He exited on the third floor and held up the box to be sure the camera captured it clearly. He marched down the hallway like he belonged. Not a single hospital employee questioned his presence. Just as he suspected, people were too wrapped up in their own lives to look beyond the surface, and the uniform ensured they'd pay him no notice.

He found the detective's door ajar and peered through the crack. He spotted Murdock soundly sleeping in his bed. Fenton should cross the room and smother the man. It would be simple. Lift the pillow and then . . . then Kait would wake up from the recliner and discover her lover gone.

She stirred, and Fenton jumped back.

Stick to the plan, man, stick to the plan.

He backtracked down the hall to the nurses' station. A tired, middle-aged nurse with frizzy hair and a round face looked up at his approach. He glanced at her nametag.

"I'm so sorry to disturb you when you're obviously busy, Laura," he said working hard to be as charming as possible.

She lifted a shoulder in an unenthusiastic shrug. "Hey, I work a skeleton crew on the graveyard shift just like you, so what can I expect?"

He made sure to offer a conspiratorial smile as he set the box on the counter. "My friend is sitting with Detective Murdock tonight, and she forgot her phone. I don't want to wake her, so I wondered if I could leave it with you. She'll come get it from you when she wakes up."

Laura glanced suspiciously at the box.

"I know, it's kind of a big box for a phone, but I packed her favorite chocolates inside." He reached under the box and pulled out a candy sampler. "Figured the hardworking nursing staff could use some, too."

"Be still my heart." She smiled, revealing crooked teeth. "You're not only good-looking, but you can read a woman's mind, too. If I wasn't married . . ."

Gross. Don't even put such a thought in my head.

She took the candy and had ripped open the cellophane before he could speak. She stared at the treats. "What's your friend's name?"

"Kaitlyn Knight."

She popped a caramel into her mouth, smacking her gums over the sticky concoction, and he wanted to strangle her. He fisted his hands and continued to smile.

She grabbed a sticky note, slapped it on the box, and then scrawled out Kait's name. "If she's not up by the time my shift ends, you want me to deliver this to her?"

"Yes, please, that would be so helpful," Fenton gushed, though there was no need for Laura's help. After the phone call he planned to make moments after taking Lily, Kait would be wide awake and seeking out the package. Of that, he was sure.

Chapter Thirty-One

SNICKERS OR Milky Way? Both bars perched in the hospital vending machine looked good to Kait. She hadn't eaten anything except snacks in the war room, and either candy bar would do the trick. Snickers, she decided. It contained peanuts, and that meant protein. She inserted coins into the slot, and the bar dropped through the machine, the solid *thunk* reverberating through the silence of the patient waiting area.

She bent to retrieve it and caught a look at her watch. 2:50, and they still hadn't heard from World of Warcraft. Nina had received the warrant and passed it on to their night supervisor who promised to phone his manager at home and get back to them. That was three hours ago, and still no word. Meanwhile, Fenton was getting away with almost killing Sam.

She ripped open the wrapper and took a bite of the candy, the sugar instantly soothing her. They'd catch him. They had to. She couldn't come this close to him for the second time in as many days and let him get away.

Her phone vibrated in her pocket. Hoping it was Nina, Kait chomped another bite of the gooey goodness and dug it out. Not Nina or a number she recognized. Could be the WoW people, she supposed.

"Kaitlyn Knight," she answered eagerly.

"I have her, Abby," Fenton said, his voice lit with excitement. "Lily's right here in my arms. We can finally be together again."

Abby?

Did he think she was Abby? Did he really have Lily?

No. No. Not likely. Not with the expert security team assigned to her. More likely Fenton was losing it. Still, a niggle of fear started in the pit of her stomach.

"Abby," he whispered. "Did you hear me?"

"Yes," Kait choked out the word, hating to impersonate her sister, yet knowing she needed to play along until she was sure he didn't have Lily.

"Will you come to me now so the three of us can be reunited at last?" His tone was sensual and repulsive.

Her stomach contents curdled, and she tossed the candy bar in the trash. "Yes. Where are you?"

"Daddy," Lily's sleepy voice sounded from the background.

No! Oh, God no! Don't let it be true.

"Yes, baby," Fenton all but cooed.

"I want Nantie Kait," Lily said.

"You mean you want Mommy?" Fenton asked.

"Mommy's in heaven. I need Kait."

"Kait. Kait. Kait!" His volume rose with each utterance of her name. "It's always about Kait."

She heard Lily whimper.

"*Shh*, pumpkin, I'm right here," Kait said loud enough for her niece to hear.

"Nantie Kait." Her pitiful cry shot through the phone.

"I'm coming, pumpkin. Just be patient. Okay?"

"'K." She fell silent.

"That's it, Lily," Fenton said sounding calmer again. "Daddy's got you. Now, close your eyes and go back to sleep."

Kait heard Fenton humming, and she imagined him rocking Lily to sleep. Kait's stomach rebelled again. Acid burned up her throat, but she had to keep it together and stay on the line for Lily.

"Kait," Fenton finally said, proving he'd come to his senses. "As you can tell, I have Lily."

Kait desperately wanted to find Lily, but his demanding tone said he expected her to react in fear to this situation. If she did, he'd be in control. She needed to remain in charge, so she said nothing.

"Fine. You obviously doubt me. I don't know how you can after hearing her, but I'm texting you a picture as proof. I warn you, you need to stay on the line with me as you look at it, or we'll disappear, and you'll never see her again. Do you understand, Kait?"

"Yes." Though she needed no proof, she went along with it in hopes of coming up with a way to rescue her niece.

"Sending the text now," he said. "Tell me when you get it."

She thumbed to her messages. "Got it."

She opened the picture of Lily sitting on Fenton's lap, and her knees lost all strength. She clutched the wall for support.

He chuckled. "I'll take your silence to mean you're looking at the picture."

"Yes," she answered, barely able to speak.

"Good. Good. Now, if you want to see Lily again, you will follow my directions to the T and not stray at all. You'll tell no one about my call, but come straight to me."

"Why would I do that?" she asked. "You're just going to kill me when I get there."

"Now, Kait. I get that you want to protect yourself, but what about Lily? Don't you want to see her before I take off with her for good?"

Kait let his words settled in. As an agent, she knew going to meet him was dangerous. Even against all of their policies. But she also knew Fenton. If she called in her team, he'd disappear with Lily. Forever. Just as he'd disappeared three years ago. This time not alone. Kait couldn't risk that. Besides, she was an agent, and that meant she had skills the average citizen didn't possess. She was Lily's best chance.

"Kait?" Fenton asked.

"I'm listening." She gritted her teeth.

"I'm sending a link to your phone right now in a text message. Click on it and be sure your GPS is turned on."

"I'm sure it's code that allows you to take control of my phone, and I won't do it," she responded out of habit.

"Really, Kait? Really? You'd risk never seeing Lily again just to keep me from accessing your phone?"

Of course she wouldn't. She'd simply let her training speak for her for a moment. "Hold on. I'm doing it." She thumbed to her GPS and turned it on, then moved to the message. With nausea still threatening, she clicked the link and waited for him confirm access.

"Okay, good. Perfect. Now I can track your movements and make sure you don't contact anyone. Next, I want you to go to the nurse's station where I've left a package for you. Take it to your car, and then remove the phone from the package. And do spend a few moments enjoying my latest present and message."

She hadn't a clue what this next message might contain, but she assumed the surprise was another heart. They hadn't confirmed the one he'd left at her house belonged to Youngblood, but they believed it did. So perhaps he really had killed the next man on his WoW list as he'd promised.

"What do you want me to do after that?" she asked.

"You'll find further instructions on the phone. Follow them exactly. When they say to stop and leave your cell, do so. No hesitation to keep your precious phone. Just leave it. Got it?"

"Yes."

"You'll also leave my special surprise and message with the phone, so when the other two monsters figure out you're gone and track your phone, they'll have something to find."

She assumed he meant Becca and Nina.

"Any questions?" he asked.

"Where will I meet you?"

"Just follow directions, Kait. Do what they say, and you'll see Lily again. Take any wrong steps or try to call in the troops, and we'll disappear. Now be a good girl, and go straight to the nurses' station. Laura is expecting you, and she'll tell me if you try to communicate your distress in any way."

Kait didn't know if she should believe he'd charmed Laura into watching her and reporting to him, but Kait knew he could easily hack into the hospital's security feeds, and she had no choice. She had to follow his directions exactly if she was ever going to see Lily again.

"IF YOU DON'T have this information to me within the hour, I'll send one of our agents out to arrest you for obstruction of justice," Nina threatened the WoW manager. Gone was the sweetness Grandmother Hale required. This was too important. Kait was too important. No one fired at her friend and got away with it. Out came the boxing gloves.

"And if you think I'm bluffing," she added. "Try calling me on it. You have one hour." She ended the call and considered throwing her phone "Stupid corporate bureaucracy."

"That bad, huh?" Quinn's voice came from behind.

She spun and found him leaning on the wall, relaxed, casual in his T-shirt and tactical pants, looking much like an agent on their FBI SWAT team. "What are you doing here? How'd you even get in the building?"

"Becca."

When stress got to Nina, she craved the chicken her grandmother used to fry. Tonight, she'd wanted it. Badly. She'd begged Becca to pick up a few pieces at a local dive while Nina waited by the phone. Now Nina wished she'd kept her big mouth shut. "Why are you here?"

He pushed off the wall. "I have some information for you."

"And your phone is broken?"

"I knew as soon as I told you what I'd learned, you'd act without thinking it through." He came closer, his expression deadly serious. "I wasn't about to put you in danger unless I was here to help."

"Please," she said, unwilling to rehash their many discussions about him needing to be the tough guy all the time. "So what's this info?"

"I tracked down the guy who gave Rhodes the portable vent. The guy I talked to also provided Fenton with the roc." He smiled tightly. "We had a conversation."

Nina could easily imagine the kind of conversation Quinn had with this guy. "And?"

"And he told me Rhodes won't fly commercially. He hates the security searches. So he calls on one of their former Navy buddies who owns his own plane. That buddy brought him to San Diego to pick up the vent."

"And he didn't ask how Rhodes planned to use the vent and roc?"

"Rhodes saved his life in Iraq. He owes him. Same with the pilot."

Nina had been around Quinn enough to know about the military code that said you never turned your back on a soldier in need—an especially true sentiment for the tight-knit SEAL teams. That doubled—maybe tripled—if you owed the other person for your life, and they found themselves in need of help.

"I wish I'd been there to *talk* to him like you did," she said.

"We did have a very long conversation." Quinn grinned, and heaven help her, she wanted to trace his lopsided smirk with her finger, then kiss it away.

Focus, Nina. Focus. "So how do I find this buddy?"

Quinn dug a scrap of paper out of his pocket and handed it to her. "He's local, but don't even think of going to see him without me."

"I wouldn't dream of it," she replied, but in reality, she'd be ditching Quinn as soon as was humanly possible and making a trip to see this pilot alone.

WHEN BECCA returned with the chicken, the greasy, crisp aroma Nina loved filled the war room, but Nina couldn't eat it. Not with Quinn hanging around. She offered it to him, and he had no problem wolfing it down while Nina called Kait to tell her about the pilot. Nina tried to phone three times, but Kait failed to answer.

"Well, shoot." Nina disconnected and turned to Becca. "I don't like this. Give me a good reason why Kait isn't answering, or I'm heading over to the hospital to find her."

"I don't have one," Becca said from the end of the table where she forked a bite of an organic salad. "She was waiting for our call. The only reason she wouldn't answer is if something was wrong."

Quinn wiped his fingers on a napkin. "Maybe she's sleeping."

"With Fenton still on the loose?" Nina said. "Not likely.

"She may not have a choice." He stuffed his trash in the bag. "You know the crash that comes after the adrenaline rush from a shooting fades."

Nina supposed he could be right, but it just didn't feel right. "Maybe, but I need to be sure."

"I could track her cell GPS," Becca offered. "It would take time to hack her account, though."

"You work on that while I head over to the hospital."

Quinn came to his feet. "I'll go with you."

Nina looked him squarely in the eyes. "No need."

"It might be a good idea to have backup," Becca suggested.

Nina swung her head around to glare at her friend.

Becca held up her hands. "I'm just saying, with the shooting, it'd be a good idea to have a second person along."

"Then *you* can come with me."

"I wish I could, but someone has to stay here to run the investigation when WoW finally delivers on the warrant."

Nina knew when she was outnumbered. "Fine. Quinn comes with me." She tossed the paper with the pilot's information on the table by Becca. "Get a team to pick up this guy. I'll talk to him when I get back."

Expecting a smug expression from Quinn, she glanced at him on the way out of the room and was glad to see he simply looked relieved.

"I love it when you take charge," Quinn whispered when he caught up to her.

The warmth of his breath, the sound of his voice, made her heart clip-clop in betrayal. She ignored the racing pulse and hurried to her car. On the drive, she turned on talk radio and pretended to be interested as they discussed the legalization of marijuana in Oregon. Quinn didn't attempt conversation, so when they arrived at the hospital, she glanced at him to be sure he hadn't dozed off. She found him watching her.

"What?" she asked, patting her hair to make sure nothing was out of place.

"Don't worry, your hair's perfect." He grinned and reached for her. "And waiting for someone to mess it up."

She pushed his hand away. "Then why that weird look?"

"I was just wondering if we'll ever be able to be in the same space without all this tension between us."

"What do you think?" She clenched her jaw so hard she thought she might fracture a few teeth.

"I think . . ." He paused and appraised her for a long moment, his eyes clouding over. "You're an all or nothing kind of girl, and I'm gonna get the nothing from now on."

"Very perceptive." She climbed out of the car before she gave him even the slightest hint that he could still get to her. She didn't wait for him, but hurried across the parking lot, her heels sending sharp pings into the still night and mixing with Quinn's solid footfalls behind her. Despite her unease at having him around, she knew he had her back, and for that, she was grateful.

Inside, she found Sam sleeping and the chair Kait occupied when Nina had visited earlier, empty. Quinn rested a shoulder on the doorframe and crossed his ankles. To a passerby, he might look relaxed, but Nina knew he took in everything around him. If danger threatened, he'd react with lightning reflexes.

She looked around the room, surprised to see Kait's purse on the floor. Nina confirmed Kait's iPad was inside. She'd never leave it for long. She had to be nearby. Maybe she couldn't sleep in the chair and didn't want to bother Sam, so she'd gone to the waiting room.

Not likely. If she couldn't sleep, she'd have taken her iPad. She could have chosen not to use Sam's bathroom and gone down the hall to a public restroom.

Nina turned to Quinn. "I'm going to check down the hall for Kait."

"Then I'm coming with you." His tone brooked no argument.

At the restroom, she knew he wouldn't care that it was restricted to women, and he would follow her in, so she held up a hand. "Stay," she commanded and searched the small space for Kait. Empty. Next, Nina checked the lounge, Quinn trialing along behind. Empty, too. Then she went to the nurse's station, hoping to talk to the duty nurse but found no one.

Nina planted her hands on her hips and considered waiting for a nurse to return or going back to wake Sam from his much-needed rest.

"I know you want the good detective to get his beauty rest," Quinn said, as if reading her mind, "but if Kait's in trouble, you're wasting precious time."

He was right. Nina didn't waste another second, but hurried back to Sam's room and stepped up to his bed. "Sam," she said loud enough to make him stir and open his eyes. "I'm looking for Kait."

He cast a groggy glance at the chair. "She was here when I went to sleep. Said she was staying all night."

Nina's concern ratcheted up. "She's not answering her phone, and I'm starting to get worried."

Sam shot up then winced and fell back. "Maybe the nurses have seen her." He pressed his buzzer and raised his bed to a sitting position.

"Yes," a tired female voice came over the intercom.

"Hey, Laura. I'm looking for Kait. The woman who was staying with me tonight. Have you seen her?"

"She picked up a package a guy left for her at the desk and took off," Laura replied over a crackly connection.

"Did you know this guy?" Sam asked.

"No, but he's an EMT. He said she forgot her cellphone, and he was leaving it along with a box of candy. He was a real sweetie. Even left candy for the nursing staff."

Nina shot a look at Sam. "Kait had her phone, right?"

"Yes."

"Are you sure?"

"Positive." His gaze swung to the table. "She set it there, so she'd hear your call."

"It's gone now." That sliver of concern Nina had been feeling grew into a full-fledged log.

"If there's nothing else?" Laura said.

"Did this guy have a crescent-shaped scar on his chin?" Sam asked.

"He did," Laura said. "A cute one that moved when he talked."

Sam cringed and sat up straighter. "How long ago did she leave?"

"About an hour. Maybe a little more."

Nina looked at Sam. "We need to look at the hospital security footage."

"I'll get dressed, and we'll find the security office." Sam swung his legs over the side of the bed, his face contorting in pain.

Nina stepped in front of him. "You're in no shape to do this."

"Too bad." He came to his feet, but had to grab onto the bedrail. "I'm not leaving Kait out there alone."

Nina blocked his path. "You could only make things worse."

"Let the man up, Nina." Quinn's voice boomed through the room. "He needs to do this."

Nina spun, found Quinn standing alert and tall. If he insisted on Sam coming along, Sam would join them. Once Quinn made up his mind to do something, he was relentless, and there was nothing she or anyone else could do to stop him.

Chapter Thirty-Two

SAM SHARED THE small security office with a chubby guard named Victor, Nina, and her Navy SEAL. She clearly didn't want Quinn around, and Sam wasn't sure why he was with her, but Sam didn't waste time getting clarification.

"There." Nina pointed at the computer monitor. "It's Rhodes dressed as an EMT."

Sam watched as Rhodes made his way into the hospital, mugging for the security cameras on the way in. The camera followed him until he moved out of range. Victor switched to the elevator footage. Rhodes smiled up at the camera while holding up the box Laura told them about.

"Dude," Victor said. "It's like he wants you to know he left the package."

"He does," Quinn said from where he stood behind Nina. "Whatever's in that box is likely the reason she took off."

"Agreed," Sam said. "Fast forward to the part where Kait picks up the box and leaves."

Victor cued up the footage.

Nina's phone rang. "It's Becca. Hopefully, she has news."

Nina stepped away to take the call. Sam kept his focus on the screen. He watched Kait open the box in the elevator, her eyes narrowing in disgust.

Quinn squinted at the monitor. "I'd sure like to know what's in there to put that look on her face."

Sam was sure it was another heart, but he was more interested in the phone she'd removed from the box and tucked into her pocket.

"Was that a phone?" Quinn asked.

Sam nodded and continued to watch as Victor switched to the parking lot view where he saw Kait climb into a white sedan—not her car—and drive off. He watched for a clear shot of the license plate as the car moved out of camera range, but the camera didn't catch it.

Quinn lifted his wrist and glanced at his watch. "Timestamp says she left nearly ninety minutes ago. She could be long gone in that amount of time."

The same thought sent Sam's head into a dizzying spin. "Do you have any cameras on the exit?"

"Sorry," Victor said. "This is it."

"So all we know is, Rhodes gave her a phone, she left at 2:55," Quinn said, "and took the south exit."

Sam didn't need this guy to state the obvious. They still hadn't a clue where Kait was, whose car she was driving, or why she took off. He looked at Nina who was ending her call and willed her to have a lead they could use.

She said goodbye to Becca and crossed over to Sam. "That was about the pilot I mentioned on the elevator. The one who chauffeured Rhodes. He claims he didn't know Rhodes was in town and only flew him to San Diego that one time. Our team is bringing him in for additional questioning."

"Maybe you should hold off taking him into custody so I can ask him a few questions," Quinn offered.

Sam could imagine the kind of questioning Quinn intended, and his offer was tempting, but Nina shook her head. "We play by the rules so nothing bites us in the butt when Rhodes comes to trial."

"Then how do you propose we find Kait?" Quinn asked.

Nina's phone dinged and she held it out. "Becca successfully hacked Kait's phone, and that glorious sound you just heard is her texting me the GPS coordinates."

"If she's with Rhodes, and he let her keep her phone," Quinn said. "He would've made sure her GPS was turned off. Which means, she probably doesn't have her phone."

"Or he doesn't have her," Sam added, though he knew it was wishful thinking.

"What about GPS on her car?" Quinn asked.

"She didn't use her own car." Sam lifted a hand to shove it into his hair in frustration, but an agonizing pain quickly brought it back down. "So the phone is our only lead."

Nina nodded. "Let's go get it. Even if she's not with it, she's resourceful enough to have left a message on it if she could."

Sam kept up with Nina and Quinn on the way to the car, but, despite the pain meds he'd gotten from the nurse before leaving his room, he broke out in a sweat. At least there was a cool evening breeze to keep him from keeling over onto the asphalt.

Nina grabbed her go bag from the trunk and slung the strap over her shoulder. *Good.* Sam wished he had his go bag, which was filled with items law enforcement officers needed on the job. Heading into the unknown, they might find the equipment could come in handy. But with Sam's car still at Kait's house, they'd have to make do with Nina's equipment. He didn't even have a gun and felt naked.

Nina unlocked the car and tossed her keys to Quinn. "You drive so I can track the GPS signal on my phone."

She dropped her bag on the backseat. Sam climbed in next to it, and she took the passenger seat where Sam saw her punch the coordinates into her car's navigation system. "That should get you there without any wrong turns."

Quinn tore out of the parking lot, and Sam rested his head. He still felt woozy, and the car motion nauseated him so he blinked hard, willing it to pass.

"I've located her phone on a street view map. Looks like an abandoned gas station."

"A logical place for Rhodes to meet her, I suppose," Sam said, feeling too sick to sit forward and look at it.

He heard Nina fumbling with something. "Her phone isn't moving on the GPS tracker at all."

No one spoke, but Sam knew they all worried about the same thing. If Kait was in possession of her phone, she was restrained, injured, or dead, and none of them were willing to put voice to those thoughts.

Quinn stomped on the gas, sending Sam's stomach rolling, but he bit his tongue and held on. He wouldn't stop Quinn or complain. The sooner they got to the gas station, the sooner they'd find Kait.

Breathing in and out, and concentrating on the rise and fall of his chest, he rested until the female voice on the navigation system announced their destination just ahead.

"Grab my binoculars from the bag, Sam," Nina called out.

He pulled them out, but instead of handing them over, he focused out the side window. Quinn cut off the headlights, and they rolled into the lot that was dark except for a lone streetlight casting a glow onto the rear of the building.

"There's a box in Dora paper just like at Kait's house," Sam said. "It's sitting on a barrel near the back."

"You think it's a trap?" Nina asked. "Maybe a bomb?"

"Doubtful." Quinn shifted into park but left the engine running. "My research says Rhodes doesn't have explosives training or experience."

"Big whoop," Sam said. "Anyone can find out how to make a bomb on the Internet."

Quinn turned and rolled his eyes. "Thought you wanted to find Kait. Sitting here like scared little girls isn't going to do that." He jumped out and marched across the space.

"Quinn, stop," Nina called after him. Sam heard the worry in her voice, but if Quinn did, he ignored it and kept going.

He studied the box for a few moments then lifted the lid and turned to look at them. "Not a bomb. A message."

Nina was out of the car faster than Sam, but he managed to grab a Maglite from her bag and follow her without passing out.

"Guy's a regular butcher." Quinn eyed Nina, and Sam could see the SEAL definitely had a thing for her, but she didn't seem to return the feeling.

Sam shone the light into the box and paid little attention to the heart. The message lying on top grabbed his attention, and he couldn't pull his eyes free.

The clock is still ticking—can you stop me before the countdown ends?

Before heartless Kait joins the others, her life wrapped up as a present for her sister.

Fenton shoved Kait down the basement stairs. She searched the dank, airless space for a way out. The narrow room held three glass-block windows, a living area, and a tired kitchenette at the far end of the space. Two doors led to other areas of the basement—maybe with an exterior door? A door for escape? She could hope, anyway.

Fenton stepped around Kait and gently laid Lily on a sagging sofa. "That's it, precious. Sleep now. We have a big day ahead of us." He then focused on Kait.

Panic raced up her spine. *Here it comes. Get ready.*

How did she prepare herself for death? An ugly, mean death like Congdon's, as Fenton had promised in the car. Her wrists bolted to the floor, the paralysis Marcie had described taking away her ability to fight. Struggling for air. Not feeling it, but her mind knowing it all.

He walked toward her. She jumped back, and he seemed surprised.

She held her breath, her body quivering in fear.

He tucked his gun in his belt, then picked up a photo album and envelope before dropping onto the nearest chair and rubbing his leg. "Sit down, Kait, and quit hovering."

Relief flowed through her body, but she fought the urge to sigh out her anxiety and let him see how panicked she was. While he concentrated on his book, she perched on the sofa near Lily and breathed.

In. Out. In. Out. That's it. You're still alive.

For how long?

She watched him. Waiting.

He rubbed his leg again, and his head snapped up, catching her eyes on him. "Enjoying looking at your handiwork?"

"Mine?" she asked confused.

"Unfortunately, one of your bullets caught me." He jerked up his pant leg, revealing an ugly scar running the length of his lower leg. "See what you did? Multiple surgeries in substandard hospitals so you couldn't find me. Now I have pain every day. Every day, Kait. You know how that makes me feel!" His shrill screeching made Lily shift and blink a few times.

Kait patted her back until she settled again.

His dark, angry eyes glared at her. "You disfigured me. I'm grotesque."

Despite his anger, she had to bite back telling him the scar was the least of his disfigurements.

He opened and closed his fists, then shrugged and looked at the photo album. He flipped through it, pausing to stare at the pages. Each successive one extinguished the anger in his eyes. With a contented sigh, he removed a picture from the envelope and inserted it in the book.

Kait desperately wanted to know what he was looking at, but after his outburst, she wouldn't ask. Instead, she focused on Lily and searched for a way to get them out of this mess. He'd locked the deadbolt at the top of the stairs and shoved the key into his pocket, closing off that escape route. Somehow, she needed to get into the other rooms to check them out. Or maybe find a weapon in the kitchenette, though she doubted he'd be careless enough to leave anything she could use against him.

He suddenly sat back, a joyful smile playing across his face. He ran his fingers over the page, then snapped the book closed and looked at her. "All this work has made me hungry. Are you hungry, Kait?"

Her stomach was still roiling, and the last thing she wanted was food, but this could be her chance to search the kitchenette. She stood and put on the best smile she could muster.

"I could fix something for us. Like a smoky melt," she said, offering him a snack that Abby had invented for him. "If you have the ingredients."

He watched her carefully. His eyes roved over her, his mood shifting yet again. Suddenly, his eyes rolled up, then slid back into place, and he stared at her as if he was memorizing everything about her. He got up and came over to her, his breathing shallow and quick.

She resisted the urge to back up and waited for him to provide a clue about the weird eye action.

"Of course, I have the ingredients for our favorite, my sweet Abby," he said, lifting a hand to touch her cheek.

Abby. He'd returned to thinking of her as Abby.

The touch revolted Kait. She wanted to slap his hand away, but he wouldn't kill Abby, so Kait would play along until she found a way out of this basement. She forced herself not to cringe and looked up at him. His eyes heated up. Desire. He wanted her as his wife. Now. Here.

She swallowed hard, forcing down the disgust burning up her throat. "I really am hungry. Shall I make the snack?"

"Yes," he answered breathlessly, but his heated expression said there were other things he'd rather do.

She escaped his touch and hurried to the kitchen, glad to scrub away the feel of him on her cheek with her palm. As she searched the drawers for anything to use as a weapon, she hoped Fenton choked on the sandwich. He had to, just had to, before he claimed his husbandly rights, or she became his next victim.

Chapter Thirty-Three

SAM HAD WASTED precious time crossing the city again to get to the FBI office. He wanted to be out there. Doing something, anything. Looking for Kait. But they'd found Kait's phone on the other side of the gas station, in the car she'd driven from the hospital. Nina needed to analyze Kait's phone, and right now, it was their strongest lead. So the three of them had returned to the FBI office.

In the time they'd been gone, Sulyard had interrogated the pilot. Not that it mattered. He offered no help. Sulyard pulled in every available agent to work the case and was putting pressure on the World of Warcraft attorneys. He'd also sent the SEAL away, and Nina seemed as much relieved as disappointed. Maybe it was a good thing the SEAL wasn't around. Gave Nina more of a focus while she and the analysts searched Kait's phone.

They all needed focus. Especially Sam, who could do little to help in the search except issue an all-points alert for Kait and Rhodes and review case files again. He thumbed through them. The same ones, over and over. For the hundredth time, starving for a lead, finding nothing.

Disgusted with his inability to help, he jumped to his feet, ignored the lingering nausea, and paced. Kait needed him now. Right now! *If* she was still alive.

So what did he do? How did he find her?

Think, Murdock. Think.

Nina stepped into the room, and Sam's gaze went to Kait's phone in her hand, like clinging to a lifesaver.

"Take a look at this," Nina said holding it out.

She displayed a picture of Rhodes holding Lily. The date/time stamp was just before Kait had disappeared.

"He has Lily?" Sam asked, his heart plummeting. "Rhodes has her?"

"Yes."

His gaze flashed up to Nina. "You're sure?"

"I called the safe house and confirmed." She met Sam's gaze, pain radiating from her eyes. "They didn't know she was gone until I asked them to check."

"This is obviously why Kait left the hospital." His heart broke at the thought of her all alone receiving this picture. Her fear. Her guilt. He should have been there for her. Gone to meet Rhodes instead of her. "Rhodes had to give her instructions on where to meet him. Did you find a text or call from him on her phone?"

"There's a call from another burner phone."

"So we can't track him," Sam said as he tried to wrap his head around this.

Rhodes has Lily, he repeated to himself, but it still didn't seem real. The depraved creep had the adorable, beautiful child while Sam sat here berating himself like he'd done the day Danny had died. A child in harm's way, and he could do nothing about it. Nothing. Again.

"Any idea how he found the safe house?" Sam asked, dreading the answer.

"Looks like he did it by taking control of someone's phone on the task force. We found a suspicious e-mail on Kait's phone that I remembered receiving. So we checked other taskforce phones, and we think he sent the same spoofed message to everyone."

A bad feeling settled over Sam, and he had to concentrate on taking in enough air to ask, "Spoofed means what, exactly?"

"In a spoofed message, the sender makes the e-mail look like it came from someone else. For example, I could send out a message that looks like it came from your personal account or from the President, for that matter."

"How's that even possible?"

She arched a brow. "You can't begin to know how detailed I'd have to get to explain it."

"Then give me only what I need for a basic understanding."

She pointed at the sender's e-mail address on her phone. "This e-mail address displayed is a legitimate one that you can find on the FBI website. The e-mail contained a link. If anyone clicked on it, a program would download that allows Rhodes to take control of the phone and give him access to files and communications. Obviously, it didn't originate at the FBI."

Sam stared grimly at the subject line, the hollow pit in his stomach growing. "I got a message with the same heading the other day. But it came from PPB. It asked me to confirm receipt of the message. I thought it was from my department. Protocol requires we respond. I didn't . . ."

"You didn't know it was spoofed, so you clicked on the link."

He nodded as a vision of Kait in shackles, a tube running down her throat with Rhodes standing over her flashed before his eyes. A vision that could come true, and now it was looking like it was his fault.

"Hey." Nina laid a hand on his arm. "Don't go blaming yourself for this. You didn't do anything that thousands of other people don't do every day. Spoofers are good at what they do. They often send e-mails warning you to be wary of such e-mails and that makes them seem even more legit."

"Still, I can tell you think I'm the leak."

She lifted a shoulder in a feeble shrug. "Did you communicate with anyone at the safe house after reading that e-mail?'

Sam didn't even need to think about it. "I contacted our officer there a couple of times. But I didn't put the safe house address in a text or even mention it in a call, so it doesn't make sense that I led him to Lily, does it?"

"All Rhodes needed was the officer's phone number to track his GPS and locate them that way."

"If you look at my phone, can you tell if I was the leak?"

"I can tell if the phone's been compromised. Without looking at the other PPB phones, I won't know how many other department phones were compromised, too."

"I need to know if I could be the one." He handed over his phone and curled his fingers, letting his nails bite into his palms. Minutes ticked by as she thumbed through several screens, then her finger stilled midair.

"Don't bother telling me. Your look says it all. It could have been me." Anger pulsed through his veins. Not directed at Rhodes, but at himself for being such an idiot. He'd not only failed to protect Lily from Rhodes, but he led him right to her doorstep. It was his job to protect Lily and Kait. He'd failed. Failed when it mattered most.

He started pacing again. "Can we use this information to find Rhodes?"

"Maybe, but the e-mail was routed through so many servers, if we do manage to trace it, it will take days."

"What about the picture of Lily?" he asked, grasping at straws. "I remember reading something about a picture showing where it was taken or something like that."

"Photos can have embedded geo trackers, but this one didn't. Rhodes is too smart to leave that feature active when taking a picture."

"So now what?" Sam asked, his steps silent on the carpeted floor.

"We keep working on Kait's phone and any other lead no matter how small."

Sam marched back and forth, his head down. He nearly barreled into Becca when she rushed through the door, waving a stack of papers.

"WoW's come through. We have the addresses." She slapped the pages on the table. "We've already confirmed Jae's research was correct. The names and addresses match Rhodes's victims."

Sam devoured the information until he spotted the man they believed Rhodes killed while they were watching WoW. "Jason Mason. Address is on the west side, but still in my jurisdiction. We need to get over there now."

Nina dug out her car keys. "You hold down the fort, Becca. I'll go with

Sam to Mason's house." Nina looked at Sam. "On the way, you can have uniforms dispatched to all three locations. Hopefully, these guys will still be alive and give us a lead on finding Kait."

KAIT WATCHED Fenton from under her lashes as the early morning sun cast the basement in hazy light. She rested her hand on Lily's back, the child's breathing offering some comfort while Kait feigned sleep for the last hour. It was the only thing she could think to do to keep Fenton's lecherous hands off her, short of revealing her real identity and guaranteeing her death. A short-lived solution. Once awake, Lily would give Kait away. Still, this bought time for Becca and Nina to find her. If they were even looking. Or maybe Sam had woken up and discovered she'd disappeared.

Lily stirred, sending Kait's heart plummeting.

"That's it, baby girl," Fenton cooed from the ottoman by the sofa. "It's time to wake up. Then we'll make breakfast and wake up Mommy. She loves breakfast. I'll bet you do, too. Then this afternoon we'll get in an airplane and go to our new house. You'll love it. We can go hiking and exploring while Mommy stays home to bake her amazing candy apple pie."

Kait cringed at his deranged fantasy.

"And you know what, baby girl?" he asked, moving closer to them. "I want us to have a brother or sister for you. Wouldn't that be nice? Someone to play with."

Kait's stomach roiled in revulsion. He'd put her in an impossible situation. Maybe that was his plan all along. So which did she do? Pretend to be her sister and let him paw her, or divulge her true identity and die?

SAM WASN'T SURPRISED by Jason Mason's office in the upscale area of northwest Portland. Nor was he surprised that the uniform had arrived to find Mason lifeless and bolted to the floor. They'd immediately phoned Marcie, and now she crouched by the body while Nina and Sam searched the room. But it was devoid of the usual office items and didn't take long.

"The same MO," Sam mused

"Except for the shards from the glass." Nina eyed the floor around Mason. "Leaving a mess is totally out of character for Rhodes."

Sam studied the vivid orange remnants littering the floor. "He must have taken off in a hurry."

"Odd that he took the heart when he said the next one would be—" Nina clamped her hand over her mouth.

"Would be Kait's," Sam finished for Nina, though he'd been trying to avoid thinking about the message they'd found at the gas station. "Which means it was this guy's heart at the gas station."

"Any idea of the time of death?" Sam asked Marcie. "We believe Rhodes killed him around 5:30 yesterday afternoon."

Marcie shook her head. "He hasn't been dead that long."

"You're sure?"

"Positive. Rigor's set in his jaw, so I'd say between one and two a.m."

Nina stepped closer. "So if Mason isn't the guy Rhodes killed after the WoW raid, who is?"

Sam shrugged. "Maybe he moved out of sequence for some reason and it's one of the other guys on the list."

"We have bruising," Marcie announced from across the room, grabbing their attention.

Sam and Nina crossed over to her. Nina bent down and turned Mason's hand, exposing the deep purple bruises circling his wrist.

Sam considered squatting next to them, but the pain in his chest kept him upright. "So Mason was awake at some point and struggled. Then Rhodes killed him and went where?"

"Maybe he's holed up with one of the other men on the WoW list," Nina suggested.

"If they're alive." Sam dug out his phone and called Vance. "We have any word from the uniforms yet?"

"They just reported in. Found both men at home asleep." Vance's voice carried the same relief Sam felt.

"Odd," Sam said, and told Vance about Mason's time of death.

"Maybe he was just messing with us and didn't kill anyone yesterday."

Sam thought about it. "Rhodes has done everything he's committed to up to this point." Which meant Kait was next. "The big question is, where is he now?"

"Well, these guys claim they haven't heard from him other than in online chats in the past. I had the uniforms bring them in for safety, and I'll take a run at them in case they're trying to mislead us."

"Not without me. I want a crack at them, too." Sam hung up and turned to Nina. "Both guys are alive. Uniforms are bringing them in, and I plan to be there to question them."

"Then let's go."

Stowing his phone, he felt like he was going to hurl. Maybe it was the pain meds wearing off. More likely, it was because Kait's abduction confirmed he'd fallen for her. In a big way. Now, he might lose her.

"Can you unlock the cuffs before you go?" Marcie asked.

Gritting his teeth against the pain, Sam bent over Mason's hand and clicked the lock. As he started to move away, he noticed letters scratched into the floor. He checked Mason's fingers and found a small cut.

"Check this out, Nina." He pointed at the floor where the letters *airp* were scratched into the wood. "Looks like Mason used one of the shards to leave a message. Airport, maybe."

She squatted next to him. "Or Rhodes set this up to make us think he's taking Lily and Kait to the airport."

"Mason has a cut on his index finger." Sam picked up the blood-tipped shard. "If we had the time to wait for DNA results, I'm sure it would confirm this is Mason's blood. Plus, it's logical that Rhodes plans to leave town with Lily." Sam wanted to say with Kait, too, but that didn't seem likely.

"His pilot buddy said he never flew commercially," Nina said. "With the pilot in custody, Rhodes won't be traveling with him."

"Okay, so what does that leave?" A million thoughts racing through his head, Sam stood, and filtered through them. "Rhodes can't risk taking Lily through security. It'd have to be a chopper if he was taking her somewhere close by, or a chartered plane for a longer move."

Nina nodded. "Which means we're talking the Hillsboro or Troutdale airports."

Feeling precious minutes tick by, Sam said, "We need information on flights scheduled today."

Nina dug her phone out. "I'll get the team on it."

"You'll need a warrant to obtain any meaningful information."

"Hey, relax." Nina dialed. "I'm a fed, and you know feds can make anything happen."

Sam tried not to think about how long it had taken to get the information from the WoW warrant, focusing instead on the fact that, at times, feds could indeed work miracles. He hoped this was one of those times.

Chapter Thirty-Four

FENTON POPPED up the toaster, the frozen pancake a luscious golden brown. He took a long sniff of the sweet aroma that said home to him. Abby cooking. Him sitting at the table reading the latest news on his computer. Coffee gurgling in the pot. He'd waited so long to be with his family, and now, here they were. It was enough to make him giddy.

He started humming, changing his tune when the Dora the Explorer theme played from the laptop Lily watched.

D-d-d-Dora. D-d-d-Dora, the song raced through his head.

How fun. He wanted to know a dozen or so of Lily's favorite songs by the time they climbed on the plane this afternoon.

He surveyed his little family. "Breakfast is ready."

"Yay, pancakes with Daddy." Lily jumped to her feet. "C'mon, Nantie Kait."

Kait? How could Lily mistake her mother for Kait? Sure, they were identical twins, but they were nothing alike. Kait was mean and spiteful. Abby warm and loving.

Should he correct Lily, or let it slide? Maybe he'd let it slide for now. He could straighten things out after their special breakfast. He pulled out the chair by the pancakes for Lily, and Abby sat next to their daughter.

He returned to the kitchen and plated the scrambled eggs. "Filled with cheese just as you like them, sweetheart." He set them in front of Abby and ran a hand over her hair. She ducked away. "Something wrong?"

Lily giggled. "Nantie Kait hates scrambled eggs. She likes pancakes. Just like me."

Fenton watched Lily for a moment. "You must not have gotten enough sleep, Lily. You keep confusing your mommy for your Aunt Kait."

Lily swallowed a bite of pancakes. "Mommy's in heaven." She shoved another bite in her mouth and chewed.

Was Lily right? Was he losing it and this was Kait sitting in front of him?

He blinked a few times then looked at her. "Aren't you going to eat your eggs, Abby?"

She took a bite and chewed woodenly, quickly washing it down with coffee. Abby would savor the eggs. Groan with pleasure over the way he'd prepared them with cheese, onions, and peppers, just as she liked.

"Kait?" he asked.

She cringed.

"No!" He rushed around the table and tugged up the back of her shirt. No sexy little butterfly tattoo.

"Your tattoo," he demanded. "Where is it?"

"I had it removed."

"Why?"

She shrugged.

"Why?" he screamed in her face.

"I'm older. It's not appropriate."

"Liar. Liar. Liar." He grabbed her hair and forced her to look at him. "Abby would never get rid of the tattoo. It was my gift to her. Lily's right. You're Kait. Pretending to be Abby."

"No, Daddy!" Lily screamed. "Don't hurt her."

"She'll be fine." He tugged harder on the thick mane of Kait's hair.

She winced. Good. Let her suffer. How dare she pretend to be Abby? How dare she? He eyed her, sending all the venom he felt through his gaze.

Lily started crying, but he hadn't a clue why.

"Shh, sweetheart," he said. "Everything will be fine." At least, it would be once Kait was dead. He jerked her to her feet and dragged her down the hallway. He heard Lily's continued sobs.

"It's okay, sweetheart," he called over his shoulder. I'll be right back."

After your devious, conniving Nantie Kait is in the shackles she deserves.

SAM'S PAIN MEDS had worn off. Every step brought excruciating pain. So what? Pacing on the street in front of Mason's house kept Sam sane as he waited for flight information. The airports were on opposite sides of the city. Heading to either of them without information would simply waste time. Precious time. So they waited. And waited, while Nina talked to Becca who researched chartered flights.

"Nothing out of Troutdale today." Nina shoved her phone in her pocket. "Two out of Hillsboro. One to Colorado in thirty minutes and one to Mexico in three hours."

"My money's on Mexico."

"Mine, too. The plane was chartered by a Toby Bradley in Hillsboro. Becca didn't have time to find a connection to Rhodes, but she did discover Bradley's employed in information technology. She also located his home address. We can head to his house or the airport. Your call."

Sam looked at his watch. "We can't make it in time for the Colorado flight. I'll get uniforms to cover that one. And another unit to watch the Mexico flight."

"While we head to Toby Bradley's house," Nina said, already digging out her keys.

"While we head to Toby Bradley's house," Sam echoed as he climbed into the car and prayed they were making the right decision.

KAIT AWOKE AND instantly knew something was wrong. Though she'd been sleeping, her eyes were open, but her body was heavy. Grounded and unmovable.

She couldn't even move her eyes, but she heard Fenton's voice as he sang to Lily in the other room. Then she heard it. The telltale draw and whoosh of the ventilator, and her memory flooded back. She remembered Fenton dragging her into this room. She'd seen the bolts secured in the concrete, the handcuffs open and waiting. She'd fought hard, but he was strong. Crazy strong, and then he stabbed a needle into her arm, and she'd collapsed.

Oh, no. No. No. No.

It was true. She was paralyzed. Like Congdon and Youngblood, and she couldn't move. Not her legs or hands, not even an eyelash or a finger.

She strained harder. Nothing.

She could feel the cold from the floor seeping into her legs, but she couldn't budge a finger. Not even a fraction of an inch. And that meant she couldn't help Lily. Panic swept through her.

God, no, she prayed, her mind whirling with fear. *Please, no. Anything but this.*

LILY DOZED OFF in front of the TV, and Fenton checked his watch. Perfect timing. Kait should be coming out from under the roc and they needed to head to the airport. He kissed Lily's cheek, and watched his precious baby for a few moments. He'd done it. Rescued his daughter. Now he'd deal with Kait.

He went to the corner bedroom and paused in the doorway. "Hello, Kait."

She turned her head and stared at him.

"Glad to see the roc has worn off. Now let me remove the tube so we can get out of here." He thought he saw a flash of relief in her eyes as he squatted next to her.

Good. Let her think he'd changed his mind. It would be all the better when he put her back under and actually took her life. After a few weeks—maybe months—of the same agonizing, mentally taxing suffering she'd made him go through.

"Don't fight me now, Kait, or it will go badly for you. When I start to remove the tube, give one big breath, and we'll have it out." He pulled the tape free, and then deflated the cuff. "Ready?"

She blinked long, luscious eyelashes like Abby's.

Not Abby, Kait. Focus now and keep it together. You're almost there.

"Okay, here we go." He slipped the tube out as her gag reflex kicked in. "Take a few deep breaths and cough. It will help."

She coughed a few times and cleared her throat. She swallowed hard and grimaced. Her throat must feel like swallowing pins and needles. A sip of water would help. Too bad. No water for her. He didn't want her comfortable. He wanted her on edge. Fearful. Begging for her life. He could barely wait until they were settled in Mexico and he had her back in the cuffs.

Not wanting to lose her now, he watched her chest rise and fall. Once satisfied she'd be okay, he crossed the room to the bag he'd taken from the trunk of her car at the hospital and dug out one of her Kevlar vests. He put one on and dropped the other one at her feet. Keeping a gun trained on her, he unlocked the cuffs from the bolts, but left one dangling from her left wrist. "Put on the vest."

Her shoulders went up, her chin out. "And if I don't?" she croaked out.

That's it. Fight. It's so much better for me when you fight. "Then my precious little Lily will have to see me kill you, and we both know what kind of scars that will leave."

"Fine." She shrugged into the vest, settling it over her wrinkled blouse.

He was disappointed she gave in so easily. He locked the handcuff to the bolt. She stared at him, defiance on her face. He wanted to slap it away, but their pilot might ask about the bruise.

He stood and glared down on her. "I'll just get Lily into her car seat, and then I'll be back for you."

"Wait," she said as if trying to buy time. "Why the vest?"

"I doubt that your cop friend or agent clones have any idea of my plan, but just in case, I don't want a stray bullet to take you out."

"I'd think that's precisely what you would like."

"Oh, no, Kait." He met her gaze, putting his hatred for her in his eyes. "Trust me when I say, you will not die that easily or peacefully. Your little episode in the cuffs was just a preview of what's to come."

Chapter Thirty-Five

SAM AND NINA advanced on the white Camry parked in Bradley's driveway. Sam had called dispatch when they'd arrived and confirmed it was a rental. Made no sense that Bradley would rent a car when he owned a late model SUV, but it was logical that Rhodes had done so to keep them from following his trail. Becca was working on finding out who'd rented it, but that would take time Kait and Lily might not have.

Armed with Nina's backup gun, Sam eased up on the passenger side and stopped in surprise. "It's Lily," he whispered to Nina. "She's asleep in her car seat."

Sam felt the hood. "Car's cold. So they didn't just arrive."

"Then they're on their way out."

Sam tried the door and found it unlocked. "Cover me while I get Lily out." Sam shoved the gun into his waistband and crawled in. As he removed her shoulder straps, she woke up. "Hey, sweetie."

"I have a daddy," she announced.

"I know."

"He's helping Nantie Kait. In the basement. We're going to the airport."

"Sounds fun," he lied. "But first, Nina and I have something to show you."

She scrunched her forehead, but she didn't question him as he lifted her out of the seat. Once free of the car, he and Nina ran toward her vehicle parked down the street.

"Take her while I go find Kait." Sam passed Lily to Nina. "Call for backup."

"Wait for them, Sam," she urged. "You can't go into the basement. Rhodes will feel trapped, and then what?"

Sam looked back at the expensive two-story house in the luxurious subdivision. Manicured lawns filled with flowering perennials seemed to belie the fact that Rhodes held Kait hostage inside. As Sam watched, the front door opened, and Rhodes stepped out, pulling Kait behind by a pair of handcuffs. Thrilled that she was alive, Sam ran his eyes over her to assess her condition. She looked tired, but she held her shoulders high beneath a

Kevlar vest. Odd. If Rhodes intended to kill her, why put her in the vest?

Rhodes tucked his gun into his waistband and dragged her to the car. A cyclone of anger twirled in Sam's gut. He took a step to go after Rhodes, but Nina's warning came back to him. *Wait for backup.*

Rhodes approached the car, but suddenly came up short at the back door. He whirled around, slamming Kait into the side panel.

"He's discovered Lily's missing," Sam said to Nina.

"Sweetie, where are you?" Rhodes continued to move in circles, dragging Kait behind him. "It's not time to play hide and seek."

"Daddy," Lily called out, but Nina quieted her.

Rhodes dropped Kait's cuffs and shaded his eyes as he continued to search.

Kait took a step back. She had to be terrified for Lily. Sam didn't want Rhodes to see him, but he had to let Kait know Lily was safe. When Rhodes turned his back, Sam stepped out far enough to wave at her and draw her attention. He mimed holding Lily, and she nodded her acknowledgement. Then he signaled for her to run away and take cover.

She turned and with a swift kick, knocked Rhodes to his knees. She bolted across the yard. Sam lifted his gun and charged, but by the time he got close enough, Rhodes was hot on Kait's tail in the neighbor's yard.

"Freeze, Rhodes," Sam shouted.

Rhodes didn't respond.

Sam kicked into high gear. Faster. Pushing to his limit, but Rhodes was gaining on Kait. She glanced back then leapt over a shrub and took a tumble. Rhodes flew through the air and crashed down on top of her. They scuffled. He came up with his weapon planted against her temple. He jerked Kait up and placed her in front of him, shielding his body with hers.

"Stop, or I'll kill her," he screamed wildly.

Sam froze in place and tried to slow his racing pulse. What a coward. Using a woman for protection. Not just any woman. Kait. His Kait. The fear in her eyes cut him to the core. He couldn't just stand here. He had to help her or die trying.

So what did he do?

With Kait's eyes imploring him to act, Sam tried to think. Every idea that flashed into his head ended with Rhodes killing Kait. Except one scenario. A crazy one. But still more promising than anything else. He knew Kait's Glock took 9mm ammo, which meant her vest would, at a minimum, stop that caliber bullet, and his plan could work. He'd give Rhodes one more chance to surrender. Then he'd act.

"Let her go, Rhodes," Sam yelled and assumed a firing stance.

"I'll kill her." Rhodes's eyes sharpened for a moment before going mean and ugly.

"And then I'll kill you," Sam warned. "You don't want Lily to lose her father, do you?"

Rhodes considered it for a moment. "Nice try, detective, but I'm not stupid." He started shoving Kait toward his rental. "I'll expect to see Lily at the car by the time I get there."

"Don't do it, Sam," Kait begged. "Let him kill me, but leave Lily where she is."

He looked her in the eyes, trying to convey the love he felt for her. "Do you trust me, Kait?" he asked, knowing it was a loaded question.

She didn't hesitate. "Completely."

At her utter and complete trust, Sam reconsidered his move. But when Rhodes shoved her forward, Sam curled his finger around his trigger. His heart stopping, he pulled. His gun discharged, the boom exploding though the quiet. His shot hit her dead center, stealing his breath. Her eyes flashed with surprise before she crumpled to the ground.

Sam ignored the worry for her and swung his weapon to Rhodes. The creep stood there his mouth gaped open, the gun dangling from his hand just like Sam planned.

"Drop the gun, Rhodes!" Nina yelled, coming up behind him. "Now!"

Fenton glanced at Nina as if surprised to see her still standing there. Then he slowly raised the gun and aimed at her.

Sam reacted, firing two rounds center mass and taking Rhodes down. Sam's only regret was that the guy wore a vest, too, and the bullets couldn't pierce his flesh and send him to eternity for the lives he'd taken. For the terror and pain he'd inflicted.

"Get his gun, Nina," Sam called to her, keeping his weapon trained on Rhodes's unmoving body.

Nina grabbed Rhodes's gun. "Clear."

Sam raced to Kait and dropped to the ground. The biggest danger she'd face was the force of the bullet stopping her heart. He pressed his fingers against her neck. Her pulse beat hard. He looked her over. Her chest moved in a regular rhythm. She was alive. Relief nearly had him collapsing beside her, but he focused on breathing and removed the cuffs from her wrists. She'd still need to be checked by a doctor, and she'd have a nasty bruise, but she was alive. And safe. With him.

Sirens sounded in the distance, winding their way closer.

"That should be Vance and the cavalry," Nina announced as she checked Rhodes's pulse. "He'll make it."

"Lily," Sam said, his gaze shooting in the direction of Nina's SUV. "Where's Lily?"

"Relax. I left her in the car." Nina slapped the cuffs on Rhodes.

Kait stirred. She moaned, and her hand went to her vest. She opened her eyes, then tried to sit up, but fell back. Her gaze connected with Sam's. "Lily? Fenton?"

"Lily's in the car, and Nina has Rhodes in cuffs."

"Don't worry, hon," Nina soothed. "She's playing hide and seek with me. I left her covering her eyes on the floor in the backseat, so she won't have seen a thing."

Kait struggled to a sitting position and winced as she ripped the Velcro from her vest. "I'm gonna have a whopper of a bruise. Hurts like crazy."

Once the adrenaline wore off, the pain would increase. Exponentially. Watching her suffering and wishing he could take it away had all but masked Sam's lingering pain from the gunshot wound.

He helped her out of the vest. "Sorry about shooting you. It was the only thing I could think of that didn't end with you being dead."

"Then thanks." She winked at him. "I so don't like the thought of being dead."

"I don't either." He caught her cheerful mood and grinned back. "I mean, I might need an FBI connection in the future, and I'd hate to have to depend on Nina. She's kind of bossy."

Kait laughed and threw her arms around him pulling him close. "Not sure this is appropriate with all your buddies charging in on us, but hey, I almost died, so I can do whatever I want."

He pulled back to look in her eyes. To touch her face. To memorize her smile. Then he grinned. "My heart almost stopped when I saw the gun to your head, so I can do whatever *I* want, too." He lowered his head and kissed her soundly, not coming up until he heard his lieutenant clearing his throat behind them.

"Umm, Sam," Kait said as she tried to pull away. "Vance is watching you."

Sam drew her closer again. "Not to worry. He nags us about developing interagency relationships all the time. I always do what I'm told, so you should expect a lot of fraternization in the near future."

KAIT'S ADRENALINE had worn off, and she was sure this was what a hangover that wouldn't end felt like. Her chest was bruised and aching, and she just plain wanted to leave the antiseptic hospital smell behind and take Lily home to crash.

Not that Lily needed to crash. She'd had a long enough nap to ensure she'd be wide awake until bedtime, as evidenced by her bouncing on Sam's knee in the small ER bay. Kait saw him wince a few times when Lily grabbed onto his injured arm, but he didn't complain. Not once. But he also didn't say anything more about their future. Something she'd expected once they were alone.

"Knock, knock." Her mother's voice came from outside the room before she poked her head inside.

"Nana!" Lily hopped off Sam's lap and ran to her grandmother who knelt to receive her.

"You're squishing me, Nana," Lily cried.

"Sorry, I'm just glad to see you."

"Did you bring our cookies?"

Kait's mother smoothed Lily's hair back from her face. "Papa has them in the waiting room."

"Can I have one?"

She tweaked Lily's nose. "I'd like to talk to Kait first, but maybe the nice detective will take you to see Papa."

"'Tective?" Lily asked.

"Me, Squirt," Sam said, ruffling Lily's hair. "She means me."

She looked up at Sam. "Will you take me to my Papa?"

"Absolutely," he said. "Just give me a second to say goodbye to Kait."

He crossed the room, sat on her bed, and looked into her eyes. His feelings for her were plain to see, but Kait wanted more. She wanted to hear him say he cared for her. "You wanted to talk?"

He leaned closer, and she caught a whiff of his musky scent. "Not with an audience and with you in the hospital."

She tried hard to keep her disappointment from her expression, but when his eyes darkened, she was sure she hadn't managed it.

He took her hand, threading his fingers with hers, but his focus never strayed. "Why don't you give me a call after you've gotten some rest, and we can meet up?"

"Sure," she said, but she had to force herself to sound cheerful.

He released her hand and brushed a strand of hair from her eyes. Her heart raced at his touch. He ran a thumb along her jaw. All of her senses fired, and she waited for a kiss. For any sign that he hadn't simply been succumbing to the heat of the situation when he'd kissed her.

"Later," he said, letting his thumb trail away before leaning close and whispering, "When we're alone."

"Later," she replied, still feeling the heat of his touch, the hint of so much more to come in the softness of his voice, telling her there was something real between them. That he hadn't simply let his adrenaline take over. That he didn't regret kissing her and promising more.

He turned to Lily, his smile wide and earnest. "Okay, Squirt, ready to go."

She clapped excitedly, then took Sam's hand. Her miniature fingers wrapped around his large hand. Perfection—a picture Kait would willingly see day after day for the rest of her life.

"Thank you, Detective," her mother said sincerely. "And thank you for bringing both our girls home safe and sound. I am forever in your debt."

"It's Sam, and it was no problem." He looked at Kait for a long moment, then departed with a chattering Lily.

"He's a good man." Her mother perched on the side of the bed.

"He is indeed," Kait said, but didn't add another word despite her mother's obvious hope of hearing more.

"Are they keeping you here tonight?"

"No, not for a simple bruise," Kait said. "I only came to the hospital because department regulations require it, but the nurse is finalizing my discharge papers now."

"I'd like to keep Lily tonight." Instead of her usual demanding stare, her mother looked down and twisted the blanket between her fingers.

Fidgeting or not, she was her impatient old self, bringing up the subject of Lily's custody before Kait even had a chance to think of a way to tell her mom she'd changed her mind. "After everything that's happened, I don't want to be away from her tonight."

"You just . . ." Her mom looked up, her eyes filling with tears that had been absent since Abby died. "You seem so tired. I thought having a good night's sleep would be good for you." She dropped the blanket and gently, almost shyly, touched Kait's hand, something she hadn't done in years. "If you're worried that I plan to take Lily and not give her back, I'm not holding you to what you said about giving me custody. In fact, I think Lily should be with you."

Kait's mouth dropped open.

"While your mouth is hanging open, I might as well say I'm sorry for the last three years as well. There's no excuse for my behavior, but I blamed you for losing Abby, and I was beyond mean to you. I thought if Lily was with you, something would happen to her, too. But when Fenton took both of you . . ." Tears rolled down her cheeks, carrying rivers of mascara that settled in creases Kait hadn't noticed before. "That's when I saw how I'd been behaving. I can't lose you, too, Kait. Can you forgive me?"

Kait knew her heart should swell from the confession, but so much had happened between them that she simply felt wary. So many hurtful words had been exchanged, and it would take time to heal, but she could offer her forgiveness.

"Of course I can forgive you." Kait grabbed a tissue from the table and handed it to her mom.

She grabbed Kait up in a hug. The sweet, flowery perfume she'd worn since Kait could remember brought back laughing, smiling memories with Abby.

Kait closed her eyes. Let her mom hold her. *I did it, Abs. I got him. Now you can rest. And I can take care of your baby like I promised—good care of her, the way you would have. Maybe with Sam. Or maybe not. I don't know yet.*

Her mother set Kait away, and Kait opened her own eyes now filling with tears.

"What's wrong?" her mother asked.

Kait wasn't about to discuss her potential future with Sam with her mother, so she offered a tremulous smile. "Nothing. Things are better than they've been in a long time."

"Have you thought at all about how you're going to explain all of this to Lily?"

"I've already told her Fenton had to go away for a while, and I'll deal with the long-term consequences after I've located a counselor for her."

"That sounds like a good plan," she said. "I'd still like to take her tonight. Not because I don't think you're fit, but because I want you to get some rest. You're a good mother, and Abby would be so proud of you."

Kait had longed to hear these words for years, but after all she'd just been through, they didn't mean what she'd once thought they would. "I'd like to think you're right."

"What about Lily tonight?"

"Let me get home, and then I'll decide."

Her mother gave a curt nod and stood. "Then I'll wait to hear from you." She turned, and after a quick squeeze of Kait's arm, she strode away.

Kait knew her mother was disappointed in her, but not in the same way as she'd been for the last three years. Who knew, maybe she was disappointed in herself for all the wasted years and their strained relationship.

One thing was for sure. Kait knew that any power her mother once held over her was gone for good. Now they could go about getting to know each other as adults and form a relationship that would have made Abby proud.

Kait rested her head back and closed her eyes again.

Love you, Abs. Always have. Always will.

Chapter Thirty-Six

AT THE DEBRIEFING on Monday afternoon, Sam watched Kait from across the table. He'd had his eyes on her for the last hour. All the questions surrounding Rhodes had been answered. Including that it was Toby Bradley who Rhodes killed after the WoW game. Attorneys felt the team had a solid case against Rhodes, and their evidence would send him away for life—something that had brightened Kait's face until Sulyard had given Rhodes's photo album to her a few minutes ago.

She turned another page while the rest of the task force collectively held their breath. She cringed and pressed her lips together, sending Sam's anger flaring. He'd thought when he'd rescued her from Rhodes that the creep had hurt her as deeply as he possibly could, but the pain kept on coming. Today, with these pictures of his victims, she had to look at her own photo in the album and relive the ordeal of her abduction. He hated to think about what would have happened if they hadn't stopped Rhodes.

Pain. More pain when all she deserved was happiness. Something Sam aimed to spend the rest of his life ensuring she found. If she'd have him. Something he wasn't one hundred percent sure of right now.

He'd wanted to go home with her Friday night and ask her that very question. But that would have been pushing things. So he'd delivered Lily to her grandfather and departed. Instead of heading to his house, he'd gone straight to the cemetery and had a long chat with Hannah. This whole incident proved life was too short to carry recriminations and guilt, and he'd left them laying with the flowers at her grave.

Now he was ready for more. Much more. A wife *and* children. Kait and Lily.

So he'd patiently waited for Kait's call, which came Saturday morning. She needed a few days to process, she'd said. He was disappointed, but he understood. She'd been through a lot.

Now, here they were. Unspoken words needed to be said, but a crowd surrounded them. Rhodes once again sat between them.

She passed the book on to Nina and looked at Sulyard who stood at the head of the table as usual. "We should be thanking Fenton for keeping these records. It will certainly aid in his conviction." Professional. Shoulders back. Agent Kaitlyn Knight through and through. Not the Kaitlyn

Knight Sam wanted to talk to.

"Murdock," Lieutenant Vance said. "Are you going to answer?"

Sam jerked his eyes from Kait to his boss. "Sorry, what?"

Vance rolled his eyes. "Sulyard asked if you had anything to add."

Sam shook his head.

"Then we're adjourned," Sulyard declared.

Hoping to talk to Kait, Sam shot to his feet and picked his way through the others. She must have had the same idea as she moved toward him. They met in the middle.

"Hey," he said, a dopey teenage boy smile finding its way to the surface. "You doing okay today?"

"I'm sore, but otherwise fine." She smiled shyly. "Are you available tonight? For that talk?"

His heart soared ridiculously high for such a simple question. "Absolutely. Do you have to pick up Lily?"

"No, she's with my mom and dad."

No. She didn't. Not without talking to him. "So you went through with the custody change after all."

She shook her head hard. "No. Lily will stay with me."

He sagged in relief. "And your mother? How's she doing with that?"

"She actually said she thought I was a good mother, and she apologized for the last three years."

"That must have been a surprise."

Kait nodded and looked at her shoes as if she suddenly felt shy around him.

He understood. This was new territory for both of them. "Why don't we meet at my house for dinner? You've never been there, and it'll give you a chance to see what you're getting yourself into."

"You mean it's time for you to let your skeletons tumble out of the closet for once?" She grinned at him.

"Not sure we have time for all of them." He chuckled.

She stepped closer. "I don't care about your past, Sam. It's your future I'm interested in."

He gave her hand a quick squeeze. "Then that's what we'll focus on tonight. Our future."

KAIT LAID HER outfit on her bed. The bright blue silk blouse and dark wash jeans were a birthday present from Nina, and the outfit included a pair of sky-high pumps. Kait stepped into the jeans, then took the soft silk blouse to the full-length mirror. Her gaze went to the deep purple bruise swirling out on her chest like a hurricane. She ran a finger over the dark center that would linger for weeks. The bruise could remind her of her ordeal, but she'd chosen to remember it as Sam's concern for her.

Sam. He waited for her, sending her pulse racing.

She hurried into the blouse then slid her feet into what Nina declared as the crown jewels of the outfit.

Kait studied herself in the mirror. She looked perfect. Like someone dressed to impress others. Not like herself at all. She frowned at her reflection.

"It's not me," she told her mirror image and kicked off the shoes. "And I'm done with that."

For too many years, she'd lived to prove to her mom that she was a fit mother. To fulfill a promise to Abby. To prove to her dad that she wasn't boring and dull. Well, no more.

She jerked off the blouse and went to her closet to find a comfortable knit top. Sam was the last person she needed to impress. He'd seen her at her worst. He knew what to expect. If this thing between them was going to work, he'd accept her as she honestly was.

"Worn Birks and all." She jammed her feet into her favorite pair of Birkenstock clogs.

She laughed, the sound so freeing as she grabbed her purse on the way out the front door. She soon pulled into the driveway of Sam's small bungalow with a tidy yard. By the time she stepped out, he'd opened the door and waited on the small stoop. He wore the same jeans as earlier but had changed the dressier shirt for a black T-shirt stretched tight across his broad shoulders. He'd shed his boots, and his feet were bare. Good. He felt comfortable around her and didn't feel a need to impress either.

As she came up the walkway, he leaned against the post and crossed his feet at the ankle while a lazy smile played across his face. She caught herself grinning broadly and couldn't remember the last time she'd felt this happy. Even before Abby's death, she'd been too busy proving to her father and herself that she wasn't a boring person and losing her joy.

"Hey," he said, the word lingering in his slow, easy accent.

She stepped up to him, her heart thumping wildly, and suddenly she was uncertain what to say. "Nice house."

"About that." His smile fell, and he came to his feet. "I should have thought to mention this was Hannah's house, too. Everything's pretty much the way she left it." He took Kait's hands. "Not in some crazy tribute to her. It's just that I don't spend much time here and didn't see the point in changing things." He drew her closer and solidly met her gaze. "Or maybe I was trapped in the past like Marcie kept saying. Who knows? But I'm done with that and ready to move on." He stared at her, his expression uneasy as if expecting her to be upset.

She extracted a hand and cupped the side of his face. "Then we should go inside to talk about what moving on means for both of us."

Holding her hand, they entered his house. The interior felt ten degrees cooler, and she shivered. Maybe from the temperature, or maybe from the excitement of what lay ahead. He led her across hardwood flooring, past white crown moldings, thick baseboards, and old built-ins surrounding the fireplace in the formal living room. They moved to the back of the house with a comfy family room open to a remodeled kitchen boasting white cabinets and dark granite counters. A spicy aroma saturated the air.

Surprised, she looked at him. "So you cook?"

"Is it a deal breaker if I don't?" He stepped behind the counter. "If it is, I'll lie and say I made the Mexican takeout warming in the oven." He gave her a fiendish grin.

She laughed. "You've had my spaghetti, so you know cooking is optional in my world."

He held up a bottle of wine, and she nodded as she settled on a barstool at an island running the length of the kitchen. She watched him uncork the wine and pour a glass for her, his movements fluid and sure. The muscles in his forearm flexed and relaxed with each twist, and she remembered how it felt to be held in those strong arms after the shooting. To feel safe. Secure.

And loved.

He slid the wine to her and grabbed a beer for himself. He twisted off the top and took a long drink. "So . . ."

"So," she responded.

He stepped up to her and set his bottle on the counter. "About us—what do you see happening?"

"Everything," she said, then bit her lip before blurting out that she wanted a husband and siblings for Lily. A confession that was bound to scare him off.

He stepped even closer and slid a hand around the back of her neck. "Just to be clear, this everything includes me."

"I want it to . . . there's just this one thing . . . I . . . I need to be certain."

He leaned back, searching her eyes a healthy measure of panic in his expression. "What?"

"It's Lily . . . you told me about Danny. About not being sure you'd be a good dad. How do you feel about that now? I mean, Lily will have such a rough road as it is. She'll need a strong dad who's there for her."

"Why, Kaitlyn Knight, are you asking me to marry you?" He grinned at her, but she could see it was covering up uncertainty.

"I'm serious here, Sam. You told me you didn't think you should be a father. Lily's in my life for good. Before we get seriously involved, I need to know if you think you'd be a good dad."

"Is that all?" He let out a shaky laugh. "Dang right. I'll be the best dad on the planet."

Her heart warmed beyond expectation. "Then that's all I need to know."

"And all I need to know is that you trust me with her."

She nodded, and he lowered his head. His lips were cool from the beer, settling over hers. She snaked her arms up around his neck and drew him closer. The kiss deepened. She considered telling him she loved him, but the whole husband and father topic was probably enough for today.

He crushed her to him and pain flared through her chest, making her pull back. The shooting came flashing back, and instead of upsetting her, the thought made her smile.

"What's so funny?" Sam asked.

"I was just thinking." She mocked a serious expression. "I finally decide to trust a guy, and he shoots me."

Sam's mouth dropped open, but when she grinned, he laughed. He settled his hands on her hips and gently drew her closer. "Then give me another chance to get things right by taking you out on a proper date."

Kait tapped her chin pretending to think about it. "We'll go out on one condition."

"Name it."

"You have to promise that whatever we do, it won't involve the use of firearms."

"I promise," he said seriously. "But I won't promise that it won't involve fireworks." He grinned, the cute little number where the right side of his mouth quirked up and the dimple deepened. He ran a finger down her cheek, leaving sparks in its trail.

Kait's breath caught in her throat, and she reveled in the sensation. It was about time she had some bright, sparkling fireworks in her life, and Sam was just the guy to provide them.

The End

Acknowledgements

Additional thanks to:

My daughter Emma for help with plot issues and technical details. My daughter Erin and son-in-law Pete for patiently answering all of my questions about World of Warcraft.

The very generous Ron Norris who gives of his time and knowledge in police and military procedures, weaponry details, and information technology. As a retired police officer with the LaVerne Police Department and a Certified Information Security Professional, your experience and knowledge is invaluable. You go above and beyond, and I can't thank you enough!

Vance Nebling, Criminalist in the Portland Police Bureau Forensic Evidence Division. Thank you for the tour of your department and for answering forensic questions when they arise. Your willingness to share your expertise is greatly appreciated.

Any errors in or liberties taken with the technical details Ron or Vance so patiently explained to me are all my doing.

And last but not least, the Portland FBI agents and staff for sharing your knowledge and expertise at the Citizen's Academy. I'm still smiling from our day on the firing rage. Who knew shooting a semi-automatic rifle could be such fun? I hope my respect for your dedication to the job comes through in my trio of FBI agents in this series.

About the Author

Susan Sleeman is a bestselling author of clean read and inspirational romantic suspense books. Awards include Thread of Suspicion (2013 Romantic Times Reviewers Choice Best Book Award), and No Way Out and The Christmas Witness (Daphne du Maurier Award for Excellence finalists). In addition to writing, Susan also hosts the popular website TheSuspenseZone.com. She currently lives in Oregon with her husband, but has lived in nine states. They have two daughters, a son-in-law, and an adorable grandson.

To learn more about Susan stop by any of these locations on the web.

Website: susansleeman.com

Facebook: SusanSleemanBooks

Twitter: SusanSleeman

Made in the USA
Middletown, DE
04 March 2015